WASHOE COUNTY LIBRARY

3 1235 02805 8266

mL

DATE DUE

JUN 0 4 2003

JAN 1 1 2008

GAYLORD   PRINTED IN U.S.A.

D0121992

THEY SHALL SEE GOD

Athol Dick_____ w__ _____ __ _____ ___, thr____ ___cult circumstances, bu_____h. *They Shall
See God* is **a**_____er from the
first page to_____

Hooked, I_____ delivers a
compelling _____ad that you
started this _____ pages.

A miracle _____hair-raising
suspense, an_____d, Dickson
has created _____long as he
writes 'em, I'_____

Athol's exqui_____nagination
from the first_____ose guided
me along th__ ___ ____ _____ __ ____ _____, and **held me in
suspense until the final page.**

HANNAH ALEXANDER
author of The Healing Touch series

. . . a brilliant page-turning plot that will leave you breathless, and **an
ending that will bring tears to your eyes.**

DEBORAH RANEY
author of *A Vow to Cherish* and *Beneath a Southern Sky*

An enthralling **"gotta-see-what-happens-next"** suspense novel.

STEPHANIE GRACE WHITSON
author of *Heart of the Sandhills* and eight other inspirational novels

Athol Dickson is **a gifted storyteller** who takes incredibly full and vibrant characters and pulls you into their lives. At first, they seem to have nothing to do with one another, but the author weaves them together slowly, masterfully, building to a crescendo finale that kept me guessing until the last page.

KRISTIN BILLERBECK
author of *Victorian Christmas Keepsake*

A kaleidoscope of clearly defined characters, hamstrung by issues of the heart, face resurfaced childhood friends, old friends dying, gentle men locked away in mental wards, a convicted murderer released from prison, and wild animals roaming their Louisiana city. Keenly written, but not easy, comfortable reading. Hang on to the end to find out what it all means.

JANET CHESTER BLY
author of *Hope Lives Here* and *God Is Good All the Time*

Athol Dickson is an incredibly **creative** storyteller with an unmistakable literary style. In *They Shall See God*, he explores the unique tensions between Christian and Jewish Americans with intelligence and sensitivity and, as always, gives his readers a **thriller** that is as **riveting** as it is hard to predict.

DEANNA JULIE DODSON
author of *In Honor Bound, By Love Redeemed,* and *To Grace Surrendered*

Athol Dickson has given us a wonderful book full of mystery, both the whodunit kind and the spiritual kind. A beautiful, sympathetic, and **informed look at both Christianity and Judaism.**

GAYLE ROPER
author of *Spring Rain*

ATHOL DICKSON *THEY SHALL SEE GOD*

TYNDALE HOUSE PUBLISHERS, INC., WHEATON, ILLINOIS

Visit Tyndale's exciting Web site at www.tyndale.com

Copyright © 2002 by Athol Dickson. All rights reserved.

Cover photograph copyright © 2001 by Jim Witmer. All rights reserved.

Published in association with the literary agency of Alive Communications, Inc., 7680 Goddard Street, Suite 200, Colorado Springs, CO 80920.

Some Scripture quotations taken from the *Holy Bible,* King James Version.

Some Scripture quotations taken from the *Holy Bible,* New International Version®. NIV®. Copyright © 1973, 1978, 1984 by International Bible Society. Used by permission of Zondervan Publishing House. All rights reserved.

Edited by Curtis H. C. Lundgren

Designed by Dean H. Renninger

"Gerontion" by T. S. Eliot. From *Poems* (New York: Alfred A. Knopf, 1920).

Library of Congress Cataloging-in-Publication Data

Dickson, Athol, date.
  They shall see God : a novel / by Athol Dickson.
    p. cm.
  ISBN 0-8423-5292-9
    1. Witnesses—Crimes against—Fiction. 2. Female friendship—Fiction. 3. New Orleans (La.)—Fiction. 4. Belief and doubt—Fiction. 5. Christian women—Ficiton. 6. Jewish women—Fiction. 7. Women rabbis—Fiction. I. Title.
PS3554.I3264 T48 2002
813'.54—dc21   2001008485

Printed in the United States of America

08   07   06   05   04   03   02
9   8   7   6   5   4   3   2   1

ACKNOWLEDGMENTS

My deepest thanks to Greg Johnson, who believed in my writing before I was sure of it myself.

This story would never have entered my mind if not for Philip Einsohn, who invited me into his temple and his world. His friendship is a great blessing in my life.

Thank you, Rabbi Sheldon Zimmerman, for encouraging me to speak up in Chever Torah. When you left, I told you I would try to build some bridges. I hope you think this is a good start.

I also want to express my appreciation to a passionate and knowledgeable group of rabbis: Debbie Robbins, Mark Kaiserman, Charles Mintz, and especially David Stern. Thanks for letting me hang around, and for sharing your Torah.

And finally, thank you, Chever Torah, one and all. You never failed to make the "stranger among you" feel warmly welcome. No character in this book is based on any one of you, but the better parts of Kate and Ruth are in you all.

The devil has striven against the truth in manifold ways.

He has sometimes endeavored to destroy it by defending it.

TERTULLIAN, *Against Praxeas*

PROLOGUE

In the south Louisiana sunshine outside the Margaret Dixon Memorial Visitor Processing Building, Gabby Cantor snored behind the wheel of her Coupe DeVille. Sooner or later, her husband would walk out of there, but the wait was boring and the katydids' somnolent hum had put her out like a light. Ten thousand of them clung to the sun-wilted leaves of the hickories and poplars looming just beyond the wire, their voices a rackety chorus, swelling and fading and swelling again, on and on and on. Then a red-winged blackbird added its oddly cheerful call to their pulsing rhythm, rousing her. She snorted softly, looked around, sat up in a dignified fashion, and began to fan herself with a *Town and Country* magazine. Gabby knew from previous visits that the processing center was air-conditioned, but she refused to go inside that awful little building again. Not one more time. So to stay awake she read the white letters on the large green sign as she had so often during the long years past. More than anything else, the words of that sign had come to symbolize the indignities life had thrust upon her:

NOTICE

This is to notify you that any individual (including minors) entering any department of corrections facility is subject to search of their property, automobile, and person. Searches include but are not limited to visual inspection of persons or property, pat-down searches of your person, inspection of persons or property by dogs trained to detect drugs, weapons, and other contraband, strip searches of your body, and searches of your body cavities. Introduction of contraband, drugs, alcohol, or weapons into a prison is a felony for which you will be prosecuted under L.R.S. 14:402.

Warden Howard Nottingham

Next to that sign another temporary one proudly proclaimed that the prison employees had already met their United Way goal for the year. Just beyond the signs, beside the gate and the ugly tan-and-brown processing center and the tall fences topped with razor-sharp wire, a man in uniform stood cradling a shotgun in his arms at the railing atop a concrete tower as beneath him Solomon Cantor emerged in blue jeans and a plain white T-shirt, carrying a cheap plastic suitcase and wearing that beard, which she hated.

For the hundredth time Gabby wondered how she would explain him to her friends.

Look at him, standing there blinking in the sunshine, dressed like a yard boy from somewhere down in Barataria. Didn't he see her over here waiting? How hard could it be to find her Cadillac with only two other cars around—old, rusted-out jalopies, the kind you'd expect a person to drive, coming to the penitentiary to visit some three-time loser. Surely he *saw* her over here. What was she supposed to do, wave?

Gabby reached down and twisted the key in the ignition. The Cadillac shivered. Sol turned toward the sound of the engine. Pretending not to notice, Gabby pressed a button and the side window whispered shut, sealing out the September heat. She turned the air conditioner all the way up to high and aimed the vent toward her lap, where the panty hose beneath her raw silk skirt clung to her thighs like a pair of hot compresses. Her wrinkled hands returned to the steering wheel, gripping it hard, the bloodred nails at the ends of her diamond-dappled fingers digging into the flesh at the base of her palms. Gabby stared straight ahead, ignoring the age spots on the backs of her hands, ignoring Solomon.

In the periphery of her vision he approached the passenger side door, crossing the small gravel parking lot with an ambling gait, an effeminately masculine John Wayne roll of the hips. Long ago, before she knew better, Gabby had sometimes wondered if he moved that way just to call attention to himself. Then she learned that Solomon Cantor had no awareness whatsoever of his effect on people.

He arrived at the door. Gabby waited for the familiar click of the latch and the soft sigh of the well-oiled hinges, but nothing happened. After several seconds, she turned toward the window. He stood out there, perfectly still, facing the car. All she could see between the ceiling of the car and the bottom of the window was his body from his waist to his shoulders—his faded denims, plain white T-shirt, and his stomach, flat like a teenager's. She snorted, the air rushing through her nostrils, a short gust of impatience. He was sixty-two years old. The thick, curly hair on his arms was gray. He had no right to a teenager's stomach.

"Well?" she called through the glass. "What are you waiting for?"

He bent and peered inside. "Where's Izzy?"

"I don't know. I haven't seen him in months."

His eyes found hers. In spite of herself, Gabby felt a familiar thrill. If Sol felt it too, he showed no outward sign. He waited, watching her, thinking who knows what. Then, finally, he opened the door and got in, the sweltering Louisiana heat trailing behind him as if he were the devil bringing hell along.

"Okay," he said, settling into the seat with his cheap plastic suitcase on his lap.

"You have to put on your seat belt."

"Why?"

"It's a law."

"Since when?"

"I don't remember."

He sat for a moment, unmoving, then reached over and drew the seat belt across his lap, working it under the case and snapping it into place.

"Okay," he said again.

Gabby shifted into gear and drove away from the parking lot outside the Margaret Dixon Memorial Visitor Processing Building of the Louisiana State Penitentiary at Angola and accelerated along the two-lane asphalt road—Louisiana State Highway 66—speeding past thick green woods on either side, past the Tunick Hills Baptist Church in a small clearing and a dense cluster of banana trees next to an old house trailer speckled with mildew, heading south toward New Orleans, toward home, as her ex-convict husband looked out the side window away from her. She decided she would wait for him to speak first, to see how long that would take. After twenty minutes, he began to whistle through his teeth softly. She recognized the tune.

Get your kicks,
on Route 66.

In spite of her resolution to the contrary, Gabby Cantor spoke.

"Guess you're glad it's over."

Solomon Cantor stopped whistling, but he did not reply.

CHAPTER ONE

The bells of a nearby Catholic church chimed midnight as the long black car glided to a stop in front of Ruth Gold's shotgun double on Iberville. Across the street, Faith Mausoleum loomed above the house, its block-long façade of gray limestone relieved only by occasional copper downspouts and a single door beneath a small verdigris canopy. Steve Cronen shifted into park but left the stereo on as the "Sirènes" nocturne flowed from the speakers. Months ago, Ruth had playfully chided Steve for purchasing a German automobile, calling him a traitor to the Jewish people. He had answered by turning on the stereo, and that had been enough for her to concede his unspoken point. The sound system in the tightly constructed luxury vehicle was better than the one in her home. When the final notes of Debussy's tranquil composition dissipated and a mellow silence settled in, Ruth sighed, hugging herself with crossed arms. Neither of them moved or spoke for several minutes.

Finally, Steve said, "It's good, huh?" She did not know if he meant the music or the two of them. Either way, the answer was the same.

"Oh, yes."

They smiled together in the darkness. Steve leaned across and kissed her. She cupped his cheek with her palm, inviting him to linger. His lips were full and yielding. He pulled back and ran strong fingers through her short black hair, stroking it as they held each other, his beautiful green eyes very serious.

She said, "You wanna come in for a cup of coffee?"

"Absolutely."

"Just a cup of coffee. Okay?"

He sighed. "Yes, rabbi."

A few minutes later, Ruth sat alone in her small living room, head back against the soft cushion of the leather sofa, her eyes closed, trying to remain awake while Steve lingered in her kitchen. Thoughts of their time together drifted through her mind. He was a wonderful man, a lawyer, filled with passion about his work. He served major corporations, defending one from another in litigation arising from leveraged buyouts and unfriendly takeovers. Living on the money earned from those cases, he filled the rest of his schedule with pro bono work for the inner-city poor. When he first explained his strategy, she had dubbed him "Robin Hood," and it hadn't taken long for her to become part of the plan. As a rabbi at the largest Reform Jewish temple in New Orleans, Ruth Gold often came in contact with the underprivileged through the temple's involvement in several homeless shelters and a food bank. She began referring people to him. Steve didn't seem to mind. In fact, he had already helped several of them find justice against uncaring landlords, corporations, and civil bureaucracies. He was her modern-day champion of the poor, her gentle friend, and, more and more, a serious contender for her heart.

Steve had proposed marriage months ago. A part of her wanted to say yes. Ruth knew she might never find another man with his kindness, passion, and devotion, but her own passion for privacy got in the way. She had not even been able to take a roommate in college when the money was tight. So she had said maybe, hoping that would satisfy him for now.

Ruth heard him opening a cabinet in the kitchen. She smiled. It was nice that he knew his way around, nice to have someone else who knew where she kept the glasses and silverware. Something about it made her feel . . . comfortable. Was that part of marriage? That cozy feeling of sharing little things? If so, it was one more reason to accept his proposal. She had been finding so many reasons lately. But the small voice continued to warn her not to give up too much.

"Hey, sleepyhead."

She opened her eyes to find Steve standing there, looking down at her as he munched an apple, so stylish in his dark blue suit, his sable hair mussed just a bit, his strong jaw shadowed with the barest hint of whiskers. For the thousandth time, she felt a flutter in her chest as she observed the way his torso sloped from wide shoulders to narrow waist.

Oh my. Such a sweet man and drop-dead gorgeous, too. Ruth Gold, what is the matter with you?

"Wore ya out, didn't I?" he asked, the apple showing white in his mouth. "Can't keep up the pace?"

She looked away, affecting disinterest. "Actually, the boredom knocked me unconscious."

He laughed, showing more of the half-chewed apple.

"Hey," said Ruth, rising to her feet. "I was saving that for Rosh Hashanah."

"Come on. There must be twenty of 'em in there."

"Oh, all right. I guess you earned it tonight."

"Where'd you find these things? They're wonderful."

"You know, it's weird. They just showed up on the doorstep."

"Huh." He took another bite of the apple. "It was a nice evening, wasn't it?"

"It was wonderful, baby. Thanks so much."

He grinned. So easy to please. She decided to say what had been in the back of her mind all night.

"I have something to ask you."

"Fire away."

"The anniversary of my mother's death is coming up." Ruth paused, unsure of how to put it. *Don't be such a coward,* she thought. *Just spit it out.* She cleared her throat. "Instead of rounding up a *minyan* to say *kaddish,* I was wondering if you'd come to Mama's grave and light a *yahrzeit* candle with me, and say *shebecheyanu?*"

He looked directly at her, all sense of levity gone in an instant. "I'm honored."

Suddenly, she felt uncomfortable. "Okay. Good. I . . . uh . . . I'll be right back."

"I'll be here," he said. The look in his eyes gave the words deeper meaning.

Ruth shuffled down the hall to her home's single bathroom. Soon after she closed the door, she heard several loud noises coming from someplace else in the house. Then she heard a crash, like breaking glass.

"Hey!" she called. "Is everything okay?"

He did not answer.

"Steve? Steve?"

She tried to hurry. Three minutes later when she returned to the living room, Steve Cronen lay on the floor in front of the sofa amidst shards of glass from her shattered coffee table, his mouth hanging open, his eyes staring blankly at the potted palm in the corner, and Rabbi Ruth Gold knew in an instant that their future was not to be.

R ubbing her eyes, Kate Flint entered the kitchen in the first soft light of the morning. She crossed to the far counter, opened a cabinet, withdrew a coffee filter, and shoved it into her coffeemaker. As she opened the freezer door to remove a bag of dark roasted coffee beans, a piece of paper fell to the floor. She stooped to pick it up. It was one of Jilly's colored drawings, a pair of stick figures holding hands with something that might have been a moose. Kate started to slip it under a magnet on the freezer door again but could not find an open spot. In fact, she could barely see the handle amidst the wild collage of colored drawings, snapshots, pizza delivery fliers, and miscellaneous scraps that had once seemed cute or important. Something had to go, but not Jilly's drawings, of course. They were precious. And not the pizza fliers. She used them at least once a week when she came home from the shop too tired to cook. What then? A pink slip of paper caught her eye, an announcement for an upcoming country retreat for the women's group at her church. Why had she saved that? She would never go. Kate took the announcement down and put Jilly's drawing in its place. Then, on impulse, she removed another church announce-

ment, this one about an upcoming class on financial management according to biblical principles. There near the top was a Bible verse she had
hand-copied for some reason. She couldn't remember why, so down it
came. In fact, there were far too many church things on her refrigerator
door. Acting on a sudden impulse, Kate removed them all and threw them
in the trash bin. There. Now her daughter's drawings had the place of
pride they deserved.

Returning to the freezer for the coffee beans, she saw the milk carton
sitting on the counter. Beside it lay an uneaten sandwich and an open jar
of applesauce. Kate sighed. Touching the milk carton, she confirmed that
it was warm. Checking the applesauce jar as well, she decided the color
looked wrong.

"What a waste," she muttered, carrying them to the sink.

Kate poured the milk out first, then shook the applesauce into the
drain. She flipped a switch and the garbage disposal whirred loudly, flush-
ing away any applesauce that remained in the pipes below. The grinding
sound went on for several seconds. *That'll get them up,* she thought, adjusting her plaid cotton robe and the banana clip that barely restrained her
thick, sleep-tousled hair. Satisfied that her sink was clean and her children
awake, Kate turned off the disposal. Then she threw away the empty milk
carton and the applesauce jar and the sandwich.

Eight minutes later, as Kate poured her first cup of coffee, Jilly
wandered into the kitchen, carrying a toy fire truck.

"Morning, sunshine," said Kate. "Where's Paul?"

"I'm hungry," said Jilly, setting the truck on the table.

"Okay. You want some cereal?"

"Uh-huh."

Kate took a sip of her French roast, then crossed the kitchen. "Uh-
oh," she said, peering into the refrigerator. "Can't make you cereal."

"But I want it."

"Sorry, honey. We're out of milk."

"But I *want* it!"

"How about a nice cinnamon roll and some orange juice?"

"Okay."

Kate smiled. Jilly was so easy to please. She'd always been the obedi-
ent one, willing to do as she was told without too much back talk. Paul,

on the other hand, was a headstrong kid. Kate sometimes wished she had given John more credit for the effort he had exerted to keep their son in line. If only . . .

She shook her head. This was no way to think first thing in the morning, even if Paul *had* wasted five dollars' worth of food last night.

Kate lined a cookie tray with aluminum foil, placed three cinnamon rolls on top, and slipped the tray into the oven. Then she poured three glasses of orange juice and carried them to the table. Jilly gulped hers down, almost draining the glass.

"Save some of that to have with your roll, honey."

"Okay."

Kate topped off her coffee and leaned back against the counter, blowing over the surface of the steaming liquid.

"Where's Paul?" she asked again.

Jilly rolled the truck around her orange juice glass. "I dunno."

"You wanna holler for him?"

"Can I?" asked Jilly, her sleepy face suddenly alive with excitement.

Kate said, "Go ahead."

Jilly threw back her head and yelled, "Pauly! Paul-*leee!* Time to wake *uhhh-up!*"

Giggling, Jilly covered her mouth. Kate smiled too. "Well," she said, "if that doesn't do it, nothing will."

After a few more minutes the timer rang. Kate slipped on a pair of oversized hot-pad mittens and removed the fragrant rolls from the oven. Still, Paul did not appear at the breakfast table. It wasn't like him. He was usually ravenous in the mornings.

Setting the cinnamon rolls on the stove top to cool, Kate pulled off the mittens.

"I'm gonna go see what's keeping him," she said, heading down the hall.

Paul's room lay at the very end, across from hers. Posters and photographs cut from magazines decorated his door, much as the collage of images had littered the front of her refrigerator. Pictures of rock stars and tanks and battleships vied for prominence. Kate wasn't comfortable with the military imagery, but everyone said it was just a phase boys went through. She hoped that was true, because without John, she'd been unable to find the energy to resist Paul's growing attraction to brutality and violence.

Knocking on his door, she called his name. Paul did not respond. Worried, she decided to break a cardinal rule and open the door without his permission.

"Honey?" she called, peeking inside. "Time to get up."

He lay on his stomach, sprawled across his bed with arms akimbo and the sheets intertwined with his legs. Kate's voice brought no response at all. She stepped into the room and flipped on the light.

"Honey? Wake up."

Still, he did not move. Drawing near, Kate saw a butcher knife on his bedside table. The overhead light sparkled on the stainless blade. She bent and touched Paul's shoulder. He exploded, springing away, slamming his body into the wall on the far side of the bed.

"It's okay!" she said. "Honey, it's just Momma. It's okay!"

Paul wrapped his arms around his head defensively. Bending over him, she saw recognition appear as he stared up at her face. She sat on the bed and cradled his shoulders, drawing him close, stroking his hair. Eventually, he snuggled his ear against her chest. She knew he was listening to her flawed heart, making sure it was beating properly. Kate shifted her position to cause him to move his ear away from her chest.

After a few moments she asked, "Did you have another one?"

He nodded.

"It's okay now. You're awake. It was only a bad dream."

She felt him begin to withdraw from her touch. It saddened her. Kate understood this was a normal part of a child's development, but still, she dearly missed the simple joy of holding her son. It was one of the only things left that comforted her. Looking around at the posters pinned to the walls and ceiling of his room, Kate thought again of the church things she had just thrown in the trash. She felt a momentary twinge of guilt, but it soon passed. After all, what comfort had those things offered?

Suddenly, Paul sat up and swung his legs over the side of the bed. His bare belly hung over the waist of his pajamas.

"Honey?" said Kate. "What's this knife doing here?"

He stared at the blade dumbly at first, then seemed to remember. "The kitchen door was unlocked last night. I think someone came in."

"Why didn't you wake me?"

"I didn't need you. I'm the man of the house."

She paused, taking it in. "You got this knife and searched the whole house alone?"

He nodded.

"Oh, honey."

He looked down at his hands. She stared at him. His knuckles turned into little dimples when he straightened out his fingers. They sat like that for several seconds as Kate searched for words. Finally she said, "You know, it's okay to ask for help at a time like that."

"I'm the man of the house."

"Yes. That's true." She rubbed his back. "And, honey? I'm so glad I've got you here to take care of me and Jilly." Looking away from her, he shrugged. She leaned close. "You want a cinnamon roll?"

"Uh-huh."

"Okay. Let's go."

They rose together. Kate Flint paused to lift the butcher knife from the bedside table, then followed her son out the door and down the hall toward the kitchen. Watching his back, she thought, *What would I do without him?* And thinking that, she felt a swirling stew of emotions, impossible to separate: some pride, some sorrow, and maybe—if she were honest about it—something less than honorable. Then, for reasons perhaps related to that vaguely unscrupulous feeling, Kate suddenly found herself thinking of another time, and another mother and child who had a different bedroom conversation filled with unspoken fears.

The bright red lipstick, so conspicuous against her mother's ashen skin, offered a false promise of health. Little Katy O'Connor knew the transparent fiction of it must go unmentioned, just as she knew she dared not ask what lay beneath the turban on her mother's head. It did not matter; Katy had stolen a glimpse of that naked scalp before, as her father gently closed the door to keep her out. Twice each day, Katy was allowed inside her parents' room, and always, her mother wore the turban and freshly applied makeup. It had been this way for weeks. Sometimes Katy could not find her mother behind those false red lips and cheeks. Sometimes her mother was merely a rag doll propped upright against the headboard. At other times those sunken eyes flickered with a strange internal glow, as if the flame of life had found some last reserve of fuel in Katy's presence. In such moments, as her mother stared out through that rag-doll face, it seemed as if she were burning up inside.

"I'm sorry you had to see those things," said Katy's mother.

Standing beside the bed, Katy did not reply.

"It must have been very scary for you."

Katy slipped her feet into her mother's terry-cloth slippers.

"Listen, honey. He can't hurt you now. You know that, right?"

Katy nodded, feeling small in her mother's shoes.

"Besides, God will take care of you," said her mother. "God loves you."

Wiggling her toes, Katy mumbled, "So that lady . . . God didn't love her?"

"Of course he did."

"Was she bad?"

"I don't know. Probably not. She was a minister, after all. A missionary."

"But she's dead."

Katy's mother sighed, closing her burning eyes. "Mommy's tired now, honey. Maybe you better ask Daddy to explain this."

Then Katy's mother had fallen asleep sitting up, as she sometimes did, and Katy watched her for a while, thinking what a good woman everyone said she was. She helped people. Sick ones at the hospital, and poor ones who lived someplace called the Irish Channel. Katy thought with wonder of the fact that even missionaries and people like her mother could die. In the time it took Katy to step out of her mother's slippers, it occurred to her that God's love was a very dangerous thing. You had to keep God happy, of course, or else he would get mad, but maybe it was better not to be so good that he noticed you especially. Maybe it was better not to stand out one way or the other. Maybe it was better to let someone else help the sick, feed the poor, be the missionary.

After that, little Katy O'Connor never tried to wear her mother's slippers again.

When they reached the kitchen, Paul joined Jilly at the table and immediately chugged his orange juice. Kate sat down and reached toward each of them. The children took her hands. Together, they bowed their heads. Kate said grace, asking God to bless the food, their day, and "Daddy, up in heaven." It was the same prayer she had prayed the day before, and the day before that. She would pray the same prayer tomorrow. She was a Christian woman, after all, and Christian women prayed. Besides, it was good to set a proper example for the children. But it had been some time since Kate Flint felt her prayers had been answered. She sometimes felt a smoldering rage about that.

After the prayer, Kate and Paul ate in silence, while Jilly kept up a silly one-sided conversation about the guinea pig in her classroom. Kate abandoned all thought of taking Paul to task for his midnight snack. How could she, when he had so courageously defended them? Even though she had been trying for two years to control Paul's spiraling weight problem, Kate felt this was not the time to mention the matter. The intruders were not real, of course. But they had been real to Paul, and such bravery should be encouraged, so she said nothing about the wasted food and rose instead to clear the table.

But Paul himself broached the subject, asking, "What'd you do with all the jelly? Throw it away 'cause I'm too fat?"

Kate turned to him, surprised. "What are you talking about?"

"All the jelly's gone. There's nothing left but applesauce."

Kate opened the refrigerator and checked. He was right. She glanced at Jilly. "You know anything about this?"

Jilly smiled enigmatically.

"Jill Marie Flint, you answer me."

Her daughter shook her head. "Uh-uh."

"Uh-uh what?"

"I dunno anything 'bout that jelly."

Kate turned to Paul. "You didn't eat it?"

"How could I eat all that?"

She knelt and searched the lower shelves of the refrigerator, then rose to her feet again. All the jellies and jams were gone. Nothing but that wasted jar of applesauce remained, and now it was in the trash. But she did not remember throwing the other things out. Come to think of it, she did not remember buying the applesauce . . . .

"Well, I'll be," said Kate. "Isn't this the strangest thing?"

Then, closing the refrigerator door, she said, "Okay, y'all, today's a school day. Let's get dressed."

None of them gave the applesauce a second thought.

"*Shabbat shalom*," said Gabby Cantor. "May I get you a nice cup of coffee?"

"I've had my limit," said Benny, lowering himself onto a chair.

Gabby leaned closer, squinting her eyes in a disapproving way. "You don't like my coffee all of a sudden?"

"Oh, no! Really, I just had an extra cup this morning with Morton, and I . . . " Benny Rothstein stopped as Gabby's eyes crinkled in amusement. "You're having fun with me again, I think."

She laughed. "You should eat something. A bagel, maybe? Hot from the oven?"

Benny cringed inside. He suspected Gabby bought day-old bagels for their Torah study. They were always too tough for his dentures to manage. Fortunately, Galia Stern arrived at the table at that moment, providing him with the diversion he needed. "Galia!" he said, ignoring Gabby. "Did you remember my copy of Plaut?"

"Here it is. Sorry I forgot last week." Galia set her huge purse on the table and, sticking both hands inside, withdrew a large burgundy book.

Benny took it from her eagerly. "Now we'll settle things."

"Oh, Benny!" said Gabby. "Are you gonna start *that* again?"

Ignoring her, Benny flipped through the book's pages, peering closely at them through thick-lensed glasses. Gabby looked at the others around the table for support. "Honestly! Who cares if it was Hallo or Bamberger?"

Benny snorted. The others smiled.

"Aha!" cried Benny, pointing to the book. "You see? I told you!"

They had the attention of half a dozen grinning people now. Galia placed a pair of tortoiseshell reading glasses on her nose and read over Benny's shoulder as the old man crossed his arms and leaned back smugly.

"*Deuteronomy and Ancient Near Eastern Literature*, by William W. Hallo," Galia read. "Gabby, you'll have to admit he's got you this time. It's not Bamberger. It says 'Hallo' right there in black and white."

Gabby shifted slightly in her chair to face away from Benny. Touching her perfectly coifed hair, she said, "I'll admit no such thing."

A couple of the onlookers began to chuckle.

"But, Gabby!" exclaimed Benny. "It's right there in black and white!"

"Galia?" said Gabby, smiling sweetly and studiously avoiding the merest glance at the open book on the table in front of Benny. "Would you care for a bagel?"

Galia shook her head.

"Anyone else?" asked Gabby, walking away on genuine alligator pumps. "Bagel? Maybe a nice cup of coffee?"

Benny watched Gabby head for the refreshment table on the far side of the room, working the crowd with the practiced grace of a veteran party hostess. Turning to Galia, he said, "Why won't she admit it?"

On the other side of the room, Gabby Cantor laughed loudly. Patting Benny's shoulder, Galia said, "That'll be the day, dearie."

When Galia Stern left Benny's side to find a chair a few tables away, Gabby returned and sat beside him. Temple Brit Yisrael's activity room buzzed with dozens of conversations as Torah students of all ages settled in at long tables arranged end to end in several rows. He and Gabby Cantor had positioned themselves right up front, to be able

to see and hear the rabbi more clearly. Benny Rothstein knew they
made an odd pair. Both of them were slightly hard of hearing, and they
shared a love of Torah study, but otherwise, they couldn't have been
less alike.

Gabby looked much younger than her sixty-two years and might have
come straight from a fashion-show runway in her taupe linen suit and
bronze-colored silk blouse. Her silver blonde hair rose from a forehead
remarkably free of wrinkles. Benny, on the other hand, wore a ragged
sleeveless sweater pulled haphazardly over a stained white shirt and baggy
woolen trousers far too short, exposing mismatched socks and scuffed
leather loafers. While Gabby's makeup was impeccable, a sprinkling of
snow-white whiskers dusted Benny's cheeks. He prepared to take notes in
a frayed plastic binder with a dull number-two pencil, but Gabby removed
a beige leather notebook and a Montblanc fountain pen from her purse.

Ruth Gold arrived, carrying four or five books of various sizes. "Sorry
I'm late," called the rabbi, as she hurried to a table at the head of the room
where she opened the books and arranged them within easy view. "Let's
get started, shall we? Everyone?" The conversations in the room slowly
died away. "Thank you," said Rabbi Gold, turning to a portable blackboard
and chalking a Hebrew word from right to left across the top in bold,
flowing script.

"Today we study a double portion, *parasha Nitzavim*, meaning 'you
all stand,' and *parasha Vayelech*, meaning 'go forward.' We will begin with
the twenty-ninth chapter of Deuteronomy, but first, a word about Rosh
Hashanah . . . ."

The rabbi made several announcements about logistical preparations
for the annual holy day, then said, "Any other announcements? Oh, I
almost forgot. We're planning to print a brochure about *Mekhkar Torah* for
new and prospective members in order to let them know what we're about.
Nancy Winset will be taking a few photographs for the brochure as we
study." The rabbi smiled across the room at a woman who held a camera
and stood against the wall. "I think the idea is to get candid shots, right,
Nancy?"

The woman smiled and nodded.

"Okay, so that means you shouldn't stare at the camera or go fix your
makeup."

Everyone chuckled.

"Other announcements, anyone?"

As one or two others stood to pitch various seminars, charities, and social events, the woman with the camera drifted about the room snapping photos. At first everyone watched her, but soon they seemed to forget she was there.

Benny shifted in his seat, impatient to get on with the Torah study. The week's *parashat* were quite similar to the vassal treaties of King Esarhaddon the Assyrian. He hoped to explore some of the parallels if they had the time, but often these announcements went on for ten minutes or longer, cutting into their study period. Unfortunately, another woman near the back rose to say something about a feminist seminar beginning in three weeks as part of Tulane's continuing education series. Benny sighed and returned his attention to the rabbi as she listened with a neutral expression on her face. Young as she was, Benny had to admit Rabbi Gold knew her Torah. Many times he had found himself pausing in mid-comment, searching his memory for a name or a verse, only to have her suggest the correct information without so much as a glance at her reference material. At first, he had been skeptical because of her age and, truth be told, her gender. Benny's Orthodox upbringing still surfaced from time to time. But Rabbi Gold was undoubtedly a scholar, and with her short, boyishly cut black hair always casually out of place, her large brown eyes so clear and perceptive, and her faultless olive complexion, he sometimes wished he were a bit younger . . . all that intelligence and such beauty to match! Oh well. His day for such notions was long gone.

A man's voice broke into Benny's thoughts. He turned to see Jonathon Laub standing about halfway back, announcing something about genetics and DNA analysis and the *Cohenim*. Would it never end? This was a Torah study, not a social club! Rabbi Gold smiled—her smile was somewhat strained in Benny's opinion—and nodded her approval. She looked toward the rear of the room. Then, just before she shifted her gaze down to the table full of books, Rabbi Gold's eyes grew wide and the light within them seemed to change, as if something vital there had been extinguished. Benny glanced around. Apparently no one else had noticed. Perhaps he was mistaken. He looked at her again. Ruth's behavior seemed normal as she rearranged the books and papers on the table in preparation for the lesson. Perhaps it had been his imagination. Then Benny noticed something astonishing.

The rabbi's hands were shaking.

As Jonathon Laub continued speaking, Benny rose and shuffled to the front table. "Are you all right?" he whispered.

She refused to look at him. "No."

"Can I get you something? A glass of water maybe?"

"I can't teach, Benny. Will you take over?"

Such an honor! "Yes, of course. But what's wrong? What can I do?"

Ignoring his questions, she hurried from the room.

The class stared silently as Benny gathered his copies of Plaut and Fox and moved behind the front table. He stood for a moment, considering where to begin. Then he remembered. Of course. The prayer. He cleared his throat.

"Excuse me, please. Rabbi Gold is . . . uh, ill, I believe, and she asked me to lead the discussion this morning. Shall we begin with prayer?"

Everyone spoke the Hebrew words together: *"Baruch atah Adonai, Eloheinu melech ha'olam asher kideshanu bemitzvotav vetzivanu la'asok bedivrei Torah."* As was the custom, Benny alone repeated the words in English: "Blessed is the God eternal, ruler of the universe, who hallows us with *mitzvoth* and commands us to engage in the study of Torah. Amen." As he spoke, Benny saw a man take his seat beside Gabby. He was in his sixties, perhaps, and large but quite fit, with wide shoulders, muscular forearms covered with wiry gray hair, and a full beard, brown with streaks of gray. The man placed a white foam cup of coffee on the table. Then he put his hand on Gabby Cantor's shoulder, leaned forward, and kissed her on the cheek.

To a less observant person, it might have seemed the casual kiss of old friends, but in fact, Benny wasn't at all sure that Gabby enjoyed the experience. And something more lay behind that kiss. Not intimacy, of course, but something powerful, just the same.

Out in the hall, Ruth Gold ran to the rest room. Stiff-arming the door, she charged inside and slouched against the lavatory, breathing hard. The reflection she saw in the mirror was no comfort. A terrified seven-

year-old girl stared back through her eyes. Her breathing quickened.
Ruth shoved against the lavatory counter and stumbled to the nearest
toilet compartment. Something cold seized her stomach as if a living
thing squirmed inside, struggling to escape. Falling to her knees, she
retched into the bowl. When she was done, she sank back against the
thin partition and wiped her lips with toilet paper.

Twenty-five years had vanished in an instant, with no way to escape
her memories . . . .

I n the August of her seventh year, Ruth Gold rode in the back seat of
her mother's Volkswagen van as they rolled toward Katy's house, two
blocks off of South Carrollton. The ancient live oaks along the avenue
loomed like widows veiled in Spanish moss. On the neutral ground, a
streetcar kept pace with the van for several blocks until it stopped to
let a pair of hippies get on board. Her mother turned onto a side street
lined with two-story antebellum homes, most of them long since divided
into rental units. They slowed and Ruth saw her friend waiting on a top
step. Katy O'Connor jumped up and sprinted toward them as her father
opened the screen door and waved.

"Poor man," said Ruth's mother under her breath.

Katy scrambled in, slamming the door, and they pulled away with
Janis Joplin singing "Me and Bobby McGee" on the A.M. radio. Ruth's
mother sang along. Katy and Ruth held hands in the back seat. It was
eleven o'clock in the morning and ninety-six degrees in the shade on the
last day they would spend together for more than twenty-five years.

They turned into the parking lot of the Northside Jewish Community
Center. A small crowd stood along the sidewalk nearby. Glancing at them
with a puzzled frown, Ruth's mother turned the radio down and slowly
cruised the bubbling asphalt. The sound of the Monkees' "Steppin' Stone"
faded, replaced by occasional shouts from outside the van as they inched
into an empty parking spot near the crowd. Katy and Ruth ignored the
noise, intent upon a game of paper, scissors, and rocks.

"Come on, girls," said Ruth's mother as she hefted a sizable cloth
bag stuffed with towels, lotions, a transistor radio, and a picnic lunch for
three. A pair of large white balls—"mod" earrings almost as big as eggs—

hung from her ears. Katy and Ruth bounced out of the van, giggling with delight at the prospect of a whole day together in the pool. Ruth's mother stared at the small crowd on the sidewalk, her face turning into a tight and angry mask. Ruth had seen that look before. She stopped giggling.

"Momma?" she said. "What's the matter?"

"Nothing. Let's go."

Her mother slipped the bag over her shoulder, grabbed them both by the hand, and pulled them toward the building. Before they got three steps, a man's voice rose from the crowd. "You there! You with the little girls!"

"Momma?" said Ruth.

"Keep walking!" hissed her mother.

Ruth stared back over her shoulder. A woman with short brown hair and wire-rimmed glasses stood slightly separated from the crowd. The woman wore dull gray clothes. Her pale face was unadorned by makeup. Ruth thought she should try some lipstick at least. It made her mother so pretty.

When the woman saw Ruth looking in her direction, she smiled. It was a pretty smile, tenderly transforming her face in an instant. A few feet away from her, a man called out, "'Suffer the little children to come unto me, and forbid them not, for of such is the kingdom of God'!" As the man shouted those words, Ruth saw the woman's face transform again, becoming sad.

All around the strange woman, people in dark clothes held big pieces of cardboard covered with words.

"Momma? Who are those people?"

"Never mind."

"But they wanna talk to us!"

The man behind them shouted, "Believe in Jesus and you will be saved! Trust Jesus!"

That was the word on the signs, *Jesus*, written over and over.

"What's a 'Jesus,' Momma?"

"It's not a *what*, silly," said Katy. "Jesus is a *who*." Ruth's mother walked faster, maintaining her grip on Katy's and Ruth's hands. Katy said, "Jesus is God. Everybody knows *that*."

Muttering something under her breath, Ruth's mother pulled them inside the Community Center.

Ruth said, "Momma?"

Her mother stopped just inside the doors and knelt between them. "Listen to me carefully, girls. I need to explain something." She crouched between them for a minute, staring at the ground. Then she sighed. "Oh, never mind. Let's just go out back and have some fun, okay?"

Both girls nodded vigorously, and the three of them set out along the hall toward the brightly glowing windows at the rear of the building. When they reached the doors to the swimming pool area, Ruth's mother paused and said, "Remember the rules?"

"No running by the pool," said Ruth.

"And no diving in the shallow end," said Katy.

"That's right. And girls? Today we have another rule. A new one. Are you listening?"

Both girls nodded.

"All right. Let's not talk about Jesus while we're here, understand?"

"Why not, Mrs. Gold?" asked Katy.

"Well, dear, because . . . well, some people might not like it if they hear you talking about him."

"But why?"

"Maybe you should ask your father when you get home. Okay?"

"Okay!"

Ruth's mother smiled at them. She was very pretty when she smiled. "You two go have fun," she said.

Squealing with delight, Ruth and Katy ran across the concrete and dove into the pool together, completely ignoring all the rules.

O ne more comment about last week's *parasha*," Benny said, "and then we really should move on to our text."

Several people chuckled. The group was notorious for getting side-tracked. Sometimes they spent the entire hour and a half without reading a single word of the week's Torah portion. Benny was determined that this would not be such a week. "So," he said, "Josephus tells us that the horrible prophecy of verse fifty-three literally came true during the siege of Jerusalem. Parents not only ate food rather than giving it to their children, but women actually consumed their children."

Hands were in the air all around the room. Benny pointed at a young lady who had not yet spoken. One must take care to allow everyone to participate.

"Clearly," said the young woman, "the author of the blessings and curses wrote them before the Jewish Wars, but it's possible this portion of the text actually came after the Babylonian siege described in Lamentations. It may be another example of the redactor's agenda to justify official responses to current events."

"So you believe these words were not actually prophecy, but were written after the fact?"

"Most likely."

"Clearly," thought Benny. *"Most likely."* He smiled and adjusted his glasses. *These young people are so sure of their theories. I only wish—* All in an instant, in the middle of thinking about something completely different, it came to him, as memories often did these days. Benny pushed his glasses farther up on his nose and stared at the man beside Gabby Cantor.

So many years. So many, many years. But yes, it was him.

Solomon Cantor had come back.

S am Gottlieb, senior rabbi at Temple Brit Yisrael, called to Ruth just as she reached the door.

"Ruth! Where are you going?"

Startled, she spun to face the older man as he approached her in the empty corridor.

"I'm not feeling well. Benny Rothstein's teaching the class. I have to go home."

Sam knew about Steve Cronen, of course. Ruth had told him the very next day. Could that really have been just a week ago? "Can I get someone to drive you?"

"No. I'll make it all right. It's just . . . I feel a little nauseous, that's all."

"Maybe it's that stomach flu that's been going around."

"Maybe."

He frowned, looking at her closely. "Listen, I'm sorry to bring this up again, but I still think you should take some personal time."

"I appreciate it, Sam. Really. I just need to keep myself occupied, you know? Give me the rest of the day to feel better, and I'll be back tomorrow."

"Okay, then. Don't let me keep you. But you might use the side door instead of this one. There are some people out front causing a disturbance."

"What's going on?"

"Some Christian fanatics standing on the sidewalk yelling at people coming in for services. We've already called the police."

Ruth mumbled a mild curse.

Rabbi Gottlieb smiled. "My sentiments exactly. But don't let them bother you too much. It's not as if our Christian friends have sent official representatives. I think they're just a few fruitcakes out for a little attention."

"Well, I'm not taking another exit to accommodate *them*."

The senior rabbi squeezed her shoulder. "That's the spirit. Take care of yourself, all right?"

Ruth left the building and followed the walkway to the parking lot. Just beyond the last row of cars, an old man stood on the sidewalk, holding a large white cardboard sign bearing the words *Trust Jesus* scrawled in big black letters. Oddly enough, he looked respectable in his dark blue suit and red tie. His clean shaven, ordinary face, gold framed eyeglasses, and neatly parted gray hair gave him the look of a doting grandfather. Several younger people stood beside him, all of them dressed just as nicely.

"'I am the way, the truth, and the life,'" yelled the man. "'No man cometh unto the Father but by me!'"

Ruth entered her car, a twenty-year-old Citroën. The man faced her, waving the sign vigorously. "'For I am not ashamed of the gospel of Christ,'" he yelled. "'For it is the power of God unto salvation to every one that believeth; to the Jew first, and also to the Greek.'"

Ruth Gold locked the door, started the engine, and sped out of the parking lot. The past and the present intermingled before her eyes and the bitter taste of bile lingered in her mouth, and—just for an instant— she questioned what was real and what was a vile illusion.

Kate Flint parked in the only spot she could afford within walking distance of the French Quarter, an asphalt lot just down river of Elysian Fields. Hurrying along the sidewalk past the peeling façades of nineteenth-century clapboard houses, she checked her watch and groaned. Late again. She quickened her pace, weaving through a small group of pedestrians, mumbling an apology as she cut in front of an old woman carrying groceries. At the corner of Esplanade and Decatur, she passed the fire station called Creole No. 9, and crossed into the Vieux Carre. She turned right on Barracks, then left on Chartres, and almost ran the last four blocks to the shop.

Sure enough, the couple from Wisconsin stood waiting by the door.

"I do apologize, y'all," she said, fumbling in her backpack for the keys. "Hope you haven't been here long."

The woman smiled and shook her head, but the man stared far away, up the street toward Jackson Square, tight lipped and grim in his outrageous Hawaiian shirt and sky blue shorts.

"I found it after you left last night. Under a pile of quilts, if you can imagine that." Kate pushed the door open and stepped inside. "Y'all wait right here till I get the lights turned on."

Deftly avoiding a spindly Queen Anne table piled high with china and crystal, Kate rushed into the shadows. Near the back wall, she paused at a rolltop desk just long enough to drop her backpack into a bottom drawer. She flipped a couple of switches and four antique light fixtures sprinkled incandescent cheer throughout The Other Day, Kate's tiny antique shop.

Smiling as she walked back toward the tourists, she said, "Here we are, right this way." Kate led them to a pile of linens, spilling out of the top drawer of a Beidermier highboy.

"Oh, it's *perfect*," gushed the woman, lifting the tablecloth at arm's length.

"It's French, of course," said Kate. "From the Thalia estate. Late eighteenth century. I have it on good authority that this cloth was used when Jefferson Davis dined with the Thalias in 1888, just before—"

"How much?" interrupted the husband.

Kate named the price and watched him frown. Five minutes later, the couple from Wisconsin headed for the front door without the tablecloth, the man in the lead, the woman following, her lips tight now and her eyes focused far away. Just before they stepped outside, Kate called to the man, "Is it that you don't *have* the money, or just that you are entirely ignorant of the value of that piece?" She felt her heart begin to pound as she clenched her teeth and watched the door close behind them.

"Calm down," she whispered, pressing a palm against her chest. "You just calm right down."

Kate Flint breathed deeply a few times, then hung the Open sign in the window and wandered back through the shop, switching on table lamps. She brewed a cup of Constant Comment, drawing the water from the lavatory in the tiny rest room nestled under the stairs and heating it on a small hot plate. Back at her desk, she opened the lower drawer, moved a Bible she had not read in months, rummaged around in a small pocket on the outside of her backpack, and extracted three small pharmacy bottles. She swallowed a pill from each bottle, two to prevent irregular heartbeats and one to thin her blood and prevent a clot from causing a stroke. Then she replaced the bottles in the side pocket of her backpack, unzipped the main pocket, and removed a copy of the *Times-Picayune*. She spread it on the desktop, turned to page nine, kicked off her espadrilles, and settled in to read about a gang-related murder in Desire. Ordinarily, she wouldn't waste her time on such things—one murder report was much like another in New Orleans—but she had read everything else already and needed something to keep her mind off her gnawing rage.

It was no use. When she thought of that idiot from Wisconsin and his mousy little wife. . . . No matter what she did, Kate's anger lingered just beneath the surface. She folded the paper and put it away. Where did these feelings come from?

She knew, of course.

Paul's overeating, his attraction to violence, and now these reoccurring nightmares . . . it was beginning to look like her son needed professional help. A couple of days ago, when Paul had gotten it into his head that someone came and stole the jellies and jams from their refrigerator, she had tried to reason with him, but crazy as that was, nothing she could say had shaken his belief.

Kate wished there were someone who would understand how she felt, but all hope of that had died with John. In the early months after his passing, she had turned to God for solace, but her tearful prayers were met with stony silence. According to the religion of her youth, that meant she was somehow being prideful or insincere, but Kate had searched her heart and found no such feelings there. She had begged too pitifully for ulterior motives. All the prayers she ever said to God had finally boiled down to one pathetic word: Please. Please. *Please!*

Where was the pride in that?

In time she had stopped asking God for comfort, accepting the silence as an answer and the ache in her chest as an unbearable punishment of some kind, something she apparently deserved. Still, she had the children. She could always count on her Paul and little Jilly.

Oh, enough of this!

Kate rose from the desk, padded barefoot across the room, opened an armoire, and removed a can of furniture polish and a dusting rag. Beginning with a Stickley side table near the door, she made her daily pass through the shop, wiping every wooden surface she could reach, working hard to get her mind off of things.

A dark oaken plaque hanging high on the shop's back wall inspired her. Five years ago, John had returned from a buying trip to London with the thing, proudly assigning it that place of honor. The inscription on the plaque read *Laborare Est Orare*—Work Is Prayer—her husband's motto. He had always thought of his work as an offering to God, but lately Kate had begun to think it was best to work *instead* of praying. When she paused, even for a moment, dismal memories bobbed in her mind like corpses in a calm and tepid sea. Besides, it did not seem to matter to God anymore whether she was working or praying, and faced with his divine disinterest, she might as well keep her mind on her business. But today she could not even seem to do that. She glanced up at the plaque. The Latin words blurred, became a meaningless pattern, then faded altogether as her traitorous thoughts spiraled down to sunken, deadly places, and she found herself adrift among the flotsam of the past.

Kate Flint stood motionless for five full minutes, the rag in her hand, her thoughts turned inward, neither working nor praying. It might have lasted for an hour if the telephone had not rung. Struggling to rise from her sorrowful reverie, she wove her way absently through the densely packed antiques, reaching her desk as the telephone rang for the fifth time. She lifted the receiver and placed it to her ear. An unfamiliar voice joined the others in her head.

"Katy, is that you?"

Kate's fingers gripped the telephone more tightly. *Katy.* John's pet name for her. But it had been more than twenty years since anyone else had called her that.

"Katy? Are you there?"

She roused herself. "Yes."

"It's Ruth Gold."

Kate said nothing as the old clocks throughout the shop ticked. What happened? When had she become Kate? The voice on the telephone continued. "Have I caught you at a bad time?"

Kate whispered, "No."

"Could you speak up? I think we've got a bad connection."

"I said no."

"Do you remember me?"

"Of course. How are you?"

"Not good, actually. Sol Cantor is out."

"Out?"

"I thought you'd want to know."

"They let him out?"

"Released early for good behavior."

"But . . . can they do that?"

"Katy, they already did."

She fell into a chair with the rag still in her hand. "Do you know where he is?"

"Here in New Orleans. I've just seen him at temple."

Temple . . . she lingered on the word, trying to decide where it fit. *Oh . . . temple. Of course. Like church.*

"Is he, uh . . . angry?"

"Someone sent a box of poisoned apples to my house. My . . . my boyfriend ate one. He died."

Kate felt a strange chill. She had read about that murder just a few days ago. How strange to find that the "unnamed homeowner" mentioned in the paper was Ruth Gold, someone she once knew. Kate said, "I'm so sorry." The telephone remained silent. After a moment, she continued, "So you think it was Solomon Cantor?"

"Oh, Katy, I don't know. It could be a coincidence. I mean, people poison food at the grocery store sometimes. Remember the Tylenol thing? People do things like that."

"Sure they do."

Ruth asked, "Has anything unusual happened to you recently?"

Thinking about Paul and his paranoia, Kate said, "No. Everything's normal."

"I guess you're married, right?"

"No."

"Got a friend? Neighbor? Someone nearby who could keep an eye on you?"

Kate said, "You're scaring me." She stared at a framed needlepoint on the wall. Red-stitched words on a blue background, faded by time: *Don't Worry*. The phone line hummed.

Then Ruth said, "I'm sorry, but I have to ask."

"My son lives with me."

"How old is he?"

"Twelve." A boy with a butcher knife.

"All right. Listen, if you need to get in touch with me, call Temple Brit Yisreal. I'm usually there."

"I'm okay. Don't worry." Needlepoint advice.

"Well, bye then."

"Ruth?" She rushed to say that name before the woman hung up, using it for the first time in . . . such a long time. "Ruth? It's nice to hear your voice."

A final pause, then, "Yeah. You too, Katy."

The woman hung up before Kate could say good-bye. Sitting alone in her shop, she thought about little girls and swimming pools and dark hallways. Then, gradually, her thoughts shifted to the applesauce and the missing jelly of a few days past. The thing was, she didn't remember buying that applesauce. In fact, she never bought the stuff. She and the kids didn't care for it, really, and Paul probably only put it on his sandwich because there was nothing else to—

Oh.

Kate covered her mouth.

No, that's just crazy.

Screaming, Jake Singer awoke.

Gripping the edges of his narrow mattress, he lay on his back panting like a sprinter, muscles tense, staring wildly at the ceiling. Gradually his breathing slowed and his pulse dropped as he realized he was safe. He swung his legs over the side of the bed and sat for five full minutes with his head in his hands. Then, without switching on the light, he rose and headed into the bathroom, where he filled his palms with cold water and splashed his face. Turning his back to the mirror, Jake leaned against the sink and stared at the blinking blue numbers of the bedside clock: 5:35 A.M. Time to get moving. Early bird gets the worm and all that.

By the time he was dressed Jake Singer had forgotten all of the details of the nightmare, except for the persistent memory of a clicking sound. For some reason, that always stuck in his mind. He wasted no time trying to remember the rest of it. Why bother? It wouldn't make any difference.

He always woke up screaming.

The dominoes curved like a row of little soldiers guarding Orvis Newton's end of the flimsy card table. He selected one and laid it down. Morton Rothstein, his opponent, leaned closer, adjusting his glasses to peer at the new number. Then the old man grunted, returning his attention to his own row of dominoes.

"I was hoping you didn't have a three."

Smiling, Orvis Newton touched his wig, pressing it in place. "Sorry."

"No, you're not," said Morton.

The elder Rothstein brother took a long time to make his plays. While Orvis waited, he looked around the roof. Mr. Disraeli, Morton's fifteen-year-old calico cat, lay atop the parapet a few feet away, snoring loudly. He had never heard a cat snore before. Morton did not seem to notice, and seemed unconcerned that Mr. Disraeli might roll over in his sleep and fall from the roof of the apartment building, a third-floor walkup, a block and a half north of Tchoupitoulas. Oh well. If Morton didn't care, Orvis certainly didn't. Besides, the cat hadn't gotten that old by falling off roofs.

Morton placed a domino on the table. A double three.

Orvis surveyed his choices. "How'd work go last night?"

"I did okay."

Orvis had learned much about Morton and his brother Benny during their rooftop games. He knew that Morton worked late nights selling roses table to table in half a dozen restaurants along St. Charles Avenue. He even knew how much money Morton usually made. It was surprising what an old man in a tuxedo could earn, playing on the sympathy of romantically inclined women, especially if he didn't mind applying a little pressure to their dates. Benny, on the other hand, didn't have to work. He had a pension from thirty years as the second-shift manager at D. F. & G. Shoe Manufacturing. For three decades he had arrived on the factory floor at four in the afternoon and returned home at one in the morning. Now Benny went to bed early and rose promptly at six without an alarm clock. Orvis knew that Benny fed the cat every morning just before he read the paper, and at eight-thirty sharp, he left to study Talmud at Temple Brit Yisrael. Most afternoons, Morton and Benny played dominoes beside the parapet on the tar-papered roof of their apartment building, sitting on plastic chairs in the shade of a salvaged Heineken umbrella, ignoring the view between a pair of former cotton warehouses as distant cargo ships slipped silently along the Mississippi past the Milan Street wharf.

It had been easy to join them. Orvis had simply walked up to the roof one day and begun a conversation about dominoes. At first, he'd been worried, thinking Benny might recognize him in spite of the wig and the horn-rimmed glasses. But he had forged ahead, telling them he was new to the neighborhood, a retired widower, just moved down from Cincinnati to live with his daughter, introducing himself as James Harrison, "but people call me Harry." After maybe ten minutes, the old men had offered to go down to their apartment for another chair, and Orvis knew he was in.

Like most old folks, the Rothstein brothers loved to talk, especially about themselves, and Orvis was a very good listener. It was why he had come. To hear them tell it, the Rothsteins were the last of a venerable family line, with ancestors dating back to the time of Bienville. Their family tradition held that two men, a father and a son, arrived in 1727 on the ship that bore the *filles à la cassette*—those nubile young ladies of good repute assembled by the French in hopes of retaining the better men among their colony. One of the women, a Jewish girl, gave birth to a healthy boy seven months after the ship arrived and claimed the younger Rothstein as the father. He was hanged by an outraged mob of drunken fusiliers, perhaps the first Jew to die unjustly in the New World at the hands of the *goyim*. The elder Rothstein raised the baby as his own, thus establishing the family's tenuous foothold on the continent.

Benny and Morton did not seem to mind the fact that they were descended from an unwanted illegitimate child, or that an American family tree at least 250 years old would die with them. The old men's lives revolved around dominoes, their ancient cat, temple life, and each other. Orvis could tell they shared a fierce affection, although of course the brothers never spoke of such things, at least not in front of strangers. He had learned, for example, that Benny had asthma, so every night when Morton returned from selling roses, he refilled the humidifier in his brother's room while Benny slept. Orvis also knew that Benny cooked a kosher breakfast for Morton every morning before leaving to study Talmud, although Benny himself never ate more than half a bagel. They'd told him it had been this way for fifty-six years. Since Benny had left the home of their parents and moved in with his older brother, they had never been separated, not even for one night, with the sole exception of World War II, when Morton had left to serve his country as a quartermaster at Fort Bragg, managing a monumental flow of boots, helmets, carbines, and fatigues. Benny had been unable to join the service because of his asthma, so he remained at home in New Orleans, working double shifts at the factory and investing every spare penny in war bonds.

Orvis had asked the neighbors about the Rothsteins. Some believed their relationship was of the baser kind, and why not? This was New Orleans, after all, a city where such things had never drawn more than a nod and a wink. He had hoped the rumors were true. It would have made his task easier. But after spending several afternoons on the roof with the Rothstein brothers, Orvis knew the gossip was unfounded. Morton and Benny simply preferred each other's company to that of anyone else.

"Morton," said Orvis, "what would you do without Benny? I mean, look at me. I'm all alone, and it's no good, I can tell you. So what if he goes first?"

Morton shuffled the dominoes, clicking them together like snapping bones. "Harry," he said, "I try not to think too much about that. And sometimes I pray we'll be allowed to go together. In a car accident, maybe. Something quick."

Orvis Newton regretted that it could not be that way.

CHAPTER
FOUR

Solomon Cantor walked Gabby's little dog. He would have chosen something larger, a Doberman or a rottweiler—something with longer teeth and shorter hair. For one thing, it wasn't right to own a furry dog in New Orleans. He remembered a guy—what was his name?—Abe something. Anyway, this guy had a collie, one of the black and white ones, not like Lassie, the other kind. This guy, Abe, he cut his dog's hair off every July. Shaved him right to the skin. Dog looked embarrassed, like it was ashamed of being naked, but at least it was big enough to do some damage if someone broke into the house.

Gabby, on the other hand, had this little dog here, this fuzzy little thing. Called it Monique. Not only did it have short teeth, it had lots of poofy fur, like a cotton ball. Reminded him of that guy in D block, the one they called Einstein, because he had gray hair that stuck out in every direction. This dog had the same problem. You could hardly see its little legs, whirring around underneath all that hair. You had to wonder how it saw where it was going, with its eyes covered up that way.

All things considered, Sol didn't care for the dog. But he did like taking it for walks.

It still amazed him, what Gabby had done. When the thing happened, they had lived in a nice enough little place over in Metarie. Three bedrooms, two baths, a study, and a wet bar. Nothing special, but not bad. He'd been doing all right with the metals recycling business. A lot of nice fat Japanese contracts, some of them over ten years old, three high-volume compactors and thirteen Peterbilt tractor trailer rigs fully paid for, with every reason to expect a new market in paper products to break in the next few years. Sure, he'd had a few problems with the Teamsters, and the hours were long, but all in all, business had been good and was getting better. Then he went down. No way Gabby could've run the business. Recycling was a man's world back then. The legal fees ate up all their capital assets and inventory in six short months. Everyone in town knew he had no choice, and they had no pity. He got pennies on the dollar. When he went up to the Farm, there was nothing left for Gabby and the boy. She had to do something, so she got this real estate deal going. One thing led to another, and here she was, rich as Midas, with him walking this cotton ball with legs in the Garden District like he owned the joint. Who would'a thought?

The landscaping was the thing that got him the most, after all those years hanging around the Angola exercise yard with nothing but little patches of weeds sticking up here and there through the dirt. He liked the way some of the yards in Gabby's neighborhood looked like rain forests, with palm trees and banana trees and huge elephant ears. The greenery made him feel free . . . that, and the fact that he never took the same route twice. On the inside, everything was routine. Even when they gave you a choice—which was almost never—you stuck with your routine. Habits became old friends, things you could count on day after day, but now that he was out he took great pleasure in walking Gabby's dog along a different route every time. The neighbors probably thought he was a hired man, dressed like he was in chinos and a T-shirt, pulling up to Gabby's house in his old truck. The beard probably didn't help either.

Gabby wanted him to cut it, but he'd had the thing so long now it felt natural. Without the beard he'd feel like Abe's collie, all naked and stupid looking.

The little thing sniffed at a trash can. On a hunch, Sol lifted the lid and looked inside. Nothing. Just paper and food scraps. Carefully, he replaced the lid, wiped his hand on the thigh of his chinos, and glanced around. It wouldn't be good for Gabby to catch him doing that. She hated what he did for a living now, driving his old pickup around town searching for abandoned scrap metal piled in back alleys and beside the road. Said it wasn't seemly, what with her trying to maintain a position in the community. Thought he should go to work for their son Izzy. Didn't understand he needed a way to make a few bucks without having a schedule. He hated schedules. Plus, after twenty-five years of saying, "Yeah, boss," to the bulls in Angola, the last thing in the world he wanted was his own son telling him what to do. A man had to hang on to *some* self-respect. He hoped Gabby would understand that soon, after they had a little more time together.

Besides, who cared if he sold scrap metal for a buck or wore a beard? As if what he did or didn't do would have any effect on whether these high society types would invite her to their tea parties.

Ridiculous.

Gabby was a Jew with an ex-con for a husband. Even if they didn't live together—yet—that was the way of things. He could be Donald Trump's banker for all they cared. These *goyim* neighbors of hers would never let her into their little world. In fact, with him around, she might even have trouble in her *own* world. Look at that rabbi the other day. One glance at him, and she ran for the door.

Still, Gabby cared about such things, and he cared about Gabby.

Solomon Cantor and the dog continued along the shade-dappled street with the tiny animal's painted toenails clicking rapidly against the slate sidewalk in staccato counterpoint to the big man's rolling gait.

This was gonna be harder than he thought.

Jesus said, 'This is my body, which is given for you. Do this in remembrance of me.'"

Reverend Cahill lifted his hand to his mouth.

Following the minister's lead, Kate placed a tiny square of unleavened
bread onto her tongue. *See, God? I'm still here, still doing what you want in spite of
everything you've done to me.* On the pew beside her, Paul and Jilly mirrored
her actions. It was Jilly's very first Communion. As the reverend began to
pray, Kate bowed her head, but her eyes were open, staring at her hands.
She wished John could be here to share the moment, but that was it in a
nutshell wasn't it? He was not here. He would never be *here* again. She had
only the meager hope that maybe he could see them. Maybe he was cele-
brating with the angels, looking down from heaven on the congregation
of Trinity Bible Church.

The thought was no comfort at all.

A silver-plated tray came their way, passed from hand to hand along
the pew. Tiny clear glasses filled with grape juice rested in slots on the
platter. Kate selected one and passed the tray on to her son. Paul held
it low so Jilly could withdraw a glass, and then he took one himself and
gave the tray to the woman at his side. Kate stole surreptitious glances at
her children, solemnly holding the blood of Jesus between the fingertips
of both hands, waiting for the minister to allow them to drink. When
everyone had a glass, the minister spoke again.

"Jesus said, 'This cup is the new covenant in my blood, which is
poured out for you.'"

Reverend Cahill drank the juice. As Kate did the same, her thoughts
turned to Ruth's poisoned boyfriend and Paul's conviction that someone
had broken into their home. What if it was true? What if someone really
had tried to poison them, too?

Kate knew it was far more likely that her son had an overactive
imagination.

"The Last Supper was a Passover celebration led by Jesus, who was
called *rabbi* at that table in the upper room," said the minister. "Jesus was a
Jew, of course, as were all of his apostles and most of those who believed
in him. Yet we often make the mistake of blaming his crucifixion on the
Jewish people, as if they were of one mind in the matter."

Ruth Gold's telephone call replayed itself in Kate's memory: *Got a friend?
neighbor? someone nearby who could keep an eye on you?* In spite of Kate's attempts
to stay focused on the sanctity of the moment, the fear continued to rise, an
alien and inappropriate emotion in the house of God. Last night, after the

kids went to bed, she had gingerly stacked wineglasses three rows tall just inside the front and back doors, hoping she would hear them fall if someone entered in the night. Then she had lain in the dark on the sofa, wide-eyed and fully clothed, clutching Paul's baseball bat, unable to rid her mind of those fearful words: *Solomon Cantor is out.* She had thought of waking Paul, so he would be there with her, ready, just in case. He really was the man of the house, after all. She had walked to the closed door of his room before deciding she was just being paranoid. Still, dawn had been slow in coming. When it did, the children rose to prepare for church as usual, unaware of her fear.

The three years since John's death had trained Kate well for the task of maintaining a strong and stable façade. She had finally learned to isolate her sorrow to rare moments, mostly when she was alone in the bathroom with the shower running to conceal the sound of her weeping. Kate resolved to control her fear in the same way. She would begin by paying attention to the sermon.

Reverend Cahill said, "The Roman soldiers in Pilate's Jerusalem garrison were from many countries around the Mediterranean. It might have been Spanish hands that drove the spikes through Jesus' wrists, or Greek. If God had wanted us to believe that Jews are guilty of Jesus' death in a special way, why not allow them to stone our Lord to death in the Jewish fashion? It is no accident that God chose the Roman cross instead, as a reminder that all the world, Jew and Gentile alike, has an equal share in the guilt of sin."

In spite of herself, Kate's thoughts returned to the missing jelly and the appearance of the applesauce. She just couldn't remember buying that applesauce. Had someone given it to them as a gift? There were lots of jars and cans of food in her pantry that had come in food baskets at Christmastime last year. She didn't remember exactly who sent what, but she'd never heard of sending applesauce in a Christmas food basket.

"So when our Bibles speak of 'the Jews' condemning Jesus, we must remember that term is a kind of literary shorthand for 'the Jewish leaders.' And we must remember that not even all the Jewish leaders opposed Christ. Our Bibles describe some Pharisees and even temple priests accepting Jesus as their Messiah and their God."

"Lies!"

The cry came from somewhere to her left. Kate turned and saw a very tall woman standing in the aisle, her arm lifted, her finger pointing at the minister. She wore a conservative gray suit. Her blonde hair lay close to her head, pulled tightly back above her ears by a hair clip.

"You are *lying* to these people!"

Reverend Cahill said nothing. Bill Lewis, an elder of the church, was already rising from his seat near the woman.

"The Jews rejected Christ!" she screamed. "They killed him! They killed Stephen! They stoned Paul! And God has abandoned them to their sin!"

Beside her, Kate felt her son cringe. Paul was old enough to understand the ramifications of the woman's words. He knew that half of the blood in his veins belonged to the people this woman had condemned. He knew that his father had been Jewish.

Two other men rose to their feet and headed for the woman. Bill Lewis placed his hand on the woman's arm. She shook him off and faced the congregation. "These are lies!" shouted the woman. "Read your Bibles! Read Acts! The Jews were a curse on the first Christians! A curse!"

Catching a movement from the corner of her eye, Kate looked at Paul. His hands were balled into tight fists. Kate touched her son's shoulder, leaning close. "Don't listen to her, honey," she whispered. "Remember, Jesus was a Jew." He looked down at his lap, where his hands remained tightly clenched.

Kate returned her attention to the woman. The other two men had reached her now, surrounding her and speaking in low, urgent tones. She stood taller than any of them. Kate thought she saw the blonde woman make eye contact with a man sitting beside her in the pew. He glanced up and seemed to shake his head slightly. Every color of the rainbow danced in his gold-rimmed spectacles, reflected from the stained-glass windows just beyond him. He wore a blue suit, a white shirt, and a red tie. His hair was gray, and his face was unremarkable, but something about him seemed familiar.

Jake Singer awoke screaming, as usual.

Flailing his arms about, Jake hit the bedside table and knocked two books, the phone, and the light to the floor and shattered an empty glass, cutting his hand. A single drop of blood fell upon the sheets.

Someone pounded at his door. He stood, staggered, and fell back upon the bed. Jake took another minute to get his bearings, then bent over and sorted through the debris on the floor, cutting himself a second time on the broken glass. Bleeding more profusely now, he found a pair of blue jeans, dragged them on, rose to his feet, and crossed the room, where he leaned against the inside of the door, nursing his hand.

A muffled voice called, "Open up, Singer. It's Ivan Slasky."

"I'm sick."

"I don't care! Open up, or I'll get the police."

Jake rubbed his forehead, smearing blood across his face. "Just a minute."

"Hurry up, Singer!"

Stepping back, Jake unlocked the door and pulled it open.

Ivan Slasky filled the frame with his sizable bulk, fists propped against his hips, flattened features arranged in a scowl. "I warned ya," he said. "I did. Ya can't say—Hey! What's the matter with yer face?"

"What?"

"Ya got blood all over yer face."

Jake touched his forehead. "It's nothing. I cut my hand."

"Okay," said Slasky suspiciously. "Well, ya can't say I didn't warn ya."

"What are you talking about?" asked Jake.

"Yer out, that's what. Ya got till the end of the week, and then I'm comin' in and throwin' yer stuff into the street."

"Aw, come on, Slasky—"

"Mister Slasky."

"Can't we work something out?"

"I done warned ya three times already. Yer screamin' all day and all night makes the other tenants nervous. Ya keep 'em up. This time I heard it myself. Sounds like bloody murder in there." Slasky craned his neck to look beyond Jake into the interior of the apartment, making no effort to hide his curiosity.

"Look, Slasky."

"*Mister* Slasky, I told ya!" bellowed the landlord. "Ya got till the end of the week!"

With that, he turned and stalked away.

Jake shut the door, slipped the dead bolt in place, and shuffled back to the bed. Stooping, he picked up the portable telephone from the pile of debris on the floor. He punched seven numbers from memory, then cursed as the phone rang too many times, knowing he would get her machine. Still, he waited for the message and the beep. "This is Jake. How come you never answer your phone? I took a nap and almost made it this time. It was different. It was good, but it was . . . very hard. I need to talk to you. Call me. Please. I, uh, just need to . . . you know." He paused, searching for better words. Finally, he mumbled, "Just call me."

Dropping the phone to the floor without breaking the connection, he fell back upon the bed, bleeding slowly, leaving an indelible stain upon the mattress.

J illy! Wait!"

Jilly ignored Kate, dashing for the front door of the house.

"Jill Marie Flint! I mean it! You stop right there!"

At the mention of her middle name, Jilly sat on the bottom step, waiting for her mother and brother to catch up. Kate and Paul walked side by side across the sparse grass of the shady front lawn, sweating in their church clothes.

"Paul, I want you to stay out here with Jilly for a minute, okay?"

"Why?"

"Because I asked you to."

"But Mom, I—"

"Just do it!" she snapped.

Paul stared at her for a second, then said, "Hurry up then, will ya? I got things to do."

"All right." She climbed the steps to the front porch and unlocked the door. Her hand shook. Perhaps it was only exhaustion. The door swung open silently. She stood for a moment, staring inside.

"Mom?" said Paul.

"Just wait a minute!" Kate hadn't meant to be so harsh. *Where does all this anger come from?* She looked down at Paul, forcing herself to smile. "I'll be right back, honey. You stay there and make sure Jilly doesn't run off."

Jilly said, "What about him? He might run off too."

"That's right, honey. You watch your brother, and he'll watch you."

Paul stared up at her, forehead wrinkled, eyes filled with questions. She realized he was not taken in by her false cheerfulness. "I'll be right back," she said, as if by repeating the statement she could conjure up protection. Just for an instant, she wished her son were the one entering their house alone. *Why couldn't he do this?* Then, coming to her senses, she beat the thought back with a shake of her head and an imperceptible guttural noise, deep in her throat.

Stepping into the entry hall, Kate left the door ajar, allowing the afternoon heat to flood into the dark, air-conditioned interior. The usual sounds filled the house: the ticking of her grandmother's cuckoo clock, the distant clunk of freshly frozen cubes rolling out of the ice maker, the soft hum of chilled air flowing from the vents overhead. Her own breath seemed unnecessarily loud. Kate wished she had been quieter with the children just now. And kinder.

She knew there probably wasn't any reason to fear Solomon Cantor. Still, if he was angry after all these years, and if he was here, he knew she was coming. In the moment that thought occurred to her, Kate felt adrenaline surge through her body, followed immediately by an all too familiar tightness in her chest. *I've got to calm down.* She had forgotten to take her medication that morning in the rush to get ready for church. If she couldn't calm herself now, the afternoon would be spent in an easy chair or in bed, waiting for her irregular heartbeat to return to normal. Kate hated her condition most at moments like this.

The living room loomed darkly behind the drawn portiere at the cased opening off the entry on her right. Willing herself to breathe evenly, Kate entered. Her needlepoint collection hung on the left-hand wall. Across the room, thick plantation shutters blocked the September sun. She saw the back of the sofa and the small tiled fireplace beyond, but the corners of the room lay concealed in shadow. She flipped the switch beside the portiere. The light did not come on.

Her heart became a rebellious thing, erratically flinging itself against her rib cage. Instinctively, she thought to pray to ease her fears, but as soon as the impulse arose, she pushed it away. She flipped the switch once more. Nothing happened. *Just a burnt-out bulb*, she thought. Clinging to that hope, Kate crossed to the floor lamp beside the sofa and turned the switch. It cast a yellow cone of light onto a copy of

Antiques Quarterly on the side table. She looked around. The room was empty.

Going out the way she had come in, Kate crossed the hall to the dining room. This time, the overhead light came on when she flipped the switch. Feeling foolish, she bent at the knees to peek under the table. Nothing there, of course. She rose and pushed open a bi-swing door and passed through the small, closetlike butler's pantry to the kitchen. It too was empty. She checked the bedrooms and the bathrooms and even the closets, passing more framed needlepoints along the way. Every room was empty. Emboldened by this fact, she returned to the central hall and stood outside the door to John's study.

It had been months since she'd opened that door. Everything inside had been left much as it had been on the day they came to take him to the hospital. Of all the rooms in the house, it was the one most completely his. She had made a few token efforts to straighten the papers still lying on his desk—mostly bills of sale, letters to other antique dealers, and newsletters from collectors and traders in various collectibles—but each time she tried to claim the room for herself, she discovered some small, personal thing—his eyeglasses, a note scrawled on the back of an envelope, a ticket stub from their last evening at the movies together—and she found herself running from the room as if the air had filled with poison. Kate had come to hate the study, even considered selling the house to distance herself from it, but the children knew no other home, and she could not bring herself to force more change upon them, so she simply avoided the room, pretending it was not there.

But she had to know for certain if someone hid beyond the door.

Kate forced herself to grasp the doorknob. She paused, longing again to call on someone, anyone, even if it was her twelve-year-old son, but there was no one else, so she turned the knob. The latch clicked loudly in the silence. Slowly, Kate opened the study door.

The smell of stale air penetrated her nostrils as she peeked inside. The study was unbearably full of emptiness. All was as she remembered—as John had left it—a room filled with common possessions, mass-produced and liberally scattered around the globe. Millions of other people had things exactly like them. But John had touched this. He had purchased that. And so, for Kate, the everyday was sanctified by the never-again, and the intimacy of these ordinary things flayed her heart to ribbons.

As Kate closed the door, she felt the urge to pray once more. But this time she did not ask for help. This time she sent curses roaring up to heaven.

R ummaging around in her oversized bag, Ruth found the *yahrzeit* candle. Just holding the thing made her weepy. Digging in her purse again, she withdrew a tissue, wiped her eyes, and blew her nose loudly. Then she lit the candle, placed it on her parents' tombstone, and sat on the concrete bench beside the path to say *shehecheyanu*. Rocking back and forth, she mumbled the prayer softly, *"Baruch atah Adonai, Eloheinu melech ha'olam shehecheyanu v'kiy'manu v'higianu lazman hazeh. Amen."*

She felt a peace creep into her heart. It was the comfort of tradition, of belonging, of knowing she was merely a link in the chain that stretched from Abraham and Sarah to the Messiah, may he quickly come. Her parents were the link before her, and after her . . . no, it was a crutch to dwell on the future. She would live here. Now. Even if it killed her.

The rabbi repeated the words in English, "Blessed are you, Adonai our God, Ruler of the universe, for giving us life, for sustaining us, and for bringing us to this season. Amen." Finished with the prayer, Ruth glanced around to see if anyone was watching. She immediately felt a twinge of guilt. So what if they watched? Why should she be ashamed of praying in public? But neither her guilt nor her shame mattered, since she was alone in that jumbled necropolis of stark white tombstones. All around her, the gravestones of dead Jews sprouted from the cracked soil like so many oversized bones—humble concrete markers just inches apart, separated only by brown weeds, dry and dead in the September sun. Ruth savored the shade provided by the Rosenbergs' monumental crypt, a pretentious exception to the rows of low-lying, understated graves found elsewhere in the cemetery. Unfortunately, even in the shadow of the Rosenbergs' flamboyance there was no escape from the humidity that wrapped New Orleans in a ponderous blanket of steam. Rummaging through her bag again, Ruth pushed a Ruger 9 mm auto-

matic aside and found a blue bandanna. She lifted her chin toward the
hazy yellow sky, wiped the sweat from her neck, and smiled, remembering her mother's honey-coated words: "Perspiration, dear. For goodness'
sake. Ladies do not sweat. We *glow*." Her mother would have had a fit
about her buying the gun. So would her father, for that matter. It would
have been unthinkable in their liberal world. But although Ruth was no
genteel lady of the Southern belle persuasion like her mother, nor a
dyed-in-the-wool member of the New Left like her father, she had inherited her parents' penchant for independent thinking. Nobody was going
to tell her she couldn't carry a gun—not when someone had killed her
beloved Steve right there in her living room.

She tried to remember that there was no proof of who poisoned the
apples. Maybe it wasn't personal. Maybe it was a random act of evil. Or
maybe it was Solomon Cantor, balancing some twisted score.

Well, whoever it is, if he comes for me, I'll drop him in his tracks.

And yes, it was definitely a salty drop of *sweat* that quivered on the
tip of her nose.

Wiping her face and neck with the bandanna again, Ruth peered at
her parents' tombstone. She could not tell if the *yahrzeit* candle still flickered. The tiny flame had dissolved into the harsh sunshine, a teardrop in
a boiling ocean. She squinted to read the names etched on the stark white
marble plaque. *Jacob Gold. Barbara Gold.* No dates, no middle initials. Just
those names, simply carved, like the Ten Words etched on tablets of stone
by the finger of God. And over there, in the small plot separated from her
parents' by a narrow concrete walkway, stood another tombstone. It, too,
was blank except for the name: *Isaac Gold.* Unlike her parents' markers, that
lack of additional information had been Ruth's choice.

How dare he?

The words of outrage flashed across her mind as always, threatening
to rob her of the peace she sought. Ruth closed her eyes. She would not
think of her brother's betrayal now. The past was as much a crutch as the
future. Why resurrect long-dead hostilities when she had so much misery
here and now? She thought instead of the medics arriving at her house,
telling her what she already knew: Steve was beyond all human hope.
She thought instead of them telling her that the strange odor she had
smelled when she had bent close over Steve Cronen's corpse—vaguely

reminiscent of almonds and musty laundry—was a telltale symptom
of cyanide poisoning.

Ruth spoke aloud, no longer caring if anyone overheard. "Momma.
Daddy. What should I do?"

She rubbed her face with the bandanna, removing more sweat from
her nose, and thought of the horrible stories they had told her as a child,
of cyanide spewing from showerheads, filling concrete rooms with the
sickly sweet scent of almond blossoms, while families, friends and strangers clawed at each other, climbing a growing pile of bodies to strain for
just one more breath at the top.

Could Solomon Cantor really have done such a thing? Murder was
bad enough, but could any Jew use *cyanide?*

She spoke again, louder, as if by giving voice to that added atrocity
she might somehow wash away the evil with a cleansing stream of syllables. "Oh, Steve," she said. "Oh Steve . . . Steve . . . Steve . . . " She
repeated his name again and again, the river of words swirling around
her parents' headstone and flowing gently toward the street.

There, a thin woman frowned and quickened her pace toward the
bus stop, shocked to hear such things emanating from the sun-bleached
graveyard. But Orvis Newton, not at all surprised, stood beside the old
iron fence and smiled.

CHAPTER FIVE

Spying from between the slats of
the venetian blinds on the front window, Ruth Gold watched as Gabby
Cantor rang the doorbell for the second time. Gabby stepped back and
cast a practiced realtor's eye across the stained-glass transom, filigreed
fascia, and fancy Victorian brackets supporting the soffit above Ruth's
front porch. Then she looked down at the pair of rocking chairs as if
considering a prolonged wait. But rather than sit, she stepped up to the
diamond-shaped wooden panel on Ruth's French door and rang the doorbell again.

Ruth whispered to herself, "Go away."

She was in no mood for visitors, especially this one. Why didn't the
woman leave? It must be obvious by now that Ruth wasn't coming to the
door. Just then, Gabby Cantor turned, catching Ruth staring out through
the slats. She broke into a wide smile, delighted to see the young rabbi.

"Oh, *hello,* dear!" she called with a little wave toward the window. "I was beginning to think you weren't in."

Ruth sighed, dropped the blind into place, and plodded to the door.

As soon as it was open, Gabby began to talk. "Dear, I just couldn't stay away after what happened. I just couldn't."

"What happened?"

"You know . . . that thing at the Torah class yesterday." Ruth stared at the woman, not really seeing her, until Gabby said, "May I come in?"

"Oh, I'm sorry. Sure." Ruth led her into the living room. "Can I get you something to drink? A glass of wine?"

Gabby smiled. "That sounds yummy, but I don't drink, dear. Had a little problem with that years ago, you know. Haven't touched a drop in ages."

"Sorry."

Gabby waved the apology away with the back of her hand. "It's all right. Ancient history."

"How about some sweet tea? I've got a pitcher made."

"That would be wonderful."

Gabby followed Ruth into the kitchen and stopped, staring at Ruth's pot rack. "My goodness! Are those Calphalon?"

"Yes."

"You must love to cook."

"They're decoration mainly. They were my mother's."

An awkward silence fell upon them as Ruth withdrew a pitcher of tea from the refrigerator.

"You know," said Gabby, "I thought the world of your mother."

"Yes?"

"We knew each other for forty years. Not well, but even if you aren't best friends, that's a long time to know someone."

"Yes, it is."

"Long enough for a whole generation to die in the wilderness."

Ruth did not answer, handing Gabby a glass of tea.

Gabby went on. "Do you think it's a coincidence that we knew each other forty years, and that's also how long it took for the first generation to wander in the wilderness?"

"Of course."

"I'm not so sure. It seems like the Torah predicts everything if you know where to look."

Ruth almost replied that the Torah was not something you used like a Ouija board, but the last thing she wanted to do was talk shop with this old woman. "She was a gracious person, your mother," Gabby continued. "I don't believe I ever saw her wear the wrong thing or say something you could take the wrong way."

"Mom had a lot of self-confidence."

"*Poise* is the word I'd use." Gabby nodded. "Yes. *Poise.*"

Standing across from her at the kitchen counter, suddenly Ruth became conscious of last night's dinner dishes still soaking in the sink between them. "Why don't we go back into the living room?"

They sat opposite each other on Ruth's ivory-colored leather sofas, recent purchases from a little shop on Magazine. Ruth wore blue-jean shorts and an Anne Klein raw-silk blouse. She pulled her legs up onto the cushion, sitting barefoot and cross-legged. Gabby wore a pair of white linen slacks and a billowy white blouse with large golden polka dots. She crossed her legs. Ruth noticed that her shoes had high, clear plastic heels. Ruth's eyes dropped farther, to the four indentations where the legs of her shattered coffee table had once pressed into the carpet.

"I suppose you're wondering why I'm here." Gabby Cantor lifted her hand to her silver blonde hair, patting it in place with perfectly manicured fingers.

"Well, yes."

"It's a little bit embarrassing, actually."

Ruth smiled, remaining silent.

"You see, Ruth, your story about getting sick the other day didn't fool us, Sol and me."

"But—"

"Honey, I'm not saying anything against you. In fact, if I were you, I'd probably do the very same thing."

"I'm not sure what you mean."

"Oh, come *on,* dear. It was obvious, if you were paying close attention, and Sol and I were watching you close as can be."

Ruth took a large sip of her tea, nervously aware of the woman's eyes on her. Swallowing, she said, "So, that's why you're here?"

"Yes . . . you know, *Erev Rosh Hashanah* seems like a good time to clear the air. I . . . I want to be sure nothing changes now that Sol has come back. I mean, I've worked hard in the community. I have a certain standing . . . ." She leaned closer. "Ruth, I know how difficult this must be for you. All I ask is that you give Sol a chance. You don't have to be friends. You don't even have to like him. But, honey, you don't have to be afraid of him, either. I promise you that."

"What makes you think I'm afraid of your husband?"

"Oh, dear." Gabby stared at her with unwavering eyes and a slight smile. "I was hoping we could speak frankly."

"Okay," said Ruth. "I admit, I'm uncomfortable with the situation."

"That's a start. Listen. I'm not comfortable either. I mean, who would be? He's not the same. He's . . . rougher, if you know what I mean. I really can't take him anywhere. My friends . . . well, it just wouldn't work. Besides, after twenty-five years of living alone, I'm not just going to take the man in, you know?"

"He's not living with you?"

"Of course not, but I'm spending a lot of time with him. I'm trying, I really am. He comes over, does odd jobs around the house. You know . . . tries to impress me." Gabby smiled. "It's sweet, really, in a childish kind of way."

Ruth swirled the ice in her glass. "I'm not sure I can offer what you want, Gabby."

"But why? It's been so *long*. Can't we just go on from here as if the past is forgotten?"

Ruth raised her eyes to Gabby's for a long moment. "Can *he*?"

The older woman held her gaze. "No. Of course not. He can't forget. He says it's even in his dreams."

"He's not the only one."

"I know, honey."

"No, you probably don't."

"But I *do!*" Gabby sighed and set her glass down on a side table. "You were what? Six years old?"

"Seven."

"Well, believe me, I do know what it's been like. Our son wasn't much older than that when he . . . well, basically, Izzy lost his father and I lost my husband."

"I didn't know you had a son."

"Oh, sure. He's grown and gone now, of course, but Izzy is my pride and joy."

"Izzy?" Ruth cocked her head. "Are you talking about Jacob Israel Cantor? The name on the new children's wing?"

"That's right."

"I'm an idiot. I thought you named it for your father-in-law."

"Well, you're *not* an idiot, dear." Gabby smiled. "We named Izzy after Solomon's daddy, and the new wing after Izzy, so anyone could've made that mistake."

Ruth nodded, and stared at her glass of tea again. She was out of small talk, out of ways to avoid the real purpose of Gabby's visit. Every word Gabby had spoken held an underlying plea, made all the more obvious by the timing of her visit on that day of all days—the day before *Rosh Hashanah* ushered in the ten days of repentance. Ruth could not deny the pressure she felt, having a woman of Gabrielle Cantor's power and influence sitting in her living room, but if Solomon Cantor wanted to . . . well, if he wanted anything at all, he would have to come ask for it himself.

The older woman's voice penetrated her thoughts. "You probably need to go to the temple to get ready for tonight, don't you?"

Ruth checked her wristwatch. "Rabbi Gottlieb gave me the morning off because . . . well . . . just because, I guess. But I do need to leave in a few minutes."

"I'll be running along then." Gabby Cantor rose to her feet and crossed to the cased opening that led to the little entry hall. Ruth followed. Solomon Cantor's wife turned, looking at Ruth with a smile. "I won't let my life go all topsy-turvy just because Sol is back. Like I said, I have a position in this city to protect. I really do." Above the smile, her eyes were hard. "I hope you understand."

Was that a threat? Ruth fought to restrain a sudden flood of anger as she moved to open the door and spoke in clipped tones. "Mrs. Cantor, you're asking too much."

"I see." Gabby Cantor's smile evaporated. She stared at the floor, aging ten years in an instant. When she looked up again, her eyes had welled with tears. "All I'm asking is to keep everything quiet. This is all so *embarrassing*." Ruth simply nodded, marveling that the woman could go from veiled threats to tears in two seconds flat. No wonder she was stinking rich.

When it became apparent that Ruth had no intention of giving in, Mrs. Gabrielle Cantor, wealthy pillar of New Orleans society, stared daggers for a moment, then lifted her chin imperiously and walked away without another word.

Ruth closed the door and sighed. It was no way to bring in the new year. Ah well, no matter. Time to clear the iced tea glasses away and head for temple.

But halfway across the room, she stopped and stared at the carpet where Steve had fallen. Dead, just there. Had it been because of Gabby Cantor's husband? For the hundredth time since it happened, Ruth tried to decide between buying a new coffee table and selling the house. She couldn't seem to sit in her living room without being drawn to stare at that spot on the floor. Should she run away, or hide the memory beneath a solid piece of furniture? Either way, she'd be true to form. Run or hide. The only choices she seemed capable of making.

She shook her head to clear it of such thoughts. *Live in the now. Live now.*

And change the locks.

Jake Singer dropped his single bag to the floor. A puff of dust rose around it, then settled back onto the threadbare carpet. It was the worst possible time to be kicked out of his apartment; he was broke from spending every spare cent on psychiatry.

This will have to do.

Walking to the window, he stared down on the street. A pair of scantily clad teenagers stood smoking cigarettes beside a mound of black plastic trash sacks. Across the way, a shabby man loitered at the stoplight, clutching a white bucket and a filthy rag. A Monte Carlo rolled slowly to a stop at the light, aglow with lustrous paint and glittering chrome, its undercarriage three inches above the pavement. The shabby man sprang into action, dipping the rag into the bucket and slopping brown water onto the car's windshield. The driver's window slipped down, and a dark young man wearing a blue bandanna low upon his forehead leaned out to yell at the man in Spanish. The man with the bucket turned to him, holding his palm out. The Hispanic driver pulled his head back into the car. Suddenly, the front end of the Monte Carlo began to hop up and down, bouncing in time to the impossibly loud Tejano music spilling through the window. Startled, the man fell back, dropping his bucket. Laughter joined the music and the car rolled slowly on, crushing the bucket beneath its bouncing tires.

Jake Singer moved away from the window and sat on the room's single chair. The Tejano music faded, replaced by the faint sound of the raggedy man's screams. Jake listened to the screams, dispassionately wondering if they sounded like his own. He sat perfectly still in the wooden chair, his fingers curled around the ends of the armrests, his feet on the floor, together. He sat that way for hours, until the sun dropped sizzling into the Atchafalaya Basin, way out west of New Orleans.

Orvis Newton stood in the darkness with his back to Bayou Saint John, facing the Christian girl's house, watching her windows closely. Every now and then he saw movement beyond the drapes. Part of him yearned to see the motion, but another part grew more angry whenever her shadow passed between the fabric and the light. It was like having a loose tooth. You couldn't help but wiggle it, but the pain increased each time you did.

Directly across from the Christian girl's house, beyond the bayou, stood the Pitot House, once owned by America's first saint, Francis Cabrini. Orvis did not know what the Cabrini person had done to become a saint, but he'd heard somewhere that all saints had died a martyr's death. Wait. No, they were talking about making a saint out of Mother Teresa and she had died of old age. Oh, well. It didn't really matter. Except he was thinking that if he had to kill the Christian girl— if she forced him to do that—it might make her a saint, in a way. That would be nice.

A car approached him, driving slowly. Orvis stood perfectly still. As the car passed by, bells across the bayou began to toll the time. One, two, three . . . it was eleven o'clock, if the priests beneath the green copper dome of St. Francis Cabrini Catholic Church were correct. *One thing about having so many Catholics in this city*, he thought. *You always know what time it is.*

He remembered that the bells had also been ringing in the distance while he stood on the Jewess Gabrielle Cantor's front gallery. A cleaning woman had opened the door, and he asked her to fetch Solomon Cantor. The Jewess had come instead. He remembered the open disgust on her face when she saw him standing there, Bible in hand. "I've come to collect a lost lamb," he had said. He had rehearsed that line for weeks. He had enjoyed the drama of it. "I've come for the one who was lost but now is found." When the Jewess heard that, she had cursed him and told him abominable things and slammed her door in his face.

Orvis Newton's ears still burned with the scorching flames of hell that had disgorged from that woman's mouth, the disgusting images, the filthy lies. She had described it in such detail, reveling in the pain she had inflicted, spewing sulphurous images of his dear sweet Nan and the Cantor man, locked like animals in carnal relations. She claimed that she had seen it herself, had caught them in the very act. Even now, Orvis could not erase the vision from his head. He did not believe it, of course. Dear Nan would have died rather than succumb to the sins of the flesh, but the picture that Jewess had woven with her words had been so graphic he had almost run away, driven to escape the evil lurking there.

Then it had occurred to him: if the Jewess said such things to a man of the cloth, whom else would she tell? Orvis had been seized with an uncontrollable urge to know and had beaten on her door until she reappeared, her face wrenched with anger.

"Who else knows?" he had demanded.

She had cursed him again and tried to close the door. He found himself pushing back in his zeal to know the full extent of Nan's transgression. It happened without thinking, as if he stood outside himself, watching from a distance, one palm flat against the carved wood paneling, the other pressing with his Bible, using the Word of God to fling

open the heathen portal. It was Orvis's first minor act of violence. Much
had become clear since then, since he shed the bonds of insincere
temperance. He had been amazed at the absence of guilt—having always
believed that the violence in his soul was dark and forbidden fruit, but
in that moment, when the compulsion had first conquered his will, the
Lord made it clear that Orvis stood on hallowed ground. His Bible
pressed against the Jewess's door had been a pleasing image, clean and
powerful enough to wash away the filth that Jewess witch had tried
to root within his brain. His Bible, pressing back against her evil. Yes.
A pleasing image.

"I'll call the police," she had said.

"Who else have you told?"

"Everyone. Everyone who helped to put him away. Even the little
girls."

Aghast, he whispered, "Why?"

"*Why*? Haven't you been listening to me?" Then she told him everything again, in even more detail.

Now, outside the Christian woman's house—the only witness who
was not a Jew—Orvis shook his head to clear it of the memory. But he
had been completely possessed by a wrathful God who would not give
him rest until the Plan had been completed.

Orvis held his wristwatch up to catch the bright light of the moon.
He did not trust the Catholics, but they were right; it really was eleven
o'clock. He had other chores to do tonight. The Christian girl could wait.

Kate peeked in from the hallway, checking on Jilly before going to bed
herself. Her daughter appeared to be sleeping, but as Kate began to
close the door, Jilly spoke from beneath the covers. "Mommy? Can I go
to Diana's house tomorrow?"

"Sure you can."

"I like playing with Diana better than school."

Kate crossed to her bedside. "You still have to go to kindergarten,
but you can go over there afterward, when you and Paul come home."

Jilly frowned. "But I don't *like* school!"

"How can you tell so soon? You only just started."

"I wanna go to Diana's!"

Kate bent to stroke her hair. "You need to learn your ABCs, remember?"

"I learned them already. A long time ago."

"Say them for me."

Jilly began to recite the alphabet, doing well until she got to, "H-I-Jake and Elmer Minnow peed."

Kate said, "Hold it. What was that last part?"

Jilly yawned.

"Don't you mean J-K-L-M-N-O-P?" asked Kate.

"That's what I said."

"Who are Jake and Elmer Minnow?"

"Just some people . . ." Jilly shut her eyes.

As her daughter drifted to sleep, Kate continued to stand and watch, thinking how wonderful it would be if she too could be five years old, playing in a world half filled with fantasies instead of dashing off each morning to the shop that John had founded. Kate sometimes felt trapped in a world of John's creation. He had even picked this house where she lived, picked it because of the bayou across the street, knowing their children would love the water. He too had loved the bayou, building toy wooden boats for the children to sail across its placid surface, teaching Paul to fish while Jilly sat in her diapers and merrily played with worms.

Although it might awaken Jilly again, Kate could not resist resting a palm on her smooth forehead. Time had stolen her daughter's memories of John. *Perhaps that's best. Heaven knows I wish it would steal mine.* But life had its own itinerary. An unexpected sight or dimly-remembered scent could tempt your mind down long-forgotten trails of misery, just as news of a murderer's release could drag you kicking and screaming into a wicked past.

Lifting her hand from Jilly's forehead Kate clinched it in midair, as if shaking her fist at heaven. She had never told anyone of this smoldering rage, this feeling that frightened her too much to confess aloud. Now she lifted both fists to her own forehead, clutching them there in a parody of prayer.

I believe! Isn't that enough? You're the creator of the universe. You can do anything, and you say you love me. Well, if that's true, prove it! Make this pain go away. Why do you make me wait? Do it now! Or is it that you want me to hate you?

Kate Flint waited for an answer, but she got no thunderous response; she did not even hear a still, small voice. What she got instead was her oldest horror, galloping roughshod through her feeble heart astride an evil memory . . . .

Katy splashed around with Ruth in the shallow end of the Northside Jewish Community Center's pool, the smell of chlorine strong in her nostrils, her thick blonde hair in braids. Ruth's mother sat in the shade of the side porch, talking to the other mothers. All the mothers looked so funny in their big sunglasses.

Katy turned toward her friend. "I can swim farther underwater than you."

"Can not."

"Can too!"

"Okay. Let's see," said Ruth.

They paddled to the side and clung to the coping, facing each other, gulping down huge breaths of air. One. Two. Three! Down they went, pushing off from the white concrete wall with arms extended straight out in front. Slipping through the water, they avoided the other kids' legs, kicking and stroking for all they were worth. Always the better swimmer, Ruth quickly pulled out in front. The bottom dropped away as they neared the deep end. Katy looked down and saw someone's flipper near the drain. Almost there! She had never made it all the way across the pool before! But her lungs began to burn for air. She kicked once more, then, giving up, rose to the surface. Treading water in the center of the deep end, Katy scanned the bobbing heads nearby for Ruth. Her friend was nowhere in sight. Then she burst to the surface, over by the diving board. Ruth laughed when their eyes met. She'd done it again. All the way from end to end!

Katy paddled across the pool and joined Ruth. They turned their backs to the side and gripped the concrete coping, hands back behind their shoulders, elbows pointing out across the water. Ruth wore a black swimsuit with shocking pink trim.

"Next time," said Katy.

"Sure," said Ruth. "You can do it."

They both giggled, filled with the mutual knowledge that she could *not* do it, and it was silly—but nice—to say that she could.

Katy said, "I gotta go to the bathroom."

"Me too."

Passing hand over hand, they moved around the edge of the pool until they came to the chrome ladder. They emerged dripping onto the concrete and dashed toward the building.

"Ruth Louise Gold! You stop that running this instant!" called her mother.

Katy and Ruth giggled and slowed to a walk.

"Where do you two think you're going?"

"Bathroom!" said Ruth as she opened the door.

Shivering in the air conditioning, the girls ran down the hall, leaving a trail of watery footprints on the tile. At the first door on the right, they turned and entered the women's locker room. Mrs. Friedman sat on a bench, wearing nothing but a white terry-cloth towel. She was awfully big and fat and wiggled all over when she moved. All the kids called her Moby Dick, because that's what she looked like when she went swimming: big and white and covered with blubber. Mrs. Friedman smiled at them. "Hello, girls," she said, her jowls bouncing with every syllable.

Ruth giggled. Katy, knowing exactly what her friend was thinking, giggled too. They covered their mouths and sprinted into the bathroom, where, still giggling, they entered two side by side toilet stalls.

Katy got done first. She flushed the toilet and opened the door and went to stand beside the sink. Ruth's voice squealed from behind the closed partition door.

"Oh no! It's Moby Dick!"

Katy laughed, watching herself in the mirror, her face alive with mischief. Then a distant scream—long and shrill and fraught with agony—filled the air, and Katy O'Connor saw her own eyes widen with fear.

Ruth's voice echoed against the cold white tiles. "Katy? Katy? What was that?"

Katy found she could not speak.

"Katy? Are you there?"

CHAPTER
SIX

Working in the moonlight, Orvis Newton tied a cord to the pistol with bloody hands. All around the parapet of the roof lay objects he had carefully selected for effect, each of them also tied to cords, each of the cords precisely the same length. The Plan would require split-second timing. Orvis allowed doubt to creep in. What if it didn't work, in spite of all this careful preparation? There were so many variables. He quickly drove such thoughts from his mind, focusing instead on a verse from the New Testament: "Stop doubting and believe." Surely after all those domino games with the Rothstein brothers up here on the roof, after all those questions, learning everything he could about their habits, fears, and behavior, the Lord would not let him fail now. If he could only get Benny to do the deed, it would be perfect, absolutely perfect.

Exactly in accordance with the Plan.

Orvis gave the knot a final tug to make sure the gun was secure and placed the pistol on top of the parapet, just like all the other objects around the roof. Bending with amazing flexibility for a man his age, he lifted the bloody cat from the tar paper at his feet. It hung completely limp in his hand. Orvis was eager to get started, knowing Morton would be coming soon. He had already sent a message to the old Jew.

Closing his eyes, Orvis Newton mumbled a final prayer then strode for the stairs, reminding himself that nothing was too complicated for God.

B enny Rothstein sat in a circle of light, enjoying Rashi's commentary on the Talmud. He licked his thumb and turned the page. Such wonderfully simple and straightforward insights, yet so filled with deeper meaning. Such a perfect way to close this *Rosh Hashanah* evening. Morton preferred Ibn Ezra, but Benny thought he was difficult to follow sometimes, even on the third or fourth reading. Benny was of the opinion that complex writing concealed incomplete thoughts. It took tremendous wisdom and clarity of mind to explain the great truths of Torah in ways that anyone could understand, and for clarity, you just couldn't beat Rashi.

But of course, it only made sense that Morton would be wrong. How could he know anything? He was a man who worked on *Erev Rosh Hashanah* when he should be home or at temple busying himself with Torah. Benny sighed. His brother would never change, God love him.

The doorbell rang. Benny frowned and checked the time on the old wall clock. So late? Who would come to call at such an hour? He marked his place and shuffled to the tiny entry hall. Standing at the door, he called, "Hello?"

There was no response.

Adjusting his glasses, he peered through the peephole. The hallway seemed to be empty, but you could never tell. Sometimes people stood to one side, out of view. He called another greeting. Again, silence. Benny shrugged and returned to his chair. Just as he settled into Rashi once more, the doorbell rang again. He arose, grumbling, and headed for the door. Again, he looked through the peephole. Again, no one was there.

Muttering to himself, he turned the latch on the dead bolt, unlocked the doorknob, and opened the door just enough to peek outside, leaving the chain in place. Mrs. Kimmelman's voice drifted faintly up from the first floor, but he saw no one in front of his apartment. Puzzled, he closed the door, removed the chain, and opened the door again, poking his head out into the hall to glance quickly left and right. As he suspected, the corridor was empty. Then, just as he began to close the door, Benny Rothstein looked down.

Mr. Disraeli lay on the floor in a puddle of blood.

Using the door frame for support, Benny lowered himself painfully to his knees. He touched the cat, hoping against hope for a sign of life, but on closer inspection, the cause of death was obvious. Someone had cut his pet's throat. Benny touched Mr. Disraeli's head gingerly. Then, grasping the cat with one hand and the door frame with the other, he raised himself to his feet with much effort, and closed and locked the door.

Benny walked to the kitchen, where he placed his pet upon the countertop and stood for a moment looking down at the lifeless body. Mr. Disraeli had been his companion for a decade and a half. Such cruelty! Who would—

The kitchen window shattered, glass flying inward across the room. Benny staggered back from the counter. Two seconds later, still more glass fell into the kitchen, littering the floor and the breakfast table. It took a moment for him to realize the cause of the destruction. Something hung outside the building, swinging in and out.

Pushing his thick glasses up on his nose, Benny Rothstein slowly approached the window. Shards of glass cracked beneath his house slippers as he drew near. Apparently, someone had suspended the thing from the roof, tied to a string just long enough to reach his third floor window. The darkness outside made it difficult to see the object, but after a moment, he recognized it as a handgun—a revolver to be exact— with the string tied to the trigger guard.

Morton Rothstein worked the tables at Delmonico, weaving his way between the diners with the air of a majordomo. The dim light concealed the threadbare sheen of his tuxedo. "Good evening, sir, and lovely lady," he said with a smile. The silver-haired gentleman eyed him warily, but the woman returned his smile. "May I say the room would dim without the beauty of your lovely bride?" Now the man also smiled.

Good.

"This is a special occasion, indeed. For us it is a rare privilege to entertain such distinguished guests."

"Laying it on a bit thick, aren't you, Morton?" said the man.

Oh dear. Repeat customers. He tried to remember them all, but there were so many. Morton said, "Not at all, sir. Not at all. It truly is a special occasion whenever you join us at Delmonico."

"When did you come over from Pascal's?"

Even worse! Someone who remembered him from one of the other restaurants. Dear, oh dear. "Actually, I've only just arrived," said Morton. It was the truth, if not the whole truth. What difference did it make if these people assumed he worked directly for Delmonico? Some people actually thought he was the maitre d'. He let their assumptions remain uncorrected. People felt special if the maitre d' visited their table, and it gave him a certain cachet, which was good for business.

He offered a little bow, carefully copied from an Errol Flynn movie. "I've brought our floral tradition along as well. Would the gentleman care to offer the lady a rose?" He proffered the flower, carefully held between the thumb and first two fingers of his right hand, with his pinkie extended just so. Success was in the details.

The woman lowered her eyes, and Morton knew he had a sale. Ladies were seldom coy in their refusals, but downcast eyes were a sure sign that they wanted the rose. The man understood as well, of course. Moments later, Morton had a ten dollar tip in his pocket. His fifth sale already.

This was shaping up to be a good night.

Morton strolled back through the dining room to the entry vestibule. Nodding to the hostess, he stepped out the front door and turned to the left, where his plastic bucket filled with the evening's supply of flowers lay concealed behind an azalea bush. He selected three more roses: two red and one yellow.

As he turned to reenter the restaurant, a young black boy appeared at his elbow.

"Mister Rothstein?"

"Yes?" said Morton, startled that the youngster knew his name.

The boy extended his hand, offering a folded piece of paper. "This fo' you."

"No, thank you, son. Whatever it is, I can't afford it."

"Ain't no charge or nothin'. I been paid."

"Well then, what is it?"

"Jus' a note or somethin', I guess."

"A note? From whom?"

"Mister, dey jus' gimme dis heah paper, say bring it over to you. I don' care if you take it or not."

Morton considered the little boy's grimy hand. If this was a swindle, it was new to him. "All right," he said, taking the note. The boy dashed across St. Charles, melting into the darkness beyond the neutral zone. Morton stared after him for a moment, alert for any sign of mischief. When nothing happened, he shrugged and unfolded the paper. Holding it at an angle to catch the light spilling out through a window, he read: *Benny in trouble. Mr. Disraeli dead. Come quickly.*

Morton read the words a second time, still thinking it could be some kind of scam. There was no signature. He did not recognize the handwriting, but whoever wrote the thing knew the name of his brother and their cat. That was disturbing.

He placed the roses back in the plastic bucket and reentered Delmonico. Approaching the hostess, he asked, "May I use your telephone, please?"

B enny went to the telephone to call the police. The line was dead. He replaced the handset and decided to leave the apartment, but before he reached the entry hall, three loud blows against the door echoed through the rooms, actually rattling the framed photographs on the nearby wall. He froze. What should he do? Then it occurred to him that perhaps someone had already called the police. Perhaps it was a patrolman at his door. He had seen them beat on people's doors just that way on television.

Benny cleared his throat and called, "Y-y-yes? Who's there?"

The silence from the hallway was more ominous than any response might have been. Benny approached the door timidly and looked out through the peephole. He lifted his eye to the tiny circular lens but saw no one. Backing away from the peephole, he stumbled over the umbrella stand. It tipped over with a horrible racket, adding to his terror. Who was out there? What would they do? He turned and shuffled into the living room. Just as he entered, a window across the room exploded inward, spraying shards of glass everywhere. Benny covered his face with both hands and screamed.

T he phone rang on and on, but their answering machine usually picked it up after the fifth ring. Frowning, Morton replaced the handset in the cradle. Who could have written the note? A neighbor, perhaps? But if there was a serious problem, why use the little boy to deliver a message, instead of coming themselves or sending the police? Unless . . .

A fire?

That would explain everything. The neighbors and the police would be too preoccupied with their own troubles to come all the way here, but someone might think to write a note and pay the boy a dollar or so to run it over to him. Yes, a fire would explain everything.

Morton hurried for the door, suddenly frightened for his brother.

Adonai, he prayed. *Have mercy on us. Keep Benny safe.*

D eafening music driven by a throbbing bass beat assaulted Benny's ears, causing physical pain. Where did it come from? He stared around the room wildly. Then he saw the oblong box hanging just outside his shattered living-room window. Some kind of radio, suspended from a string like the pistol, twisted and swayed in the air. It bumped against a remaining shard of glass, sending it crashing to the floor. The music—if that word could be used to describe the brutal noise—was excruciating. He covered his ears and stumbled toward the window, intending to retrieve the radio and turn it off, but as he crossed the room more glass exploded inward, just to his right.

This time, he was too close.

The flying shards sliced through his shirt and the side of his face. There was no pain, but soon the glistening blood from a dozen small cuts soaked his clothing. He turned toward the shattered window and saw the silhouette of a man's head swaying there. *Hashem, be merciful!* Then the terrible thing swung into the room again, just long enough for him to see that it was only a cheap plaster bust suspended from a string.

He heard the sound of another window being smashed, somewhere in the back of the apartment. Then another. Then another. The horrible crashing noise and the rap music blaring from the radio filled his mind with confusion. Abominable words assailed his ears, recorded oaths of hate and anger. He stumbled for the hallway door, but as he reached for the dead bolt he remembered the loud pounding he had heard outside just moments before, so violently shaking the door on its hinges. What if they were waiting for him just outside? What if their intention was to flush him out of the apartment? Crying in terror, his sobs engulfed in the swirling cacophony of shouting voices and breaking glass, he lurched on down the hall with his hands over his ears, leaving bloody smears against the wall each time he staggered.

Then the lights went out.

Still wailing loudly, Benny plunged into the kitchen, stumbling against the breakfast table. Grasping the window frame with one hand, the old man leaned far out into midair, three stories up. He saw heavy objects hanging all along the wall to his right and left, swaying on the ends of strings stretched tightly up to the roof. Lamps, skillets, telephones, and butcher knives moved slowly back and forth. It was insane! He fumbled clumsily for the revolver, dangling just beyond his reach. Benny almost touched it, but the weapon jerked on the end of the string, hopping upward six more inches. He tried to grab for it again and felt himself start to slide out of the window. Thrusting his free hand back, he gripped the sill with trembling fingertips. Benny twisted his head upward and saw someone staring down from the rooftop, a dark silhouette against the moonlit sky.

Feeling his tenuous grip on the window slowly slipping, Benny screamed into the night, his terror drifting out across the city, high and thin.

"What do you want?"

Morton emerged from a taxi and looked up at the building, relieved that he saw no smoke or flames. But where was that awful racket coming from?

He glanced around nervously. Such music was the trademark of the gangs that stalked these streets sometimes. He had seen them, passing slowly by in strange automobiles, the music roaring from their windows, an audible poison, polluting the air with messages of hate. But tonight the street was empty.

He stooped to pay the cabby and hurried to the front door of the building. Just as he entered, a familiar voice screamed into the night, sounding raw and naked. Every hair on Morton's neck stood suddenly to attention.

"Benny!" he shouted. "I'm coming!"

The old man rushed to the stairs as quickly as he could. He climbed, gripping the banister for support, cursing his feeble body. Up one step at a time, each taking far too long, prayers mumbled with every breath, he climbed. On the second floor he stopped, gasping for air. When he could go on, he grabbed the banister again and pulled himself along, hand over hand, his eyes cast up at the landing above.

Finally, Morton reached the third floor. He paused, palm pressed against his side, breathing deeply. Then, ignoring the pain in his lungs, he forced himself down the hall, passing the neighbors who stood in the open doors of their apartments, staring nervously toward the source of the horrible sounds . . . toward his own door at the end of the corridor. Arnold Liebowitz, his next-door neighbor, spoke to Morton as he passed. "I called the police!"

Ignoring him, Morton shouted, "Benny! I'm here! I'm here!" as he reached the door. Chest heaving, he looked down at the floor. *Hashem, have mercy! Is that Benny's blood?* It took three tries to get his key into the lock. Finally, he pushed it open.

A wall of noise hit him as he stepped inside. Screaming at the top of his lungs, he called his brother's name, but his old man's voice was no match for the thunderous roar echoing through the apartment. He stumbled over something on the floor and fell hard. Reaching around on his hands and knees, his fingers found the umbrella stand. He set it upright. He rose. He flipped the light switch, but the darkness remained.

Where was his brother?

Feeling his way along the hall, Morton Rothstein approached the living room. He could just make out the shape of things in the moonlight trickling through the open windows. Why did Benny have the windows open? It made no sense in the heat of September. And what *was* that terrible noise? Then he saw the plaster bust swinging outside the window. He stood in the shadowy hallway, staring across the room, trying to make sense of a pale white head hanging by the neck outside his window.

Perhaps a closer look.

As he stepped from the hall, a new sound joined the cacophony in the living room. In addition to the blaring rap music and Benny's wails of grief, the 130-year-old clock on the wall began to chime. Morton Rothstein glanced toward the clock, and in spite of all the noise and confusion, his last thought on earth was: Rosh Hashanah *is halfway over*.

Then his brother Benny, sobbing on the floor in the corner, lifted the revolver and shot him dead.

CHAPTER
SEVEN

Orvis Newton had parked the Vista Cruiser carefully this morning, so the passing parade of Jews come to observe *Rosh Hashanah* could easily read the message painted on the driver's side door: *Sister Nan Smith Crusade for Jews*. He was there with a faithful few, including Martha Douglas, who had let her passion overrule her discretion at the church service last Sunday. Orvis sighed. It was hard to blame the girl. This was emotional work.

He lifted a hand to shade his eyes. The entrance to the temple danced in rising waves of heat on the far side of a sea of automobiles. Sometimes he got just a little bit depressed. It seemed that nothing changed in spite of all his preaching and his prayers, but this was the start of a new week, and Orvis Newton had a mission. He stood on the public sidewalk outside the temple with his little band of true believers, ready to walk and talk and spread the gospel. Glancing to his left, he smiled up at Martha Douglas.

Her height was an asset here, attracting even more attention to their ministry, and he could use her passion to inspire others. Orvis's tactics frightened many brothers and sisters, but so long as you kept moving and stayed on public property, they didn't have a law that could touch you. It had been true back when he and Nan first came to this place, and it was still true today. Just keep moving, and you could preach forever. That was why he insisted all the men must wear black athletic shoes. They were easy on the feet but looked appropriate with a suit. He hadn't found a similar solution for the ladies yet. Athletic shoes just did not look proper with their skirts, so the ladies still wore dress shoes, even though they were uncomfortable after six or eight hours on the concrete. Orvis wore respectable clothing while doing the Lord's work, and he insisted his missionaries do likewise. The unsaved wouldn't listen if you looked like a truck driver.

He glanced across the street at Audubon Park. All those years ago, he and Nan had shared many a picnic over yonder under that exact same live oak. Sandwiches wrapped in wax paper, RC Cola cold from her metal ice chest, and prayers for the godless Jews. His poor, sweet Nan. The Lord never gave her easy work, or him either for that matter. Apostle to the Hebrews in this day and age? It took the patience of Job. Yet, after everything the Jews did to the Savior, after the terrible persecutions they had inflicted on Christians and all those centuries of denying Jesus, God still chose to reach out to his children with the message of salvation.

Great is his mercy!

Orvis felt his heart swell with emotion. He lowered himself to one knee and bowed his head and thanked the Lord. Then, lifting his eyes, he surveyed the people rapidly filling the parking lot. They had been coming for almost an hour, coming by the hundreds, in their fancy cars and suits. A woman pulled a burgundy van into a nearby parking stall. As soon as she stopped, the side door flew open. *How can she fit so many children in that vehicle? My lands, there must be a dozen of them in there.* He stood and spread his arms wide. "Jesus saves!" he shouted. "'Suffer the little children to come unto me'!" Smiling, he waved at the Jewess and her children.

He tried to look friendly so they would listen.

At three the following morning, after *Rosh Hashanah*, Rebecca Betterton awoke for no reason. It happened to her often these days. She'd be sleeping just fine, dreaming even, and *bam!* she'd be awake all of a sudden. Roy said it was because she drank too much caffeine, but Rebecca wasn't convinced, at least not tonight. She thought maybe it was because yesterday had been *Rosh Hashanah*. Sometimes she still felt a tiny twinge of guilt when the days of awe came around, as if God were telling her to go to temple. Nothing like good old fashioned Jewish guilt to keep you up nights.

Roy's snoring didn't help much, of course. If a person wanted to know why they called it "sawing logs," all they had to do was listen to her husband sleep. Then again, after twenty years you'd think she'd be used to that. So, rather than lie in bed with her eyes squeezed shut, counting to one hundred over and over, Rebecca decided to get up and go to the kitchen for a glass of milk. That was all—just a glass of skim milk. The last thing she needed now that she'd finally found a diet that worked was to start late-night snacking again.

Afterward, as she rinsed the glass in the sink, Rebecca decided to slip into the bedroom to get her book, so she could read for a little while in the easy chair in the family room. Roy never seemed to notice when she walked around the house at all hours, but she tried to be quiet just the same. This time, though, when she stepped into the bedroom she saw someone standing right outside the window, looking in.

Naturally, she screamed.

That woke Roy up, all right.

Her husband flopped around like a fish out of water, tossing sheets every which way. When he finally settled down, he turned on the bedside light and saw Rebecca, frozen in place, pointing at the window.

"P-p-peeping Tom!" she said.

Roy jerked open the bedside table drawer, grabbed his pistol, and ran outside in his boxer shorts. Meanwhile, Rebecca dialed 911. The police lady wouldn't let her hang up the telephone after she heard what was happening, so they had a nice chat about the crime problem in New Orleans while her husband searched the backyard. Whoever it was had disappeared when she screamed, so Roy came back in and put on his robe before the police got there. Thank goodness he did; otherwise, they might have thought *he* was the man peeking in people's windows.

The police made her tell the story of how she came in and saw the person. She had to tell it three different times. Then one of the officers stayed in the house while the others searched the backyard. Pretty soon, a helicopter flew over, hovering, making a lot of noise, and shining a bright light down on everything. Rebecca asked if the helicopter was really necessary. The neighbors were going to absolutely kill her in the morning. The policeman said they wanted to catch the perpetrator. Was she really sure she saw a person outside, or could it maybe have been a shadow from those nandinas or something? So then she had to tell the story a *fourth* time, as if she could have mistaken a nandina's shadow for a rapist or a murderer or whatever that horrible man was!

Honestly.

At 4:30 in the morning, the police finally left the house, and *goodness*, was she glad to see them go! Ray went right back to sleep of course; he really could sleep through anything, but Rebecca put on her yellow rubber gloves and mopped the entry foyer with disinfectant because of the dirt and grass the police tracked in. Who knew where their shoes had been?

When she was done, Rebecca sat in the easy chair with her book like she originally planned, only now she couldn't read. Even after the sun was up, all she could do was sit and think about that awful person out there, staring in people's windows.

R unning late, Ruth wheeled into the parking lot of the Jewish Community Center. She had risen early to go grocery shopping for a sick neighbor. In her haste to catch up, she didn't notice the people with the signs until she stood outside her Citroën, locking the door.

"Jesus saves!" yelled a man. "Trust your Messiah!"

Lifting her hand to shade her eyes, she scanned the parking lot. There he was, over on the far sidewalk among a small group of people. The same old guy, with the same suit and cardboard sign, the one she'd seen outside the temple last *Shabbat*, and again yesterday at *Rosh Hashanah*. So. It wasn't enough to harass Jews at temple on one of the high holy days; now they were going to do it here, too? Ruth clenched her teeth and turned toward the front doors.

What kind of people would act this way, especially at this time of year? How would they feel if the Anti-Defamation League showed up with signs in front of their churches next Easter? Yesterday, the parking lot at temple had been crammed, and the shuttles from the Catholic church's parking lot down the street had let people out just about where those lunatics were standing. It was a miracle they had avoided violence, even on *Rosh Hashanah*. A miracle, and a testimony to the forbearance of her congregation.

She doubted that the Christians would have been as patient.

Slipping her purse strap over her shoulder, Ruth marched across the lot, ignoring the maniac's shouts. Much as she'd like to give him a piece of her mind, there were other, more pressing matters that required her attention. Heat rose from the asphalt, trailing along her bare legs and arms with scorching fingers. *Good. Let them bake their brains out. If they have brains to bake.*

A small black man in a navy blazer and neatly pressed khaki slacks stood in the cool of the corridor just inside the doors of the Community Center. She smiled and offered her hand. "Lieutenant Washington?"

"You must be Rabbi Gold."

"Sorry I'm late."

"No problem. I was a little bit late myself."

"Before we talk about the other thing, can I ask you a question?"

"Sure."

She stared out through the glass door. "Did you see those people out front with the signs?"

"Yeah?"

"Is there anything we can do about them?"

"What do you want to do, rabbi?"

"Make them go away. At least until *Yom Kippur* is over."

He shook his head. "Long as they stay on the public sidewalk and move around a little, there's not much we can do."

She sighed. "They'll probably get tired of standing in the sun and leave soon anyway."

"Could be."

Still staring at the fanatic in the sunshine she said, "It's so strange . . ."

"What's that?"

"They were standing right there, holding signs just like that, when it happened."

The policeman shifted his eyes, watching her carefully. "When what happened?"

"That's what I wanted to tell you about." Suddenly, she turned away from the door. "Let's go down the hall, Lieutenant. I have something to show you."

"Okay." The lieutenant walked beside Ruth along the corridor, their footsteps echoing against the tile floor. "Do you work here?" he asked.

"Sort of. My real job is down at Temple Brit Yisrael, but the J.C.C. board of directors decided they needed some cross-pollination with the rabbinate, so to speak, and I got elected last year." Ruth continued as they walked. "It's really a figurehead position. There were some disagreements a while back, some of the temples complaining that the swimming pool was open on the Sabbath, stuff like that. So I guess you could say my job description here is 'peacemaker.'"

Washington said, "Isn't there something in the Bible about 'Blessed are the peacemakers'?"

"Nice thought," she said, "but wrong part of the Bible in my case." She stopped outside the ladies' locker room and nodded toward the door. "We were right in there when we heard her scream."

"We?"

"Yes. My friend Katy O'Connor and me."

"The other girl who was with you when Nan Smith was murdered."

"You've done your homework."

"I read the file. Okay. So y'all heard a scream. Then what?"

The scream had echoed in the locker room, lingering on and on . . . or had it merely echoed in her mind? Ruth sat still in the toilet stall, looking up at the white rectangle of ceiling visible above the partition walls. After a moment, she said, "Katy? Katy? What was that?" Her own voice sounded thin and scared.

Katy did not answer.

"Katy? Are you there?" A long silence as her heart beat faster and faster with fear for Katy and herself.

Finally Katy spoke. "I'm here."

Katy's trembling voice gave Ruth the reassurance she needed to reach up and open the toilet-stall door. Peeking out into the locker room, she said, "What was that?"

"Somebody screamed."

Ruth pulled up her swimsuit and slipped the straps over her shoulders. "Should we go see if they're okay?"

Katy shook her head.

"Oh, come on," said Ruth. "Don't be such a 'fraidy-cat.'"

"I wanna go back outside."

"What if it was one of the kids trying to scare us? Everyone'll laugh if we run outside."

"I don't care!"

"All right," Ruth marched to the door and pulled it open. "You go ahead and run away, but *I'm* gonna go see what happened."

"Wait!"

Ruth turned. "Well?"

Katy's lower lip quivered. "I want you to go back outside with me."

"You don't need me. You know the way."

Katy stamped her bare foot. It slapped against the cold tile floor. "No! I want you to come with me!"

Suddenly, Ruth understood. Her friend was worried about her. She smiled. "I'll be okay."

Katy glanced at the door that led outside to the swimming pool and sighed. "Oh, all right. I'll go."

Ruth reached out to Katy, and together the little girls left the locker room, holding hands.

Red brick lined one side of the long hall, and a wall of glass faced a central courtyard on the other. Now that they were actually out in the hallway, Ruth wished she had gone back to the pool with Katy, but now it was too late to do that without admitting she was scared, so on she went. Up ahead lay the doorway to the kitchen. Ruth and Katy moved slowly, still holding hands. As they neared the door, Ruth heard strange, soft sounds coming from just around the corner, sort of gargling noises, like what her mother did with the mouthwash in the mornings, only this gargling stopped and started instead of going on and on like her mother's.

"Ruth," whispered Katy, "maybe we should turn around now."

It was a good idea. Except Ruth wanted to see what was making that sound, and to find out, all they had to do was walk a few more feet and peek around that corner. So instead of listening to her friend, Ruth pulled Katy forward.

Ruth and her friend Helen Blumenthal sat at a table beside the window of the Palace, watching pedestrians hurry along Canal between Royal and Chartres. Their meeting place was convenient to both Helen's psychiatry practice in the central business district and Ruth's temple near Audubon Park, just a short drive up St. Charles. Normally lunch with Helen on the day after *Rosh Hashanah* would be a welcome break in Ruth's hectic schedule, but today the rabbi tapped her foot rapidly against the tiled floor beneath the table, holding herself rigidly upright on the edge of her seat, a full six inches from the support of the chair back.

"Ruth," said Helen, "you have *got* to relax."

"Relax? Didn't you see those self-righteous anti-Semites at temple yesterday?"

"Sure I did."

"The bigots! And on *Rosh Hashanah,* no less!"

"I can't believe you're letting a few zealots get to you."

"It's not just them."

Dr. Blumenthal waited.

Tapping her foot even faster, Ruth stared out the window. Across the street the Le Meridien doorman whistled for a cab, enduring the heat in a black uniform trimmed with gold buttons and epaulets. "I thought it was all behind me," said Ruth. "But Cantor doesn't even have the decency to go live someplace else."

Helen pushed a drop of condensation around on the tabletop with her fingertip. "Gabby probably feels she's too well-established in the Garden District to move, don't you think?"

"That doesn't give him the right to come back here and ruin our lives all over again! Do you understand that Steve and Morton are dead and Benny has been arrested?"

"Yes. I understand that, Ruth."

Ignoring the patronizingly professional tone that had crept into her friend's voice, Ruth stabbed her pecan-encrusted catfish with her fork, breaking it into tiny pieces. Normally, she didn't eat nonkosher meats, but like many Reform Jews, she wasn't rigid about keeping kosher, and today, the catfish was a small gesture of acrimonious defiance against a God who allowed murderers to go free and good men to die and anti-Semitism to endure for centuries. Unfortunately, like most acts of rebellion, the temptation was sweeter than the reality. Ruth found her appetite vanishing amidst angry thoughts of Solomon Cantor and grief at the deaths of Steve and Morton. Especially Steve. If the two of them had been allowed just a little more time, who knows? They might have married. Even children were a possibility. But not now. Now she might never . . .

Stop this! It's senseless. Live in the now.

Ruth preferred anger to grief, so she returned to thinking about Solomon Cantor. "Morton and I were both involved in the trial, but when I pointed that out to the lieutenant, he said it still looked circumstantial to him! Circumstantial!" She jabbed the fish again, her fork hitting the plate hard enough to cause a nearby diner to glance their way.

Helen leaned forward and placed her hand on Ruth's. "Take it easy."

Ruth dropped the fork on the plate. It clattered against the china, causing still more diners to look in their direction.

"How can I take it easy when people in my congregation are dying and the police won't listen?" She felt her friend's eyes on her as she stared out the window at the passing people on Canal.

Helen said, "I haven't seen you this upset since Isaac."

"That has nothing to do with anything."

"Didn't you say *shehecheyanu* at the cemetery for your mom the other day?"

"What about it?"

"Are you okay about that?"

"Yeah. I'm fine."

"And Isaac?"

Ruth looked away. "I'm *fine*, Helen. Change the subject, okay?"

"All right," said Helen, pausing for a moment, then, "It could be a coincidence, right?"

"What?"

"Well, technically speaking, Steve wasn't a witness at the trial."

Ruth turned to stare at Helen. "So what?"

"I'm just saying, if Solomon Cantor is killing people, he's certainly choosing strange methods. Couldn't Steve have been the victim of a random evil act? Couldn't Benny have simply overreacted to the harassment of a gang?"

"You sound like that lieutenant!"

"Well, it's true about Steve. And Morton Rothstein . . . I mean, there's no doubt that Benny killed him, right?"

"He was set up!"

"Set up? You mean someone vandalized their apartment that way specifically so that Benny would kill his brother?"

"Not someone, Helen. Sol Cantor."

"But why?"

"Because Morton and Benny were witnesses at the trial. He wants revenge."

"No, I mean why kill him that way?"

"Why not?"

"Oh, come on, Ruth. Don't pretend it's so simple. I mean, there are so many ways both of your 'murders' could have gone wrong. In fact, the first one did, if you really were the target. And what if Benny hadn't reacted to the vandalism that way?"

"But he did, Helen."

"Yes, but what are the odds?"

"Helen, listen to me." Ruth leaned closer. "Sol Cantor has been back two weeks, and Morton and Steve are dead. You wanna talk to me about coincidences? You wanna talk about odds? Talk to me about *that!*"

"Please lower your voice."

Ruth sat back, gripping the edge of the table as if holding on for dear life. She opened her mouth to speak, then closed it again and shook her head. Then, speaking softly she said, "I'm sorry."

"You're going through a tough time."

"Yeah. Maybe that's it. Steve and I . . . you know, we were . . . we . . ."

Helen reached across the table, covering Ruth's hand with her own. "I know."

Ruth fought back tears and tried to smile. "I just feel so vulnerable."

"Maybe it would help if you did something about that."

The rabbi lifted her chin. "I bought a gun."

"A *gun?* Ruth, you can't—"

"Don't start. I bought it, I'm taking lessons on how to use it, and that's that."

"But you still feel vulnerable."

"Uh-huh."

Helen thought for a moment, then removed something from her purse. "How about if you changed your locks? Maybe have some stronger ones installed?"

"I guess maybe."

"Here. Call this guy." Helen passed a business card across the table. Taking the card, Ruth read: *Jake Singer. Locksmith.*

Solomon Cantor watched Ruth walk away toward the river through the dense crowd on the east side of Canal. When she reached the end of the block, he shifted the dilapidated pickup into gear and pulled out into traffic, cutting off a Chevrolet Suburban with Mississippi plates. Ignoring the blaring horn, Sol kept his eyes on Ruth. She turned left onto Chartres, entering a narrow valley between eighteenth-century brick and stucco town houses. Fortunately, the street was one way in Sol's direction. He waited for a hole in the traffic on Canal, then gassed the old truck across the avenue and into the French Quarter. The rabbi strode quickly along the damp slate banquette. Sol rolled along behind, tapping on the brake to avoid overtaking her. Each time his boot touched the pedal the truck rocked on its worn-out springs like a boat in choppy water. After trailing her for three blocks, Sol saw a steel barricade up ahead, forming the lowermost border of a rectangular glimpse into Jackson Square. Lush greenery leaned in from the right-hand frame, coyly bobbing in a river breeze beyond delicate wrought-iron balconies. On the left, the faux limestone façade and dull slate mansard of the Cabildo defined the view. A woman emerged from a nearby door and pitched filthy water onto the street from a white plastic bucket. Steam rose ghostlike from the puddle she left behind. Just beyond the barricade at the vanishing point of the image, seven or eight men holding brass musical instruments at various angles sprawled on park benches. The merry notes of their Scott Joplin rag drifted through his pickup truck's open window. Sol frowned.

Jackson Square lay in the rabbi's path, cutting off the road. If she intended to cross the square in front of the Cabildo and the Cathedral, he'd have to turn left on St. Peter, loop all the way over to Bourbon and back down St. Ann, hoping to catch up with her on the other side.

Sure enough, she crossed Toulouse and entered the square. Sol began to panic. He couldn't lose her now, not after sticking so close all day long.

If only he could ditch the truck and follow her on foot.

Just as he was giving up hope, a guy in a Volvo pulled out of a parking place up ahead on the right. Gritting his teeth, Solomon Cantor flipped on his turn signal and began to parallel park for the first time in two and a half decades.

T he computer screen reflected pale blue on the lieutenant's face, creating an island of light among the shadows of the darkened office as

his fingers tapped at the keyboard. Venetian blinds pared the stark sunshine into the slimmest of parallel stripes stretched side by side across
the floor. The lieutenant preferred to think in a darkened room. It mini-
mized distractions. He moved slightly and one of the slender bars of
light sliced across his neck, sparkling on his small gold earring. Except
for that, Washington was dressed like a banker. His perfectly trimmed
hair and professionally manicured fingernails underscored his upwardly
mobile, middle-class image. He wore the earring to violate the stereo-
type. Washington had learned long ago that it was helpful to keep
people guessing. Set up certain expectations, then toss in one little thing
that contradicted all the rest, and sit back with your mouth shut. They'll
usually make up for their uncertainty by talking too much. It was one of
the secrets of his success.

Like his clothes and his mind, the lieutenant's desk was neat as a
pin, his inbox empty, his outbox stacked with the day's reports ready
for filing in the morning. The only personal item on the desktop was a
nameplate that read *Lieutenant Lincoln Washington*, a gift from his mother
in honor of his most recent promotion. It sat front and center, cast in
bronze, a proud declaration of rank and a dare to anyone who thought
he had the juice to give him grief about his name. His friends called him
Link. His enemies—and like any cop, he had a few—called him Lieutenant, at least to his face. A couple old buddies from the neighborhood
still called him Prez, but he had discouraged that within the department.
It was disrespectful, both to him and to the great men whose names he
bore. Well, disrespectful to Abraham Lincoln, anyway. George Washington he didn't care about so much. He had owned slaves.

The lieutenant's personal notes lit the computer screen. Every afternoon he updated his database, transferring his thoughts and any particu-
lars he had jotted down in his notebook since the previous day. That way
he could cross-check his facts later, looking for common elements—
anything that might indicate a pattern. Once or twice, he'd found connections between cases he'd thought were unrelated. More often, his system
just allowed him to keep the facts organized within each individual case.
Organization. Another secret of his success.

Poking at the keyboard with three fingers, Washington came to
the hour he'd spent with Rabbi Ruth Gold that morning, over at the

Northside Jewish Community Center. He lifted his neatly manicured fingers from the keyboard and sat back, remembering how that went. She had been a few minutes late and had seemed distracted at first. Probably because of the people demonstrating out front. Well, not demonstrating exactly, but close enough. After talking about her options in that situation, which were limited, she'd taken him deeper into the building and walked him through the events surrounding a twenty-five-year-old murder. He'd been a little impatient, feeling it was not a good use of his time since the perpetrator had already served his sentence. But the lady was a rabbi at the city's largest Jewish congregation, and his captain had made it clear that she deserved the white-glove treatment, so he did his duty, whether it was useful or not. At least the rabbi was a good-looking woman. That kept the time from being a total waste.

Still, after about twenty minutes he had been ready to get back to work. Then the rabbi had mentioned a theory about a couple of other deaths during the last two weeks. She figured they were killed by the perp of the old homicide, for revenge.

Link had made a few calls on the way back to the precinct and had learned the circumstances of the deaths. An elderly man shot by his own brother—also his roommate—who mistook him for an intruder. Apparently, the shooter had good reason for his mistake, due to some vandalism and harassment that had occurred just before the shooting. Pretty open and shut, actually. The shooter was still in custody, but Link figured he'd get man-two at the most; they might even drop the charges. When you added it up with a guy who ate a piece of poisoned fruit, you came up with nothing but coincidence, which is what he later told the rabbi. That was when he learned she had a temper. Link smiled. Man, what a temper. Still, just because she felt strongly about it was no reason to waste department resources.

Link typed, *No action*, pressed the Enter key, and moved on to his next case.

CHAPTER
TEN

Katy?"

The exotically attractive woman who had just stepped into her shop smiled tentatively, as if unsure of her reception. Kate stared openly at the woman's olive skin, short black hair, and huge, dark brown eyes.

"Katy, it's me. Ruth Gold."

"Wow," said Kate. "You've changed."

Ruth smiled, walking closer. "Well, I hope so."

"But I mean, you're . . . beautiful."

"So are you."

"No." Kate's hand rose, shyly pressing a loose strand of her thick blonde hair back in place. Suddenly she felt pretty grungy in her faded blue jeans, tie-dyed T-shirt, and Doc Marten sandals.

"Phooey! You're gorgeous, girl." Ruth unleashed a dazzling smile. "I love this hippie thing you've got going."

Both women laughed nervously. Kate couldn't stop thinking, *Can this incredible woman really be the little girl of my memories?* Finally, she realized she was staring and said, "Would you like a cup of tea?"

"Sounds good. Thanks."

As Kate went about the business of heating water, Ruth wandered through the little shop, pausing here and there to examine an object or a piece of furniture. She bent to get a closer look at a small three-cornered hat in a display case.

"Isn't that something?" asked Kate.

"Is it real?"

"You mean really old? Yes."

"It's like the ones they wear in those old paintings of Paul Revere and the Revolution and all that."

"You have the period right, but we found it in England, not America. Made by a Liverpool company sometime between 1768 and 1782."

"How'd you find that out?"

"Lots and lots of research."

"You must really like antiques to put all this together."

"Actually, my husband made the initial purchases. That was the hard part, getting a whole shop full of interesting things all at once. Now it's just a question of filling the gaps when I sell a piece."

"On the phone the other day you didn't say anything about your husband."

"He died."

"I'm sorry."

"Thank you."

Kate brought Ruth her tea. Ruth smiled, accepting the cup and saucer. The two of them sat across the aisle from each other, Kate on a settee made in Boston in 1847 and Ruth on an original Queen Anne side chair. Ruth said, "In a way, you could say I'm in the business of research-ing old things, myself."

"Really? What do you do?"

"I'm a rabbi."

Kate stared at her. "They have women rabbis?"

"They do in my denomination."

"Which one is that?"

"Reform."

"Oh. My husband was raised Conservative."

"He was Jewish?"

"Uh-huh."

Ruth looked at Kate appraisingly. "Did you convert?"

Kate met her eyes. "No. He did."

Ruth looked away.

Kate said, "I mean, he had already converted when I met him in our singles group at church."

"I see," said Ruth, still looking away.

Sensing disapproval in the woman's body language, perhaps even offense at the thought of a Jew converting, Kate thought, *If you only knew how little all of that matters to me these days. . . .* She decided to change the subject before she found herself trying to explain such things to a stranger.

"So. You're a rabbi. Who would've guessed?"

"My dad, for one. He was a rabbi too, remember?"

"I don't think I ever knew that."

"Yes. If there's a single reason for my choice, I guess that'd be it. He raised me to love Judaism."

"So if your father was a rabbi, I guess that means rabbis can get married?"

"Of course. There's no vow of celibacy. That's a Christian thing."

Kate blushed. "Sorry. I guess I should have known that."

"It's okay. Most people don't know much about our faith."

"Well, I should know more. But John, my husband, didn't have any Jewish friends and didn't talk much about his background. And I haven't met very many Jews, except for him and his parents."

"Oh, I'll bet you've met a lot."

"Not to talk to . . . I mean, about religious things. Sometimes I wish I could ask my in-laws a few questions, but they don't really invite that kind of thing, you know?"

"You aren't close?"

"No. Actually, when John became a Christian they had a falling out. And they didn't like him marrying me. That pretty much shut down all communication until the kids came along. Then they thawed out a little, but we're still not real friendly, you know?"

"It's . . . hard, sometimes."

"Well, it hurt John, and that's what bothered me most. But I *am* very interested in . . . well, in Judaism and all, and I'd *like* to have Jewish friends. I really would."

Ruth cocked her head, a small smile playing around the corners of her mouth. "You seem uncomfortable, Katy."

"Not really."

"Are you sure?"

"Well . . . I guess I do feel a little bit awkward."

"Why?"

"I don't know. Like I said, I've never met anyone like you before."

"You make me sound like I'm from another planet."

"I'm sorry, Ruth. Really. I don't know why I'm saying these things."

"It's okay."

"I do know a Jewish couple, now that I think about it. They live down the street. Their little boy used to play with Paul sometimes."

"Used to?"

"Yes. Until there was a—a problem, one time. I took the kids for a picnic over at City Park, and Paul's little friend brought his own lunch, you know, but when we got there, I let the kids play while I got everything ready on this table, and I, uh . . ."

"What? You slipped him pork or something?" asked Ruth, smiling.

"Of course not. But I did notice his roast beef sandwich looked awfully bland—I mean, it was just meat and bread—so I put some cheese on it."

Ruth shook her head.

Kate said, "Well, the little boy went absolutely berserk when he bit into it, and when his mother found out, she got very upset. I'm still not sure why."

Ruth said, "Orthodox Jews aren't supposed to mix meat and dairy products."

Kate gave her a blank look. "Why not?"

"It's in the Bible," said Ruth. "We're told not to boil a kid in its mother's milk."

"And from *that* you get to no mayonnaise on roast beef sandwiches?"

"The connection seems clear to me."

"Really?"

"Really."

The two women fell into an uncomfortable silence, sipping their tea. Then Ruth said, "How'd we get on this subject?"

"I don't know. Let's talk about family. Are your folks well?"

"They've both passed away."

Kate nodded. "Mine too."

"But you said you have a son."

"Yes, Paul. He's twelve, and looking just like his father."

"Any other kids?"

"Jilly. She just turned five."

"Then you're blessed."

Kate nodded. "Oh, yes."

"I assume you're raising them as Christians?"

It was a good question. She had taught the kids to pray before meals and before going to bed. She took them to church every Sunday, but those were merely habits. Family traditions. What did she have to offer beneath the surface? Should she continue to lead them down the same dead-end path she had taken, or teach them the bitter truth now to keep their hopes from being dashed like hers?

"Katy?"

"Sorry. I was just thinking about something. What did you say?"

"I asked if you were raising your children as Christians or as Jews."

"Oh yeah. They're Christians. I mean, that's what I am, and like I said, John was Jewish, but he was a Christian too."

Ruth smiled slightly. "That's like saying your car was a Ford, but it was a Chrysler."

"Well, you know what I mean."

The rabbi nodded. "I suppose." Finishing her tea, she set the saucer on an eighteenth-century French dresser. "Katy, have you had any unusual experiences the last two weeks?"

"Unusual? How do you mean?"

"It could be anything, I guess. A feeling of being watched. Seeing the same car over and over again in traffic. Phone calls in the middle of the night. Anything like that."

"I've been frightened ever since you called about Sol Cantor being out, but other than that there's been nothing." Kate paused. "Except . . ."

"What?"

"It's nothing. Stupid, really."

"Come on, Katy. What?"

Kate told her about the applesauce she couldn't remember buying and the jelly that had disappeared.

"Has anything else like that happened?" asked Ruth.

"No."

Ruth fixed her dark eyes on Kate. "You remember what I told you about Steve?"

"Who?"

"Steve. My boyfriend. The one who was poisoned."

"Oh, yes."

"Well, now there's been another death. Do you remember Morton Rothstein?"

Kate searched her memory. "I think so . . . wasn't he that tall man who saw Mr. Cantor after we did?"

"Yes."

"I liked him. He brought us candy during the trial, I think."

"That's him. He's dead."

"How?"

Ruth explained.

Kate said, "Sounds to me like his brother went crazy."

"It wasn't Benny who broke the windows."

"How do you know?"

"The glass was all inside the apartment."

Kate understood immediately. "So the windows were broken from outside?"

"Had to be. But the police said they didn't find anything *inside* the house that could have been used to break the windows. No rocks or bricks or anything."

"Maybe they used a baseball bat or something like that."

"The Rothsteins lived on the third floor."

"Oh," said Kate. "How strange."

"Tell me more about this applesauce."

"I'm sure it's nothing, really. It's just that I can't remember buying it."

"Have it tested. The police would probably do that for you."

"I already threw it out."

"Oh."

"Well, even if I still had it, what would I say? 'Please test this stuff, because I don't remember picking it up at the grocery store'?"

"But you said someone took all your jellies to get you to eat it right away, and your son found evidence that someone broke into your house."

"I said someone *might* have taken the jelly for that reason. And all Paul found was an unlocked door."

Ruth exhaled deeply. "Why is everyone ignoring what's happening?"

"Ruth, I—"

"No. Forget I said that. You're just being honest. But think about it, Katy. I get apples filled with cyanide shipped to my house and you find applesauce that you didn't buy in your refrigerator. Steve is dead. Morton is dead. And all of that has happened within two weeks of Sol Cantor's release." She leaned forward, staring directly into Kate's eyes. "We've got to try to catch him."

Kate laughed.

"I'm serious, Katy! The police won't believe me, so that means it's up to us."

"Oh, I don't know . . ."

"He's after you, Katy! He's already killed two people. It's just dumb luck that we're alive. We're the only witnesses left."

Kate lowered her eyes. "Ruth, I appreciate what you're trying to do."

"That sounds like a no to me."

"I live a quiet life. I'm not the kind of person who gets involved in things like this."

"You *are* involved, whether you like it or not!"

"But don't you think this theory of yours is a little bit far-fetched?"

"Far-*fetched*?"

"Well, don't you think?"

Ruth rose to her feet. "I do *not*! And I'm sick of hearing that from everybody!"

"Ruth? Calm down a little, okay? Maybe in your line of work you come in contact with this kind of thing—"

"What are you saying, Katy?" snapped Ruth. "That I work with murderers because I'm a rabbi?"

"All I meant was—"

"I know what you meant! People like you have been saying the same thing to people like me for centuries!"

"Ruth, let me explain. I—"

"No need to explain. I understand completely."

Ruth Gold spun on her heels and marched to the front door, jerking it open. As she was about to exit, she turned back. "At least you didn't tell me some of your best friends are Jews!" After she slammed the door, the tiny brass bell tinkled for five full seconds as Kate Flint sat motionless on the antique settee, trying to understand what had just happened.

R abbi Gold rushed uptown on St. Charles, away from the Vieux Carre, with Solomon Cantor right behind. He figured something bad must have happened in the antique shop. She had come charging out like the place was on fire. It had been all he could do to keep up with her. Then, when they had passed his parked truck, he'd had to hop in, get himself out of the parking place, and loop around on Royal in time to catch her as she pulled away from the parking garage on Dauphine in her funny little car.

Now, a streetcar rumbled along in front of her, an antique throwback to the era when the thirty-story glass towers on the left and right would have been impossible to build. Sol found downtown confusing. Very few of the skyscrapers had been there when he'd gone into the joint. He felt like a throwback himself sometimes, his truck bed filled to overflowing with rusty pipes and storm-bent television antennas and leaky dishwashers and other roadside salvage he could not even identify. In a way, it was the perfect disguise. Sol had learned that nobody looked past the junk to the old man driving the truck. In a culture rich enough to treat dishwashers and television antennas as disposable, he was one of the city's lower castes, a useful parasite, picking roadside fleas from the glossy coat of society.

They emerged from between the looming towers of the downtown area. The streetcar veered onto the neutral ground, but the woman's

Citroën continued along at a leisurely pace. Sol felt pleased. Earlier that morning, she had driven with cavalier abandon. He had found it difficult to keep up in a thirty-year-old truck with a front end badly in need of alignment and shock absorbers that simulated the undulations of the Canal Street Ferry when the river was high.

She slowed. He thought she was about to park in front of a furniture store, but then she sped up again. He found himself only two cars back. Too close. If the rabbi saw him, everything might be ruined. Sol slowed and stopped in the middle of the block. The car behind him honked. He ignored it, but the thought crossed his mind that the honker was taking a heck of a chance. You never knew who was driving in front of you these days. He'd once heard a couple of Latin kids up in Angola laugh about beating an old guy with a tire iron because he was tailgating.

Uh-oh. Looks like she's stopping up in front of that flower shop.

He slowed in order to stay five cars back. The clown in the car behind him honked again. Sol reached up and tilted his rearview mirror to get a better look at the driver, but the reflection of the sky and the live oaks in the car's windshield made it impossible to see him. What an idiot this guy was. Of course, the way things were these days, there was no guarantee it was a guy. Women were acting crazy as men. Crazier sometimes. Sol had definitely noticed that since he got out.

Up ahead, the rabbi emerged from her car and entered the flower shop. Sol pulled to the curb. The jerk behind him stepped on the gas, offering an uncomplimentary gesture as he passed. Sol ignored the obscenity, his thoughts solidly concentrated on the woman in the flower shop. In prison, he had learned to disregard the incidental clutter, and focus on survival. Out here, that habit came in handy.

Her felt tip moved across her notebook, making a scratchy sound they could both hear clearly in the unnaturally quiet room. Then the psychiatrist swiveled in her chair to face him more directly. "Why do you think your nightmare was different this time?"

"You know, I've been asking myself that. I'm not really sure."

"Any theories?"

He smiled. "I thought that was your job, Doc."

"I'll take all the help I can get," said Dr. Helen Blumenthal, returning his smile. "Come on, what do you think?"

"I've got no idea, really. Unless it's just these sessions, finally making a difference."

Again, her felt-tip pen moved across the paper. Jake Singer sat patiently, watching her. When she was done, she looked up and smiled. "Okay. Let's talk about what you saw this time."

"Okay."

"You said you felt different. Was there anything else?"

"Yeah. The, uh, the end was different too, I guess."

"Okay." She swiveled away from him, looking out the window. It seemed to make him nervous when she made eye contact. "How so?"

"Well, like I said, I got numb all of a sudden. A nonfeeling feeling, you know?"

She waited, knowing he was rehashing their earlier dialogue as a delaying tactic. Staring out the window, she saw the Mississippi far below dotted with barges, and beyond, the low buildings of Algiers shrouded in steamy humidity. She tried to suppress her growing excitement. The patient had enjoyed a genuine breakthrough of some kind. That had been immediately clear from his demeanor when he entered her office. Unlike Jake's previous visits, he was quite alert, made some eye contact, and displayed an increased willingness to engage in dialogue. The ongoing depression he usually presented seemed to have lifted a bit. She was very curious to learn the reason, but she never allowed herself to reveal her own emotions to patients. Emotional response was contagious, and this was about *his* feelings, not hers, so she waited, watching a tugboat push a barge up the muddy river far below her downtown office.

He cleared his throat. "And, uh, the clicking stopped."

"That's never happened before?"

"No."

"Anything else?"

"Well, yeah. This time, I just kind of *knew* that I was about to see the reason. I was almost there when Slasky's stupid poundin' on the door woke me up."

"When you were almost 'there,' how did you feel?"

"I already told you. I didn't feel anything."

"Are you sure?"

"Yes!" His voice had risen.

Turning away from the window, she looked at him. "What are you feeling right now?"

"Nothing! I'm just trying to get you to understand."

His eyes were lowered, respiratory rate elevated slightly, skin tone somewhat ruddy. One hand wore a gauze bandage, the other was curled into a fist. For the thousandth time, she wished she could simply ask, "What's going on inside your mind?" But of course, that would be foolish. She said, "What do you want me to understand?" He sat without answering, his eyes on his lap, unconcerned about the silence building between them. She repeated her question.

"I'm . . . afraid, I guess," he said.

"Afraid right now, or back then, in the dream?"

"Now."

"Why?"

"I don't know!"

"Do you want us to stop?"

"No!" He said it quickly, urgently, looking up at her with eyes wide.

"All right. Don't worry; we still have some time."

A pause, then he said, "I think the fear . . . I think it comes from knowing what's about to happen."

This was new. Always before, his fear was of the unknown. She asked, "What's that? What is about to happen?"

"I can't remember."

"But in the dream, you knew?"

"Uh-huh."

Again, she wrote on her pad while he waited silently. The glass wall groaned, shifting slightly in the wind, joining the scratching sound of her pen. There was almost always a wind this high up. Helen stopped writing and glanced at him, then lowered her eyes to her pad. "This place where you are in your dream . . . do you know where it is?"

He started to shake his head, but stopped. "You know, I did sort of know!"

"Where were you?"

"I'm not sure exactly, but it was a place. A real place." He looked straight at her. "How did you know?"

She smiled. "Lucky guess. How could you tell it was a real place?"

"It was like . . . some place in the real world. Not just a place I made up in a dream."

"I see. And you were afraid?"

"Well, sure."

"But a minute ago you said you were numb. You had that—" she glanced at her notes—"that 'nonfeeling feeling,' remember?"

"Uh-huh. It was like being paralyzed, except I could move, okay? And I was, like, far away from myself." He paused, then added, "But I was still scared."

"Why?"

"I told you! Because I knew what was going to happen!"

"What was that?"

"I don't know! Something bad!"

"Was it going to happen to you?"

"No! You don't understand!"

He erupted from his seat and strode across the room to stand before the wall of glass. Placing both palms against it he bowed his head and leaned forward, pressing out toward the empty sky, hundreds of feet above the city. She worried about the pressure he was putting on the glass. She thought about the fact that they were alone up there in the wind. From thousands of miles to the south where the wind came from, clear across the Gulf of Mexico, no one else was living as high in the air as she and her patient. All the way from South America, this wind had come without touching a single man-made object so high up. It was a lonely thought. Certainly not something to share with Jake Singer. Not with him pitting his weight against the tensile strength of that glass, pressing against it, so high above the ground. She knew the glass was strong enough to resist the pressure, but still Helen had to fight the urge to warn him not to push so hard. Nothing could save him if he fell through. A new thought occurred to her. On her pad, she wrote, *Suicidal?*

CHAPTER
ELEVEN

J illy clutched a piece of colored cardboard covered with glued-on kernels of popcorn and rice. As soon as they got home, it would join the art gallery already stuck to the front of the refrigerator, right beside the one with her handprint colored to look like a turkey. That one was from Sunday school, last year at Thanksgiving time. This one was her very first art from real school.

"Pauly?" she asked. "Do you really think Mommy will like it?"

"Sure."

"Really?"

"Uh-huh."

"Really truly?"

"*Yes*, Jilly. Stop asking me that."

Mommy didn't always like her art. She always said she did, but sometimes you could tell she was just saying that to be nice.

"Pauly?" she said, looking up at him. "Do you like my picture?"

"It's all right."

She held it out in front to look at while she and Pauly walked. She had made a cross with the popcorn. A cross standing on a little hill of rice.

"Pauly? Why did Mommy take all the church stuff off the 'frigerator?"

Her brother ignored her.

"Why did she do that?"

"I dunno."

"Do you think Mommy still loves Jesus?"

"I dunno."

"Do you think she'll let me put this on the 'frigerator?"

"Sure."

"But it's about Jesus. Maybe she won't."

"Will you please just be quiet?"

Jilly held her art out in front to look at it again. They were almost home, and she didn't have to watch where she was going, because she knew every single crack in the sidewalk by heart, especially the ones where the roots pushed up through the concrete. Then, right in front of the house, Pauly grabbed her arm.

"Wait a minute," he said.

"Huh?"

Pauly had a funny look on his face.

"Whatsamatter?" she asked.

"Shhh!"

"Whatsamatter, Pauly?"

But Pauly didn't answer, so she looked at the house, where he was looking. She loved their house. She loved the big white columns, and the pretty green shutters and the two funny windows up there on the roof. She loved the great big tree that put its shadow all over everything and the way the moss hung down like Granny's hair. She especially loved the way you had to go upstairs to get to the front door. From up there, you could look down on the bayou across the street and everything. Then Jilly saw that the front door was open. *That* wasn't right.

Pauly knelt down beside her. "You go over to Diana's house and see if she can play, okay?"

"But I wanna put my picture on the 'frigerator."

He smiled. "Can I put it there for you?"

"No! *I* wanna do it!"

Pauly got mad. "Listen, you little squirt. Mom's not here, and that means I'm in charge."

"You're not the boss of me!"

"Oh yes I am! I'm the man of the house."

"Are not!"

"I am too!" He grabbed her arm. "Jilly, you can keep the picture and put it on the refrigerator later if you want to. But go show it to Diana and her mom first."

He gave her a push, and she almost fell down.

"Hey! I'm gonna tell!"

"All right," said Pauly. "You can tell later, too. Just go to Diana's house now."

"You pushed me," she said, looking at the open front door. "An' you're lettin' all the cold air get outside." She took a couple of steps toward Diana's house, then turned to look back at her brother. "Mommy's gonna be *real* mad!"

But Pauly wasn't paying attention, because he was already halfway up the stairs, heading toward the open door.

R uth sat beside Benny Rothstein's bed, holding his shriveled old hand and doing her best to appear interested in the conversation. The guards had raised an eyebrow when she arrived with the flowers from the shop on St. Charles. Benny was probably the only person in the security ward of the hospital with a floral arrangement in his room. Ruth was glad she'd brought them. Visiting the sick and the elderly was a *mitzvah* she sometimes avoided. Enduring their ramblings while maintaining the appearance of interest often took great patience, not to mention the skills of a Shakespearean actor. She might have skipped this particular good deed, but early that morning as she had searched for a commentary on her office shelf, Ruth noticed the leather-bound copy of the *Bereshit* Talmud tractate that her father had given to her on the day of her ordination. It was a rare and beautiful Hebrew book, almost two hundred years old, and had been in his family for half a dozen generations. She thought of her father's words as he offered that precious gift: *"Always remember, the Torah is not just a thing you read; it's a thing you do."* So, remembering, she had made the time today for Benny Rothstein.

"Of course, Morton was only thirty-seven then," said Benny. He frowned. "Or was he thirty-eight? I don't seem to be able to recall things as well as I once did. . . ."

Ruth smiled again, willing herself to nod at appropriate moments. Benny seemed to require nothing more. The ward nurse had warned her that he had been talking for hours without pausing. It was a strange reaction to the shock of Morton's death, which at least allowed Ruth some time to think. Unfortunately, she did not enjoy her own thoughts. In fact, after the way she had behaved at Katy O'Connor's shop, she didn't like herself very much at all.

" . . . so off he went," said Benny, "flying down the mountain on a pair of the longest skis you ever saw. You know, they made them much longer back then, and you had to hold on to a knotted rope to get up the slopes. . . ."

Ruth nodded. Why had she stormed out that way? The woman had meant nothing by what she said. Obviously, Katy had been uncomfortable, but why automatically assume her discomfort was about Judaism? After all, it was natural for both of them to be uneasy, getting together again after all those years, strangers now, but best friends when they had last seen each other. How should you behave in a situation like that? Normally? Impossible. There was nothing normal about it.

" . . . dropped the bomb, and thank goodness that ended that. He came home three months later. I had to put a few pounds back on him, but otherwise, he was none the worse for wear and tear. Just a little tired, that's all. I think they worked him too hard at that commissary. In fact, you know, I think it was two years before . . ."

Ruth felt . . . ashamed. There. That was a word she'd been avoiding all afternoon, but now it was out. She was ashamed for treating Katy that way, just as she had been ashamed to pray aloud at her parents' graves, and ashamed of the way she'd treated Gabrielle Cantor, assuming nothing but the worst intentions when the old woman might very well have come simply to beg for peace for its own sake. Ruth's emotions seemed to swing so wildly from anger to shame and back again. She did not understand herself. She did not like herself. She wished to change.

I will change! I'll begin by apologizing to Katy.

It was a *mitzvah* to repent, it was the time of year to repent, and that was exactly what she would do as soon as Benny fell asleep. The nurse said he always fell asleep eventually, sometimes in midsentence.

" . . . Morton should be here any minute."

Ruth wondered whether Benny might not be better off in his new-found fantasy world. After all, his other option was the horrible reality that he would never see Morton again because he had killed his brother two days ago. Benny Rothstein did not even seem to notice that the door to his room was locked and the window was barred.

She sighed.

Benny said, "Are you unhappy?"

"I—"

"Because you seem worried about something. Do you want to talk about it? Don't waste your time worrying, Ruth. If I had a penny for every day I wasted worrying about something that worked out just fine, why, I'd be a wealthy man today. You know, it's never what you worry about that ruins things. It's always something else. Something you never imagined."

Ruth frowned, thinking, *That's exactly what I'm afraid of.*

"Sometimes, your own worries are your worst enemy. Did you ever make something happen, just by thinking that it might? I did. I remember . . ."

The old man's voice dipped below her consciousness as his words struck home. *"Did you ever make something happen, just by thinking that it might?"*

Oh yes, she thought, *I've done that very thing.* Then Ruth's mind drifted away as it seemed to be doing more and more these days. With the Day of Atonement approaching and the raw image of Steve's death ever-present in her mind, Ruth's misery grew day by day, manifesting itself in irrational anger at innocent people, fueled by the restless flame of memory, mercilessly shining on the most painful moments of her past . . . .

just want to know if it's true!" she screamed, twenty-six years old and fresh from rabbinic school at Hebrew Union College in Cincinnati. She confronted her brother in the middle of the Mississippi River on the Canal Street Ferry with her fists planted solidly on her hips, measuring her words for effect.

"Is . . . it . . . *true?*"

Isaac's wide eyes searched hers, and she knew the answer before he spoke a word. "Who told you?"

"Mom and Dad, of course." She faced the river and gripped the dull green rail tightly. "How could you do this to us?"

"What?" asked Isaac. "I couldn't hear."

The gulls screeched overhead. For one crazy moment, she thought they were laughing at her. Furious, she screamed, "I said, how could you do this to us!"

An Asian couple standing a few feet away lifted their eyes from the putty gray waters, stealing surreptitious glances in their direction. No doubt they mistook the situation for a lovers' quarrel. Isaac was just four years younger than Ruth and looked old for his age. He touched her sleeve. She yanked her arm away. "Please," said Isaac, his eyes imploring her for mercy. "Please try to understand."

"Understand what, exactly? That you've turned your back on everything? That you've joined *them* in spite of all they've done?"

"It's not about them, Ruth."

"Of course it is!"

"No. Please, just listen—"

"I will not! I've heard it all before—but from them, Isaac. I never thought I'd hear it from you."

He tried to respond, but Ruth had pushed away from the railing and stalked across the steel plate deck of the ferry. Isaac followed, entreating her for a chance to explain. People stared from their parked cars and standing positions along the rail as she strode as far forward as she could, stopping beneath a Louisiana state flag at the bow. It flapped in the wind, displaying a proud female pelican, her widespread wings sheltering three hatchlings in a nest. The motto on the flag mocked her: *Union, Justice, and Confidence.* Overhead, the gulls glided and laughed, joining in the mockery.

Isaac arrived at her elbow. "You think this was easy for me? Come on. I'm still your brother, Ruth. You've got to listen to me. You've just got to!"

Turning to him, she said, "No."

"No? That's it? Just no?"

"That's it, Isaac."

"How can you be so closed-minded? Didn't they teach you anything at that college? Reform Judaism is supposed to embrace any—"

"*Don't you lecture me about Judaism!*"

He froze with his mouth open, staring at her.

Glancing around, she lowered her voice, but her words were still vicious, boiling up out of control. "What gives you the right to do this to us?"

"I'm not doing anything to you, Ruth. I've just chosen to—"

"I *know* what you've chosen! You've chosen to betray your family and your people. And if that's the way you want it, that's how it will be! You're no brother of mine!"

With those words, Ruth Gold, recently ordained rabbi, stormed away between the cars to the far end of the boat, leaving her brother alone at the bow. She stood above the churning water, watching logs and small islands of debris drift downstream as her fury slowly dissipated. They docked at Algiers. Ruth remained where she was, vacantly observing a dry-docked Russian ship at the Powder Street Wharf while the cars drove off the ferry. There was a whiff of rotten fish in the air. Garbage from every port on the planet languished in the water along the riverbank, cast adrift by sailors who spoke no English and did not care a whit for the local ecology—here a white plastic bleach bottle from Norway, there a mayonnaise jar from Brazil—you never knew what kind of offerings the Mississippi would deposit in the open arms of the Big Easy.

Other cars rolled on board. Soon they embarked again, returning to New Orleans. The giant engines rumbled beneath her feet, vibrating the metal deck. When they reached the landing at the end of Canal, she walked back to the bike rack. Her ten-speed bicycle was the only one there. Apparently Isaac had taken his and disembarked on the other side of the river. So Ruth walked alone up the ramp, and still, the gulls above her laughed.

T he hours dragged on and on. Kate couldn't seem to avoid looking at the clock. Now and then someone came in and browsed through the shop, but she found it difficult to show any interest. That probably explained the fact that she hadn't sold a thing all day.

Kate just couldn't get Ruth off her mind.

What had happened? What had she said? After all those years, to finally see each other, and to have it end that way . . .

A small woman with braided gray hair and a large macramé bag opened the front door and peered inside.

Don't stand there all day, thought Kate. *Get in or get out.*

The lady began moving through the shop, slowly examining everything. Kate made no effort to greet her. Somehow, she couldn't shake this sense of gloom. It had been hours since Ruth had stormed out, but here she was, still trying to figure out what she did wrong.

"How much is this?"

Kate looked up to find the woman holding a turn-of-the-century, arts-and-crafts ceramic tile. "One hundred and twenty dollars," said Kate.

"For *this?*"

Kate stared at her for a moment, then said, "You're right. It's two hundred and twenty."

"But you said one hundred and twenty—"

"Yes. Thank you for noticing my mistake."

"I didn't notice any—"

"Did you want the tile?"

"Not at that price. I just—"

"All right, then. I'll be here if you need me."

The woman glanced from the tile to Kate to the tile again, eyebrows furrowed in confusion. Kate swiveled around in her chair, facing away. Seconds later, she heard the tinkle of the bell as the front door opened and shut.

Kate sighed. Ruth Gold's accusations of anti-Semitism were the perfect highlight of yet another meaningless day here in this suffocating sarcophagus with her dead husband's dead dream presiding over her own dead hopes.

Maybe God is dead too. Maybe that's why I can't seem to care about anything anymore . . . except the children, of course.

She rose and walked toward the front, intending to flip the sign around from Open to Sorry. The telephone rang when she got to the far side of the shop. Typical. Rolling her eyes, Kate hurried back across the sales floor and lifted the handset on the fourth ring. "Mrs. Katherine Flint?" The voice on the line was crisp and professional.

"Yes?"

"This is the New Orleans Police Department calling."

Kate felt a chill rise from the small of her back, icy fingers tracing the contours of her spine. "Yes?"

"Ma'am, are you alone?"

"Yes," she said. "Why?"

"Uh, Mrs. Flint, we have a car coming your way."

"Why?"

"The officers will explain when they arrive, Mrs. Flint."

A thought occurred to her then, came from out of nowhere. Premonition or prophecy—what was the difference? All that mattered was that somehow she knew.

"It's my children, isn't it?"

"Mrs. Flint, there's been an incident at your home. It involves your son. If you'll wait just four or five minutes, we'll have a patrol car there and they can explain every—"

Kate dropped the telephone to the floor, grabbed her backpack, and ran to the door. The policewoman's voice rose from the telephone handset on the floor beside the desk. "Mrs. Flint? Are you there? Mrs. Flint?" But she was already outside, running as hard as she could along the sidewalk toward her car. She pushed her way through a walking tour, slowing just enough to avoid slamming into the startled tourists as they gawked at an eighteenth-century Creole cottage, leaving scattered stares and snide remarks in her wake. The crowds were merely animate objects, holding her back. She shoved between two men in front of her walking slowly, shoulder to shoulder. There were still more loiterers ahead. Kate stepped from the curb, charging headlong down the middle of the narrow street, running with the cars, oblivious to everything but this certainty she felt that something was horribly, horribly wrong. One of her sandals flew off of her foot. She kicked off the other and kept running, barefoot.

As she ran, Kate replayed the woman's words in her mind over and over again. *"There's been an incident at your home. It involves your son"*—*Oh, God, please. Don't take Paul away from me! Don't do that to me too!*

A horn honked behind her. "Get outta da street, lady!" shouted the driver. "Are you crazy?"

She leapt back up onto the blue slate sidewalk. Turning a corner, she crashed into a young man carrying groceries in two plastic sacks, knocking him sideways into the lush climbing vines of a huge plumbago. He fell hard upon the pavement, blossoms drifting to the sidewalk all around like pale blue snowflakes. Without apology, Kate ran on, past creosoted telephone poles densely papered with multicolored handbills, past the rust-encrusted, cast-iron filligree of French Quarter fame, past the incurious eyes of Vieux Carre residents, the bartenders and waiters and prostitutes and panhandlers and upwardly mobile professionals and hippie holdouts who populate the Quarter for love of history or love of culture or lack of anyplace else to go. Reaching the small parking lot at last, she dove into her Jeep and roared onto the street, only to find the way blocked by a delivery van. She screamed and pounded the horn, but the man in the brown uniform ignored her as he transferred box after plain brown box from the van to his hand truck. Finally, in desperation, Kate steered her right two tires onto the sidewalk and inched by. Once clear, she stomped on the accelerator and hit fifty miles per hour on the narrow streets, barely pausing before running stop signs and red lights all the way across town. She was thinking of Ruth's dead boyfriend and poisoned applesauce and an old man shooting his brother. She was blaming herself. *Oh, how could I have left them alone?* And she was blaming God. *Don't you do this to me. Don't you dare do this to me again!*

On her own street, Kate didn't bother to pull to the curb. She stopped in the middle of the road and leapt from her Jeep, leaving the engine running and the door open and charging between the two patrol cars parked in front of her house. A policeman in the front yard held his palms toward her as she ran up the sidewalk. "Hold it right there, lady," he said. Without pausing, she feinted left, then dodged around him on the right and hit the stairs, taking them two at a time.

"Paul!" she screamed, entering the house. "Paul! Jilly! Where are you?"

A couple of patrolmen standing in the entry hall turned toward her with startled expressions. "Mrs. Flint?" asked the tall one.

"Where are my children?" she cried. "What's happened to them?"

From deeper inside the house she heard, "Mom?"

Paul! She spun and saw him standing in the doorway to the kitchen. "Thank God!" she called, rejoicing, running to her son. She engulfed him with kisses. Paul stood awkwardly, embarrassed. She pushed back. "Where's Jilly? Is she okay?"

"Ma'am?" A policeman touched her shoulder. "Could you ask him to give us that now?"

"What?" Kate looked up at the patrolman blankly.

"The knife, ma'am. He won't put it down."

Kate looked back down at Paul. For the first time, she noticed the butcher knife in his right hand. "Oh, honey," she said, reaching for the knife.

Paul took a step back, holding it up between them.

He began to shake. She extended her hand toward him, palm up. "Come on, honey. It's all right now." Still trembling, he slowly placed the knife in her hand. As soon as her fingers closed around it, he turned and ran from the room.

"Tough kid," said the policeman.

W hich is just one example of a time I worried and it didn't do any good. There are lots of other times. I'm afraid I don't take my own advice sometimes."

Ruth saw Benny's eyes droop, then close, and just like that, he was asleep. She gently disengaged his hand from hers and placed it on the bed. Checking her watch, she realized there was no way she could get over to the Quarter before Katy closed her shop. She would just have to go find her house. What had she said her married name was? Ruth had always thought of her as Katy O'Connor.

Half an hour later, after finally remembering the name and looking up *Katherine Flint* in the telephone book, Ruth drove slowly through Katy's neighborhood. Pausing at each intersection, she leaned closer to the windshield to read the street signs in the gathering dusk. There. That was the street. She turned from Harding onto Moss and immediately saw the patrol cars.

"*Hashem* have mercy," she whispered. "What now?"

A Jeep stood empty in the center of the street, its driver side door wide open. Ruth was unsure what that meant, but it couldn't be good. She pulled the Citroën to the curb, scanning the nearby houses for Katy's address. Her heart fell as she realized Katy's was the house with the patrolmen standing on the lawn. She left her car and hurried toward them.

In John's study, in the center of the carpet, lay a pile of garbage. Except it wasn't garbage. It was pages from his books, torn out and wadded up; the Good Samaritan print that had hung on the wall, ripped out of its frame and torn in half; and a seat cushion sliced to ribbons.

Sitting cross-legged on the floor beside the pile, Kate reached for the cover of John's family Torah, the one he had displayed proudly on the antique bookstand in the corner, the one with his family's births and marriages and deaths, recorded in the hand of his great-grandfather, grandfather, and father for over a century. Kate's and John's names and their wedding date had been written in that book by John's father, as well as the date of Paul's birth, which was also the date the family Torah had been given to John by his parents as they stood outside the viewing room in the maternity wing of Touro Infirmary. It had been a tangible sign of hope for reconciliation. It had meant the world to her husband. Jilly's birth date was there too, in John's own handwriting. She withdrew the Torah from the mound of debris and opened the cover. The few remaining pages had been ripped from top to bottom, and the family record was missing. She had never thought to add John's death to the dates recorded there. Now it was too late.

"Ma'am, it'd be better if you didn't touch any of that stuff yet," said a patrolman. "They'll wanna dust it for fingerprints."

Ignoring him, she pawed through the pile on the floor, searching for the missing page. She found hundreds of torn pieces of Hebrew Scripture. Sifting through them, she felt a slight moisture. Kate lifted her fingertips to her nose and detected the unmistakable scent of lighter fluid. Eyes wide, she looked up at the officers standing nearby. One of them said, "We think your son scared him off before he had a chance to start the fire."

"This person was here when Paul came in?"

The policeman shrugged. "It's just a theory. Explains why he didn't start the fire."

Kate felt the floor fall away as the room tilted at crazy angles. Closing her eyes, she let the horror wash over her. *He was going to burn down our house . . . burn our home . . . and Paul and Jilly almost walked in on him.* Kate swayed back and forth clutching the cover of John's ruined Torah to her breast. *I can't take any more. Why are you doing this to me!*

Then a woman's voice said, "Katy?" and she turned and saw Ruth Gold standing in the entry hall, peering timidly at her with worried eyes.

When Ruth entered, Katy sat small and unprotected on the floor, rocking to and fro with grief. Meanwhile, three policemen stood around doing nothing. The louts.

"Katy?" she said.

Katy's eyes met hers, and just for an instant Ruth felt a memory there—something dim and barely present, but warm and familiar: a sudden, glorious flood of lemonade and Moon Pie sandwiches and hopscotch on hot summer afternoons; a scent, drifting on the breeze, touching something buried deep inside, then fading away before she could recall . . . what? What was this strange longing that swelled like a river and threatened to surge beyond the levees she had thrown up around her heart? Then Katy looked away, and the emotion receded, replaced by dismay as her own eyes fell to the tattered book Katy cradled in her arms. Was that a *Torah?*

The rabbi started across the room, but one of the officers blocked her way.

"Let me go," she said.

"Ma'am," he said, "who are you?"

The policeman stared at Ruth, waiting for an answer. She cleared her throat, searching for the words. Emboldened by what she had seen in Katy's eyes, she almost said, *I'm her friend.* She thought how good it might be to say those words out loud. But when they came, the words she spoke were simply: "Ask her."

Outside the house, the engine of Solomon Cantor's pickup idled roughly, rattling the accumulated metal odds and ends in the truck bed like a manic percussion section. A bent steel rod whacked away on a rusted tubular headboard, while a broken folding chair tapped against a square piece of expanded steel. Sol switched off the engine to silence the racket as he watched the Flint woman's house intently. After a while, two of the policemen came out and drove away, leaving just one of the patrol cars at the curb. Still he waited. He had been there over an hour when a plain white Crown Victoria rolled to a stop at the curb, followed by a white van with the words *Crime Scene* printed on the side door. Two men in coats and ties emerged from the car—one small and black, the other large and white. They started for the house, followed by a pair of women who also had come from the van. The women wore dark blue coveralls with *Police* in large white letters across the back. They carried brushed aluminum suitcases. Sol winced inwardly at the sight of the coveralls. He'd worn the things every day for a quarter of a century. Of course, his had been bright orange instead of dark blue, but it still depressed him just to look at them.

He said a little prayer for the woman who lived in that house, and for her children. *I should have followed her instead of the rabbi. But I can't be everywhere.* Sol leaned back against the cracked vinyl seat and sighed.

A rising tide of crimson had begun to flood the azure western sky. A commercial jet rumbled away from the city. Sol had flown in an aircraft only twice: on his way to Vietnam, and on his way back. Like the coveralls, airplanes held depressing associations for him. Of course, after he got out of prison he had sometimes been perversely thankful for his time in Southeast Asia. It had been very helpful to know that there were much worse experiences than Angola. Some of the younger inmates had thought prison was hell. They had no idea.

He lowered his eyes and rolled them toward the house without moving his head. One of the uniformed cops stood on the balcony, staring at him. That was bad. Sol roused himself, started the engine and drove away, the odds and ends in the truck bed playing a mad little symphony in his wake.

CHAPTER TWELVE

The large detective's thundering bass voice dominated the house, filling it with his Left Bank accent as he explained the situation to the two women from forensics and led them down the hall toward John's study. Meanwhile, in the living room the lieutenant asked, "So y'all go back a ways?"

"Thirty years," said Ruth.

Kate nodded, sitting beside Ruth on the sofa, facing Lieutenant Washington. For the first time, it occurred to her that Ruth was someone who had known her before, back when she was still that little girl she sometimes remembered, before she became this stranger, this widow of John Flint, this mother of two children. Kate's parents, like her, had been without brothers or sisters. She had never been one to make friends in school—not after what happened—so in all the world, there was only this strange rabbi who had known her as a child.

"Mrs. Flint?" said Lieutenant Washington. "You all right?"

"Yes." She tried to smile. "I'm fine."

"I heard there was a little trouble with your boy before. Is he okay now?"

"He's fine," snapped Kate. "We're all fine!"

He stared at her.

She blushed. "I'm sorry. It's just . . . no. No, you know he's not okay. He needs a little support, you know? Uh . . . a man around the house."

The lieutenant's eyes softened. He nodded and shifted them to Ruth. "So, Rabbi Gold, you're still thinking there's a connection between the deaths of these friends of yours and what happened here to Mrs. Flint?"

"Of course. Sol Cantor *is* the connection."

"Between you and Mrs. Flint?"

"And Benny and Morton."

He checked his notebook. "Uh, Morton Rothstein. The guy who got shot by his brother."

"Yes. Morton Rothstein. Can't you even remember him without your notes? He was a decent man. He deserves to be remembered."

"Rabbi Gold," he said, "people are murdered every day in this city. I mean clearly, undeniably murdered. Stabbings, shootings, beatings, and whatnot. Just this afternoon we had three people turn up dead in a tenement over in Desire. All of 'em with their hands tied behind their backs, shot in the head. Had another fella killed the same way over there just last week. I do my best to remember everybody. We all do. But that's a lot of dead people. I'm probably not gonna be able to recall all of their names and keep up with the people who *might've* been murdered, too."

"Might have? These people weren't—"

"Ruth!" said Kate, her voice trembling. "It's not important. Please."

Ruth turned fiercely, but something she saw in Kate seemed to stop her cold. "All right," she said. "We can discuss it later."

The lieutenant watched them both. "Let's say for a minute that you're right. Say they were murdered by the same man, and now he's after Mrs. Flint. What do you think he hopes to gain by all this?"

Ruth threw up her hands. "You're the expert. You tell us."

"I have no idea. This, ah . . . " His eyes dropped to his notebook again, then back up at them. "This Solomon Cantor has served his time. Twenty-five years. Hard to believe he'd get out and go right to killing everyone

associated with his case. After all those years, most people would've made
peace with the past."

"Most people wouldn't have done what he did to begin with, Lieutenant."

He held Ruth's eyes for a moment, as if considering her point. She
returned his stare defiantly. Finally, he said, "Why don't you tell me what
you remember about that?"

"I told you everything yesterday," Ruth said.

"Never hurts to hear it twice. Especially when you have a memory
as bad as mine."

Kate laughed once, too loudly, then covered her mouth as if she'd
said something wrong. Ruth glanced at her sourly, then back at the
policeman. She said, "It's late, and Katy's had a very stressful evening.
I think you should go."

The lieutenant shrugged. "Okay. If y'all don't wanna give me anything
else to go on . . . " He rose and straightened his tie, preparing to leave.

Kate said, "No! Ruth, we have to tell him! Maybe you left something
out." She looked up at the man. "Isn't that right, Lieutenant?"

He shrugged again. "It's a possibility."

"See?" said Kate, her eyes unnaturally bright. "See? If there's a chance
we know something else that might help, then we have to tell him."

"All right," said Ruth. "Go ahead then."

Kate opened her mouth to speak, but fear rushed up her throat, choking off the words. Ashamed of her weakness, she dropped her eyes to her
lap. She had spent her life avoiding the memory of that day. Tonight, after
what had happened here, she found she couldn't bear to speak about it.
The silence lingered, each second adding another drop to Kate's inner
pool of unbearable shame. She reached for Ruth's hand, hoping for some
kind of support. But as their flesh came in contact, Ruth lifted her hand
away. Did she do that on purpose, or was it an accident of timing? *Oh God,
can't I even have a friend?* And then she heard Ruth speak softly.

"Never mind, Katy," she said. "I'll tell him how it was."

Katy had been the first to look.
  When they got there, Ruth stood frozen in place, pressed against the
brick wall, watching Katy inch closer to the corner. When Katy finally

peeked into the kitchen, Ruth saw her shoulders and back go stiff as
a board.

"Katy," she whispered. "What is it?"

The gurgling sound filled Ruth's ears, now that they were so near.
But Katy remained silent, eyes fixed on whatever lay beyond Ruth's sight.

Ruth forced herself closer to her friend. Bending at the waist so that
only her head would be exposed to whatever it was, she slowly peered
around Katy, leaning farther and farther, until she saw it too.

A woman lay faceup on the kitchen floor, not ten feet away. It was
the woman from outside in the parking lot, the one who stood with all
those people who had yelled at them about Jesus.

She was bleeding.

Golly.

There was a lot of blood.

But that wasn't what *really* scared Ruth. And it wasn't the sight of the
big man standing over the woman. No, the thing that made her scream
and turn and run away as fast as she could go was the butcher knife he
held pointed right at her.

The lieutenant said, "Okay. So how do the others fit in? The two old
men?"

Ruth said, "Sol ran away after we discovered him standing over Nan
Smith's body. He ran past Morton as he was coming out of the library.
Morton testified about seeing the knife in his hand, and the blood on
his shirt."

"And the other one?"

"Benny heard our screams. He came up the hall behind us."

"From the pool area?"

"From that direction, yes. We were running back that way, and he
stopped us to find out what was wrong. We told him what we'd seen.
He sent us on outside and ran back the way we'd come."

"Did he see Cantor too?"

"No. But in the trial Benny testified that he heard Nan Smith speak
about Sol just before she died. She said something like, 'Tell Solomon I'll
be waiting.'"

"Was that all?"

"No. Apparently, she also said, 'I forgive him.'"

Washington grunted noncommittally and scribbled something in his notebook, then looked up again. "Mrs. Flint? You have anything to add? Any other witnesses you remember? Anything like that?"

Kate felt she was forgetting something important, but as Ruth had recounted their mutual horror, she had slipped into a deep pool of misery and could not seem to rise again. She shook her head.

Ruth nudged Kate gently with her elbow. "Tell him about the applesauce."

Surfacing, Kate looked at Ruth blankly. Slowly, she said, "Oh, that's nothing."

"Come on, Katy!"

"Okay." Kate recounted the story of Paul's applesauce and peanut butter sandwich, while the lieutenant listened carefully.

When she was done, he said, "Anything else?"

"No."

"Okay. If you threw the applesauce away, there's nothing for us to go on, but that's very interesting information, Mrs. Flint. Especially given what's happened here today." He rose, slipping the notebook into his inside coat pocket and straightening his tie. "I have to admit the connection to the Smith case seems pretty strong."

"Finally!" said Ruth, lifting both hands and letting them fall back to her lap. "Now what are you going to do about it?"

"We'll continue to check the house for fingerprints and other evidence. A forensics team already went over the Rothsteins' apartment. Frankly, we've been thinking the vandalism there was anti-Semitic. Gang related, probably."

"You still believe that?" asked the rabbi.

"I'm not sure what to think right now. If we find a match between that scene and this one, we'll have a whole different ball game."

"Are you gonna arrest Sol Cantor?"

"We can't until we get some hard evidence."

"Will you at least keep an eye on him?"

"We'll do our best. But our resources are limited. It takes at least three well-trained people to maintain surveillance on a suspect around the clock. Until we have more than circumstantial evidence to go on, it's hard to get the department to allocate the manpower."

"That's ridiculous!" exclaimed Ruth. "He almost burned Katy's house down! Is he gonna have to murder one of us before you find it in your hearts to 'allocate the manpower'?"

Lieutenant Washington looked down at his shoes, sighed, then spoke to Kate. "We'll leave a man outside in a patrol car tonight. He'll have a cell phone so you can call him if you need to, and he'll come runnin'."

"So you can 'allocate' someone to watch us, but not a murderer?"

"Ruth," said Kate, "he's doing the best he can." She turned to the lieutenant. "How about Ruth? Will someone watch her too?"

"Absolutely," he said, looking at Ruth now. "I'll get a man to follow you home, then stick around until morning. Y'all can rest easy tonight."

Ruth said, "I still don't see why you're willing to have your people watch both me and Katy, when you could just watch Sol Cantor instead."

"What if you're wrong, Rabbi? What if it's some other guy, and he comes back tonight while we're watching Mr. Cantor sleep like a baby?"

Neither woman spoke. The lieutenant took a deep breath and turned to Kate. "Listen, I'm thinkin' if this guy meant to harm you, he could've done it today. But he didn't. This here—" he waved his hand toward the study—"this isn't the kind of thing a guy usually does if he's plannin' a murder. I mean, why warn us in advance and make it harder on himself?"

"He's crazy, Lieutenant," said Ruth. "There's no telling what he'll do."

"What makes you say that?"

"Because he's murdered people, of course."

"Rabbi," said the lieutenant. "Everybody's capable of murder, given the right set of circumstances. Even assuming you're right, and there is a murderer behind this vandalism, it doesn't mean he's crazy. I would've thought someone in your line of work knows that better than most."

Ruth turned toward Kate. "I wonder why people keep telling me that?"

Kate offered a small smile.

Washington said, "The fact is, people do randomly poison food and medications, and Mr. Rothstein was shot by his brother, and—while I'll admit what happened here is suspicious from a timing point of view—there doesn't seem to be a common pattern to these events."

Ruth said, "If there's one thing I *have* learned as a rabbi, it's that there's always a pattern in life. We just don't see it yet."

"Uh-huh," said the policeman, turning to go. "Well, I suggest you ladies make sure you have good locks, and use them. Mrs. Flint, I'd add a dead bolt to that side door if I were you."

"Katy," said Ruth, "a friend of mine recommended a locksmith just this morning. I'll give you his card."

Kate nodded mutely. The lieutenant said, "Mrs. Flint, you have anyone you could leave your children with for a few days? Someone out of town?"

A cold and merciless anger came from nowhere, pouring into Kate's chest, filling her up until there didn't seem to be enough room inside to take a breath. The lieutenant stood beside the sofa, looking down at her and waiting for an answer. She tried to control the irrational sense of persecution his question had caused, but John was gone, and God had abandoned her, and here was this stranger telling her to send away the children. Now Ruth was watching her too. Why didn't they go away? Why didn't everyone just leave her alone with her children? They were all she had left.

The lieutenant added, "I just thought it might be a good precaution."

"I can't let them go, Lieutenant," she mumbled. "They need me."

Raising an eyebrow, he said, "Oh. Sure. Of course they do, Mrs. Flint."

CHAPTER
THIRTEEN

Orvis Newton knelt at the Jewess's back door, working a screwdriver between the latch and jamb in broad daylight, when he heard someone's brakes squeal and God told him to stop. Obeying immediately, he slipped through the thick stand of cane behind the Jewess's house, jogged up the alley, looped around the block, and strolled into view of her front door just in time to see the so-called rabbi admit a man carrying a toolbox. The man was young, perhaps thirty, and appeared to be in good physical condition.

Orvis whispered, "Thank you, Lord." If he had gone on as planned, that young fellow might have caught him in the act and ruined everything.

Orvis decided to wait. Glancing around to be sure no one was watching, he slipped behind the row of tall shrubs along the mausoleum wall across the street. From there, he made a note of the crudely painted sign on the dilapidated van parked at the curb: *Jake Singer, Locksmith.* Soon the young man emerged from the house and knelt beside the front door latch. As Orvis watched him work, he smiled with the certainty that no lock or barrier could stand against the Lord's anointed.

Half an hour later, Orvis saw a strange thing. The Jewess emerged from the house carrying two glasses of what appeared to be iced tea. She handed one to the locksmith. They spoke standing up for a few minutes; then to Orvis's surprise, she and the locksmith settled side by side on the front steps, sipping from the glasses. Their conversation seemed to become intimate. At one point, the locksmith appeared to be crying, and the Jewess placed her arm around his shoulder. That interested Orvis enormously. Obviously, this locksmith was no stranger. They seemed to have some kind of relationship, and Orvis Newton was highly interested in anyone who had a relationship with this Rabbi Gold.

The locksmith wiped his eyes. The rabbi patted his back and stood, leaning down to say something. The locksmith nodded and made an attempt to smile, then rose and returned to work on the door. The rabbi went inside.

Orvis decided to follow the locksmith when he left.

The locksmith drove directly to one of the taller downtown buildings, with Orvis close behind in his Vista Cruiser. After parking near the locksmith's van in the underground lot, Orvis rode up with him in the elevator, keeping his eyes on the floor and wondering why the man had not brought his toolbox along. They stepped out together on the forty-ninth floor. Orvis pretended to head for an office down the hall in the opposite direction. He walked thirty feet and then turned just in time to see the locksmith enter a psychiatrist's office.

ours later, Jake Singer fell asleep with the rabbi's words lingering in his ear like gentle kisses. When he had learned she was in the rabbinate and a friend of Dr. Blumenthal's, it seemed the fates had led him straight to her. With the slightest of excuses, he had unburdened his heart to that beautiful woman of God, and against all reason she had listened as if she cared. My, how she had listened. Jake had felt as if the world shrank down to just the two of them, alone there on the steps. He had told her of the nightmares, the sense of uselessness, the depression. He had explained the growing excitement he had felt since beginning his sessions with her friend, Dr. Blumenthal, of how he longed for resolution . . . longed to understand the sleeping dragon coiled around his heart. He had even cried in front of her, then apologized, and she had draped an arm around his shoulders as if nothing in the world could be more natural than that. She told him not to worry. *"Lots of people cry in front of rabbis,"* she had said. *"I'm used to it. Tell me more. Tell me everything."*

Now the evening news crackled softly on the radio as Jake Singer's sleeping form writhed on sweat-stained sheets like a man afire, eyes flitting rapidly behind closed lids. He gripped the edge of the bed, moaning softly.

Jake was there.

He saw it.

He understood.

In the instant of this epiphany, as the radio newsman somberly announced the attempted arson of a woman's home near Bayou Saint John, Jake awoke to the living nightmare of his life. But for once, he awoke without screaming. Far from it.

This time, Jake Singer awoke laughing.

A fter waiting for hours in the parking garage downstairs, Orvis again emerged from the elevator on the forty-ninth floor. He wore a navy blue blazer embroidered with a red-white-and-blue shield. The security guard he had left bound and gagged on the first floor would not be needing the jacket anymore that evening. Orvis strode to a glass door about halfway down the hall. Glancing left and right, he stepped back and swiftly kicked the lower edge of the door, just above the latch. A spiderweb of cracks radiated out from the point of impact, but the tempered glass held. He kicked again at the same spot. The glass shattered. With a final look up and down the corridor, Orvis draped a handkerchief over his hand, reached inside, twisted the latch, pushed on the ruined door, and entered the offices of the Wellness Mental Health Group.

He crossed the large reception area slowly in the dim light trickling through the shattered door. The air smelled of fruit and spices emanating

from a small clay vase filled with potpourri on a low table between a pair
of sofas. On the far side of the room, Orvis Newton passed through
another door. When it closed behind him, he stood in total darkness.
Running his hands along the rough, corded texture of the vinyl wall
covering, he found a switch. Still working with the handkerchief over his
hand to avoid leaving fingerprints, he flipped it on. Fluorescent lights
immediately saturated the hallway where Orvis stood in brilliant white.
Blinking, he began opening the doors on the left and right, glancing
quickly into the adjoining rooms, then moving on. Behind the fifth door,
Orvis found what he sought.

Hundreds, perhaps thousands, of manila folders with multicolored
tabs rested in the long, narrow room on metal shelves that lined the walls
and reached from floor to ceiling. He groaned. This might take all night.
Still, he had come too far to stop now. He began his search.

Forty minutes later, Orvis re-entered the elevator and pushed the
button that would send the cab down to the lobby. As he descended, he
scanned the file marked *Jake Singer*. It was very interesting reading. Turning the pages, he raised a thumb to his tongue to moisten it. He paused.

Holding his thumb and fingers beneath his nose, Orvis sniffed, smell-
ing the unmistakable odor of lighter fluid.

CHAPTER
FOURTEEN

Kate kept the kids home the next day, calling their school and explaining that the family was dealing with an emergency. In the middle of the sleepless night, she had finally faced the fact that the safest place for Paul and Jilly right now was with their grandparents in Atlanta. Although the mere thought of living in the house alone had turned her heart to lead, Kate had been ready to accept the loneliness for the sake of her children. Then the sun had dawned, bright and cheerful, and she had forgotten her foolish resolution, convincing herself that Paul and Jilly would be safe enough with her so long as reasonable precautions were taken.

Besides, they needed their mother.

Now, as Kate scrubbed the carpet in John's study on her hands and knees, Paul came into the room. Crossing behind her, he opened one of the windows. Kate sprang to her feet and rushed across the study.

Pushing her son aside, she slammed the window down with unnecessary force and twisted the latch savagely, then took a moment to stare outside before closing the draperies. When she turned back toward Paul, he stood silently, looking down at his feet. Only then did Kate realize how her actions must have seemed.

"Oh, honey," she said, moving toward Paul and taking his corpulent hand in hers. "I'm sorry. It's just that we need to be careful about open doors and windows right now."

He flinched away from her touch. "I just wanted to help you air out the room. It smells in here."

"I know. But we have to be careful."

"Why? Who did this to us? Why did they ruin Dad's room?"

"It's . . . a bad man. He did something really awful when I was just a little bit older than Jilly. They put him in jail, and now he's out."

"What did he do?"

Kate paused, wondering how much to tell him. She did not want to add fuel to the smoldering anger and mistrust that had grown steadily stronger in her son ever since John's death, yet she longed for the time when Paul would be able to bear more responsibility. She was so tired of carrying the burden alone. And why should she? In the last year his voice had begun to change, sometimes slipping down an octave for an entire sentence or two. He had grown three inches, and not all of his weight increase was fat. Paul was becoming more and more like John every day. Maybe she should trust him with the truth. Maybe taking him into her confidence would help him build his own.

Or maybe such honesty would drive Paul even further toward a fascination with violence.

In the end, it was the hope that Paul could help her as John once did that swayed Kate's decision. She needed his help so desperately. Searching his face for a reaction, she said, "He killed a lady."

Paul's eyes grew wide. "Why?"

"They said it was because she was trying to tell him about Jesus."

"Like those Indians down in Brazil? The ones who killed the missionaries?"

It took her by surprise. Sometimes his immature logic, direct and uncluttered, connected things that would never have occurred to her, cutting through cultural clichés like a hot knife through butter.

"In a way, that was the problem, I think."

The telephone rang in the background. Paul said, "You mean he was like those Indians?"

"No. I mean the lady *thought* he was."

Puzzled, Paul lifted his eyes to hers, then understanding dawned, and he nodded. "She insulted the man."

Jilly called from the kitchen, "Mommy! It's Wooth."

Wooth? Oh, *Ruth*. Kate smiled and patted Paul's shoulder. "We're gonna be fine, honey, but we do need to be careful for a little while, okay?"

He nodded.

"That means don't go out front without letting me know first. Keep all the doors and windows closed and locked all the time. And help me watch your little sister."

"I will. I'll take care of both of you."

It felt so good to hear him say those words. But as Kate went into the kitchen to answer the telephone, she felt her momentary sense of relief giving way to something far less comfortable, something that felt a bit like shame.

S olomon Cantor had cashed in yesterday's load at the salvage yard for $143.89. Not bad, considering he had collected the stuff while keeping an eye on the rabbi.

Encouraged by this small success, he had begun cruising the back alleys and Dumpsters of the city's industrial neighborhoods at dawn this morning and found a coil of copper wire worth about fifty dollars. Then, as he drove across the Ninth Ward, he had spotted a couple of sections of old cast-iron fencing propped up against a pair of trash cans. Antique dealers paid good money for those, so he stopped and tossed them in the back. After that, he dropped by Gabby's place for a cup of coffee. She was unusually friendly. She even gave him a kiss on the cheek as he walked in the door. It was shaping up to be an even better day than yesterday, except for one thing: When Gabby kissed him, Sol could have sworn he smelled alcohol on her breath.

If that was true, she had fallen off the wagon for the first time in years.

Now, as Solomon Cantor turned left at the corner of Prytania and Washington, he saw a police cruiser pull up behind his truck. He accelerated slowly across the intersection. The cruiser followed. Careful to remain below the speed limit, Sol pulled to a stop at Magazine, stuck his arm out the window with his hand in the air to signal the right turn, then eased around the corner. Flicking his eyes to the mirror, he watched the cruiser pull in right behind.

Uh-oh.

Rocking along in the dilapidated pickup, Sol ran down the list in his mind. Miss a meeting with his parole officer? No. Forget to get the truck's tags updated? Nope. Got his license? He shifted in the seat to reach for his wallet. Opening it one handed, he saw the document. Yep. He'd had a beer with lunch, but they'd never notice that. And there were no weapons in the truck, so he was okay there.

All right, let 'em come. I'm ready.

They followed him until he stopped on his own at the little junk shop near the corner of Magazine and Bordeaux. The cruiser pulled up behind him as he got out of the truck. Deciding not to make it easy on them, he went ahead with his work, pulling a section of fencing from the truck bed while two officers sat in the cruiser, one of them on the radio, both of them watching with that dead look the cops like to use. Sol had the other section of fencing out before they opened their doors and came his way. One of them, the younger one, stood several paces back with his hand resting on his side arm. The other one walked right up and said, "Solomon Cantor?"

"That's me."

"Are you aware that you failed to signal a turn just now?"

"I used hand signals."

"No, sir. Not when you pulled to the curb here."

He smiled. "Gee. You got me there, Officer."

"May I see your license and registration, please?"

He stared at the cop for a moment, just long enough to let him know he was complying because he wanted to, not because he had to. It was one of the first things you learned in the joint. Never let the bulls think

you'd jump whenever they said. The cop had already opened his mouth
to tell him again when Sol reached for his wallet. Taking his time, he
withdrew his driver's license.

"The registration's in the glove box. Want me to get it?"

"Yes, sir," said the cop.

He opened the side door and the glove box and stuck his hand inside.
That was when he noticed the younger cop had his holster unsnapped
and his fingers wrapped around the grip of a Beretta.

"Remove it very slowly, Mr. Cantor," said the older one.

Doggoned if he wasn't about to pull *his* pistol, too. Smiling, Sol did as
he was told. When the piece of paper was all the way out, he held it up
between his thumb and first finger. "All right?"

"Yes, sir."

He passed the registration slip to the older cop, the younger one
watching every move. While the older one read the paperwork, Sol
caught the younger one's eye and winked. The kid's face didn't change
a bit. Maybe he was tougher than he looked.

"Okay, Mr. Cantor," said the cop with his registration. "You mind
telling us what you're doing here?"

"Making a delivery."

The cop gestured toward the iron fencing. "That?"

"Yeah."

"Who you delivering it to?"

"That shop right there."

"Where'd you get it?"

"I found it."

"You found it."

"Yep."

"Where did you find it, sir?"

"Over in an alley in the Ninth Ward somewhere. I don't remember
the exact place. Somebody left it out for the garbage pickup."

"It looks too expensive to throw away."

"You'd be surprised what people throw away."

The cop glanced at the younger one, who nodded, walked back to
the squad car, and got on the radio again. Meanwhile, Sol and the other
officer stood silently. After a minute, the lady who ran the junk shop

stuck her head out the front door. She took one look at Sol getting rousted right in front of her place and jerked her head back inside.

Oh, that's great. Just great.

"Listen," said Sol, "if I was gonna steal something, you really think it'd be this junk here?" He nodded toward the pile of scrap metal in the back of his truck.

"Nobody's made any accusations, sir."

"Yeah, right."

The kid put the microphone down and got out of the squad car. His partner caught his eye. The kid shook his head. The older one, writing in his book, said, "All right, sir, I'm citing you for failure to properly signal a turn. You'll find instructions for how to respond on the back of the citation." Handing him the book, he said, "Please sign here."

Sol took the thing, scrawled his signature across it, and gave it back.

Tearing the ticket out of the book, the cop said, "So you're in the junk business, Mr. Cantor?"

"The recycling business. I used to have a big operation, but there was a little setback." Sol smiled. "I'm startin' over on the ground floor."

"I see you have a lot of metal items here. Ever deal in other kinds of junk?"

"Like what?"

"Oh, I don't know. Anything really old . . . say, old books?"

"What are you talkin' about?"

"You know, like pages from old Bibles that you can frame and sell. That kinda thing."

Sol stared at the cop, trying to figure out what he was talking about.

The guy didn't seem to mind not getting an answer. He smiled and touched the brim of his hat. "Have a nice day, Mr. Cantor."

R uth?"

"Hey."

"Hey yourself," said Kate, shifting the telephone handset to her other ear. "Did you get any sleep last night?"

"A little," said the rabbi. "You?"

"No, not really." She paused. "The lieutenant wasn't very encouraging."

Ruth made a guttural sound. "The least he could do is assign a cop to watch Cantor."

"Yes."

The line hummed in Kate's ear, then Ruth said, "I'm sorry about yesterday, at your shop."

"Oh, me too!" said Kate. "I was so insensitive—"

"No! It was me. I was *hyper*sensitive."

"Well . . . maybe we could try again."

"I'd like that."

"How 'bout dinner? You could come over and I'll fix us something nice to eat."

"Actually, I was thinking we could kill two birds with one stone. I'm teaching a Torah class this Saturday morning at temple. Would you like to come?"

Torah class? At a Jewish temple? The idea made Kate nervous, but she didn't want to admit as much to Ruth for fear of offending her again.

Ruth said, "I just thought you'd find it interesting."

"It does sound interesting. But I need to be at the shop on Saturday."

"It's early, before the shops in the Quarter open."

So much for that excuse. "Okay, but what about the kids? I don't want to leave them alone."

"You can bring them. We have day care right down the hall."

"What time Saturday?"

"Eight-thirty."

She frantically cast around for another good reason to decline, her mind a blank. Maybe with more time she'd come up with something. "Can I think about it?"

Kate waited while the telephone line remained silent. Finally the rabbi said, "Look. Don't come if you don't want to. It's not important."

"Ruth, come on. I'm honored that you've asked. It's just a really new idea. I mean, studying the Bible with people from another religion? Gimme a chance to get used to that, okay?"

A sigh, then, "Yeah. That's fair."

"Thanks. You said something about killing two birds with one stone?"

"Uh-huh. The other thing is . . . well . . . Sol Cantor might be there."

"*What?*"

"He came last week."

"Why? How could he?"

"His wife has been coming to the class for years."

"Well, that changes everything. I don't want to see *him*."

Ruth's voice came in a rush. "Katy, don't you see? We can show him we're not afraid. Let him know we're standing up to him together. It'll be a way to warn him off."

"Or make him more angry."

"Okay. Even that. But maybe if he gets angry, he'll make a mistake. Something the police can use against him."

"Oh, Ruth, I don't know."

"It's the only way we can make this stop. We have to stand up to him!"

Katy did not respond.

After a moment, Ruth said, "I'm scared, okay? Just seeing him last week frightened me so badly I threw up."

"Well, how do you think *I* feel?"

"But that's why we need to face him together!"

Katy said, "I don't know."

"Please do this, Katy. *Please*. I . . . I . . . you have no idea how difficult it is for me to say this, but . . ." Ruth stopped talking. Kate waited. Finally, the rabbi continued, "I don't think I can do it without you."

"I'm gonna have to think about it, Ruth. There are my children to consider."

When she spoke again, Ruth's voice was cold and formal. "All right. You think about it."

"Okay. But, Ruth? Even if I don't come to your temple, we could still get together. Right?"

"We'll see."

Kate heard a click as Ruth hung up. Softly, she replaced the telephone handset, trying to sort through her feelings. Something important had happened when she saw Ruth standing in the hallway last night, something she didn't want to lose. Maybe, even after half a lifetime, it really was possible to have a new beginning. But the mere thought of facing Solomon Cantor again filled her mind with visions of hate-filled faces screaming as she entered the courthouse, mobs of reporters poking at her with microphones and tape recorders, and her father, pushing away the men in suits and lifting her up and running for the car. Surely there was a way to reconnect with Ruth without walking that labyrinth of fear again. Their time together before the . . . the thing that happened, that time had been the most wonderful part of her childhood, memories second only to her marriage and children. But it had all come to such a tragic halt.

Kate shuffled across the hall to John's study to finish clearing away the debris before she locked his room away again. For the thousandth time, she wondered, *Why does God let these things happen?*

E ver since she saw the Peeping Tom, Rebecca Betterton's insomnia had been worse. Sometimes, she caught two or three hours of sleep. Mostly, she was up all night.

She just knew that man was a mass murderer, or something worse, like one of those old Nazis they said were still hiding down in South America, conducting experiments on the natives. Roy told her not to worry so much. "You probably scared him worse than he scared you." When she asked him what *that* was supposed to mean, Roy laughed and told her the peeper got more than he bargained for. Rebecca knew Roy thought she was fat, but he never came right out and admitted it. Instead, there were always little hints. So she dieted and exercised. Not actually lifting weights or anything. More like right now, watering the plants. And it helped. She'd lost a lot of weight since her thirties. At least two pounds for every year. If Roy thought she was fat now . . . well, he should have seen her then.

She shifted the garden hose to sprinkle a palmetto next to the potted plant on the patio. It was a good thing she had vacation time already scheduled. She didn't see how she'd be able to work with this thing hanging over her. The library was stressful enough. Imagine trying to keep your mind on your business, knowing that anyone at all could be the stalker. Rebecca shuddered.

Of course, the best thing would have been for this to have happened next year. Because next year she'd be retired, along with Roy, and they'd be touring America in the Winnebago. She flipped the hose back and forth, soaking the soil all around the tree. Oh, it was gonna be glorious, just rambling around with no itinerary, free as a couple of birds. Plus, the windows on the Winnebago were too high off the ground for anyone to peep in. That would be a blessing.

She finished with the palmetto and moved off the patio to squirt the planting bed beside the wall. The begonias were a little bit yellowed around the edges. Maybe she was watering too much. Begonias were hearty plants, well adapted to the Southern heat and occasional drought. She should probably back off a little, but frankly, this was the only excuse she could think of to go outside. It was far too warm to sit and read, even in the shade, and she wasn't about to go for a walk, so she watered the plants.

Moving down the planting bed, Rebecca Betterton drew near her bedroom window, and again, her thoughts turned to that frightful night. *My goodness, who knows what that nasty man had in mind?* She shuddered again. Horrible. Just horrible. She wished Roy would take it more seriously.

The nandinas below the window seemed to droop, their branches bowed slightly toward the ground. That was strange. She directed the flow of water at their base, thinking they were wilting from lack of moisture, but no, the soil was quite moist there. And . . .

What was that?

Bending at the waist as best she could, Rebecca Betterton inspected the soil beneath the nandina right outside her bedroom window. Because the water stood in puddles, it took a moment for her to recognize what she saw. The police had searched this planting bed that night and found nothing—no sign at all of the man she had seen. But now there were footprints outside her window. Deep, large *footprints*.

Rebecca dropped the hose and backed away, eyes wide with horror. *He's been back!*

Since learning of the office break-in when she had arrived at work that morning, Helen Blumenthal's emotions had run the gamut from dread to outrage. For some reason, she couldn't help thinking the crime had been committed by one of her patients. She had almost canceled her sessions. It was irrational, of course. Her partners saw just as many unstable individuals as she did, so why not suspect their patients? Plus, what evidence did she have that the crime hadn't been committed by an outsider—

someone looking for drugs, perhaps, with no connection to the practice? Canceling sessions made no sense at all, and there were ethical obligations to consider. Helen felt it would be wrong to postpone this next patient in particular. She sensed that he was near a breakthrough in his personal struggle for healing. To slow the momentum now could cost weeks or months of further work, so she would forge ahead.

Helen paused to breathe deeply for a moment before entering her office. It really was surprising how strongly she'd been affected by the burglary. *Breathe. Breathe. Yes. There.*

She went in feeling somewhat calmer.

He stood when she entered and shook her hand. Always before, he'd avoided physical contact, but this time he not only stuck out his hand, he looked her right in the eyes.

Extraordinary.

"So," said Dr. Helen Blumenthal. "I hear you came back to the office yesterday afternoon."

"Yeah."

"Did you forget that we'd already had our session yesterday?"

"Of course not. I just wanted a refill of those green pills, you know?" He shook his head. "Come on, Doc."

"Of course. Do you still want the prescription?"

"No," said Jake brightly. "Actually, I don't think I need pills anymore. I feel pretty good."

"Why is that?"

He laughed.

Helen said, "What's so funny?"

"Well, think about it. I mean, usually when you tell a person you're feelin' good, they say somethin' like, 'Hey, that's great.' You know. Somethin' like that. But instead, you say, 'Why is that?'" He chuckled again. "That sounds like, you know, 'What's your excuse?'"

"That's not what I meant."

"I know. I'm just pullin' your leg a little."

Was he overmedicated? She didn't recall prescribing anything that would explain this sudden presentation of well-developed social skills. She wished she could check his file, but it hadn't yet been found in the mess down the hall.

"So, Doc. Figured it out yet?"

"Figured what out?"

"You know. Why I'm doin' so good today."

"No, I haven't. Do you know why?"

"Sure."

She waited. He rose and walked across her office to stand before the floor-to-ceiling window with his back to her. This time, he did not push at the glass. This time he stood with his hands clasped confidently behind his back, staring down at the Mississippi hundreds of feet below as if he were master of all he surveyed. The sunlight streaming through the glass engulfed him, reducing him to a black silhouette against a halo of clean, crisp white. He said, "I finished it."

In spite of herself, Helen leaned forward eagerly. "The dream." It was not a question.

"Uh-huh."

She waited, calling upon every ounce of professionalism to remain silent. After a full minute, he spoke. "I told you last time I was scared of what I might do."

"In the dream. Yes."

He turned to look at her, although she still could not see his features. "Now I know what I've really been afraid of all these years."

"Yes?" she said. "What is that?"

"Me."

"What does that mean, Jake?"

"Come on, Doc. I know you're thinking it too."

"Thinking what?"

"You think I'm gonna do myself in."

Instantly, Helen remembered one of the last notes she'd made in his file, the file her assistant had been unable to locate prior to this session, and it occurred to her that Jake might be the one who had ransacked the offices after all. *Breathe. Breathe.*

"Why should I believe you're suicidal?"

"I don't know why, but I know you do."

"I never thought about the possibility until you mentioned it." *I'm lying to a patient.* She felt sick.

He stared at her. "I saw you write it in my file yesterday."

"We won't argue the point. It's counterproductive." She refused to show her emotions. "Why don't you tell me about the dream?"

He crossed the office and sat abruptly, swinging a leg over one arm of the chair, rocking it back and forth. She did not like the way he stared at her. Something new looked out through Jake Singer's eyes. He said. "Are you afraid?"

"What makes you think that?"

"Slight flush at the neck, noticeable increase in respiratory rate, arms crossed at the chest, legs crossed as well, pushing back into your chair as if to withdraw . . . all the classic signs are there, Doc."

"You're reading too much into too little, Jake." Watching him closely for a reaction, she said, "Someone broke into our offices last night and vandalized our files. It's a bit disconcerting, that's all." His reaction betrayed nothing. She uncrossed her arms and legs and leaned forward. "Let's talk about why *you're* afraid."

"Well, let's see. What could it be? What could it be?" He rose again, pacing the office, pausing to touch a lamp, removing a book from her bookshelf, then replacing it, talking the whole time. "Maybe it's because I know I *am* suicidal. Or maybe I've just realized I have multiple personalities and one or two of me aren't to be trusted."

He smiled.

"Look, Jake. I'm glad you've reached some kind of resolution in the dream, but if you don't share it with me, I don't see how I can help."

The patient continued to pace the office, handling her things, presenting obvious controlling behavior, which was completely out of character. She waited silently, watching him, fascinated. Finally, he stopped before the full-length window again. There, with his back to her, Jake Singer began to speak. He told it all . . . his whole dream from start to finish. And as he spoke, the fine hairs at the nape of Dr. Helen Blumenthal's neck slowly stood on end.

Mommy!" cried Jilly. "Mr. Smith is here!"

Kate opened her eyes and looked around the room in confusion, thinking, *What am I doing here?* She sat up. A novel fell from her lap to the floor. Rubbing her eyes, she began to remember. She had made an early

dinner, then settled in to read for a while and . . . she must have
dozed off.

She checked her watch. It was 9:45! Impossible. But glancing at the
windows, she saw the blackness of night and realized it was true. She had
been asleep for almost four hours.

"Mommy!" cried Jilly, standing in the doorway.

"Hmm?" She rubbed her eyes, still a bit groggy.

"Mr. Smith is here!"

"Who?"

"Mr. *Smith*, I told you!"

Slowly, Kate began to understand that they had a visitor. Mr. Smith?
Who could that be? She stood and shuffled to the entry hall, still rubbing
the sleep from her eyes. Without thinking it through, Kate flipped on the
outside light and opened the front door. A man stood on the porch with
his back to her. With a sudden flush of fear, Kate remembered she should
have asked him his business before opening the door. Too late now.

"Mr. Smith?"

He turned and smiled, his eyes merry. "No, ma'am. I'm afraid we've
had a little confusion there."

"We have?"

"Yeah. I guess your little girl hasn't learned the word *locksmith* yet."

"Oh! You're the *lock*smith!" She laughed. "Great! Thanks for coming."

"I'm sorry it's so late. Must've been some busy burglars around town
last night or somethin', 'cause I had a whole mess of calls today."

"Better late than never. Come on in."

"Thank you."

Kate closed the door behind him. The locksmith walked to the
center of the hall, carrying a small toolbox. He was about six feet tall,
with nice wide shoulders and narrow hips, and full, sandy blond hair
worn long in front and combed back from his tanned forehead. He wore
a pair of dark green trousers and a plain white shirt with a button-down
collar open at the neck. When he looked straight at her, Kate felt a small
thrill at the sight of his pale blue eyes, generous lips, and square chin.
Her pleasure was somewhat dampened by the sight of a silver Star of
David hanging from a small chain around his neck. He was a Jew, and
she could never—

He spoke, interrupting her thoughts. "Your message mentioned something about a break-in?"

"Yes," she said, "that's right."

"Did they ruin the lock?"

"Uh, no. We're not really sure how they got in, actually."

"Well, it's a shame. Burglaries make you feel really strange, don't they?"

"Yes." She didn't care a bit about what he was saying, but found the way he said it utterly fascinating.

"Do you have spare keys?"

"Just one."

"Do you keep it in the house? Is it still here?"

"I . . . uh . . . I do keep it here. But I don't know if it's still where I left it. I never thought to look."

"I'm surprised the cops didn't ask you to check. That's what a lot of burglars do. They take your keys."

"Really? Why's that?" She felt like a teenager, asking questions when she didn't care about the answers, just to keep listening to his voice.

"Well, then they can use 'em to get back in later, without having to work so hard at it."

She remembered the open door Paul claimed he had found several days before, that night when he made the applesauce sandwich and prowled the house with a butcher knife. Was that how Solomon Cantor got in? Had he come before, found the door unlocked, and stolen her spare key? She looked at the locksmith with new appreciation.

"I'll go look for the spare."

"Can if you want, but . . . ," he shrugged. "In a minute, it won't matter because the keys won't work on your doors anymore."

"Oh, right," she smiled. "I guess that's why you're here."

"Yes, ma'am."

"My name's Kate," she said, extending her hand.

He transferred the toolbox to his left hand and took hers in his right, giving it a gentle shake. Spotting a flesh-colored bandage on the skin just above his thumb, she took care not to squeeze very hard.

"Jake Singer," he said. "Pleased to meet you, Kate."

She looked up at him, completely satisfied to stand and stare.

"Uh, did I wake you up?" he asked.

"No."

He cocked his head. "Really?"

She blushed. "Well, yes, you did actually. How did you know?"

"You've got a little sleep line." He touched his cheek. "Here."

She covered her cheek with her hand. "Oh no!"

"Hey," he smiled. "It looks good on you."

An awkwardness settled over them, a sudden reminder that they were total strangers.

"Uh, there's the door. Right there," said Kate, indicating the door he had just entered.

Jake nodded solemnly. "I see."

She smiled. "Well, I *meant* that's the one I need a new lock for."

"Of course you did. How 'bout the back door?"

"Yes. It'll need one, too. And there's one on the side."

He knelt beside the door, inspecting the dead bolt. "If you really want brand-new dead bolts, I'll have to come back. I used my last set in the truck on the stop before this one. But this here is a good strong lock. You don't want a new one. You just want me to change the pins, so the old key won't work on it anymore."

"I do?"

"Sure."

"Okay. I guess that's fine. Just make it so he can't come in, all right?"

"You got it, ma'am."

"Please, call me Kate."

Hours later, Kate sat in a chair beside her bed. Only a reading lamp beside her lit the room. On her lap was an open Bible. She stared at it, not really sure why she bothered, seeking hope but aware of a stubborn sense of futility.

Are not two sparrows sold for a penny? Yet not one of them will fall to the ground apart from the will of your Father. And even the very hairs of your head are all numbered. So don't be afraid; you are worth more than many sparrows.

Kate didn't agree with those people who used the Bible like a crystal ball, asking a question then opening it at random to read the first verse their eyes fell upon for the answer. Still, it seemed providential that her Bible had opened to this particular passage. She wished she could believe it. She really did. But whatever her alleged value to God, it did not seem to be sufficient to keep her from falling to the ground.

Still, where else could she turn?

Solomon Cantor terrified her. Kate had begun to believe Ruth's theory about him. After all, *someone* had ruined John's family Torah and tried to build a bonfire inside her house. Who else would want to do such a thing?

But the truth was, another kind of fear dominated her thoughts. She had seen something in Ruth's eyes yesterday. It had crackled across the room between them like a tiny spark of electricity. Kate had felt she could reach out to this beautiful woman who had once been her best friend. She felt it was . . . ordained, somehow. Yet a minefield of differences lay between them. The moment Ruth had mentioned coming to her temple, an unreasoning terror of the unknown had seized Kate's mind. She remembered the bitter barricade of mistrust and anger that had once stood between John and his parents. They had lashed out sometimes, actually calling him a traitor. They had accused the church of brainwashing him, as if it were some sort of cult. They had accused Kate herself of playing a role in the "indoctrination" of their son, ignoring the fact that he had chosen the Christian faith long before they met. John had done his best to help Kate understand their animosity. He had spoken of evils in the Dark Ages and of anti-Semitic affronts in the present. Still, as she considered Ruth's invitation, such hostility was hard to forget.

What if I say the wrong thing? I don't even know how to dress. Should I take my Bible, or will the New Testament offend them? What if they say something bad about Jesus? Should I speak up? If I do, will they throw me out?

A part of her understood that these were trivial concerns compared to the danger posed by Solomon Cantor, but Kate did not control her fears.

Quite the reverse.

She breathed deeply, closing her eyes. She wondered if Ruth felt these things, too. Did fear and hope war within her when she thought of Kate? Maybe so. Maybe that explained Ruth's odd behavior . . . approaching then suddenly pushing away, hot and cold, like some kind of manic-depressive. Kate felt certain there was more to Ruth's invitation than simply putting up a united front against Solomon Cantor. She felt Ruth must be trying to reach out to her in the only way she knew, by sharing such an important part of her life. Hope struggled to seize control of Kate's thoughts as she considered the possibility that Ruth wanted to be friends. In the end, hope was stronger than fear.

She roused herself and looked around the bedroom as if it were a new and unknown place. Laying a ribbon between the pages, she gently placed the Bible on the small table beside her chair. She rose to her feet, crossed the room, and found her backpack lying on the floor beside the dresser. Lifting it, she searched inside and retrieved a small piece of paper. She went to the telephone and dialed the number on the paper. The paper trembled in her hand.

"Hello?" The voice on the telephone was languid with sleep.

"Oh, I'm sorry, Ruth. I forgot how late it is," said Kate.

A pause. "That's okay. What's wrong?"

"Nothing. I just wanted to let you know . . . " Her eyes fell upon the book on the table nearby. "I've decided to come."

Another pause, longer this time. Then, "Why?"

Kate thought about how to put it. Sometimes the simplest way was best. She thought about saying, *I need a friend,* but when she opened her mouth, what came out instead was, "I think God wants me to be there."

"That's . . . interesting."

"Okay," said Kate. "Uh, I'll see you then? At 8:30? At your temple?"

"All right."

Kate hung up the phone feeling unsatisfied. Ruth had seemed distant. It was not at all the reception she had hoped for, given the courage it had taken to make the call. Fear crept in once more, eroding hope's feeble claim upon her heart.

Orvis Newton found the ladder lying beside a neighboring house. He set it against the temple bricks and pulled on the rope to extend the upper portion over the edge of the roof. As the ladder telescoped upwards, metal on metal rattled loudly enough to wake the dead. Not that they needed a wake-up call. In New Orleans, the dead walked every night.

Orvis left the ladder and ran across the grass and slipped into the shadows of a small cluster of trees nearby. He waited. After almost ten minutes, he decided no one had heard the racket, or else nobody cared. He jogged back over to the ladder, grasped the sides, and climbed, carrying a crowbar in his right hand. Twenty feet in the air, he stepped over the edge. His black athletic shoes crunched on the gravel of the flat rooftop. He paused and looked around. The view was good from here. He saw a few lights in the adjacent houses. He saw the deep darkness of the park across the street. In the distance, he heard the call of a wild animal. It sounded like a mule, except deeper throated. A water buffalo, perhaps, lowing at the moon in the zoo across the park.

Be patient, he thought. *You're next.*

In the patches of open sky between the low-lying clouds, the glow of the city lights obscured the stars, but that was to be expected. Once the people of Babel had built a tower to the heavens in a vain attempt to become like God. Now all of New Orleans cowered beneath a man-made canopy of lights, pretending that God did not exist.

Orvis walked across the roof and looked down into a central atrium, a rectangular pit completely surrounded by the building. Windows glowed on the ground floor, dimly illuminating a concrete bench against the wall below. Seeing the bench, he nodded. *This will do nicely.* He knelt upon the roof, feeling the pea-sized bits of gravel bite into the tender places just beneath his kneecaps. Orvis welcomed the pain. It was one of the only things that he had left to offer. Gritting his teeth against the agony in his knees, he lifted the crowbar high above his head and struck the roof with all of his strength. The tongs of the crowbar bit easily into the tar paper beneath the gravel. He pulled, and was rewarded by the sound of the bar tearing up the roof. He lifted the crowbar and drove it down again. And again. And again.

Soon, the roof was crisscrossed with rips like the gaping wounds inflicted by a giant bird of prey's talons, or the claws of a demon. Standing, Orvis Newton surveyed his handiwork. A raindrop hit his hand. Orvis looked up and smiled.

Oh, that's very good. That's perfect.

BAM! BAM! BAM!

Ruth squinted at the target, then grimaced with frustration. None of her rounds had touched it. She removed the clip and turned to the countertop at her left to reload. As she pressed the bullets in one by one, Jerry McCone said, "You're still jerkin' the trigger, Ruth."

"I know." She spoke too loudly with the headphone-like ear protectors on.

"And you're not givin' yourself time to re-aim after the recoil."

"I know."

"Okay. Just so you know."

"I do, Jerry. I know."

She pressed the clip back into the handle of her automatic and turned toward the target. The full-scale, human-shaped piece of cardboard stood just five yards away—the closest range Jerry would allow—and it bore a

black piece of paper with concentric white circles positioned where the
heart would be. At first, Ruth had been a bit uncomfortable with the idea
of a target shaped like a person; she'd been *very* uncomfortable, actually,
but Jerry had asked the obvious question.

"What'd ya buy that weapon for, Ruth?"

He'd been right, of course, so she had reminded herself of what it
says in the *Baba Rabbah* portion of the Talmud concerning self-defense:
"Thine own life comes before the life of thy fellows." And by now, in
her fourth lunch-hour session of target practice at Jerry's Gun Shop and
Indoor Range, she'd become used to the target. In fact, after what Sol
Cantor had almost done to Katy's house, she'd actually begun to put his
face on the thing. Perhaps that wasn't healthy, but if not, why did she
always feel so much better after target practice? She lifted her automatic,
cupping the hand holding the weapon with the palm of her other hand.

"Remember," said her instructor, "place the target in the groove of
your rear sight first. Then bring the forward sight up and align it with the
groove, . . . "

"I know that, Jerry."

"Okay. So if you know all this stuff, why don't you just do it?"

"I'm trying!"

"It just seems like a lot of money to waste if you're not gonna do it
right."

She turned to give him a dirty look. He grinned, his long bushy hair
wildly askew beneath his ear protectors, teeth big and white against his
jet-black beard. The overhead lights sparkled in his orange-tinted aviator
glasses. He looked like Abbie Hoffman, from back in the sixties. Another
hippie throwback, like Katy. Suddenly angry, she turned back toward the
target and fired. She paused and fired again. Paused and fired again.

"All right!" said Jerry. "Finally!"

Ruth lowered her weapon and stared. All three rounds had fallen
together near the center of the target. "I did it," she said, astonished.

"You sure did."

Ruth raised the gun and squeezed the trigger four more times. All
four rounds fell within the outer circle on the target.

"That dude is history, man," said Jerry as he flipped a switch to bring
the target forward. It floated toward them like a ghost, drawn along an

overhead wire. As Jerry replaced the black-and-white target, Ruth turned to the counter to reload. It was odd that she'd finally managed to hit the target that time, when she hadn't even been concentrating. Maybe that was the secret. Learn the fundamentals, but don't try too hard. Just flow with the moment, like driving a car.

Jerry flipped the switch again, and the target sped away to the sound of a whining electric motor. This time, he stopped the man-shaped piece of cardboard a little farther away.

"Okay, let's see if you can do the same thing."

Ruth stepped to the firing line, clutching her gun with both hands. Ignoring the acrid scent of cordite in the air, she aimed the gun, intending to think about Solomon Cantor, to get her mind off firing the gun by focusing on him, but instead, Ruth thought about last night's call. What had Katy said? Oh, yes: *"I think God wants me to be there."* Ruth gritted her teeth. She knew what *that* meant. Asking Katy to come to temple had been a mistake. Deep down, Christians were all the same. No different than those obnoxious ones who stood out by the parking lot with their cardboard Jesus signs.

Ruth fired. A hole appeared within the outermost circle of white.

All Ruth had wanted was a little moral support next *Shabbat*, someone to be there while she taught the class with Solomon Cantor grinning up at her like some . . . some . . .

She fired again, the bullet slamming closer to the center this time.

So she'd asked Katy to come, thinking that of all people on earth *she* at least would know how Ruth felt. *She* would have something to gain from facing Sol down.

Her finger squeezed once more. Another hole appeared between the first two.

But no, Katy had to call and say *God* wanted her to be there.

BAM!

Maybe she should call her back and retract the invitation. Maybe she should say, "We have enough of your kind outside our walls; we don't need another one inside."

BAM! BAM! BAM!

Ruth pulled the trigger until the hammer clicked impotently on an empty chamber. She'd used up the clip. Lowering the weapon, she squinted at the target. All seven bullets had hit within the outer circle. Three were dead center, inside the bull's eye.

"Wow, man," said Jerry, the hippie gunshop owner. "When you get somethin' figured out, you really get it, don'tcha?"

H ello, I'm Rabbi Shumish. You must be Mrs. Betterton."

"Yes . . . ," she said, noting the nice suit he wore and his friendly smile.

Orvis Newton extended his hand. "It's a pleasure to meet you."

She took his hand, filled with a growing sense of guilt. A rabbi on her front porch, after all these years . . . she wondered if he knew she was Jewish, and did he know how much time had passed since she'd been to temple? Did he know Roy *wasn't* Jewish? What would he think of her if he knew everything?

"Mrs. Betterton," he said. "I'm with the National Jewish Restoration League. Maybe you've heard of our work?"

"I, uh, I think so . . . "

His smile grew wider. "Excellent! Then you probably have some idea why I'm here."

"Well, no. Not really."

Smiling, Orvis held his hands up, palms out. "Don't worry. I won't ask for money."

"That *is* a relief." They shared a little laugh together.

"Mrs. Betterton, I understand it has been many years since you left Temple Brit Yisrael, and you don't attend a *shul* here in town?"

Oh no. He does *know!* Feeling herself blush, Rebecca said, "Yes. That's true."

"Please, the last thing I want to do is intrude upon your personal beliefs, and if this subject is uncomfortable for you in any way, I'll be happy to leave immediately, but . . . ."

"Yes?"

"Well, you may recall that the NJRL was formed with one single goal: to reach out to Jews around the country who feel disenfranchised by the religious experiences of their youth, or who have—for any reason whatso-ever—decided against participating in the faith."

"I see."

"Yes. It is our hope that people like you will reexamine the founda-
tions of your heritage and reconsider Reform Judaism."

"Why?"

Orvis frowned. "That's a fine question, Mrs. Betterton. I don't know
if you're aware of this, but since World War II, the number of Jews in
this country who actively participate in our religion has declined almost
30 percent."

"I didn't know."

"It's true. Interfaith marriages, disenchantment with a faith perceived
as irrelevant to today's problems, cultural assimilation, and conversions
have taken a terrible toll."

"Oh, dear."

"American Judaism is facing its most dire emergency since . . . well,
since the Holocaust."

"I really had no idea."

"Mrs. Betterton, I want to say that I am not here to proselytize.
We leave such offensive practices to other faiths."

"Good."

"Yes. And if your reason for not worshiping at temple has anything
to do with conversion to another faith, I want to ask you to please
forgive this intrusion and I'll be on my way. . . ."

"Oh no, Rabbi. It's not that."

Orvis smiled. "Happy to hear it. In that case, I wonder if I might
spend just a few minutes explaining what I believe you can gain by rees-
tablishing a connection with Judaism?"

This must be God's doing. God has sent this man.

"Of course, Rabbi," she said, "how rude of me to keep you standing
out here on the porch." She stood aside and allowed him in, noticing his
black silk *yarmulke* for the first time. "We've had a problem with a Peeping
Tom here recently, so naturally, I'm being very careful."

Smiling, the man who called himself Rabbi Shumish said, "As you
should be, Mrs. Betterton."

As sunset approached, Ruth labored at a large table in the temple
library, surrounded by open volumes of Talmud and Torah commen-

taries. Preparing for the *Shabbes* Torah study was usually the high point of
her week, an opportunity to immerse herself in texts and commentaries,
to walk Herod's Temple with Hillel and Shammai, to dialogue with
Maimonides and Ibn Ezra, to reflect upon the mind of God, and in one
sense perhaps, to see his face and live. But not this evening. This evening,
the face of God was obscured by the faces of Sol Cantor, Katy Flint, and
the small crowd of proselytizers waving signs outside her temple. Still,
she had a class to teach in the morning, and less than an hour before
Shabbat services would begin. She redoubled her efforts to extract something of interest from the texts.

"Ruth?"

Sighing, she lifted her eyes. Helen Blumenthal stood at the door,
tall and perfectly chic as usual in a simple black shift with a single strand
of pearls. Somehow, being around Helen always made Ruth feel like a
tomboy. "Hi, Helen."

"Am I disturbing you?"

"Well, I do have to get this finished."

"I'm sorry, but there's something I need to say."

Ruth paused, then lowered her pen and gestured toward another chair
at the table. "Have a seat."

"Thanks." Helen crossed the room, the expression on her face betray-
ing the importance of her visit. She seemed uncomfortable. Very uncomfortable. *This is going to be serious*, thought Ruth, as she waited for her friend
to speak. Although Helen clearly felt compelled to tell her something,
she sat silently across the table, kneading her hands like a woman in pain.

Finally Ruth said, "What's the deal?"

"I'm having trouble deciding where to begin."

"You seem upset."

"Yes." She nodded. "I am. For some reason, I get around you and all
my training goes out the window. This is a work thing, so I'm supposed
to be calm and detached, you know? Objective."

"How about beginning there? Why so upset?"

"I . . . that is, I . . . " She lifted both hands together and dropped them
to the tabletop with some force, uttering a mild curse. "I can't tell you! I'm
upset because of a patient, but I can't tell you exactly what I want you to
know."

"I see."

Helen looked directly into Ruth's eyes, as if entreating her to understand on some level deeper than words. "Are the police still watching
your house?"

"No. They stopped that after one night. Why?"

"You must be careful, Ruth. This patient . . . I believe a patient I'm
seeing may be dangerous."

"To me?"

"Not specifically. At least, I don't have a specific reason to think
you're in danger. I'm talking about all of us. Everyone here at temple."

"So it's someone here? Part of the congregation?"

"I can't answer that."

Ruth leaned forward. "Helen, if you know about a threat to this
congregation, you have a duty to reveal that information."

"I don't. That is, I don't have knowledge of a specific threat to a
person. That's the problem. It's more of a . . . a professional guess."

"Okay. Can you tell me anything more? Something I can use to
protect us? Anything?"

"No! I mean yes! I mean . . . oh, this is impossible!"

Ruth reached across the table, covering Helen's hands with hers.
"Listen to me. You have an ethical obligation to your patient. A person's
health may depend upon your respect for that obligation. That is very
important. But you also have a moral duty as a Jew to protect human life.
If these facts have come into conflict, your only choice is to *make* a choice.
Do you understand?"

Helen nodded.

"Underneath all of that," continued Ruth, "under your obligation to
your patient and your duty as a Jew, you have a responsibility to yourself.
To protect yourself, if you can, from a future filled with regret. If you
waver between your obligation and your duty to the point of indecision,
you'll be letting circumstances decide for you. That's the worst thing you
could possibly do, because if the result is . . . well . . . tragic, then you'll
always know that the tragedy might've been avoided, but you were too
cowardly to try. You'll live with that for the rest of your life. Helen, you
must decide what to do and then *do* that, whatever it may be."

"What if I make the wrong choice?" whispered Dr. Helen Blumenthal.

"In that case, you will regret your error for a while. But if you make a decision now, before circumstances remove your options, you'll have your self-respect, no matter what happens. At least you'll know you did your best."

Rabbi Gold kept holding her friend's hands. Finally, Helen nodded and looked up. Ruth gave Helen's hands a squeeze and leaned back against her chair again.

Helen said, "You should have gone into psychotherapy."

Remembering her talk with the unhappy locksmith the day before, Ruth smiled. "Sometimes it feels like I did."

As the final announcement blared over loudspeakers telling everyone the zoo was closed, Jerry Broudain began his first patrol through the area. Jerry's route included the northeast end of the zoo, with the swamp exhibit and its albino alligators. He paused to look through the glass at the pale reptiles, wondering if they really were the only ones of their kind in the world. That's what the zoo brochure claimed, but Jerry had his doubts. Then again, what did he know? He was only a part-time security guard.

Moving on, Jerry checked the restaurant by the pond.

They made pretty good jambalaya there, for a zoo. Better than the chili cheese dogs or so-called nachos, which were nothing but chips with melted Velveeta on top. Jerry went to the San Antonio Zoo one time, and those so-called nachos were about all they had to eat in the whole place— except for hot dogs, of course. That had surprised him, because there were lots of Mexicans around San Antonio. You'd think they'd take more pride than that. Velveeta on chips wasn't real Mexican food.

The shutters were padlocked and the doors dead-bolted at the restaurant, so Jerry began a slow stroll along the boardwalk.

You had to look sharp. One time, a couple of kids stowed away on the shrimp-boat exhibit till after hours. Ol' Chester found 'em foolin' with the monkeys about 3 A.M., and Jerry like to never heard the end of it. Now he made a point of stopping by the shrimp boat and giving it a good hard look every evening.

The little boat swayed gently in the pond, its hull caked with duck-weed along the waterline. Darkness had settled in, so Jerry shone his flashlight into the cabin. Nothing. He moved on down the path to the boat works. They had a little pirogue there, and a couple other kinds of boats, sort of a demonstration of how Cajuns get around in the swamp. Although he was Cajun on his father's side, Jerry hated boats. He hated swamps, too, for that matter. Everybody thought he ought to be able to reach around in the bayou and grab catfish with his bare hands, just because his last name was Broudain. He sniffed and rubbed his nose. Lousy swamps bothered his sinuses. Headaches, runny eyes, the whole thing. No sir. Jerry Broudain was living proof that you could take the boy outta the swamp *and* the swamp outta the boy.

All around him the katydids and crickets were tuning up for the evening. He paused to listen. That was one thing he did like about nature. The birdcalls and insect sounds. Most peaceful thing in the world, hearing katydids strumming along, over and over, louder and louder. Made Jerry think of hammocks and Sunday afternoon naps under a shade tree. . . .

Soaking in the sounds, he closed his eyes. Then a twig snapped behind him. He didn't have time to turn before something sharp pricked him in the thigh. He looked down and saw a little steel thing stuck to his uniform trousers, with something fuzzy and red sticking out of the end. It looked like a . . . uh . . . it looked . . . uh . . . uh . . .

There, that was done.

The last guard lay safe in the men's rest room, sleeping like a baby with duct tape over his mouth and around his wrists and ankles, safely away from the death that would soon stalk Audubon Zoo. Wiping his hands on his slacks, Orvis Newton rose and walked outside to finish the job. He felt good about setting the animals free. Funny thing, though . . . some of them, like the chimpanzees, had been too timid to leave their cages. They might've been in the zoo for as long as a couple of decades, maybe even longer. After all that time, you'd think they'd be racing for the door, but when he'd left their cage wide open they'd huddled on the far side of the enclosure, afraid to move even after he was well away. Oh, well. Maybe that was for the best. In a few minutes, the big cats would be loose. After that, the chimps would be better off in their cages than out here with the carnivores.

It occurred to him again that this was an awful lot of trouble to go through for a woman he had never met. But this way had been ordained, and Orvis would move heaven and earth to conform to the Plan. Anything else would be the basest kind of murder, with no redemptive value for Orvis or for those who had to die.

Everyone had to understand that this was the holy will of God.

The other night, after he'd followed that young man to her office, the psychiatrist had looked familiar, but he had not been able to remember where he'd seen her before. Eventually though, it came to him. Each Friday night after their so-called worship services, while he and his faithful stood outside the temple sharing the gospel, she emerged from the building and marched right past them. Unlike the others, she did not try to avoid Orvis and his followers. She always took the shortest route between the temple doors and her destination, even though that route took her very close to his evangelists. And unlike the others, she never ignored them or responded in anger. In fact, the psychiatrist was one of the only Jews so far who had dared to make eye contact with Orvis Newton. Not that she had encouraged his evangelistic efforts in any way. Each week, she simply offered a friendly smile, shook her head in a bemused kind of way, and walked right by. But the thing that had impressed Orvis Newton most, the real reason he remembered her, was the psychiatrist's destination. For several Fridays in a row, when she passed them, she had crossed the street and disappeared into the shadows of Audubon Park, all alone.

It was a foolish thing to do, but of course, now Orvis understood that she did it at the direction of the Father himself. It was all part of the Plan.

Heading for the feline section, the liberator of the Audubon Zoo walked calmly, using bolt cutters to quickly open every cage he passed, leaving a pandemonium of confused creatures wandering along the paths behind him or rising to the skies on long-unused wings. The odd picture he presented was made even more bizarre by the ten-pound brisket he towed along the ground behind himself at the end of a length of twine. He had placed small hunks of raw beef here and there along the way, but everything depended on the big cats pursuing the trace of blood all the way across the park. For that he needed a continuous trail of scent.

Orvis paused in front of a cage containing two Bengal tigers. As he

cut the locks, he thought of Mr. Disraeli, the Rothstein brothers' cat.
He enjoyed the irony of using a little cat in one part of the Plan, and big
cats in another. After all, everything was interconnected in the original
version. Why not in his version too?

An hour later, Helen Blumenthal stopped next to Ruth and they stood
together by the front door as the congregation filed out into the
night. It had been a moving worship service, and Helen felt strangely
peaceful in spite of the fanatic Christians outside, shouting Bible verses
like protest slogans at the departing Jews. Beside her, Ruth sighed.

"Listen," Helen said, "I want to thank you. You're really something."

"Aw, shucks."

"No, really. I sit in my office all week long, listening to other people's
problems. Sometimes they fill me up. I start to feel like I'm overflowing."

"I know what you mean, believe me."

"I'm sure you do." Helen touched Ruth's arm. "Thanks for being there
for me, Ruth."

"You're welcome."

She gave the rabbi's arm a little squeeze, then turned to leave the
building.

"Can I give you a ride?" asked Ruth.

"No, thanks. I think I'll walk."

"Feeling Orthodox this evening?"

Helen laughed. "That'll be the day. I'm not gonna walk all the way
home. Just over to the streetcar stop."

"Be careful."

"I will, but it's not me I'm worried about." She looked hard at Ruth.
"You be careful, too, hear?" Ruth nodded. Helen continued to stare at her.
"I wish I could tell you more."

"I know. Don't worry."

Helen shrugged. "Hard not to."

"I know."

They stood silently for a moment, as the zealots on the sidewalk
shouted chapter and verse. Then, with a rueful parting smile, Helen said,
"See ya," and set out across the parking lot.

She reached the street, where she waited by the curb while several cars passed by. "Jesus can save you, daughter!" shouted one of the lunatics above the roar of a passing panel truck. He was young and dressed in a nice black suit. "Come unto me all ye who labor and are heavy laden, and I will give you rest."

The young man started moving her way. Helen hated dealing with these people every week, but they always stood directly between the temple and the park, and she refused to let them intimidate her into walking one inch out of her way. Shifting her weight from foot to foot, Helen gauged the traffic flow. If it didn't clear soon, she'd be forced to deal with this nutcase. Suddenly, Helen smiled at the words of her inner dialogue. *Lunatic. Nutcase.* Some psychiatrist she was.

He had nearly reached her when the traffic opened up. She rushed to the far side of the street. *Safe at last,* she thought, setting out across Audubon Park. Helen knew most people wouldn't dream of walking in the park after dark, but it was almost ten, and cutting diagonally over to the closest streetcar stop on St. Charles would save her several minutes. With residents meeting her at the hospital for rounds promptly at six tomorrow morning, she couldn't afford to stay up a minute later than necessary. Besides, this shortcut was safe. She'd taken it many times after *Shabbat* services without so much as a wino asking for a quarter. What could happen?

Helen walked with a sure and steady pace along a narrow asphalt path lined with oaks. Her footsteps tapped loudly on the pavement, competing with the surge and fall of the katydids' rhythmic hum in the treetops. A single cloud raced across the ebony sky, its glowing underbelly gently caressed by the city lights. Then, without warning, a man on a bicycle sped out of the darkness and swished past her.

As he passed, something hit her side with the force of a soft punch.

Helen yelped and took a frightened step away from the path. The remnants of a burst balloon fell to the pavement at her feet. She felt something damp trickling down her side. The man on the bicycle did not glance back as he rode back into the blackness from which he had come, his torso low over the handlebars.

Helen stood still a moment, waiting for her heartbeat to return to normal. Then she felt her side. Her hand came away covered with a cold, viscous liquid. In the moonlight it was difficult to tell for sure, but when she lifted her fingers to her nose, Helen thought she smelled the heavy scent of blood. The stuff had dribbled down her leg and pooled at her feet. She uttered a mild curse. What kind of person would ride around pelting people with balloons filled with blood?

"Creep!" she shouted into the darkness.

Then, muttering to herself, Helen Blumenthal resumed her journey through the park.

CHAPTER
SIXTEEN

Rabbi Ruth Gold lingered alone just inside the doors, waiting for Rabbi Sam Gottlieb to walk her to her car. The last of her congregation had left five minutes ago. Peering outside, she saw one last kook standing beside a ten-speed bicycle in a streetlight's glow on the far side of the parking lot. She sighed, wondering for the hundredth time why there wasn't something they could do to protect themselves from this harassment, but she supposed you had to allow freedom of speech, even for zealots. *Especially* for zealots. She thought of a quote that went something like, "I disagree with everything you say, but I will defend to the death your right to say it." It would be good to remember that as she walked across the parking lot tonight.

"Okay," said Sam, striding up the hall. "Ready if you are."

He opened the door and held it for her. Sam was a gentleman of the old school, and frankly, she found his manners pleasant. "Thanks," she said.

"My pleasure."

"'For by grace are ye saved through faith,'" shouted the man from his position under the streetlight. "'And that not of yourselves: it is the gift of God: Not of works, lest any man should boast'!"

"Lovely evening, isn't it?" asked Rabbi Gottlieb, elaborately ignoring him.

Ruth smiled. "Yes. Except for a touch of air pollution."

Sam chuckled as they strode across the empty asphalt toward her car. In the distance, she heard a lion roar. It was normal, this close to the zoo. But the animal call seemed louder than usual. She was about to mention that when the man yelled, "'Now the righteousness of God without the law is manifested, being witnessed by the law and the prophets; Even the righteousness of God which is by faith of Jesus Christ unto all and upon all them that believe!'"

Sam said, "I wonder if—"

He was cut short by an enormous roar, rumbling deep and strong and very near.

There was no point in remaining angry about the creep on the bicycle. That would only grant him more power. So Helen tried to occupy her mind by remembering the words about faith that Rabbi Gottlieb had spoken during the evening service. She was not sure if the concept of faith had relevance to her life. In fact, for Helen Blumenthal, faith came hard.

She was the eldest daughter of three, the offspring of a man who fled Hitler in 1938, along with his parents and older sister. Her father had retained his German accent until his death of lung cancer at the age of fifty-three, when Helen was in high school. Her mother had died of a stroke soon after, leaving Helen to care for two younger sisters. As soon as both girls had graduated, Helen entered college, beginning the long path to her medical degree. Nobody had helped her. She worked nights and weekends at any job she could find, getting by on two and three hours' sleep for months at a time, until, she finally had achieved her dream.

Tonight, the rabbi had spoken of the need to credit God with who we are. Helen wondered where God had been when her father lost his home to the Nazis at the age of thirteen. Where was God when an eighteen-

year-old girl inherited the duties of her dead parents, raising her sisters
without help? Where was God while she slaved on the graveyard shift in
an all-night diner for fifty-cent tips, and endured the pompous abuse of
professors all day? God certainly seemed to have little mercy for the never-
ending stream of lost and dispossessed patients passing through her office
week after week, each one a walking example of the futility of faith.

What's that?

She stopped, listening.

Oh, nothing. Just a big cat at the zoo, roaring at the moon.

Resuming her pace, Helen glanced back over her shoulder. She
thought she heard something else, a curious sound, like a drumbeat, but
different, like a . . . a horse, maybe. Yes. A galloping horse.

How odd.

Through the trees ahead, she saw the headlights of cars on St.
Charles. *Good,* she thought. Something about this evening's walk made
her nervous. The park seemed different tonight. She hadn't been able to
shake the feeling of being watched, ever since that freak on the bicycle
had . . . no. She would *not* dwell on the negative. Slipping the strap of her
purse a bit higher on her shoulder, Helen increased the length of her
strides. Then she heard that galloping sound again. What on earth could
it be?

A monkey jabbered in the trees to her right.

A monkey?

What was she thinking? Of course it was a bird of some kind. She'd
heard somewhere that the call of the redheaded woodpecker sounded
similar to a monkey's chatter. The galloping seemed closer now, but it
had changed, become more complex, as if there were two or three horses
running together. She stopped and turned around in spite of herself.

The sound came closer.

She sometimes saw equestrians in the park, dressed in jodhpurs and
small-brimmed black helmets. Maybe a couple of them had remained
after dark, like the man on the bicycle. Louder and louder the hoofbeats
pounded until they broke from the tree line and Helen Blumenthal saw
two zebras loping across the field.

She stood, slack-jawed, eyes defying her mind to believe the scene as
half a dozen other zebras joined the first two. The herd ran close together,

gliding smoothly over the ground with legs stretched far in front, striding across the grass at top speed. Then something else burst from the cover of the woods, something slightly shorter, running as quickly as the zebras, but without making a sound. There! She saw another. The two shorter animals remained near the trees, out of the moonlight's reach. Helen could just make out their shadowy forms, racing in pursuit of the zebras. They ran differently, with a smooth, catlike grace.

Then she remembered the roar she had heard before, and a primal fear washed over her.

Turning from the primitive drama unfolding across the field, Helen fled toward the tree line on the opposite side, directly toward St. Charles. Again, she heard the crazy high-pitched laughter in the treetops. The zebras had reached the woods near the avenue, but rather than plunging in, they turned to their right, loping alongside the trees, keeping pace with a Mercedes-Benz just thirty yards away. Perhaps the traffic frightened the huge creatures as much as the big cats at their heels. Whatever the reason, their turn was a poor decision, because the cats cut across the field diagonally, reducing the zebras' lead by half. Helen realized if she continued running on the path, the cats would pass between her and the street. Breathing raggedly, she veered to her left, hoping the lions or tigers—or whatever they were—would follow the zebras in the opposite direction.

They did.

As she entered the tree line, Helen heard another roar, followed by a sound that could only have been a zebra slamming into the trees across the field. She did not pause to watch the deadly drama but stumbled into the woods, hoping to find another way to St. Charles. As she wove her way among occasional clumps of undergrowth, she glanced left and right, alert for the slightest movement. Still, she was unprepared for the sudden arrival of a herd of piglike creatures crashing through the brush. Taking shelter on the downstream side of a large pecan tree, Helen stood motionless as they parted and flowed around her, at least two dozen of them, racing by with feral grunts.

What's happening?

Fighting a growing sense that this was a hallucination, she continued through the woods, moving quickly. Her toe caught on something. She fell hard. Desperately, she pushed herself up to a sitting position and then to her feet. With one step, however, she was back on the ground, screaming in pain. She reached for her leg in the darkness and felt hot blood coursing across her panty hose. She moved her hands farther and found the gash, just below the knee. Apparently she had fallen on a piece of broken glass or something equally sharp. She could not see the wound, but knew from the amount of blood that it was serious.

Somewhere nearby an animal screamed. She had no idea what it was, but the meaning of the shriek was unmistakable.

Running her hands across the soil nearby, she found her purse. Its strap was detachable, designed to allow the purse to be converted into a clutch for more formal occasions. Working mainly by touch, Helen removed the strap and wrapped it around her upper thigh, pulling it as tight as possible, and tying it off. She felt below her knee again. Good. The blood flow was reduced. Dragging her leg and feeling ahead carefully to avoid another encounter with a sharp object, she inched across the ground. She reached what felt like a sapling, grasped it in both hands and fought her way to her feet.

I can do this, she thought, remembering the flash of pain the last time she'd placed her weight on the injured leg. Gritting her teeth, she took a step. The pain was bearable now that she expected it. She took another step, and another. Good. She would make it.

Orvis Newton faced the park with his hands lifted to the heavens, a streetlight glimmering in his wire-rimmed glasses. "'The wolf and the lamb shall feed together, and the lion shall eat straw like the bullock, and dust *shall be* the serpent's meat'!"

"You have to admit he knows his Bible," said Rabbi Gottlieb.

"Sam, what should we do about that animal we heard?" asked Ruth.

"Don't worry about it. Probably just some kids fooling around."

"I don't know . . ."

"Sure. I'll bet some kid got the bright idea of playing jungle noises on his boom box." Sam gestured toward the evangelist. "Or maybe this character is using sound effects. Come on. Let's get going."

The rabbis walked the rest of the way to Ruth's car while the man across the parking lot stood yelling one lion verse after another. Ruth had her keys ready as usual and opened the door immediately when they reached the Citroën. Sam gave the top of the car a pat.

"When are you going to buy a real car?"

"Soon as I get a real raise."

He smiled. "Well, I was going to lobby for one with the board next week, but it turns out we have to spend your money to keep out the rain."

"You know," said Ruth, "I've been wondering about that. Why would anyone vandalize our roof?"

"The police think maybe someone was trying to break in from up there, out of sight of the road and all."

"I guess that makes sense."

"Apparently it happens fairly often. So anyway, it looks like you're gonna hafta wait a while to get rid of this piece of junk."

"Hey," said Ruth. "Watch how you talk around my baby."

He laughed. "Well, this is one baby that belongs in a nursing home. How long has it been since—"

A roar from very nearby cut him short.

Sam and Ruth turned toward the park just in time to see three zebras burst from the shadows beneath the live oaks. The animals galloped across the narrow strip of grass beside the curb and onto the street, straight toward the evangelist on the sidewalk. Oblivious to their approach, the man stood with his arms and face raised toward the sky.

"Look out!" screamed Ruth.

It was too late. The zebras charged up the street and, with inches to spare, parted and ran past the man, who lowered his arms and spun around, astonished. As Ruth and Sam and the evangelist looked on, the zebras continued across the parking lot and around the side of the temple out of sight.

"Wow," said Sam.

The evangelist, apparently at a loss for an appropriate zebra verse, simply continued to stare toward the corner of the temple.

Sam said, "I wonder how they got out."

"Who cares?" said Ruth. "What I want to know is, what are they running from?"

At that, both rabbis turned back toward the park. While they had been looking in the other direction, a grizzly bear had emerged from the trees. It ambled halfway across the road, where it decided to pause and inspect a smell on the pavement. Seeing the bear, the driver of an oncoming Chevy Cavalier stood on his brakes and managed to halt just five feet away. Stunned, he sat behind the wheel staring at the creature. The huge bear, easily as big as the little car, lifted its snout from the pavement and sneezed. Meanwhile, the evangelist continued to gaze after the departed zebras with his back to the road, unaware of the approaching grizzly.

"Hey!" shouted Ruth. "Mr. Christian fella! Look out!"

"'Mr. Christian fella?'" asked Rabbi Gottlieb.

"Well, I don't know his name!"

"But, 'Mr. Christian fella'?"

"Will you please put a lid on it and and help me get his attention?"

Both of the rabbis shouted and waved at the man until he finally shifted his eyes toward them.

"Look behind you!" yelled Sam.

The man turned slowly. Meanwhile, the bear seemed to catch his scent. Nose high in the air, nostrils flaring, the grizzly was on the move again, its pigeon-toed rolling gait carrying it closer and closer to the hapless evangelist.

When the man perceived the threat, he lifted his hands toward the sky again and began to speak. "'The Lord is my shepherd; I shall not want. He maketh me to lie down in green pastures. He leadeth me beside the still waters.'"

He lowered his head just enough to check on the grizzly's progress. It was much closer. The evangelist's voice rose half an octave. "'He restoreth my soul. He leadeth me in the paths of righteousness for his name's sake.'"

Again he shifted his gaze from the black sky above to the burly brute approaching. By now, the bear was less than ten feet away. Even on all fours, it towered over the man. "'Yea, though I walk through the valley of the shadow of death, I will fear no evil, for thou art with me. Thy rod and thy staff they comfort me.'"

As Ruth and Sam watched, frozen in place, the huge beast pressed its snout against the man's pants and inhaled deeply. Its head was as wide as the evangelist's hips. The man's hands shook visibly, but he continued to lift them to the sky as Ruth's whispered voice joined his: "'Thou preparest

a table before me in the presence of mine enemies. Thou anointest my
head with oil; my cup runneth over. Surely goodness and mercy shall
follow me all the days of my life, and I will dwell in the house of the Lord
for ever.'"

As if the end of the psalm were its cue, the bear swung its head
toward the man in the Cavalier, who shouted, "Shoo! Shoo, you bear!"
from behind the windshield, making waving motions with his arms.
Without taking further stock of the evangelist, the grizzly ambled onto
the parking lot in slow pursuit of the zebras. Seeing the creature coming
their way, Ruth and Sam dove inside her car and slammed the door.
The bear paid no attention to them whatsoever but continued across the
asphalt, its immense haunches swaying with every step, its huge claws
clicking against the pavement. Ruth and Sam followed the creature's
progress with bated breath. Only after the animal had turned the corner
out of sight did they realize that the evangelist was shouting at them and
shaking his fists.

"You see?" he screamed. "Death stalks us all. How will you meet your
Maker?"

Rabbi Sam Gottlieb glared at the man on the sidewalk and said,
"I suppose it's wrong of me to regret the way that turned out."

Lowering her forehead to the steering wheel, Ruth began giggling
uncontrollably.

SEVENTEEN

Something else had entered the woods.

For the last minute or two, Helen had heard it back there, moving when she moved, stopping when she stopped. She considered climbing a tree, but that really didn't seem possible with her injured leg. Besides, how did she know the thing couldn't climb too? So she concentrated on making slow, steady progress, inching toward the sound of traffic in the distance. Maybe the thing back there was hiding from the lions, just like she was. Maybe it wasn't interested in her. But if that were true, why did it mimic her movements? That was a concern . . . definitely a concern.

Helen paused in a sliver of moonlight to lean against a large tree and check her wounded leg. She was coated in blood—some of it hers, some from that madman's balloon. The hemorrhaging had slowed substantially, but not enough to risk loosening the purse strap around her thigh. Yet, with the pressure unabated for at least five minutes now, she had lost sensation in her leg, making it even more difficult to walk. Her foot drooped badly, forcing her to exaggerate each step, raising her knee higher than usual to allow her toes to clear the ground as she inched forward. Each time she lifted her knee, it aggravated the wound, which accounted for the continued bleeding.

A crack.

The muffled sound of dry leaves, stirred by a passing body.

So close.

Helen Blumenthal strained to see through the darkness. Above her, something flitted through the treetops—a bird perhaps, or maybe a squirrel. She glanced up. It was useless. The thick canopy obscured most of the sky, with the light of the moon penetrating here and there, but only in slender shafts angling down to the leafy floor of the woods. Helen lowered her gaze.

A pair of bloodred spots of light hovered in the darkness just fifty feet away. They were widely spaced and at least three feet above the ground. Her breath caught in her throat as the horrible truth hit home. Whatever it was, it was big, and it was staring straight at her. As she watched, the red spots moved, swaying slightly from side to side, coming closer.

She panicked. All thought of the pain in her leg vanished as she turned and stumbled away, lifting her knee high with every step, making pitifully slow, awkward progress. Behind her, she heard heavy breathing, like a dog panting in the summer heat. But this breathing was slower. Deeper. Louder. A branch cracked under the weight of the thing. It was closer. Much closer. Helen began to cry. She glanced back over her shoulder as the beast passed through a moonbeam. What she saw froze her heart.

Slowly, gracefully, row after row of black stripes on an orange background slipped through the pale bar of light.

The tiger was four times her size, and it was inexorably drawn to the scent of the blood that covered her body. Helen ran, forgetting her dangling foot. Almost immediately, she tripped, hitting the ground hard. A flash of pain shot up her right arm. Crying with terror, she rose to her hands and knees. Immediately, she collapsed again, as liquid fire surged up from her wrist. She gingerly probed with her left hand, finding the radius and ulna of her forearm intact. In less than two seconds, her mind automatically ran through the other possibilities, diagnosing a fracture of the scaphoid at the base on her thumb. Glancing back again, she saw the tiger standing still, watching her. She used her left hand and right elbow to crawl away. Her agonizing efforts brought her to a small opening in a dense cluster of underbrush. Pushing through, Helen gritted her teeth against a web of thorny vines clawing at her flesh as she fought her way deeper into the bush.

The tiger charged.

Helen's wounded leg trailed behind her, still out in the open, just inches away from the protective cover of the thornbush. The massive cat bounded across the space between them, soft paws falling faintly on the leaves, eyes focused only on her foot. She screamed at the top of her lungs, clawing the ground with her one good hand to scramble deeper into the underbrush. The tiger lunged from less than ten feet away. Helen reached back with both hands and gripped her knee, pulling her exposed foot inside the thornbush despite the searing agony in her thumb. With a final, graceful stride, her famished suitor was upon her, its front claws fully extended, its huge paws stretching for her.

Helen yanked hard on her leg just as the tiger's claws sank into her ankle. She felt nothing, the lack of circulation blocking all sensation. The tiger tugged, pulling her backwards a few inches across the ground.

I'm dying, she thought. *This is what it's like.*

She gripped a small tree trunk and pulled against the tiger, playing a monstrous game of tug-of-war with the beast. Crooking the elbow of her wounded arm around the tree and grasping her wrist with her good hand, Helen strained with all her might. At that instant, the tiger released its grip, intending perhaps to claw her again farther up, but the force of Helen's pull on the tree yanked her leg from the space between the tiger's claws before they could close again. The tiger bellowed its rage, filling the night air with a ferocious roar. Helen yanked again on the tree trunk, dragging her leg inside the meager security of the dense thornbush. The tiger squatted on its haunches, reaching into the narrow opening to bat at her with three-inch claws.

A car honked on St. Charles, and the sound of a distant siren filled the air as Helen Blumenthal, doctor of psychiatry and respected member of New Orleans society, cowered within a thornbush in Audubon Park less than six feet away from a Bengal tiger. It paced the soil outside her tenuous shelter, searching for a way to consume her. For five, ten, fifteen minutes, the tiger paced, pausing to push at the brush, withdrawing when a thorn pricked its paw, trying again a few feet away. Finally, the carnivore crouched just beyond the small opening, settling down like a sphinx to stare in at her. There was no anger it its eyes, no animosity at all. The tiger looked at Helen Blumenthal in exactly the same casually interested way that she herself had often contemplated a filet mignon just before slicing it into bite-sized pieces.

Propping her head against the small tree trunk, Helen returned the animal's gaze. Curiously, she found herself relaxing. She knew it was the loss of blood, knew she must fight against unconsciousness, but still, it was so peaceful there, listening to the breeze in the treetops and the sounds of the city nearby. She began to think of the tiger as a beautiful creature, magnificently muscled and perfectly formed for its purpose. Once it had been the absolute monarch of its environment; then it had fallen to a pitiful state of imprisonment. But now, here in Helen Blumenthal's environment, the tiger was sovereign once more.

She closed her eyes, just for a moment.

Orvis slipped through the woods of Audubon Park as silently as any other predator. Walking his bicycle between the trees, he knew he was probably not alone. He had just seen half a dozen teenagers, lurking in the woods, dressed all in black, with pale faces and metal-studded lips, noses, and eyebrows. Doubtless they were escaping middle-class parents by engaging in pathetic late-night orgies of sex, drugs, and alcohol. There might well be others with even more sinister reasons for their presence in the park. But Orvis was unafraid. The Lord had delivered him from the grizzly bear, had he not? Orvis was immune from evil.

Tomorrow morning, he had no doubt the media would serve the jaded people of New Orleans a macabre dish that even they could not stomach. They would find the wrath of nature turned upon them. For over three centuries they had lived with the constant threat that the Mississippi would breach its banks and inundate their homes, but tonight Orvis had unleashed nature's fury on the Crescent City in a way no one had ever anticipated. All he had to do was follow along, making sure the predators did their work completely. If not, he was more than willing to help.

Helen opened her eyes again. Above her, through limbs and leaves, she saw the night sky glowing pale and soft with the coming sunrise. Lavender and violet hues hung like stained-glass panels mounted in the jigsaw webbing of crisscrossed branches. She felt herself sliding on her back across the ground, being pulled by her feet.

The beast had her.

She could do nothing more. She did not care. Something sharp, a branch or a stone, struck her hip and slid up her back as she was dragged across it, finally bumping against her head.

Helen thought about the strangest things. Her kitchen, which she loved. Who would get her kitchen utensils? She remembered learning to cook, watching her mother on the afternoon before each *Shabbat*, up to her elbows in flour, baking *challah*, egg bread. She thought of a trip she took long ago to San Francisco, with a boy from college—what was his name? His parents had lived high on a hill. She remembered looking down on the bay. How lovely it had been, topped with fog like a giant bubble bath.

The creature grunted with the effort of dragging her through the dim woods. Helen lifted her head slightly and looked toward her feet. She had only enough time to see the beast's hands wrapped around her ankles before another stone struck her in the hip and knocked her onto her side.

Hands?

Wasn't that important? She thought, *What was the name of that boy?* His parents had put them up in their quaint three-story row house, sandwiched within a steep block of other row houses. She remembered thinking that the homes looked like paddle wheelers on the Mississippi berthed side by side, with steering cabins proud and high above the river. Funny, going to San Francisco had made her homesick for New Orleans.

She felt herself stop. *Now it will eat me*, she thought. The sky above was lighter now, the tree canopy less dense. Helen found she loved the sky. She loved the trees. Life was everywhere, and it was wonderful.

The thing circled her. She felt it best not to watch. Now she heard its breath again. It drew very near. She knew the pain would be intense, but she thought she would be able to bear it somehow. The physician in her doubted she would remain conscious for more than a few seconds, and besides, this was life, too. A natural conclusion. As much a part of everything as all the rest. So come along and get it over with. It's time to move on.

Helen felt pressure against her rib cage. It lifted her onto her side. From her new position, she saw that she lay at the top of a short slope down to a narrow lagoon. The thing pushed again, and she went over the edge, sliding down. She rolled into the murky water, feeling it lap against her ears and cheeks, almost covering her face. Looking up, she saw the figure descending after her, its silhouette against the dim glow of the approaching dawn.

She smiled, recognizing the shape of what she saw, finding a hope she had abandoned. Hands, not claws. That was important.

"Help me," she whispered, fully expecting to be understood.

But the thing squatted beside her, gripped her head in its hands, and slowly turned her facedown into the water.

Too weak to fight, Helen Blumenthal surrendered herself to a confusing jumble of thoughts. In her final seconds, a thousand images filled her mind. She saw the ornate plaster ceiling in the third-floor bedroom of the San Fancisco row house on her first night of love. She saw fanciful images of riverboats lining the shores of the insignificant lagoon in Audubon Park, where she lay dying. She saw the faces of her parents, her sisters, herself in the mirror, wearing a black shift and pearls. She thought of everything she had planned to do, all the places she had hoped to visit some day. She thought of her clients, the special ones who existed in cruel, restricted places through no fault of their own, compressed smaller than life by all the evil in the world. They relied upon her. She had so much work left to do. If she died now, it would all have been for nothing. She was not finished! She was not ready! Who would do the work? How would it go on? Everything would stop . . . .

And then, in a last terrified grasp at life, she opened her mouth to explain her need to live for the sake of everything, but her lungs filled with water, and there was nothing left to say, as the swirling mud gently washed her open, unseeing eyes.

EIGHTEEN

Rebecca Betterton sat alone at the kitchen table, crying.

The other day, when she had seen the footprints outside her bedroom window, she had run inside and locked all the doors. Then she called 911 and reported an intruder. Roy returned home just as the patrolmen arrived. He let them in through the front door. Meanwhile, she stood in the kitchen talking to the nice police operator on the telephone. Two policemen entered with their fingers wrapped around the grips of their holstered pistols. That just about frightened her to death. Then she saw Roy standing behind them, and knew everything would be fine.

But there had been some confusion. Somehow, the policemen got the impression there was an intruder in the house right *then*, at that moment. She had tried to explain that it was all a mistake—the intruder had never actually come in, but he'd *been* here. They could go out back and see his footprints for themselves. The policemen walked all through her house anyway, while Roy stayed with her in the kitchen. Roy had been very quiet. When the police finished searching the house, they'd asked her to take them outside to see the footprints, so she and Roy and the officers went out the patio door and over to the shrubs below her bedroom window, where she pointed out the impressions in the soil.

That was when Roy had said the footprints were his.

The policemen asked him if he was certain, and he explained about checking all the windows the morning after the Peeping Tom, to make sure there were no signs of someone trying to break in. She felt *so* embarrassed, saying, "Why on earth didn't you *tell* me you were going to do that?" The policemen exchanged a look and said they had to go. Roy walked them all the way to their car, and the three of them stood out there talking while she watched from inside the house. When he came back in, Roy hadn't had much to say. In fact, he hadn't said much the whole rest of the evening. Finally, she asked him if he believed there had been a Peeping Tom. He'd said he supposed so.

He *supposed* so!

Was that any way for a man to support his wife?

Roy hadn't said much to her yesterday, either. In fact, that nice Rabbi Shumish had said more in fifteen minutes than her husband said all evening. Now here she was, sitting around the house while Roy was off playing golf with his friends. Whacking at a little white ball while his wife lived in fear, all alone. She sobbed out loud, staring through the bay window in the breakfast nook, twisting a soggy paper napkin in her hands. What if the intruder came back while Roy was gone? What if he came *inside* this time? What would she do?

Rebecca tried to imagine what it would be like to be dead. There seemed to be three possibilities. Either nothing happened and you just stopped, or you went to heaven or to hell. She didn't believe she might come back in another life. Not for a minute. That was just silly. And if this world is all there is, why then, what difference does it make? When you're dead, you're not going to care anymore, right?

But what if there *was* a heaven and a hell?

Rebecca twisted the napkin tighter and tighter. To tell the truth, she wasn't sure where she'd end up. Her parents had done their best to teach her about the Jewish faith. Her daddy had been a native New Orleanian, but her mother had emigrated from Hungary in 1937. Neither of them cared much for the Orthodox ways of their youth, so they had joined the Reform temple over near the park and raised Rebecca to believe it was her right to choose which parts of her heritage made the most sense. When she was sixteen, she quit going to temple. They tried to force her, but she turned their own logic back on them, saying she had a right to choose which parts of her faith to observe, and she chose to have nothing more to do with it.

Then she met her first husband, Sidney Friedman. He was originally from Brooklyn, New York, and had been raised in an ultra-Orthodox family, with the black hat and the long locks of hair at the temples and the fringes of his *arba kanfot* dangling loose below his shirt. When Sidney moved to New Orleans as a young man, he abandoned all that, probably because here he stuck out like a sore thumb. A few years later, they met and married, and a year after that, little Aaron was born.

Rebecca Betterton's dreamy smile at the memory of her son soon became a frown. That was when Sidney showed his true colors. Suddenly, he was nailing a *mezuzah* to the doorframe and running around town wearing his *yarmulke* in public.

"What are you doing?" she had asked, afraid she'd be seeing the fringes of a prayer shawl dangling from under his shirt any day.

"My duty as a father," he had replied.

Sidney had tried to get her to join an Orthodox synagogue, but she wasn't about to sit behind the *mechitza*, screened off from the men like some inferior person. She had told her husband he would wait a lifetime before he got her to worship God Almighty from the back of the *shul* behind a curtain, while Sidney and his buddies lorded it over the women up front. He said it wasn't a symbol of superiority; it was because the women's beauty might distract the men. She said the men should get a grip, for goodness' sake. Besides, most of the women weren't that good-looking if you wanted to know the truth. After a couple of weeks of the silent treatment, Sidney had proposed a compromise. That was how Rebecca had found herself rejoining Temple Brit Yisrael after almost ten years. She and Sidney had paid their dues and attended services almost every *Shabbat*. Aaron grew up playing at the Northside Jewish Community Center on

Saturday afternoons after temple, and going to the children's classes on Sunday mornings. When it was time for his Bar Mitzvah, Rebecca had been so proud to see him standing on the *bima* in his *yarmulke* and *talit*, reading Hebrew like a little rabbi. Funny how the traditions she'd despised when she was Aaron's age had seemed so comforting that day.

Then she had met Roy.

Every Monday morning he had come to the library where she worked to read that week's edition of *Tools Today*. Roy owned a wholesale tool distribution company over in Algiers, and he liked to start his business week by catching up with the latest industry news. Somehow, they got to talking. Over the months, she had learned he was a widower with three grown kids. He lived alone in a nice house by the lake. One thing led to another, and she found herself looking forward to Monday mornings. He wasn't Jewish, but that didn't matter. About a year after she first met him, she told Sidney she wanted a divorce.

She hadn't been to temple since.

That was twenty years ago. Now Sidney had moved back to New York, where he was probably dressing like a nineteenth-century Polish person again. Her son Aaron had a condo in downtown New Orleans with a river view. And Rebecca was sitting alone in her half-million-dollar house, watching the bird feeder and bawling her eyes out while her *shaigetz* husband played golf. If the intruder came again, she might be killed, and it had been over ten years since she'd said the *shema*, much less *kaddish*. With such a life, who knew what might happen after she died?

Rebecca thought of that nice Rabbi Shumish who had come to visit. He had seemed so understanding. He had even called her a couple of times to see how she was handling the Peeping Tom thing, suggesting that she should meet him at temple this *Yom Kippur*, so she wouldn't be there alone. Such a kind man . . .

Sniffling, Rebecca rose and crossed to the wall cabinet next to the telephone. She opened it and peered at the calendar hanging on the inside of the door. Just as she thought, *Yom Kippur* was only five days away. It was probably too late, but she still knew a few people who went to Brit Yisrael. Maybe she could get a ticket to the services.

Yom Kippur.

The Day of Atonement.

Roy probably wouldn't like it, but who cares? With this terrible person lurking in her flower beds, if anyone needed to get right with God, she did. It occurred to her that she could say the *shema* right then. Why not? It was *Shabbat*, after all, and it wasn't as if she had forgotten the words. She bowed her head, standing by her kitchen counter, and whispered, "*Shema Yisrael Adonai, Elohim, Adonai echad.*" She thought about the meaning of each word: Hear Israel, the Lord God, the Lord is one. She stood for another moment with her head down and eyes closed.

Then she said it again, louder.

Kate sat in her Jeep, staring through the windshield. Although the temple was a lovely building with soaring rooflines and beautiful stained glass, she barely noticed the sight before her. Instead, her lips moved slightly as she prayed, her open eyes focused inwardly, searching for help. *Take the fear away. Please.* She stopped praying. She continued to stare at the temple building from inside her car, knowing God would not answer. He never did.

"Mommy?" said Jilly. "Aren't we gonna go inside?"

"In a minute, honey."

Paul sat in the small backseat playing a handheld video game, the small machine beeping and buzzing while Kate tried to think of reasons not to be afraid.

As she waited, many other vehicles entered the parking lot. Casually dressed people emerged from them and strolled to the temple. Some carried books—Torahs probably—but mostly they were empty-handed. She noticed that a few of them fit her stereotypical notions about Jews— they were the ones with curly hair and prominent noses—but there were no more of them than you might find in any crowd. She saw far more blondes and average-looking brunettes and redheads with pale skin and freckles. She even noticed one skinny black woman wearing a *yarmulke*. She made Kate think of one of Moses' wives, a woman from the ancient African country of Cush, just south of Egypt. Chances were good that any Jew descended from Moses was partly black. Yet even in Moses' time, there was prejudice against black people, because Moses' own sister and brother spoke against him for marrying the Cushite woman. Kate

wondered if the people entering the temple knew those things. Probably
a few of them did, but maybe only a few. The idea that she knew about
Moses' Cushite wife gave Kate confidence. It occurred to her that the
Torah was the first five books of *her* Bible, too. She had studied it many
times. And Ruth *had* asked her to come here today. Ruth was a rabbi, one
of the people in charge, apparently, so she had a friend in high places.

Maybe she *could* do this thing.

Kate reached for the door handle. Feeling a little more self-confident,
she said, "Come on, kids. Let's go." But her fragile resolve vanished the
moment she stepped outside, where a very tall blonde lady stood twenty
feet away, yelling at her.

R uth lingered just inside the doors, waiting for Katy. The things she
had seen the night before now seemed impossible. Zebras and a grizzly bear in Brit Yisrael's parking lot? If Sam hadn't seen it too, she'd have
written the whole thing off as a dream, but it had been real all right. Last
night, after she and Sam Gottlieb had returned to their senses, they'd
reported everything to the police, who told them they'd already received
similar reports from dozens of other people. This morning Ruth had
heard the details on the morning news. Someone let a lot of the animals
loose at the zoo last night. A zebra had been found dead, the victim of a
lion attack. People who lived near the park had been warned to be alert
and stay indoors, since many carnivorous predators remained at large.

Lions and tigers and bears.

Oh my.

Ruth grinned, but it really was a serious matter. According to the
news reporter, except for the big cats, all of the animals had been well fed
when they escaped, but with time they would become ravenous. Then
anything could happen.

Suddenly, Ruth remembered her friend Helen. She lifted a hand to
her mouth. How could she have forgotten? Helen had gone into the park
last night, just fifteen minutes before those animals appeared! What if . . .
no, it was too fantastic. Ruth found herself struggling to suppress a rising
sense of the surreal.

How had she slipped into this other dimension where childhood friends resurfaced, old friends perished, gentle men were locked away in mental wards while murderers were released from prison and wild animals ruled the city? The irony was, nobody else seemed to believe that anything had changed. Ruth resolved to call Helen after the Torah class to make sure her friend was all right.

She looked out through the glass doors. Normally, she would be in her office, frantically trying to pull together a few last-minute facts for the Torah study, but Ruth had a feeling Katy would appreciate seeing her as soon as she entered the temple.

Wait. Was that her, stepping out of that Jeep on the far side of the parking lot? Yes. Hard to miss that beautiful blonde hair. Ruth watched as one of the Christian fanatics accosted Katy. She felt a momentary twinge of guilt. *I should have warned her about them.* But then Ruth saw Katy approach the woman—that tall one with the loud voice—and actually speak to her in a friendly way. Several congregants passed through the doors, greeting Ruth warmly, but she barely noticed, her attention focused on Katy across the parking lot.

Look at that. She's actually smiling *at that woman!*

Here was a family getting out of a Jeep, very nearby. What an opportunity! As the beautiful blonde woman ushered two children out onto the parking lot and locked the door of her vehicle, Martha Douglas called to her in a very loud voice. "Do you know where you'll spend eternity?"

The blonde woman turned toward her and said, "Yes."

Obviously her answer wasn't true. How could a Jew know where she was going when she died? If she really knew what eternity had in store for such as her, she'd become a Christian right away. Fortunately, Martha knew how to handle the woman's response. It fell neatly into one of the patterns Reverend Newton had taught her.

"Where will you be?" asked Martha.

Gathering the boy and girl beside her, the woman said, "Well, heaven, of course."

"Why should God let you into heaven?" Martha knew the Jew would probably say something like, "Because I've obeyed the Torah all my life," or "Because I'm one of God's chosen people."

The woman looked down at her little girl. "Tell her why, Jilly," she said.

The little girl said, "'Cause Jesus Christ is our Lord and Savior!"

That was a shocker!

"I thought y'all were Jewish," said Martha. The woman smiled. It seemed to Martha that her smile was a little bit strained, like she wasn't really happy, or maybe she was nervous about something. Martha said, "So I guess you're here to help out with the crusade?"

"Crusade? No. I was invited to come to a Bible study thing. A Torah study, or something."

"With *them*?"

"Uh-huh."

"But they're Jews!"

"Well, yes, that's true."

"But, I mean, you're a Christian. You can't go in there and study the Scriptures with them like there's no difference."

"I can't?"

"Of course not. What if they get the idea that you think it's okay not to believe in Jesus?" Martha looked at the woman more closely. "They don't believe in Jesus, you know."

"I know, but—"

"Have you really thought this through?"

With one hand on the shoulder of the little girl—the older boy stood too far away for his mother's touch—the woman stared at the temple building, where a middle-aged couple was entering through the covered portico. The man carried two large books and wore a blue crocheted yarmulke low on the back of his head. The blonde woman said, "Maybe I haven't given it enough thought."

"No, I don't think so."

"It's just . . . I was invited by one of their rabbis. She and I used to be friends, and I thought it would be rude to . . . you know . . . to turn her down. I mean, since she asked."

"Listen," said Martha Douglas. "If you go in there, you'll give those people the idea that you think it's okay not to believe in Jesus. What's worse? Being rude, or risking the damnation of your friend's immortal soul?"

"Maybe you're right."

Martha was surprised to see the little girl frowning up at her with obvious displeasure. Something about the little girl's expression gave Martha a vaguely uncomfortable sense that she might be making a mistake, but she could not think it through. Martha had never been an organized person. She often wished that she could be more logical, better able to think in a systematic fashion. Instead, the Lord had made Martha a feeling person. She had very strong feelings. She cared about others. She cared deeply about the Jews inside the temple, for example. Sometimes Martha suspected that one or two of the other members of the Nan Smith Crusade for Jews were there for personal reasons that had little to do with saving people, but she knew her own heart and her reason for witnessing this way. She loved the people in that building. She loved everyone everywhere, and she wanted everyone to share the source of her love. It was just that she felt too shy to actually get to *know* people. Maybe that was because she was six feet two inches tall. Men were intimidated by her, and women . . . well, women treated her like she was a man. Martha hadn't had a real friend since she was eleven years old—the year before she started growing fast. Besides, she never felt as if she had enough time to get to know people. She didn't know much about relationships, but she did know it took a lot of time to have one, at least for her.

Now that Martha thought about it, maybe it would be a good idea for this woman to go into the temple, after all. Wasn't that exactly what Reverend Newton kept saying he wished they all could do?

"You know," said Martha, "if you go in there with the right attitude, it might be okay."

"What do you mean?"

"Well, they won't let us in, but you've been invited. By a rabbi, even. It could be a chance to get right in the middle of them all, and then tell them about Jesus!"

"Oh, I don't think I could—"

"Sure!" said Martha, warming to the idea. "It's a golden opportunity."

"Mommy," said the little girl. "I think we should go inside."

The blonde woman looked up at Martha. Looked her right in the eyes. Not too many people did that. It made Martha nervous. Then the woman said, "What's your name?"

"Martha Douglas."

"I'm Kate Flint, Martha. You know, I had the strongest feeling that it wasn't right to do this. And you helped me understand why. I think you were right the first time. We just need to go."

"But Mommy—"

"Be quiet now, Jilly."

"Well," said Martha reluctantly, "if that's how the Lord is leading."

"Yes. I never felt right about going in there. Thanks for helping me see why."

"You're welcome."

Kate Flint cocked her head to one side. "Have we met before?"

"I don't think so."

Kate Flint paused, still looking at her. Martha felt uncomfortable under her scrutiny. Finally, Kate said, "Well, I guess we'll be going. Thanks again for showing me what I should do."

"You're welcome," said Martha. "Hey. Why don't you stay and help us witness?"

"I would, but we have to go to work now, don't we, kids?"

"Whatever," said the boy. The little girl frowned, saying nothing.

The beautiful woman and her son and daughter had already gotten back in their Jeep before Martha realized something was not right. If that woman could bring her kids to study the Torah with a bunch of Jews, why couldn't she do the same in order to join their crusade? It was a puzzle, but Martha did not spend much time trying to work it out. Instead, she turned back toward the temple and started looking for another Jew to save. Martha had never been much good at puzzles.

I can't believe she did that, thought Ruth, watching Kate and her children drive away. I can't believe she left!

"Hello, dear," said Gabrielle Cantor. "I hope we're not interrupting."

Ruth turned to find Gabby and Solomon Cantor standing five feet away. First Katy, and now them. What a miserable day. But she forced a smile and said, "What can I do for you?"

Sol scratched his graying beard. "Listen," he said, "I noticed last week that you were in a big hurry to get outta the room when I came in."

"Sol!" laughed Gabby as she looked around nervously. "Couldn't you be just a *little* more tactful?"

"No, Mrs. Cantor," said Ruth lifting her chin a bit and looking straight at Sol. "That's okay. He's right."

"Thought so," he said. "But I want you to know you've got no worries with me."

"When you came to the study, did you know who I was?" asked Ruth.

"'Course I did. You're one of the little girls who testified against me." He smiled, his eyes openly appraising her. "You're not so little now."

Ruth felt her stomach begin to roil.

"Ruth, dear," said his wife, "we feel just *awful* about the way things went last week. And we want you to know you can expect absolutely nothing but friendship from us. The past is past."

"That's nice, Mrs. Cantor, but—"

"Please! Call me Gabby. Remember?"

"Yeah," said the man. "And you can call me Sol."

"Thank you," said Ruth. "But like I told your wife before—"

"What?" he said, interrupting her.

"Uh, like I told your wife before, I—"

"When did you talk to her?"

"Sunday, I think. Or it might've been Monday. I don't remember, exactly. Whenever she came over to my house."

Sol turned to his wife, speaking in a low voice. "You never told me you went to her house."

Patting his arm, Gabby said, "Now, Sol, I just wanted to smooth things over—"

"Oh, *right*." Turning back to Ruth, he said, "Rabbi, I hope she didn't try to throw her weight around."

Gabby Cantor began to speak in an imperial tone. "Solomon, I hardly think—"

Raising his voice slightly, Sol interrupted. "You promised me you'd leave her alone." He leaned closer to Ruth—looming over her. "Lemme know if she bothers you again. Sometimes Gabby can be a little pushy."

Ruth knew he was correct, of course. Gabrielle Cantor had indeed come to her house to throw her weight around, and it had indeed been offensive, but Ruth didn't care about that anymore. She refused to give this man the satisfaction of being right. She said, "Gabby wasn't pushy, Mr. Cantor."

Sol stared at her for a moment, trying to communicate something with his eyes. Finally he said, "I'm just saying not to worry about us. Gabby and I wish you well, no matter how she acts."

With that, he took his wife's elbow and steered her away, down the corridor toward Wiltz Hall. Perhaps with any other couple, Ruth would not have noticed, but suddenly to her it appeared that Solomon Cantor was pulling his wife along like a wayward child. She imagined Sol's blunt fingers digging into the crisp linen of his wife's sleeve. Gabby Cantor looked back over her shoulder, and the rabbi could have sworn that Gabby's eyes were a window to the pain and humiliation in her heart.

It was too much.

"Hey!" shouted Ruth. Her voice echoed in the sedate hallway, a shocking violation of the calm of that place. "Hey, Cantor!" she shouted again. A middle-aged couple near the door stared at her, dumbfounded. Ruth didn't care. "You let her go!" she shouted, filled with righteous indignation. "Let go of her!"

Sol turned slowly, Gabby Cantor's elbow still in his grasp. Ruth strode up the corridor toward him. She did not remember making the decision to do so; she simply found that it was happening. Sol stood his ground, his facial expression relaxing into a neutral mask behind his beard. "What's the matter, Rabbi?"

Marching toward him, Ruth called loudly, "We won't have this kind of behavior here, Mr. Cantor."

"*What* kinda behavior?"

She was upon him now, a mere two feet away, in his face, staring up with her fists planted firmly on her waist. "We won't allow a man to drag his wife through our halls, Mr. Cantor. I'm afraid you'll have to leave."

"Are you crazy?"

"No, I am not. But I *am* serious. Now you leave this temple immediately."

Sol looked from the rabbi to his wife in confusion. "Gabby?" he said.

His wife said, "Ruth, honey, please don't make a scene."

"It's all right, Mrs. Cantor. I saw the way he handled you."

Solomon Cantor seemed genuinely puzzled. "What did I do?"

Gabby said, "That's just Sol, honey. That's just his way. You have to make allowances." Ruth stared at the older woman as she patted her husband's arm. "He's forgotten how to act is all. He doesn't mean anything."

A small cluster of people had gathered a few feet farther down the corridor, just outside the Wiltz Hall doorway. Two of them clutched Torahs to their chests for protection. Everyone stared at Ruth as if she'd lost her mind.

"But, Mrs. Cantor, he was *pulling* you down the hall."

Gabby Cantor laughed nervously, glancing around and patting Sol on the arm again. "That's my Sol, all right. Always in a hurry."

"In a *hurry*? You can't be serious!"

"Honey," whispered Gabby, "you need to relax a little bit. You seem very nervous."

"Is there a problem here?"

Ruth turned to find Sam Gottlieb standing behind her.

"Oh no, Rabbi," said Gabby Cantor. "Ruth just misunderstood something is all."

"Ruth?" said the senior rabbi.

"Sam, this man was dragging Mrs. Cantor down the hall—"

Gabby laughed again, her eyes flicking back to the crowd. "Oh dear. I hardly think he was *dragging* me."

Suddenly Ruth understood. This woman's fear of public opinion was greater than her fear of her husband, and with that realization, Ruth knew she was in trouble.

Sol smiled.

"But he *was* dragging you," said Ruth to Gabby, pleading with her. "He had you by the arm and he was pulling you. I saw the look you gave me."

"Rabbi Gottlieb, we have a simple misunderstanding here," said Gabrielle Cantor. She turned her eyes to Ruth. "I'm sure Rabbi Gold didn't mean anything by it."

Sam looked from Ruth to the Cantors, and back to Ruth again. "Ruth?" he asked.

Ruth shook her head, filled with doubt and confusion. Had she imagined it? Was she wrong? She felt the senior rabbi watching her but avoided his eye. "Okay," said Sam. "Let's just forget about this. What do you say?"

"Fine by me," said Sol Cantor, his eyes locked on Ruth.

"Ruth?" asked the rabbi.

Blushing, Ruth nodded.

"Good!" said Sam Gottlieb. He moved between the Cantors, wrapping an arm around each of them. "Now then, it's almost time to begin. Shall we find our seats while Rabbi Gold prepares to dazzle us with her scholarship?"

Solomon Cantor turned to Gabby. "I think maybe we better sit this one out, don't you?"

Gabby nodded. "Whatever you say, dear."

Standing in the corridor, Ruth watched them walk outside, arm in arm, as Rabbi Gottlieb stared at her and slowly shook his head.

Orvis had watched the conversation between Martha Douglas and the Christian girl from several yards away. He had been encouraged that it lasted so long. If Martha could convince the girl to join them, maybe he would not have to harm her after all. But apparently, it was not to be. The Christian girl had driven away.

Feeling the familiar depression settling in again, Orvis crossed the street to the park to sit in the deep purple shade of what he had come to call "Nan's Oak." The Bible said that Jesus often withdrew to be alone, and Orvis's disciples were accustomed to him doing the same. With his back against the gnarled trunk and his large Bible open on his lap, the evangelist pondered the inevitable circle of history that had passed beneath this tree so long ago, and again, here and now. Orvis thought of Nan lingering over picnic lunches here with him. To be in the same place once more, engaged in the same work, and doing it in Nan's name . . . what other proof of divine providence did he need? From the Garden of Eden to the New Jerusalem of Revelation, all was a circle and just as there was a Tree of Life in both places, Nan's Oak had been a mute witness to Orvis's passion, then and now. He thought of the warm touch of Nan's hand in his as they had knelt in prayer beneath the sheltering boughs of this gentle giant. Their hearts had been in perfect accord; he was sure of it.

True, Nan had insisted that their touch was merely that of a sister and brother in Christ, but Orvis felt certain that her shy denial of their rising ardor had been a chaste attempt to wrap her tender emotions in a cloak of piety until the proper time—an entirely appropriate response from such a godly woman, but it was hardly indicative of her heart's true desire.

Using a thick red marker, Orvis drew lines through several verses in his Bible, blotting them out. For Orvis, the Word of God had been reduced to stark simplicity. After twenty-five years of wondering why the Lord would let his dear Nan die, Orvis finally understood the Plan, and nothing else mattered. In fact, all else was a distraction, meant for other men, lesser men, those who had not received a revelation such as his. He turned the page, and crossed out more unnecessary words.

Oh, Nan. Darling, if only you had listened. If only you had not gone inside that day.

Tears came, as they had so many times before, falling to the open pages of his Bible. Orvis knew that his beloved Nan would have surrendered to his entreaties for marriage sooner or later, just as he knew she would have seen his way was best when it came to evangelizing Jews. Had she not been so cruelly taken —and by a Jew—oh, the irony!—Nan would have learned the hardness of the Jewish heart, the stiffness of their necks. You could not draw them to the cross simply by modeling Christ's love, as Nan had hoped in her precious naïveté; you had to goad Jews to salvation. After all, Christ had been a tiger when faced with such as them: whipping their backs and overturning their tables in the temple, pronouncing woe upon them and calling them hypocrites. *That* was how you treated Jews. It was the only way to penetrate the hardened shell that Satan cast around their hearts. Sooner or later, Nan would have understood if she had been given more time.

Fortunately, he and he alone knew that Nan had been unwise in the end. All the world saw her as the spiritual founder of his ministry, the source of his wisdom and his methods. Of course, Orvis had carefully cultivated that perception, knowing that it might not be strictly true but also knowing that a martyr's memory could bring more financial contributions than any living minister. And Orvis knew if Nan had been allowed a long life, she would eventually have seen the truth and blessed his methods.

A long life. His dearest Nan had deserved that, and so much more. But now, behold, the very Jews who had stolen his beloved were plotting in their synagogues to rob him even of her reputation with their filthy lies.

Orvis felt the familiar rage rising to displace his tears. He tried to focus on his Bible. The Word had always been a friend in moments such as these, whenever anger threatened the peace of God, so now he turned to the Scriptures again. Taking up his thick red marker, Orvis Newton continued blotting out the extra verses, the ones that did not matter anymore. With each new stroke of the pen, he felt renewed commitment to God's Plan.

Driving away from the temple, Kate could not suppress a nagging insistence that she had made a mistake. The tall woman's argument had made sense while they were standing there in the temple parking lot, but it rang hollow now. What if Jesus had thought the same way? What if he had declined dinner invitations from those whom the religious people of his day called "sinners"?

Maybe she should turn around and . . .

No.

Let God find someone stronger, someone who could think on her feet and have the courage to go into a foreign place without being consumed by fear. Right now, she should head for the shop. She should be there now, getting ready to open. In fact, she shouldn't have let Ruth talk her into this at all. Her job was to be a good mother, nothing else.

Passing Audubon Park, Kate noticed several police cars and what appeared to be a hearse parked on the grass at the edge of a small wooded area. Yellow tape stretched from tree to tree, fluttering in the breeze. That morning she had heard on the news about the animals escaping from the zoo, which was just on the far side of the park. She had heard they found a dead zebra, but obviously they hadn't brought the hearse for a zebra.

Someone must have died. Someone went to the park to run or something, and instead, some animal killed them.

Kate shuddered.

Whoever they planned to put in that hearse had been a fool to be in the park after sunset. Look what happened when you went where you didn't belong. It was an old lesson, something Kate had learned firsthand years ago from a missionary bleeding to death in a kitchen.

It dragged her right through here," said the patrolman.

Lieutenant Washington nodded, staring at the ground. "Yeah. Kinda looks that way."

"Kinda? Shoot, Lieutenant, you can see the marks right there. See how them leaves is brushed away along here? That trail leads straight to the lagoon."

"Yeah. I can see that, DuFeaux. Why don't you get some more tape strung up? I want it thirty feet back from this, uh, this trail here, on both sides." Washington straightened his Italian silk tie and gazed back toward the deep brush of the woods. "Run it on into those woods."

"How far in there, Lieu?"

"Far as that trail seems to go, and then a few more yards."

Just then a sound rose from the trees, starting low but quickly rising until it drowned out the noise of the nearby traffic on St. Charles Avenue. It was clearly an animal call, but neither the lieutenant nor the patrolman had any idea what kind. They stood side by side, staring at the grove of oaks, listening. The patrolman chewed a large wad of gum, the muscles at his temples bulging with each smacking clench of his jaw. He was twenty-three, with almost two years on the job, and already he'd seen a dozen murders and dealt with sociopaths of every description, but nothing could have prepared him for this. He turned to look at Lieutenant Washington, his eyes settling onto the smaller man's little golden earring.

Trying to keep the fear out of his voice, Officer DuFeaux said, "Think whatever killed her is still in there?"

Washington shrugged. "Maybe. Something sure is. Take a couple of guys and go see." Washington turned toward the cluster of men and women at the edge of the lagoon. DuFeaux followed his gaze toward the three or four uniforms looking on as a forensics team examined the body down at the water's edge, out of sight. A man and a young woman stood with them, staring over the edge of the lagoon. Both wore pale olive shirts with the Audubon Zoo logo over their hearts. Beyond them, two fountains in the center of the lagoon shot continuous streams of water skyward, filling the air with a peaceful sound.

Washington asked, "Isn't Terry wearing a .357 over there?"

Patrolman DuFeaux grinned. "Yeah. We call him 'Dirty Terry' sometimes."

Washington did not return DuFeaux's grin. "Take him with you. Tell him to keep his hand on his weapon and his snap off."

"Could we wait for some more guys to show up? Maybe call in for some rifles?"

Washington shrugged. "Sure. If you don't mind letting the perp get away."

"Perp? Come on, Lieu. You can't really call it that."

"Why not?"

"It's an animal. Animals ain't perps, exactly."

"You sure about that?"

"'Course I am. It's instinct for them."

"No. I mean, are you sure the killer was an animal?"

The patrolman gaped at the lieutenant. "You saw her leg, Lieu."

Washington nodded.

"Them cuts was parallel, all up and down her calf," continued DuFeaux, smacking his gum. "Like them zoo people said, it had to be claws that did that. Big claws."

"Yeah," said Washington, waving his hand toward the forensics team at the edge of the lagoon. "But why'd it drag her over there?"

"Who knows? Ask the zoo guys."

"I did. They have no idea."

"What's the big mystery? I seen big cats do it on TV all the time. It's a security thing. They kill things out in the open, then drag 'em back to the bushes so's they can relax while they eat."

Washington stared at DuFeaux. The patrolman waited, his temples bulging in time with his jaw's constant motion. When Washington said nothing, DuFeaux said, "What?"

"Look at the trail, DuFeaux."

The patrolman stared at the ground. "Yeah . . . so?"

Washington sighed. "*Look* at it. What do you see?"

"Uh . . . there's blood there, and over there, too, and there's this long, smoothed-out streak in the dirt. I figure that's where her body slid along the ground." He looked up at the lieutenant. "Right?"

"Is that all you see?"

"Well, yeah," said the patrolman defensively.

Washington snorted. "Just go get Terry and string the tape."

"What? What did I miss?"

"You missed what's missing, DuFeaux."

The patrolman studied the ground again. "Missing?"

"Anything with claws big enough to slice a leg open like that oughta leave a pretty big paw print, don'tcha think?"

"Oh . . . yeah. There's none of them."

"Nope."

DuFeaux pondered that fact for a moment, then brightened. "Hey! Maybe it was backing up when it dragged her through here, so's her body covered up its paw prints."

"Now you're thinking, DuFeaux. But shouldn't there be at least one or two prints along here somewhere?"

He stuck out his jaw. "Maybe not."

Washington rubbed his eyes wearily. "Okay. You're right. That's possible. Not likely, but possible. So what about that TV show?"

"Huh?"

"See anything else here that doesn't make sense?"

The patrolman scratched his head. "Uh . . . ."

"Come on, DuFeaux. You said it yourself a minute ago. Where do big cats like to eat?"

"In the bushes . . . " He smacked at the gum for a moment, thinking. "Hey! It dragged her out into the open. That's the wrong way!"

Lieutenant Washington said nothing. Instead, he set off toward the lagoon, where the unidentified woman still lay facedown in the water with her mutilated leg on the shore.

Watching him go, DuFeaux stopped chewing and blew a bubble. It popped. He licked the thin pink membrane off his lips and began chewing again, wishing he had a rifle.

H ey, Orvis! I tol' you stay off dat phone now. I ain't kiddin'."

Orvis Newton hung up the telephone and waved at the little man sitting in the barber's chair at the far end of the shop. The little man was Salvatore "Sally" DiConcino, owner of the barbershop next door to Orvis's storefront ministry headquarters in New Orleans' desperately poor Irish Channel. Sally usually didn't object to his using the telephone, so long as his calls were local and he didn't monopolize the thing, but all morning Orvis had been calling television and radio stations, telling them about the great things the Sister Nan Smith Crusade for Jews was doing at Temple Brit Yisrael. The evangelist had tried to make them understand the historical importance of the ministry, the awe-inspiring connection between his work today and Sister Nan's work at the very same spot a quarter century ago. Only one station had seemed interested. They said they'd get back to him, maybe arrange an on-camera interview at the temple for later in the week. He smiled, thinking how proud Nan would have been.

Orvis owed everything to Nan. Without the memory of her spotless reputation, he would never have been able to keep the ministry alive all these years, preaching to the poor in the Irish Channel, feeding them with the Word of God. But lately, since he had renamed the ministry and narrowed the focus to Jews, interest in the ministry had fallen off. Some of his oldest supporters, the ones who had known Nan personally, had passed away. Trinity Bible Church, one of his oldest ministry partners, had cut off its support when it learned about his sidewalk evangelism campaign to save the Jews. Orvis needed new sources of revenue. For that, he needed to resurrect the city's memories of Sister Nan Smith.

The evangelist leaned back against the vinyl cushion of the barber-shop sofa, stretching his legs straight out in front and tilting his head to study the cracked plaster ceiling. Above him a fan hung motionless, one of its broken blades dangling precariously above his head like the sword of Damocles. Soon the Jews would celebrate the Day of Atonement— *Yom Kippur.* Their temple would swell to overflowing with those who attended services only on the high holy days. His ministry would be on the scene in a very special way. Not just with signs and slogans. No, Orvis had something much more appropriate in mind to honor Nan's sacrifice. He had already made the necessary arrangements with a man who owned a small farm north of Lake Pontchartrain. It could be a golden opportunity to reach hundreds of marginally religious Jews, and it only came around once each year. Plus, it should get him at least three minutes on the local news.

But he needed help. To impress the media, he needed many others. Maybe he could find some support at Trinity Bible Church tomorrow. They had thrown Martha out, but he would return to show goodwill. Nothing could stop him from fulfilling this glorious mission. Of course, he must also fulfill the next part of the Plan. Both ministries were essential, and to keep them going he had been living on three hours' sleep each night for weeks. In fact, Orvis sometimes went two days with no sleep at all. The Lord provided all the energy he needed. And fortunately, the next part of the Plan could be delegated to others, so he could continue with the preparations for the Day of Atonement undistracted.

Orvis checked his watch. Oh, how he wished he could be there to see the Plan unfold!

TWENTY

Kate strolled along Chartres, leading the children past five nearly identical French Quarter town houses and the Richelieu Hotel. They had closed the shop for fifteen minutes to dash up the street to a corner grocery for a late lunch; now they were returning with three po'boys and a large bag of chips to go. The nagging sense of uneasiness still tugged at the fringes of her consciousness as it had all morning, ever since she left the parking lot of Temple Brit Yisrael. But by now, she had almost convinced herself it was nothing more than guilt for opening her antique shop an hour later than usual. The responsibility of earning enough money to support the kids had been a heavy burden since John passed away. She had no right to pass up valuable sales hours just to make Ruth happy.

Lost in her thoughts, Kate almost collided with a slender iron pole supporting a delicate wrought-iron balcony.

"Hey, Mom," called Paul. "You need glasses?"

"Mind your own business, wise guy," she growled.

In spite of himself, Paul grinned. Kate adjusted her backpack and picked up the pace, with the kids tagging along behind. As they drew near the shop, Kate saw a white piece of paper slipped between the wooden door and the frame. She removed it and read:

> Katy,
>   Sorry I missed you. I'm downtown shopping. Can you meet me at Tower Records at 5:30? I thought we could go somewhere for dinner.
> Ruth

"How come she calls you Katy all the time?" asked Paul, reading with her.

"That's what everyone used to call me when I was little."

"Like we call Jilly 'Jilly,' even though her name is really Jill?"

"Uh-huh." She opened the door and entered the shop. The kids followed her inside.

"But you're not little anymore," said Paul. "Why does she still call you that?"

Something in his voice made Kate turn to look at her son. "Does it bother you?"

"I don't like her having her own name for you."

"Why not?"

"I don't know," he said brusquely. "Forget it."

He passed her and continued toward the back, flipping on lights as he went. Jilly followed him. Kate watched them go, thinking, *He's jealous of Ruth. Who would've thought it?*

"Paul," she called, "wait up." He turned, his face set in a neutral mask. She approached him. "Listen. You know how much I love you?"

"Yeah, sure."

Kate hugged him. He stood passively within her embrace. She said, "There's nobody more important to me than you and Jilly, honey."

Pushing away, he mumbled, "Whatever," and walked into the tiny bathroom beneath the stairs and closed the door.

After lunch, Kate entered the stockroom and slipped on a man's

cotton dress shirt smeared with paint and wood stain. She had comman-
deered the shirt from John's closet years ago to wear whenever she refin-
ished reproduction furniture for the shop. John had laughed the first time
he saw her in it, delighted that the tail hung to her knees, but today, Kate
did not think of him in her preoccupation with the ill-defined uneasiness
that had descended on her at Ruth's temple. No nostalgia, no interior
monologue, no argument she could offer seemed enough to penetrate this
anxiety.

What she needed was to lose herself in some hard work.

Kate had hardly begun sanding a reproduction Stickley armchair when
Paul poked his head into the stockroom. "There's a guy here to see you."

"Customer?"

"Naw. It's that guy from before. The locksmith."

She felt an immediate rush of adrenaline. "Tell him I'll be right out."

When Kate emerged from the storeroom five minutes later, she had
removed John's old shirt and tucked her T-shirt into her faded jeans. Her
long blonde hair was freshly brushed and newly applied lipstick accentu-
ated her full lips. Paul took one look and rolled his eyes. She frowned and
waved her son away, indicating without words that he was to stay right
there in the back of the shop.

Jake Singer stood beside the front door, examining the lock.

"Hello," said Kate, walking his way. "This is a surprise."

He spun at the sound of her voice. "Hey, Mrs. Flint."

"Call me Kate, remember?"

"Sure. And I'm Jake."

"I remember."

"You do? Good! I mean . . . I hope it's okay that I dropped by. I
remembered you saying y'all might need new locks at your shop, and
I was in the neighborhood, and . . . " He shrugged.

Kate tried not to let her disappointment show. "Oh. So you're here
about our locks?"

"If you're still interested."

"Oh, sure. Yeah." She waved at the door dismissively. "Go ahead and
change that one."

"Thanks."

The man knelt and opened the door, inspecting the lock closely.

Meanwhile, Kate returned to the back of the shop and sat dejectedly
at her desk.

Standing nearby, Paul said, "What's the deal with that guy?"

"Don't you have some homework or something?"

Paul stared at her. "You like him?"

"Just sit down at that table over there and crack a book, okay?"

"Oh, Mom."

"Go on now, mister."

Paul moaned but did as he was told.

Kate pretended to work on her ledger, idly punching numbers into
a calculator, but she couldn't keep her eyes off the gorgeous man at her
front door. After about twenty minutes, he rose and walked toward her.
She felt her pulse leap as he approached, until she knew her cheeks must
be fire-engine red.

"I got you a new deadbolt installed up there," said Jake Singer,
wiping his hands with a rag. "That lock was as old as some of this furniture, I'll bet."

Kate laughed too loudly.

He grinned, watching her. "Is that your son, or does he work for
you?"

"He's my son. Paul."

"How old is he?"

"Twelve." She smiled. "And a half."

"I would've guessed sixteen or seventeen, maybe."

"Really?"

"Yeah, from the way he carries himself and all. Seems like a nice kid."

"Thanks."

"Seems like I remember a little girl too. She answered your door the
other night."

"Yes. Jilly. She's under that buffet over there."

He bent at the waist to get a better look at Jilly under the buffet, flat
on her belly, giving her doll a ride in a truck. The Star of David at his
neck dangled freely outside his shirt for a moment, then fell back against
his skin when he straightened. Looking back at Kate, he said, "Cute as a
bug. Bet you've got your hands full with the two of them."

"Uh-huh."

They fell silent for a moment. *I'm no good at this*, thought Kate. *I should say something.*

Jake said, "Well, I was thinking, you're down here in the Quarter and all, and you've got the kids with you . . . do you think they'd like to go to the aquarium? I mean, you too, of course."

Filled with emotions she did not understand, Kate stared at her reflection in a nearby mirror, which was spotted with black where the silver had fallen away over the last two hundred years.

Jake rushed to fill the silence. "Or else we could take them to see a movie. That remake of *Moby Dick* is showing over on Canal."

Still, she did not speak.

"I'm sorry," he said. "Maybe I should go."

"No!" she almost shouted. "No, it's okay. I just . . . I . . . uh . . . I have plans for tonight is all." *Why did I say that? This isn't right. It isn't right.*

"Okay. How about tomorrow? I think the aquarium's open until six on Sundays. We could grab a bite to eat afterward."

The loneliness inside her whispered, *Go ahead.*

"Okay," she said. "That sounds like fun."

"Great! I'll come by your place and pick you up about three-thirty. That'll give us a couple of hours at the aquarium, and then we can go someplace for dinner. How's that?"

"Okay, but nothing fancy, foodwise. Sometimes the kids get a little rambunctious."

"No problem. I'll eat anything."

After Jake Singer had collected his tools and gone, Kate sat for a while, struggling with conflicting emotions. *No good can come of this*, she thought. *He's a Jew, and I'm a Christian. What am I doing?* But then she caught a glimpse of her own reflection in the black-speckled mirror; she was smiling.

uth arrived home at five, pulling into her usual parking spot by the curb and emerging from the Citroën with her arms full of books. Her head was throbbing.

Sam Gottlieb had cornered her in her office after *Mekhkar Torah* and read her the riot act about the scene with the Cantors in the hallway. She knew she had been wrong, so why chew her out? It was the first time Ruth had ever seen the senior rabbi so close to losing his temper. To top it all off, Katy got chummy with those anti-Semitic jerks outside the temple, then turned around and left without even bothering to come inside! If Katy had just done the right thing, given those people the cold shoulder and come directly inside, who knows what might have happened? Cantor might have backed off, knowing they were united against him, or he might have lost control in front of everyone and . . . and . . . but no, *she* was the one who had lost control and ruined everything, while Katy joined the opposition!

Her head was absolutely killing her.

Carefully balancing the books under one arm, Ruth twisted the key in the lock and opened the door. Since Steve and Morton had been killed, she'd been afraid to enter her home alone, even with the new locks. Katy's break-in had confirmed her fears. And the police were useless. They'd removed her protective surveillance after only one night, promising to drive past her house every hour or so. As if that would keep her safe.

Remaining outside, she bent to peer through the open door, searching the living room for signs of an intruder. A white piece of paper lay on the floor just inside the door below the mail slot. She entered cautiously and set the books on a table near the door. Stooping, she picked up the paper and read:

> *Ruth,*
> *Meet me in the Quarter at Tower Records at 5:30. It's important.*
> *Katy*

Ruth considered ignoring the note. Katy had stood her up; why shouldn't she do the same? But reason immediately prevailed. If she wanted Katy's help, that was the last thing she should do. With a sigh, Ruth turned and stepped back outside, latching the door behind herself and returning to her car. What on earth could Katy want at Tower Records? Was this her way of apologizing? Ruth certainly hoped she wouldn't expect her to go shopping on *Shabbat*.

TWENTY-ONE

As Ruth drove across town, rubbing her temple in a vain attempt to relieve her aching head, she thought about the terse wording of Katy's summons. That's what it was, really—a summons. If Katy had any respect for her time, she would not have set up the meeting this way, with no advance notice and no chance to postpone. While sitting at a stoplight, Ruth lifted the note from the passenger seat and scanned it again. Each time she read the thing, it made her more angry, yet there she was, driving toward the French Quarter just as Katy wished.

Katy reminded her of Isaac, the way she remained so calm and maddeningly reasonable when Ruth lost her temper. Isaac had been that way, too. And he could usually get Ruth to do what he wanted, just like she was doing what Katy wanted now, in spite of a monster headache and being deliberately stood up at temple this morning. Yes, Katy and Isaac had a lot in common. Too much, in fact. Ruth thought about a time—oh my, was it really ten years ago?—in her second year out of Hebrew Union with her second *Yom Kippur* in the rabbinate fast approaching. She'd been very worried that things might not go well. Then Isaac had come home for the holidays and . . .

W hat do you mean you're out of tickets?"

"I'm sorry, Isaac," said Ruth. "You should have called to tell us you were coming."

He had appeared without warning at her one-room apartment over the Silversteins' garage, Ruth's first home of her own after returning to New Orleans. He was supposed to be in Princeton, New Jersey, studying economics, but there he was at her doorstep instead, eyes flashing with the intensity of his annoyance. Isaac was beautiful when he was angry. She used to tease him by saying that, but it was true. Her brother had received their mother's huge green eyes, which glowed with an inner light whenever he felt passionate about anything. He had also inherited their father's strong, square chin and placid disposition. Even when he was angry Isaac remained calm. Sometimes she hated that about him.

"Since when do I have to tell you I'm coming home for the holy days? I *always* come home for the holy days."

"Well, naturally, we assumed this year would be different." She stood in her doorway, blocking his view of the interior of her apartment.

"Why?"

"Come on, Isaac. You can't be serious."

"Of course, I'm serious! I wanna know why you thought you didn't need to get me a ticket." When she didn't answer, he said, "Aren't Mom and Dad going?"

"Of course."

"And Aunt Gilda? You gonna drag her out of the rest home like last year?"

"Yes. If she's able."

"Okay. What if she's not? Do I get to use her ticket?"

"Why do you want to, Isaac?"

"What kind of question is that? I'm still part of this family! I'm still a Jew!"

"No, you're not, Isaac. You threw that away."

His head jerked back but his shoulders remained motionless. It was an odd reaction, as if she had struck a physical blow. For a moment they stood still, staring at each other, and then Isaac turned and left without another word.

T he light turned green. Ruth lowered her window, wadded the note into a tight ball, and flung it into the street.

A few minutes later she found a parking spot near the Mint—naturally there was nothing any closer—and set out on foot along Decatur. Her headache had not abated. If anything, the traffic noise and her bitter memories had made it worse. She pressed the fingers of her left hand against the bridge of her nose as she walked, wary of idle teenagers standing in recessed doorways. You never knew what could happen with so many drunks and addicts hanging around. Then she remembered the gun in her purse. Relaxing a bit in spite of her pain, Ruth allowed herself to speculate on why Katy had summoned her. Tower Records was such a strange place to meet. She sincerely hoped Katy was not planning to take her to the nearby French Market. The noise and tourists would absolutely drive her over the edge. Besides, the last thing her hips needed was a beignet at the Café du Monde.

She hurried past a walk-up daiquiri shop, shaking her head at the idea of selling frozen rum drinks to go and filling the sidewalks with even more drunks. As if the police didn't have enough problems. A group of kids, runaways no doubt, stood along the wall, slurping the colorful concoctions; every one of their faces was pierced by metallic objects and caked with pasty white makeup, their hair shaved off in some places and long, stringy, and multicolored in others. Ugly children drinking liquor on the street: so much for the gentility of the Vieux Carre.

Ruth passed the Pontalba Apartments and rushed along in the shade of the banana trees bordering verdant Jackson Square. Over toward the cathedral, astride his perpetually rearing horse, Andrew Jackson doffed his weathered bronze hat. Once draped with confetti from a cheering crowd

after his victory over "the bloody English," the old general now wore a
less noble substance deposited by pigeons. Were she Andrew Jackson
high upon his pedestal, Ruth would keep her hat on.

Ten minutes late by the clock on the cathedral, Ruth increased her
pace. Tower Records was just ahead on the left. Her head throbbed with
each heartbeat. She should be at home in bed with the blinds drawn.
Willing herself to ignore the pain, Ruth dashed across the street through
an opening in the traffic. She stepped through the glass doors into the
music store and paused to look around. The girl behind the cashier counter to her left seemed to be marking time until she could join the kids
at the daiquiri shop. Metal studs lined the tops of her eyebrows. Black
lipstick adorned her mouth. Gauging by her pale complexion, Ruth
assumed the child had not been touched by sunlight for several years.
A tattooed wreath of dark blue thorns wrapped her neck.

She smiled gloriously. "Welcome to Tower Records."

Surprised by the girl's friendliness and the beauty of her smile, Ruth
returned her greeting weakly, forcing herself to smile as well.

Katy did not appear to be on the ground floor, so Ruth ascended
the stairs. On the second floor, she opened a glass door on the left and
checked the classical music department. No Katy. Turning back, she
walked past an information counter. The young black man working there
had shoulder-length hair wadded into thick, ropy strands. It swayed to
and fro as he bobbed his head in time to the reggae music pulsing from
the speakers. He smiled. Everyone was so friendly here. Ruth returned his
smile, amused to think how clean-cut he seemed compared with the cashier and the kids she'd passed outside.

The pounding in her head seemed to synchronize with the beat of
the music. Ruth rubbed her temples. Why was she here? Oh yeah. She
needed Katy's help.

Looking down at the first floor, she noticed the multipunctured
cashier speaking on a tiny cellular phone. Obviously, the girl didn't
earn enough money at the music store to pay for such a device. Ruth
wondered if her parents had provided it for her in a desperate effort to
keep her safe. *Call us if you're ever in trouble, honey. We'll come, no matter where
you are.* The metal studs in the girl's eyebrows glittered in the light. Ruth
tried to imagine the pain of a parent with a daughter who scarred herself

forever with tattoos and scraps of steel. She felt anger rising and turned away, warning herself to take care. *With this headache, I need to keep my mouth shut around Katy, or I'll overreact again for sure.*

Julio Jones checked the clip on the automatic weapon. He couldn't believe his luck. Jet could've picked anybody for this, but here he was holdin' a real Uzi. Julio wiped his nose with his palm, then wiped his palm on the front of his T-shirt. A dull blue swastika covered the back of his hand. Each of his knuckles bore a single tattooed letter: H-A-T-E on one hand and F-E-A-R on the other. He leaned to the left to catch his reflection in the car's rearview mirror, liking what he saw: eyes lined with black, steel ring through his nose, head shaved with just a little tail of black hair starting high in back and falling to below his shoulders, like them samurai warriors in that movie they snuck into last night. Julio lifted the Uzi so he could see what he looked like, holding it next to his face in the mirror. He gave it a little shake, thinking, *Yeah! Julio Jones— samurai warrior!*

"Put dat down, stupid!" yelled Jet, turning to look back at him from the driver's seat.

"Don't call me stupid, man," snarled Julio. He lowered the weapon and sank back. Sometimes he hated Jet. Always bossin' him around, actin' like he was in charge. But Jet did have good connections. He could get crack when everyone else was tapped out, and now he gone and come up with this deal here, an Uzi and a couple hundred bucks, just for poppin' a couple of chicks. One of them was even a Jew.

If Jet only knew, thought Julio, exposing gray teeth with a crooked grin. *I woulda done the Jew for free.*

Julio thought Jet looked kinda like Elvis Presley, with his black hair slicked back and a paisley shirt from the Goodwill store. Right now, he was talking to Candy on a cell phone. Jet was excellent at boostin' phones. He was pretty good at boostin' cars, too. He'd had this cherry red Nova fired up in under twenty seconds without no key. They ripped it off over in Storyville 'bout ten minutes ago. Julio found a bunch of rap CDs in the front seat. Jet had pitched that monkey music into the street soon as they drove away, and tuned in an industrial station on the radio.

He was all bent outta shape 'cause they was late or somethin'. Kept sayin' they was gonna miss the chick, and then they wouldn't get paid the other half o' what this guy owed. Julio wished he knew who the man was, but Jet wouldn't tell nothing 'bout the business arrangements, 'cept the man was someone he met over in Audubon Park the other night. He got mad when Julio asked for more than that, so Julio gave up on tryin' to find that out and just went along for the ride, glad for what he got. It didn't pay to get Jet mad.

Jet hung up the phone. "Candy say de Jew just walked in."

"Okay," said Julio, turning toward the window to watch the tourists on the sidewalks as they drove by. Nothin' but fat dumb cows waiting to be milked. Julio and everyone he knew made their meat off o' them fat dumb cows.

Aw-right. They was coming up on Daiquiri Debbie's. Julio sat up straight and craned his neck to see past the tourists on the sidewalk. Hey. There they were. Some o' his runnin' buddies catchin' a rum buzz.

"Hey, Jet," he said. "There's Slit an' Elmo an' the rest o' them guys. Over there doin' daiquiris."

"Yeah, whatevah," said Jet, driving with his wrist draped casually over the wheel. "Just keep you eye peeled for dem women, you. We late."

"All right. Sure."

Jet talked funny, 'cause he was one o' them swamp boys from over by Abbeville or somewhere.

"Dey be comin' up on de banquette heah. By de record store."

"I know that, Jet. You don't gotta tell me that."

"Well, you lookin' out de wrong way."

"I was just lookin' to see if the boys was there, all right? Man, you act like I'm stupid."

Jet said, "You say it, you." Then he reached down and cranked up the stereo. Nine Inch Nails roared from the oversized speakers behind the backseat, playing a classic and cutting off any chance of further conversation.

Man, it was loud! Julio felt his anger soar with the raging eighteen-inch woofers. He slipped his finger into the trigger guard of the Uzi and stared at the back of Jet's greasy head, thinking, *One o' these days, man. One o' these days.*

Jilly had lost her shoes somewhere in the shop, and Kate and Paul had searched everywhere, finally finding them beneath a burled walnut Edwardian buffet, so now Kate and the children approached Ruth's strange rendezvous at about fifteen minutes till six. Kate worried that Ruth would take their tardiness as a sign of disrespect, especially after what had happened at the temple this morning. They hurried along the southwest side of St. Peter in the cool ribbon of late afternoon shade falling onto Jackson Square from the Pontalba Apartments. The September heat and humidity siphoned excess water from Kate's pores until her tie-dyed T-shirt was soaked at the armpits. They turned right on Decatur and were soon within sight of the music store. It occupied two floors in a yellow-and-white building called the Marketplace on the river side of North Peters, across from where Peters and Decatur and Conti formed a grassy triangle, and a statue of Jean-Baptiste le Moyne de Bienville stood facing downtown, with a friar and an Indian chief at his feet. For the life of her, Kate could not fathom why Ruth would pick such a place to meet. It was hardly a picturesque location. Ruth could just as easily have selected some shade-dappled restaurant courtyard with table service and the soothing sound of water trickling from a cast-iron fountain.

She surveyed the sidewalk across the street, searching for Ruth, half hoping she would not show up. A bearded man, caught her eye; he was sitting in an old pickup truck parked at the curb just beyond the statue of Bienville. For an instant, he seemed to look right at her. When their eyes met, Kate felt a twinge of recognition, but then he looked away, and she decided it was nothing at all. Just her nervousness rising to the surface.

Kate really did not want to face Ruth after standing her up at temple. Still, standing her up twice in the same day would be even worse, so Kate decided to try a little prayer, to ask God to keep Ruth from being angry. But ever since Jake Singer's visit to her shop, uninvited images of him had invaded her mind like honey softly swirling to the bottom of a teacup. Now, visions of his pale blue eyes and full lips slowly prevailed in her mental ebb and flow, until the desire to see him again completely saturated her mind, edging out all thoughts of Ruth and God. Although she knew it was wrong, Kate's prayers sank beneath a pervasive sea of loneliness, and she thought only of Jake Singer.

"Mom?"

Kate looked at her son. He returned her gaze with a puzzled frown. She realized she had closed her eyes, right there on the busy sidewalk. *Snap out of it*, she thought. *You've got things to do.* Kate scanned the passing crowd unsuccessfully for Ruth. Probably she was waiting in the air-conditioned music store. They should cross the street.

"Kids, I want both of you to take my hands. We'll run across together, all right?"

Jilly immediately grasped her hand, but Paul rolled his eyes.

"Come on, Paul," said Kate, holding her hand out to him.

Just as he reached for her, she heard an awful noise and glanced back at the road. For the next ten seconds everything seemed to happen in slow motion.

It was almost six o'clock and Katy still wasn't there. Ruth was out of patience. She stared out the store window, mentally cursing the name-less Jamaicans who had recorded the marijuana-induced, half-beat reggae currently assaulting her ears and rattling the window glass. Why did they play the music so loudly in this store? Didn't they know their customers were trying to select other recordings at listening stations all over the sales floor? Ruth was certain you could hear the reggae right through a pair of headphones. What if you were trying to pick out a nice Gershwin recording or something else?

Wait. The glass was vibrating to a different rhythm.

She soon understood why. Peering outside to her right, Ruth saw a bright red car. Pedestrians turned to watch as it passed, some of them covering their ears. She could now hear the car's music more clearly than the reggae inside the store, and it was still half a block away. She marveled at the stupidity of the people in the car. Their hearing would be destroyed in no time if they kept that up. Ruth lifted her hands to her temples and rubbed, willing the headache to die. Where was Katy?

There! Just beyond that car. That was her on the far side of the street. Ruth headed for the door.

An old red car with all four of its windows down approached Kate and the kids along Decatur. Incredibly loud music spewed from its interior, an indistinguishable cacophony of sounds: steel grating on steel and harsh screams that seemed to have no relationship to the relentlessly pounding primitive beat. The car rolled by slowly, no faster than the tourists strolling to and from Jackson Square. It passed the dented old pickup truck filled with junk across the street. Kate saw the bearded man stare at it, his eyes filled with a fierce hardness.

Inch by inch, the car drew closer to the curb, until it almost collided with a mule-drawn carriage. The carriage driver cursed the car, shaking his fist in the air. The car swerved at the last second, narrowly missing the carriage full of frightened women, pulling even with Kate's position. Holding tightly to her children's hands, she watched as the car rolled slowly past, belching out snarling, unintelligible voices. Standing between her son and daughter, holding their hands, Kate drew the children away from the curb as she looked inside the passing car. She saw two men, one driving and the other in the backseat. The man in back lifted a small object from his lap and leaned toward the far window. His body concealed the object until they had driven on a little ways, but then, through the car's rear window, Kate saw it was some kind of gun, and it was aimed across the street.

She lifted her eyes to the other side of Decatur just as Ruth Gold emerged from the music store.

Julio loved Nine Inch Nails. The music touched the anger inside him, validating it, making it seem so natural. He leaned back with his eyes closed, finger on the trigger, muzzle pointed at the seat in front of him, shaking his head erratically to the beat. His long pigtail flopped around, slapping him on the cheeks, neck, and shoulders. He loved the feel of it, so long and ropy, as he rocked from side to side, completely immersed in the sounds pulsing from the huge speakers behind his seat.

Suddenly, he felt hands slapping his shaved cranium. Enraged, he opened his eyes to see Jet twisted around up front, trying to drive with his knees, slapping him and yelling at him, all at the same time.

"Hey, man!" screamed Julio. "Cut it out!"

Jet yelled something back at him. Even though they were less than three feet apart, Julio couldn't hear a word.

"What?" he screamed. "What?"

Jet continued to yell, growing red in the face. He looked so ridiculous, Julio started laughing. Falling back against the seat, he roared his laughter and pointed at Jet, the Uzi forgotten in his lap. Jet twisted farther away from the steering wheel and renewed his attack. Halfway over the seat, he slapped at Julio with both hands. The car swerved. Jet slipped back into place and barely avoided ramming a mule-drawn carriage filled with tourists. As soon as he had the car pointed down the road again, Jet turned and shouted something else at Julio. Julio cupped his ears with his hands and screamed, "You gonna hafta speak up, man!" Then he dissolved into laughter at the fury on Jet's face.

Next thing Julio knew, Jet had a pistol pointing straight at him.

This wasn't funny anymore.

"Okay, okay!" shouted Julio, lifting the Uzi and pointing it out the side window. "Relax, will ya?"

As they drew near the store, he saw a woman come through the doors. She looked like one of the women in the pictures Jet had showed him before. Yeah. She was definitely the Jew.

Get down!" screamed Kate. "Ruth! They have a gun! Get down!"

It was impossible to scream loudly enough with the traffic noise and the poisonous music spewing through the air. Across the street, Ruth smiled and waved. Kate released her children's hands and lifted her own, high above her head, palms down. Urgently, she shoved them toward the ground, over and over again, shouting "Get *down!*" Ruth's smile faded. Kate pointed to the car, shouting *"Gun!"* Ruth didn't seem to understand. For some reason, she pressed both of her hands to the sides of her head.

People near Kate began to hurry away, casting worried glances back at her. For the first time, it occurred to Kate that she might be wrong. What if she was making a fool of herself? Then she heard a rapid series of popping sounds, like the cracking of knuckles, faint and almost indistinguishable from the blaring music.

Why *is Katy waving that way?* wondered Ruth. *Oh no. She brought the children. The last thing I need with this headache is dinner with a couple of kids.*

Summoning her self-control, Ruth waved back. Now Katy was trying to say something to her, shouting over the music.

"Hello!" called Ruth. "Y'all wait there! I'll come over!"

Katy shouted something in return, but it was impossible to make themselves heard over the awful noise from that car. Ruth resumed rubbing her temples with both hands. What in the world was Katy doing, flapping her arms like a bird? What a nut! In spite of her headache and her anger at the woman, Ruth smiled. Then she saw the look on Katy's face. She seemed . . . terrified?

Suddenly, Ruth Gold forgot her headache.

Movement at the edge of her field of vision caught her attention. She turned just in time to see the tall, glass storefront crash to the sidewalk. Turning farther, she saw the reason. Small holes appeared in irregular rows along the center of the glass. Instantly, Katy's hand gestures made sense.

Ruth dove for the ground.

Bent over double at the waist, Kate tried to drag Jilly and Paul toward the nearest cross street, backing up along the sidewalk with a child's hand in each of hers. Jilly came easily, although she screamed hysterically, but Paul seemed paralyzed, unable to take his eyes off the mayhem across the street. He seemed hypnotized by it. Drawn to it.

"Paul!" she screamed. "Paul! Come *on!*"

Ruth Gold lay facedown on the sidewalk, hands covering her head, cheek pressed against the heat of the herringbone brick as glass fell all around her. She felt it hit her leg. The pain would come later. At that moment, she felt nothing but a deep, irresistible anger.

Just as she had somehow known instantly what was happening, Ruth also knew with certainty *why* it was happening. Sol Cantor was behind this. But Ruth had prepared herself, both psychologically and physically. As soon as the glass stopped falling, she rose to her feet. The car had moved a few yards beyond her, but the maniac in the backseat continued to fire, leaving a meandering trail of bullet holes in the shop fronts as they rolled along. Everyone on the sidewalk lay flat on the ground. Some lay motionless; others crawled for the shelter of nearby parked cars or trash barrels. Jabbing her hand into her purse, Ruth clutched her tiny automatic and removed it. As she had been trained to do, she slipped the safety off, cocked it, spread her feet, and cupped her right wrist with her left hand. She squeezed off two shots, allowing time between rounds to correct for the recoil. To her great satisfaction, two holes appeared in the back window of the car. Then the window seemed to disintegrate. But she had not fired again. How was that possible?

Confused, she glanced across the street. A middle-aged black man in Bermuda shorts and a pale blue polo shirt stood on the far sidewalk, aiming a handgun in a posture that mirrored her own. Unlike Ruth, he did not stop firing until his weapon was empty.

It was as if she had stared into a mirror. For the first time, Ruth became consciously aware of her actions, and a pestilent cloud of revulsion enveloped her. *What have I done? What has he driven me to?*

Ruth glanced down at the people on the ground. Nobody looked at her. Cries of fear and moans of pain rose from the pavement in both directions. She stared blankly at the weapon in her hand. Mechanically, she jabbed it into her purse and set out along the sidewalk, stepping over the prone bodies at her feet. Behind her, she heard more firing—individual reports, louder and much more slowly paced than the rapid pops of the weapon that had caused all this destruction.

In less than ten seconds, Ruth left the glass-strewn portion of the sidewalk and marched along Decatur. Anyone coming upon the scene for the first time would ignore her, thinking she was simply fleeing the mayhem. She looked perfectly normal, except for the smear of blood on her leg and the shock and terror in her eyes.

TWENTY-TWO

Solomon Cantor had watched it start through his bug-smeared windshield. He had the truck door open right after the first rounds hit the storefront, but before he was entirely out of the truck, the black guy across the street opened fire. Solomon decided to stay put. After all, what could he do for the girls without a gun of his own? It was soon apparent he had made the right choice. The rabbi was up and walking away slowly, like she was window-shopping, and across the street, the other one and her kids were nowhere in sight, so they were fine, probably running for their lives.

Sol felt terrible. He should have seen this coming.

Meanwhile, the red car rolled into the side of a delivery truck parked at the curb. The black guy in shorts approached it slowly, holding his gun hand stiffly out in front, moving forward crablike, with quick steps followed by long pauses. He yelled something at the car. One of the guys inside threw a weapon out onto the street, then stuck both hands out the window. The black guy yelled something else and the hands came farther out.

A couple of uniformed patrolmen ran up to the car from the far side of the street. They yelled at the black guy, pointing their guns first at the car, then at him, then at the car again. The black guy lowered his weapon and fished something like a small wallet out of his back pocket. He showed it to the uniformed cops. Oh, so he was a cop, too. The uniforms focused all their attention on the car again. The black guy yelled something, and the rear door opened. A skinny white kid with a shaved head got out and stood in the middle of the street with his hands in the air. The cop in the shorts yelled again, and the kid kneeled on the pavement, then lay facedown.

Well, that's that, thought Sol.

He twisted the key in the ignition, slowly pulled away from the curb, and rolled down Decatur. The uniformed cops and the black guy in shorts did not look up as he drove slowly by.

C rouched down face-to-face with her children, Kate flinched with each bark of the guns. She felt adrenaline hit her bloodstream, her pulse rising to three times its normal rate, her chest throbbing as if her heart would leap through her ribs.

Jilly still screamed at the top of her lungs and wrapped both arms around Kate's neck, but Paul strained upward from their huddle on the sidewalk, trying to see the action on the street. "Get your head down!" shouted Kate. When Paul ignored her command, she placed her hand behind his head and shoved him to the pavement with all her might, but by then it no longer mattered. The firing had stopped, and for half a second Kate fantasized that the world was underwater, suddenly slow and muted. It was as if time stood still. In that moment, the pulse in her ears thundered so loudly that she marveled to think that no one else could hear the erratic *beat, beatbeatbeat, beat.* It was the only sound in her entire world—the sound of her own mortality, her imperfect heart.

Then the street erupted.

Cries of pain and terrified screams and thin wails of grief rose skyward. People ran in every direction. Police sirens whined in the distance, joining the impossibly loud warble of burglar alarms from half a dozen businesses. Activated by falling glass from a nearby storefront, the antitheft system of one parked car honked on and on and on. Kate rose to her feet amid the chaos, hesitant to expose herself yet frantic to get away. Ignoring a wave of dizziness, she took in the red car with the side door open and the young man standing in the center of the street with his hands clasped on top of his head and the armed black man in shorts crab-walking toward him.

"Come on!" she hissed, literally yanking the children to their feet. "Come on!"

Together, they rushed along the sidewalk, skirting dazed tourists still crouching low or lying flat on their faces. Kate glanced ahead and saw Ruth crossing the street to their side, barely avoiding a speeding panel truck. Up on the sidewalk again, the rabbi plunged into a crowd of tourists, bouncing off a burly man as if she had not seen him standing squarely in front of her. She staggered, then set out again, passing Jackson Square, her arms hanging limp like a rag doll. Obviously, something was terribly wrong.

"Hurry, kids! Hurry!"

Now, hundreds of people who had not been in the line of fire rushed toward the scene, drawn by curiosity, shouting excitedly. Kate tried to keep her eyes on Ruth as she fought her way upstream against the flood of onlookers. Occasionally, as if their hands in hers were insufficient evidence of their presence, she glanced at Paul and Jilly.

"Ruth!" shouted Kate. "Ruth! Wait!"

Although the blaring music and the shouting crowd were farther behind them now, Ruth did not seem to hear. Kate pulled the children faster. Her arrhythmia was worse, her heart running wildly out of control. She began gasping for breath although her pace was not that fast. Near the Old Farmers' Market, Kate called again from less than ten feet behind. The rabbi did not turn or stop. Kate released Paul's and Jilly's hands and ran up alongside Ruth. "Where are you going?" she asked, struggling to keep pace.

Still no reply.

Thinking the rabbi might have been temporarily deafened by the gunfire and the noise, Kate grabbed her shoulder. Immediately, Ruth spun and lashed out with her fist, catching Kate just below the rib cage and knocking out most of her wind. Kate doubled over, clutching her belly, gasping for air. Ruth stared as if Kate had suddenly materialized before her eyes. "Oh no," she said. "Oh no."

Then Paul was there, slamming into Ruth, knocking her sideways, pounding her with his fists. The rabbi struggled against him, trying to grab his wrists to stop the blows. Kate tried to tell Paul to stop, but she could not breathe. Finally, Ruth managed to envelop the boy in a bear hug. As she gripped him tightly in her arms, Paul continued pounding her back with both fists.

Moving him back and forth as if they were dancing, Ruth said, "It's okay; it's okay," over and over, like a mantra.

Kate lowered her eyes to the pavement between her sandals, fighting to draw a breath. A curtain of darkness descended on her mind. Swaying, she knew she would fall. Her pulse clamored for attention, drowning out everything else. Jilly gripped her leg, trying to help. The moment passed, and Kate stumbled to a nearby cast-iron bench as Ruth watched over the top of Paul's head. The sickly sweet smell of rotten fruit drifted past them from the Farmers' Market, carried on a river breeze. Kate sat heavily, beginning to breathe again. Ruth released Paul, and he moved to stand beside his mother, with one palm on her back. When Kate had recovered well enough to speak between breaths, she looked at Ruth and said, "Are . . . you . . . okay?"

Ruth sobbed once and nodded.

"Need . . . go back . . . tell . . . police."

Ruth blanched. "They'll arrest me!"

Kate focused on her breathing. Thirty seconds later, she felt she could stand. "Okay," she said, rising to her feet. "We'll go to my shop. We can call them when we get there."

"But—"

"*Will you just do as I say!*" screamed Kate.

An elderly couple moved away from them, wearing troubled looks beneath matching wide-brimmed hats. Lowering her voice, Kate spoke through gritted teeth, "You can't be alone right now. You're a mess. You're acting crazy."

Ruth looked down. The right leg of her pants was soaked in blood. Her blouse was torn and filthy. "Okay," she said meekly.

"Good. Come on, kids."

Still a bit out of breath, Kate set off, thinking of the heart medication in her desk drawer. Jilly followed, but Paul stayed put, continuing to stare at Ruth, his hands balled into fists.

"Paul?" said Kate. "Come *on*."

He did not move. Standing between his mother and Ruth Gold, Paul blocked the rabbi's way. Ruth faced him. In a voice devoid of all emotion, too soft for his mother to hear, the boy said, "If you try to hurt my mother again, I'll kill you."

ey, Lieu!" shouted a patrolman. "You better come hear this!"
Lieutenant Lincoln Washington rose from his crouched position beside the spot where the body had lain and clambered up the side of the Audubon Park lagoon. Behind him, the twin fountains had been shut off at his command. Washington had pretended his concern was the slight wave action they caused, claiming it might disturb a piece of evidence at the shoreline, but his real reason for issuing the order was less professional. He couldn't stand to listen to the peaceful sound of the fountains while the pale corpse of a beautiful woman lay rocking in the water.

"What is it, O'Flaherty?" he yelled.

The patrolman stood fifty feet away beside the open door of a squad car. He called, "They got a ten seventy-one over in the Quarter."

"So what? I'm busy."

"They sayin' these guys was tryin' to hit some Jewish broad."

"Yeah? So?"

"Well, I was thinkin' 'bout that case you're workin'. That Jewish broad."

Washington sighed. "There's a lot of Jewish women in this town, O'Flaherty."

"Yeah, but they calling this one a rabbi."

As Washington hurried to the car, a monkey of some kind screamed from the nearby woods. At least Washington *hoped* it was a monkey. *Man, oh man*, he thought. *This town is going crazy.*

Katy, the kids, and Ruth arrived at The Other Day less than fifteen minutes after the shooting stopped. Several people had stared at them as they hurried up Ursulines and turned onto Chartres. On the two-block walk, Ruth had been dazed and unsure of her surroundings. Twice she had slowed and stared at the ground until Katy took her hand and gently encouraged her to keep walking.

When they entered the shop, Katy said, "Paul, pull the blinds," and Paul dutifully went about the business of obscuring the view into the shop, while Katy led Ruth to the rear. Meanwhile, Jilly kicked off her shoes and crawled under the Edwardian buffet to resume playing with her precious fire truck as if nothing had happened.

"Sit here," ordered Katy, guiding Ruth to a chair. The rabbi moved stiffly, like a robot. Katy opened a drawer, removed a small brown plastic bottle, and shook out a single tiny pill, which she quickly popped into her mouth. Then she knelt at Ruth's feet and gingerly pulled up the leg of her pants, exposing a long but shallow cut on Ruth's calf. "It looks worse than it is," she said.

Looking down, Ruth grimaced. "Think I'll need stitches?"

"No. Just some disinfectant and a bandage." Katy rose and entered the tiny rest room, emerging a moment later with a first aid kit the size of a large book.

"Oh no!" cried Ruth as Katy withdrew the iodine. "That stuff stings!"

"Don't be such a wimp. Aren't you the one who was shooting at gangsters a few minutes ago?"

Ruth's face hardened as Katy poured the liquid onto a fresh piece of gauze.

"Ready?" asked Katy.

"Go ahead."

Katy gently dabbed the cut. Ruth sucked her breath in loudly each time the cloth contacted her leg. "You sound like you're having a baby," said Katy. "Using the Lamaze technique."

"Having a baby couldn't possibly hurt this much."

"Wanna bet?"

"No. I just want you to stop torturing me!"

Katy chuckled.

"This is funny?"

"I was just thinking of you shooting at those guys."

"You think that's *funny?*"

"Well, you have to admit it's a little out of character."

"Oh, I don't know," said the rabbi seriously. "There've been several times I've *wanted* to shoot a man. I just didn't have a gun handy."

Katy burst out laughing. She couldn't seem to stop. Ruth wished that she could join in the laughter, to let it wash away the tension of everything: Steve's death, Benny's horrible mistake, her encounter with Sam at the temple, and now a drive-by shooting. It would be good to douse it all in laughter, even if it was really just hysteria bubbling up from a primal source. It would be good to cleanse herself of fear, to let the laughter grow until she no longer felt this soul-sick sorrow, but instead, all Ruth could do was watch Katy from behind a frozen mask.

Then Katy leaned forward, still laughing, and hit Ruth on the shoulder.

"Hey!" cried Ruth, with a rush of anger. "What's the idea?"

"You punched me!"

Ruth looked across the room, where Paul stood watching. "Yeah.
I guess I did."

Following her gaze, Katy turned to see hostility in her son's eyes.
She stopped laughing. "What's going on?"

"Nothing," said Ruth.

"Don't tell me that. What is it?"

"Nothing, Katy. Let's just drop it."

"Paul?" asked Katy. "What's going on here?"

Paul took a step closer, still glaring at Ruth. "Don't do it again."

"Paul!" said Katy. "What's the matter with you?"

"She hit you."

"She didn't mean to!"

"I don't care. I have to protect you. I have to watch out for Jilly, too.
Besides, I don't *like* her! She calls you Katy! She shot at those guys. She
has a *gun*, just like those men in that car!"

Ruth buried her face in her hands and moaned.

"Paul," said Katy softly, "you owe Rabbi Gold an apology."

He said nothing. Ruth's hands remained over her face.

"Paul? I think you should say you're sorry."

Paul Flint turned and walked away. Soon, the high-pitched whine of
falling bombs drifted from the back of the shop, where the boy lounged
at Katy's desk playing a game on her computer.

"I'm sorry," said Katy.

Staring at the bandage on her calf, Ruth said, "You know, this was no
coincidence."

"What do you mean."

"The men in that car were trying to kill us."

Katy watched Paul as she spoke. "How could that be? I didn't even
know I'd be there until I found your note."

Ruth looked at her blankly. "What do you mean, 'my note'?"

Still watching Paul, Katy seemed far away.

Ruth tried again, "Katy, listen to me. I didn't leave you a note. *You* left
me a note!"

Katy finally looked at her. "I'm sorry. What were you saying?"

Ruth stood and began limping up and down the aisle among the furniture. The instant she rose, Paul looked over from the computer, watching her suspiciously.

Ruth ignored him. "When I got home from temple, there was a note lying on the floor, just inside my door. It was signed by you. It said to be at that record store at five-thirty."

"But I got a note like that too!"

"We were set up," said Ruth grimly.

Katy stared at her as the thought sank in. "Oh no."

"Oh *yes!*" said Ruth. "This is great! Now we can prove he's trying to kill us!"

"How?"

"Don't you see? We have your note! We can show it to the police. They can check it against Cantor's handwriting and prove he wrote it! Maybe he even left fingerprints!"

"That's right!"

Ruth stopped pacing and faced her. "Let's look at it."

Katy turned to her desk, then back toward Ruth. "I threw it away."

Ruth stared at her. "Where?"

"In the trash can."

"So dig it out."

"They picked up the garbage already. They pick it up every day in the Quarter."

Ruth fell onto an eighteenth-century Windsor side chair with a groan.

"Well there's always *your* note," said Katy.

Ruth shook her head dejectedly. "I had a headache, and I thought you were rude to ask me to come on such short notice. And I was mad about what happened at *Mekhkar Torah* anyway, so I—I pitched it out the window of my car."

Katy waited a moment, then said, "I'm sorry I didn't show up at your Torah study. I was going to be there, but something came up and I couldn't make it."

Ruth stared at her. "Come on, Katy. Don't lie. I know why you weren't there. I saw you outside the temple with your friend."

Kate blushed. "She's not my friend. I met her there, when I was on my way inside."

Ruth did not believe her for a second. She needed Katy's help, but it was difficult not to unload on her, to make her sit and listen to all the insults and pain those people and others like them had inflicted. Still, she couldn't risk alienating Katy . . . not when she might be the only other person alive who truly understood the truth about Sol Cantor. *Maybe if I put it tactfully* . . .

"I wish you hadn't spoken with her."

Katy cocked her head. "Why?"

"Those people have caused a great deal of trouble."

"Oh."

"But I . . . I appreciate your not coming in and disturbing our Torah study."

"Disturbing?" Katy seemed confused.

"Yes. I know that probably took some restraint on your part and—"

"Restraint? What are you talking about?"

"I just meant that you probably thought about, uh, proselytizing, and I appreciate your restraint in not doing that during the class."

Katy spoke softly, watching Jilly as if concerned that her daughter might overhear. "What kind of a person do you think I am, Ruth?"

"Well, you had such a friendly conversation with that woman . . . "

"I'm trying to have a friendly conversation with you, too. Does that make me Jewish all of a sudden?"

Ruth and Katy stared at each other. After a moment, the rabbi took a deep breath and said, "Maybe I've made a mistake."

Katy said nothing.

"I'm just confused, Katy. I mean, sometimes it's like I can see *you* in there, behind your eyes. You know—the girl I remember from way back when. Other times, you seem so . . . different."

"I feel that way around you, too, but please don't lump me with some strangers just because I was civil to them. Shouldn't a Jew, of all people, know better than that?"

"You're right. I'm sorry." Glancing down, Ruth noticed that Katy's hands were shaking.

"Can I say something?" asked Katy.

"Of course."

"Okay. I think what those people are doing is wrong, but I understand their point of view. I—"

"You understand?"

Katy drew a shaky breath. "Let me finish, please."

Crossing her arms, Ruth leaned back in her chair. "All right."

"I was going to say I understand why they're doing it. They really believe they have something you need, Ruth. Something that will make your life better and get you into heaven."

"Who are they to think their way is any better than mine?"

"Please keep your voice down," said Katy, glancing at Paul.

"Maybe we'd better change the subject."

"Oh, come on, Ruth. Can't you hear a different point of view without getting mad?"

Ruth did not answer at first; then she said, "Go ahead."

"All I'm saying is, sometimes honest conviction looks like arrogance to outsiders. If you really believed you had something that could make everyone's life better, not just here and now but for all eternity, wouldn't you want to share that good news with the world?"

"I wouldn't try to cram it down people's throats!"

"But wouldn't you want to share something like that? I mean, if it was true, wouldn't sharing it be the only right thing to do?"

Ruth erupted. "How would you feel if we showed up outside your church next Easter with signs that said 'The Messiah hasn't come yet,' or 'Trust Moses'?"

"Mom?" called Paul.

Katy looked his way. The boy stood on the other side of the desk watching them, his eyes hard and wary. She said, "We're just having a conversation. Keep playing your game."

"I'm sorry," hissed Ruth, "but the question stands. How would you feel if we came to church with signs and slogans?"

"I'm not defending what they're doing. I'm just saying—"

"I know what you're saying, and I'm not buying it. If those people really cared so much about us, they'd give us some respect and behave with common decency."

Katy sighed. "Maybe those particular people are there for the wrong reasons."

"*Maybe?* They might as well be Moonies or Hare Krishnas! What do they think our temple is, the airport?" She slapped the arm of her chair. "They shouldn't be there at *all*, Katy!"

Paul stood again. Katy glanced at him and shook her head sternly, warning him off as she spoke to Ruth without looking at her. "What happened to you, Ruth? Why are you so angry?"

Again, Ruth let a silence fall between them. Finally, in a dull and lifeless voice, she said, "You wouldn't understand."

Julio lay strapped down on a gurney in the full sunshine, sweating like a pig. "Man," he whined, "come on. Take me to the hospital."

A big white guy leaned over him, his face kinda hovering with the clouds in the background, looking down like God in heaven. *Hey*, thought Julio, *maybe I'm already dead.*

"Shuddup, punk," said the cop. "You ain't goin' nowhere yet."

He wasn't God. God would've let him go to the hospital, at least. Julio closed his eyes. Man, it hurt! His side really hurt.

"This the shooter?"

Julio opened his eyes at the sound of the new voice.

"That's right, Lieu," said the cop who wasn't God.

Another face leaned over him—a black face, perfect. Julio closed his eyes and turned his head away. He wasn't gonna talk to one o' *them*.

"I'm Lieutenant Lincoln Washington. What's your name?"

Julio laughed. Then he winced.

"I know, I know. It's a funny name, but I'm stuck with it. Hey, you in pain?"

Julio scrunched up his face and nodded. "I took a bullet, man. Right in the chest." Julio wished he could look down to see his wound, but the straps across his forehead, chest, and arms made that impossible. He knew he was shot, though, because his chest hurt, and there was blood on his shirt.

Lieutenant Lincoln Washington continued, "Yeah. Looks pretty bad to me. Hey, you wanna make it, or you wanna die right here?"

Julio kept his eyes closed, but it was something to think about. These guys didn't seem like they was in a hurry to get him fixed up. He really *could* die here, maybe. But he didn't wanna beg no black man for mercy, either. He decided to stay quiet.

"Okay. That's fine with me," said the lieutenant. "You just lay there and bleed to death while we wait."

Julio lay still for several minutes, thinking, *They gotta take me to the hospital soon. They can't lemme die here. Not really. That ain't fair.* The cops were all talking about other things: wives, kids, one of them showing pictures of his baby around. Nobody paying attention to Julio here, dying in broad daylight. *Man, they really gonna lemme die!*

He opened his eyes and said, "Hey!"

The lieutenant came over again, taking his time. "Yeah?" he asked.

Julio cleared his throat. "Julio Jones, awright? That's my name. Now will ya take me to the hospital?"

"Sure thing. We just have a couple of details to go over first."

Julio moaned.

"Hey," said the cop, sounding real concerned. "Something the matter?"

"I'm dyin' here!" said Julio.

"Yeah, I know," he said. "But other than that?"

A couple of the other cops laughed. Julio gritted his teeth against the pain. Then he said, "What I gotta say to get ya to take me to the hospital?"

"Well, you can start with why you shot up the street here, Julio."

"I already told that fat mick over there. We was supposed to waste some chicks."

"Who?"

"I dunno no names, man. Just some chicks."

"If you don't even know their names, why were you trying to kill them?"

"Money, man. We was gettin' paid. What else?"

"Okay. You're doing good, Julio. I see a nice ambulance ride in your immediate future. Just a couple more questions."

"Man," he whined. "It hurts!"

"I know, and I'm real sorry. Tell me this: If you don't know who these women are, how did you know who to shoot?"

"He showed me pictures."

"He? He who?"

"Jet, man. The guy you wasted."

"Hey, Julio. Don't blame that on me. I wasn't even here."

"Who was it then? It was a nig—I mean a black fella—like you, what shot Jet an' me. I saw him."

"You got that right, Julio. It was Detective James Whitman. He was mindin' his own business, walkin' to the music store on his day off." The cop raised his voice a little, talkin' to someone else. "Prob'ly gonna buy that new Wynton Marsalis CD, right, Jimmy?"

A voice in the distance said, "There it is, Link."

Somebody else said, "You gonna love that one, man."

The cop looked back at Julio and said, "Then you came along and ruined Detective Whitman's day."

"*I* ruined *his* day? You're jokin', right?"

"Well, maybe a little, Julio. But you have to admit, it's gonna be hard for Detective Whitman to buy Mr. Marsalis's new CD now, what with the store shot up and all."

Julio shut his mouth. This cop was messin' with him, an' it was startin' to make him mad.

"Julio? Those pictures . . . the ones of these women you were supposed to shoot?"

"Sure, man! Come on!"

"Where'd Jet get them?"

"Some old white guy was all he said. Wanted them women dead pretty bad. Said it had to happen outside the record store. That's all I know. Now will ya please just—"

The cop interrupted. "Do you have them? The pictures?"

"No," Julio moaned.

"Know where they are?"

"Jet burned 'em."

"He *burned* them? That's a strange thing to do. Isn't that strange, fellas?" A chorus of voices called their agreement. "Why would he burn the pictures, Julio?"

"I dunno! Maybe he didn't wanna leave no evidence. Jet's real smart thataway."

"Oh, I don't know, Julio. Him being dead and all."

After a pause, Julio said, "Well, yeah."

"You know what, Julio? I only have one more question, and then we can take you to the hospital."

"Okay," he said, moaning a little.

"I heard you called one of these women a rabbi. Why would you do that?"

"Jet said she was a Jew."

"Yes?"

"Well . . ."

Washington waited, but Julio seemed to think he'd answered the question.

"Well, what, Julio?"

"Well, there ya go. She's a Jew."

"That still doesn't tell me why you called her a rabbi."

"'Cause she's a *Jew*, man!"

"But that doesn't mean she's a *rabbi*."

Julio stared up at the lieutenant with a quizzical look. "It don't?"

Lieutenant Lincoln Washington looked down at him for a moment. Finally, shaking his head, he moved from beside the gurney and spoke to the patrolmen standing nearby. "All right, get this idiot out of here."

An emergency medical technician came over and stooped and unstrapped Julio. Then two burly uniformed cops lifted Julio to his feet. "Hey!" said Julio. "Ain'tcha even gonna lemme lie down on the way?"

"Nah," said one of the cops. "That ain't how we usually do it." The other one laughed.

"Well, sure it is," said Julio. "I seen it on TV lotsa times. Someone been shot in the chest or whatnot, ya gotta let him lie down on the way to the hospital."

"You got us there," said the first one. "That's standard procedure for scumbags that been shot in the chest, all right."

Deciding to ignore the scumbag comment, Julio said. "Okay . . . so lay me back down."

"Why?" asked the cop innocently.

"'Cause I been shot in the chest!"

"Yeah, but that's healed up already. Now all you got is a coupla bruised ribs and your buddy's blood all over that nice clean shirt."

"Hey!" said the other one. "It's a miracle!"

Julio Jones whined all the way to the backseat of the patrol car.

Someone pounded loudly on The Other Day's front door.

Paul said, "I'll get it!" and took off running.

"*No!*" hissed Ruth.

Paul turned, a surprised look on his face. Ruth turned to Katy, pleading. "It could be the police."

"You'll have to talk to them eventually," said Katy.

"But they might arrest me for shooting at those guys."

Katy stared at her for a moment, then spoke to Paul. "Let's not answer the door, honey."

Whoever stood outside knocked again, louder this time.

Ruth said, "Do you think it's them?"

"I have no idea."

"Could it be a customer?"

"Maybe. They do that sometimes."

The door shook in its frame with the force of the third knock.

"Customers never knock like that," said Katy, moving toward the door. "It's probably the police. Come on, Ruth. We should let them in."

"No! What if it's Sol Cantor?" Even Jilly had stopped playing to watch the door. After a moment, Ruth said, "Thank goodness you shut the blinds, Paul."

"Why are we hiding?" he asked.

Katy approached the front door. "We're not hiding, Paul. At least, not exactly."

"Katy!" hissed Ruth. "What are you doing?"

"Don't you want to know who it is?"

"No!"

"Well, *I* do."

Before Ruth could object again, Katy peeked through the horizontal slats covering a window several feet from the door. Immediately, she let the slat fall back into place. When she turned, Ruth could tell the news was not good. Kate walked back to the rear of the shop and placed her lips next to Ruth's ear. "It's that detective," she whispered. "The one from the other night."

"Lieutenant Washington?"

"Yes."

Ruth considered the news for a moment, then said, "Maybe he's here about the break-in at your house."

Katy shook her head. "There's another man with him. I think it's the man who shot at the car with you."

Ruth stared at the locked door. "*Hashem*, be merciful," she whispered. "They're here for me."

"I guess so."

"What can they do to me for firing my gun like that?"

"I don't know."

Swallowing, Ruth spoke in a very small voice. "Let's just wait for them to go away. Can we do that, please?"

"Ruth, you're gonna have to see them sooner or later."

"Katy, *please!* I just need time to think!"

"All right," said Katy. "We'll wait a while."

They hid inside the shop until darkness settled on the French Quarter. Only when the afterglow of sunset had completely faded did Katy venture out, skulking beside the ancient stucco façades of half-timbered Creole cottages and the slender wrought-iron columns standing guard outside the more "modern" eighteenth-century French town houses. Crossing Esplanade and Frenchmen, she rushed up Elysian Fields toward the parking lot where she kept her Jeep. Meanwhile, Ruth and the kids watched for her, peeking out through the venetian blinds. When Katy pulled to a stop at the curb, they dashed outside immediately.

The shooting had changed everything. Now Ruth feared the police more than she feared Solomon Cantor. When they arrived at her parked car several blocks away, she asked Katy to circle the block twice in case the police had staked out the vehicle. Both of the children had dropped off to sleep in the backseat. Searching the darkness between the passing streetlights, Ruth whispered, "I'm gonna park a couple of blocks from home and sneak in the back way. There's an old alley there, all full of weeds. Nobody uses it anymore. Maybe I can get in without being seen."

"Why not just go see the police tonight? You shot at those men in self-defense. I'm a witness to that. I'll go with you."

Ruth shook her head. "Tomorrow. I don't want to run the risk of spending the night in a cell. I need to sleep in my own bed one more time first, get my bills paid, let the neighbors know I might be away for a while—stuff like that." They drove another half a block before Ruth said, "Hiding from the police while Sol Cantor walks the streets in broad daylight . . . you'd think I'd be surprised."

"So why aren't you?"

Ruth continued to stare out the window. For the second time that evening, she told Katy, "You wouldn't understand."

A fter putting the children to bed, Kate lay awake for hours. Paul's behavior toward Ruth worried her. So did Ruth's decision not to go to the police. She should have insisted that they see Lieutenant Washington when he came to the door, and she should have spent more time with Paul, to comfort him and help him feel safe.

Of course, the problem was, he hadn't *been* safe.

Rolling over, she yanked the sheet up beneath her chin, her mind at war with itself. She needed sleep, but now that she had nothing to do to keep her thoughts at bay, the horror at the French Quarter descended upon her full force. She should never have placed her children in that situation. In fact, maybe she *should* send them away, out of town, to their grandparents.

But how would I make it without Paul and Jilly?

This final thought rose unbidden, too quickly to be suppressed. She did not believe she could live a single day without the children at her side. Of course, her survival was less important than their safety. *Of course.* Still, who else could possibly devote enough attention to their safety? No one else. Only her. So the children must remain with her. For their sake.

Yes.

For *their* sake.

That decided, she made a deliberate effort to think about something restful and positive. She thought about praying, but just as fantasies of Jake Singer had distracted her before, now she found herself dwelling on

Ruth Gold. Kate could see the rabbi's point in a way—those evangelists were awfully insensitive—but did that justify Kate's not going to a Torah study with Ruth's people? Maybe she had been wrong to turn away from the temple, but if so, why was she so uncomfortable with the thought of going there? The mere idea of setting foot in that place made her feel almost as uneasy as the idea of living without the kids. Not that the two things were in any way connected, of course, but at the thought of the kids, she began to worry about their safety again.

So on and on it went, her mind desperately fleeing one dismal place only to find itself trapped in another, until finally, reeling beneath successive waves of guilt and apprehension and struggling to remain alert for sounds of an intruder, exhaustion overwhelmed her, and she slept fitfully.

How odd to find that he missed the dream.

Ever since Jake Singer saw the end and knew, his nights had been uneventful. Now, when he lay down and closed his eyes, he fell asleep and . . . nothing. Next thing he knew it was morning. He just opened his eyes and there he was, like a normal person.

It was confusing.

Jake rose from his bed in the Hotel Poisson, feeling good about the day, like something important might happen. You never knew how things would turn out, of course. Sometimes you made plans and nothing worked the way you had in mind, but lately, he'd been doing okay. Pretty much whatever he did turned out the way he hoped. That was good, because he hated it when life took over and twisted things around. It was important not to let that happen, important to stay in command.

Kate Flint had agreed to go out with him this afternoon. He'd get to know her better; then who knew what might happen?

Smiling, he entered the tiny hotel bathroom and stepped to the sink. From a motley collection of toiletries on top of the water closet, he extracted shaving cream and a disposable razor. He splashed water on his cheeks and sprayed foam onto the palm of his left hand. Looking at the mirror, he smeared the shaving cream on his jaw. This was the hard part. The trick was to get the stuff onto his face and shave it off without making eye contact. Two mornings now, since the dream had stopped, he'd confronted this man in the mirror. Both times he had survived it okay, but Jake knew if he slipped up and looked himself in the eye. . . . In a way, that was worse than the dream. He mustn't look, or—

Jake froze in position, completely still, the razor forgotten, hypnotized by the eyes in the mirror. His mind slipped into an endless loop, asking the same question over and over again:

What is that thing in there?

TWENTY-FOUR

Rabbi Ruth Gold's own snores woke
her. She was fully clothed in her darkened living room, her head lolling
on the seat back. A sliver of sunshine slanted through a gap in the drapery. Languidly, she checked her watch. Five till seven in the morning.
What? Why was she on the sofa in her clothes at such an hour? With
head cocked to one side against the yielding cushion, her eyes shifted to
the empty place where her coffee table once stood. Slowly, she remembered that Steve was dead and Morton Rothstein was dead and Isaac was
dead. And she might have killed a man on the streets of the French Quarter. She felt the misery seep in once more.

She had arrived an hour after dark the night before, parking a block
away and sneaking like a thief into the back door of her own home. Afraid
the police were watching from the street, she had decided not to turn on
the overhead lights. She had prepared a cold dinner of brie, grapes, and

sourdough bread in the glow from the open refrigerator. She had eaten standing up. Then she had settled onto the sofa, elevated her wounded leg on some pillows, and considered her options.

Repent.

Return.

Teshuva.

There really was no other choice.

But how could she know what was required until she knew exactly what she had done? Last night she had been afraid to risk the noise of a radio or the glow of a television in case the police were outside, but now, after willing the final gauzy curtain of sleep from her mind, Ruth turned on her television with the remote control, flipping through the channels. She found a news program right away. The lead story was the continued search for animals released from the Audubon Zoo. Residents of the area were warned to remain inside as much as possible, and to keep doors and windows closed. Pets should be brought indoors as well. Several danger-ous animals were still unaccounted for, including a Bengal tiger, three lions, and a pair of black bears. Dozens of harmless but exotic creatures still wandered the city, adding their calls to the wail of sirens and the rumble of commercial jets overhead. The reporter mentioned the dead zebra again. There were many reports of missing or viciously slaughtered pets, and several people had encountered carnivorous animals in the streets, alleys, and backyards of uptown New Orleans, but so far, said the announcer, only one person had been harmed—an unidentified woman found dead in the Audubon Park lagoon.

As those final words sank in, Ruth felt a new kind of fear. She seized the telephone on the side table and punched Helen Blumenthal's number. How could she have forgotten to call? The phone rang three times, then Helen's answering machine picked up with her no-nonsense doctor's voice announcing, "You've reached Dr. Helen Blumenthal's residence. I can't come to the phone right now. If this is an emergency, you can page me at 504-555-2537. If this is a personal call, please leave a message and I'll get back to you as soon as I can. Goodbye."

Helen's voice sounded so normal; Ruth felt herself calm down. Hundreds of people used the park every day. Maybe thousands. What were the odds that the dead person in the lagoon was her friend? Ruth spoke into the telephone, "Uh, Helen, I just heard about that person they found in the park, and I thought, you know—" Ruth paused, thinking—"well, you might not know about the person in the park. Uh, anyway, they found someone over there who was . . . you know . . . dead. Look, I know this is silly, but would you call and let me know you're okay? No, wait. You can't call me. I'll probably be in jail. I mean, at the police department. Oh . . . I've made a mess of this! Listen. I'll see you later and explain everything, all right? Bye."

Ruth hung up, feeling foolish. That message would only make Helen worry. Oh, well. Too late to change it now. Besides, on the television the French Quarter drive-by shooting was being featured as the second story. Chewing on a fingernail, she leaned forward to watch the screen. They aired footage of two men wearing dark blue jackets with *Coroner* printed across the back in white letters. Horrified, she watched them push a gurney bearing a body in a black body bag to a city hearse.

Oh no. Did I kill that man?

The sight of that plastic bag twisted her insides until Ruth bent double, pressing her face against her knees as if in urgent prayer. But she was too afraid to pray. Atonement came only with confession, repentance and restitution, but how did one confess and repent to a dead man? How did one repair a lost life? Her thoughts spiraled downward into a morass of sorrow as she waited for the news announcer to state the specific cause of death. Maybe her shots had missed. Maybe the black man who had fired from the other side of the street was responsible. Or maybe it had happened some other way. She awaited the most important fact in the universe: How did he die? But they moved on to the next news story without adding the details she needed most. Oh, curse them for the vapid idiots they were, with their bleached smiles and empty eyes! They had left her in hell, while *Yom Kippur* approached with the hollow footfalls of a dead man. Confess. Repent. Atone. Return. How was it possible if she had killed?

Sitting up, Ruth wiped her eyes and stared once more at the empty place in the center of the floor. She could delay no longer. To know, she must contact the authorities.

Surrender herself.

Give herself up.

No matter how she phrased the concept, it came out sounding like the end of her world.

Y ou have *got* to get a grip on yourself, Beck," said Roy Betterton, sipping
the last of his coffee.

For the third time, Rebecca Betterton said, "All I'm asking is for you
to come along. What's wrong with that?"

"I'm not a Jew. And you've never been much of one either." Roy
smiled, pointing to his breakfast plate. "Look. We're eating bacon here.
I don't think I can give that up, baby."

Rebecca sniffled.

Roy said, "Stop that! This isn't something to cry about."

"But you're being so unsupportive."

"Oh, for Pete's sake!" He threw his napkin onto the table. "So if I don't
agree with you I'm unsupportive? That's not fair. And neither is crying.
You know what that does to me."

She smiled through her tears. "It always works, doesn't it?"

"Not this time, Beck," he said. "I mean it. I'm sixty-two years old,
and I've been a Catholic all my life. I'm not about to start going to some
synagogue—"

"It's a temple."

"Whatever. You're not gonna get me in there, is the point. Especially
on the busiest day of the year. Isn't it enough that I fight the crowds at
Saint Paul's every Easter and Christmas?"

"Maybe if you went to church on regular Sundays—"

"Don't change the subject!"

Rebecca Betterton said, "Well, *I'm* going—with you or without you.
I just hoped we could do this together."

"Why, Beck? How come you're getting interested in your roots after
all these years?"

"You don't want to know."

"Well, of course I wanna know. Why else would I ask?"

She stared at him, thinking, *He'll just get mad if I say it.*

Roy stared back. Finally, he said, "Listen. If there's something going
on that I don't know about, a problem or something, maybe I could help."

"You can help by going to temple with me on *Yom Kippur.*"

He threw up his hands. "Why? That's all I'm asking. Why do you
wanna go all of a sudden?"

Desperate for his support, she blurted it out. "I'm afraid that man is

going to do something terrible to me, Roy. I'm afraid of dying without
making things right with God, but I'm also scared to go back to temple
after all these years. So I'm asking you to help me. To come with me."

He stared at her like she was crazy. "You're still worried about that
Peeping Tom?"

Rebecca Betterton nodded.

"But that was days ago, and we haven't seen him since."

"I know, but—"

"*But* nothing, Beck. You gotta get a grip here. We live in a big city,
with all kinds of creeps running around. Sometimes our path crosses theirs
is all. If we're lucky, nothing happens; they go on and so do we." He
leaned forward, covering her hand with his. "That's what you gotta do,
Beck. Put it out of your mind and go *on*."

"I know. But I can't help this feeling I have."

"What feeling?"

Shaking her head, she lowered her eyes to her lap.

He looked at her for a moment, then removed his hand from hers.
"Well, I'm not gonna support this kind of thing, that's for sure. You don't
need religion. What you need is some kinda psychologist or something."

He stood up.

"Where are you going?" she asked.

He looked at his watch. "I gotta game with Jim Howell in thirty
minutes. He thinks he can get Sears to buy our chisels."

Five minutes later, Roy drove away with his golf clubs in the trunk,
while Rebecca sat alone in a square of sunshine slanting in through the
bay windows of the morning room, thinking, *Maybe I should call it the
mourning room.*

Ruth lay on her side, legs pulled to her chest, head in her hands, rocking
back and forth. The phone rang. She let the machine get it. After her
outgoing message and a beep, Sam Gottlieb's voice rose from the speakers, sounding tinny and thin, like a person talking in a barrel.

"Ruth, it's Sam. Are you there? Ruth? Ruth, we need to talk. Are you
there?"

She continued to rock, ignoring the senior rabbi's voice.

"Okay," said Sam. "Well, we really need to talk. Gabby Cantor came
to see me last night. She came to my house. She's very upset about what
happened before *Mekhkar Torah*, Ruth. She, uh . . . well, she asked me
to bring it up before the board. She said you've been abusive to her and
Mr. Cantor before. She said something about trying to work things out
over at your place, but you wouldn't cooperate? Well, anyway, I know
there's two sides to every story, especially with Mr. Cantor's background
and all, so I thought I'd give you a call. Ruth? I wish you were there.
Uh, obviously I'm not going to take this to the board without hearing
what you have to say, but Gabby Cantor's one of our biggest donors,
you know, and we have to treat her with kid gloves. . . . Anyway, you'd
better call me as soon as you can, okay? This is serious. Okay. Well,
uh, call me."

Ruth barely heard the hum of the machine after her boss hung up the
phone, so tightly were her palms pressed against her ears.

R ising mist roiled along the pavement, gathering in the gutters until it
overflowed the curbs and curled against the base of the windowless
limestone façade of Faith Mausoleum, directly across the street from
Ruth Gold's house. Soon six inches of cotton white hovered above the
sidewalks, lapping against the upturned lawn on one side of the road
and the blank mausoleum wall on the other, a heavenly river flowing
inch by inch between lush levees of Saint Augustine and harsher banks
of cold unyielding stone. Solomon Cantor's liberally dented pickup
floated up to its axles in the milky stream, with a tangled collection of
metallic debris threatening to spill over the edge of the truck bed. The
windshield perspired with condensation. The engine had cooled to
match the densely humid surrounding air. Inside the cab, with red-
rimmed eyes locked on Ruth Gold's front door, Sol sipped coffee from
a thermos and wondered why anyone would choose to live across the
street from a mausoleum. He thought about all the bodies just behind
that wall, packed into their little concrete cells like larvae in a wasp's
nest.

He shuddered.

At eight o'clock sharp, Kate dropped Paul and Jilly off at their Sunday school classes in the children's wing of Trinity Bible Church. She delivered stern warnings not to leave the rooms until she returned for them, then made her way upstairs to the single parents' class, where she ate two sugar cookies, drank black coffee from a small foam cup, and listened to Sally Baker present a lesson on patience from the book of Job. It was difficult to stay awake.

At nine-fifteen, she met Paul at his classroom, and the two of them set off through the crowded hallways to get Jilly in time to find a good seat near the front for the second service. As they drew near the classroom, Kate saw Jilly's Sunday school teacher, Ann Riggins, chatting in the hall with another woman. Usually Ann stayed in the room with the children until the last parent had come and gone.

"Excuse me, Ann?" said Kate.

The woman turned with a smile.

"Where are the kids?"

"Hey, Kate. How are you?"

"Ann, where's my daughter?"

Ann blinked at Kate's abrupt demeanor. "She's outside. It's such a lovely day, we decided to take the class out to the playground."

"But who's watching them?"

"I finally got a helper for the class. He's out there with them now."

"Who is he?"

"Orin something. Or maybe Owen . . . I'm so bad with names."

"You don't know him?" snapped Kate. "How could you leave the children with someone you don't even know?"

Turning on her heel, she stalked away with Paul close behind.

"I've seen him at church before, Kate!" called Ann. "It's not like he's a total stranger!"

Ignoring her, Kate rushed to the end of the hall and burst out onto the playground. Fifteen feet away, a gray-haired man sat in the shade of a live oak tree on a low planter made of bricks. He wore a nice blue suit with a white shirt and a burgundy-colored silk tie. A group of children sat in a small semicircle at his feet, listening with rapt attention as he spoke. Startled by her dramatic entry, several of the children shifted their attention to Kate. The man followed the children's gaze, looking her way as well.

"Well, hello there," he said. "Mrs. Flint, isn't it?" Kate glanced from him to Jilly, who seemed quite safe and content. *How does he know my name?*

The man said, "We'll be done in just a minute, okay?"

Kate nodded, staring at him and thinking she had seen him before.

The man said, "All right, children, where were we? Oh, yes, so God told Abraham to take his son Isaac to the mountain and sacrifice him there. Do y'all know what *sacrifice* means?"

A little boy said, "It means to let them tag you out so's a runner can make it home."

The gray haired man laughed. "That's right, but they didn't have baseball in Abraham's time. Does anyone know what *sacrifice* meant back then?"

"I do!" said a girl in the back. "It means to kill somethin'."

Kate marveled that this fool would teach that particular Bible story to five-year-old children. She was about to interrupt when he said, "That's exactly right. And Abraham didn't want to do it, because he loved Isaac, just like your daddies love all of you. But Abraham also loved God, and God said it had to be done. Abraham knew that God loved his son Isaac even more than he did, so Abraham figured the Lord would find a way to make everything all right."

Kate watched the kids closely. They sat wide-eyed, their attention fixed on the storyteller, but they did not seem to be afraid. Maybe the man knew what he was doing after all. He glanced up at her, the dappled sunlight gleaming on his glasses, obscuring his eyes.

Suddenly, she remembered. He was the one sitting beside that woman who stood in the middle of Reverend Cahill's sermon last Sunday and . . . Kate's eyes widened. That woman! It was *her*—the tall one in front of the temple yesterday. Martha something or other. And this man, he had been there too, yelling Bible verses at the people in the parking lot.

"So Abraham and Isaac and two helpers rode their donkeys to a big mountain, where God told them to go," continued the man. "And Abraham told the helpers to wait at the bottom of the mountain while he and Isaac climbed all the way to the top. He told the helpers that he and Isaac would be back when they were done. Do you know why it's important that he said that?"

"'Cause he thought Isaac would be okay?" asked a boy in front.

"You're so smart! Yes, that's exactly what Abraham thought. Remember, he knew God loved him, and he knew God loved Isaac, and Abraham had faith that God would find a way to make everything all right. So he and Isaac climbed the mountain, and when they got to the top, Abraham laid Isaac down and tied him up, and then he lifted a knife up over Isaac, like this." Here, the man raised his clasped hands together above his head, as if lifting the knife above a prostrate body. The children watched in awe. "And . . . do you want to know what happened next?"

A chorus of cries rose from the children: "Yes!" and "Please!" and "What?"

But the man lowered his hands and smiled. "Well, I'd tell you, but we're out of time." All of the children protested loudly, begging him to go on. The man laughed. "It's a real cliff-hanger, all right. Tell you what. Y'all be sure to come back next Sunday, and I'll not only tell you the end of this story, I'll tell you another one that's even better. Okay? Now then, y'all go play for a few minutes till your parents come."

Instantly, the children leapt to their feet and raced to the far side of the fenced enclosure, where they swarmed over the slide, swing set, and seesaw. The gray-haired man rose with a flexibility that belied his obvious age. Dusting off the seat of his slacks, he approached Kate and her son. "You must be Paul," he said, holding out his hand. "I've heard a lot about you."

Paul shook his hand and offered a desultory greeting.

"And Mrs. Flint. I can't tell you what a pleasure it is to see you again," he said, holding his hand out to her. "I'm the Reverend Orvis Newton, but you just call me Orvis."

Kate took his hand. It felt rough and dry, like an old leather gardening glove. "How do you know my name?" she asked.

Placing his left hand over hers, he smiled and peered closely into her eyes, as if by doing so he could unlock some secret she held hidden deep inside. Kate found it difficult to look away. Behind his gold-rimmed glasses, one of Orvis Newton's eyes was the washed-out gray of Spanish moss. In the other, a greenish cast came and went, like the reflection of a fish's scales darting just below the surface. Kate found herself watching that eye closely, unable to define its color.

"You really don't remember me?" asked Orvis Newton.

"I think I do. Weren't you at Temple Brit Yisrael yesterday and at our church service last week? With that tall woman who disrupted the service?"

He smiled. "I guess Martha caused a bit of a commotion."

"She yelled at Reverend Cahill," Paul said disapprovingly. "They kicked her out."

"She was wrong to do that, Paul," said the man. "We should have admonished Jim privately."

Admonish Reverend Cahill? thought Kate incredulously. *Who does he think he is?* Withdrawing her hand from Orvis Newton's grasp, she wrapped her arm around Paul and pulled him closer, away from the man. "We need to go. Paul, would you get Jilly, please?"

With a last look at Orvis Newton, Paul headed for the other side of the playground.

"I wasn't talking about last Sunday, Mrs. Flint," said the gray-haired man. "We first met a long time ago, when you were a child."

"Really? Were you a friend of my parents?"

He laughed. "Oh no. I don't think your father approved of me."

Kate gave him her full attention. "Why not, Reverend Newton?"

"Let's just say we had a theological difference of opinion. And please, call me Orvis."

"Daddy's theology was pretty vague. What was your disagreement, exactly?"

He looked at her. "Are you sure you don't remember?"

She returned his gaze, fascinated with his multicolored eye. "No. I'm sorry."

"No matter. You will in time, I expect."

Paul and Jilly approached, holding hands. In the tree above them, a bird called exotically. Kate looked up just in time to see a flash of purple among the leaves.

"It's nice the way your children behave toward one another," said Orvis. "John would be proud."

She turned to him. "Did you know John?"

"Not exactly, but I've tried to keep up with you over the years."

"How? Who told you these things?"

He smiled, and the green flashed again in his iris. "I've just picked them up here and there. Please don't be concerned. I can't help but be interested in you. Because of our past."

"When did we meet, exactly?"

"As I said, when you were a little girl." He checked his watch as the bird called loudly again. Kate glanced up and saw a parrot, or maybe it was a macaw. The creature was three feet long from head to tail and covered with the most astonishing array of colors.

"Look at that!" she said pointing.

Reverend Newton looked up. "What?"

The bird had disappeared beyond a thick clump of leaves. "There's a big parrot up there."

He looked back down at her, amusement in his chameleon eye. "Yes, of course."

"No really! It was right there."

"I'm sure it was." He glanced around. "I'm sorry to be so mysterious, but I really need to be going, Mrs. Flint. Tell you what: Next time we meet, I'll take the time to answer all of your questions. Maybe we could get together again soon?"

"It's right up there, behind those leaves!" said Kate, her face turned upward, searching for the giant bird. It was important to her that Reverend Newton see it too.

He looked up again. "Are you sure? Could be a kite or something. Kids lose them in trees all the time."

"I'm telling you I saw a huge parrot."

"Sure. I believe you. Tell you what. My ministry is sponsoring a community outreach event next week." He removed a well-worn wallet from his hip pocket and extracted a small white card. Pulling a pencil from another pocket, he wrote on the card. "Here's the address and time. Maybe you could join us? We can talk about old times, okay?"

"I don't know . . . ," she repeated, still looking up.

"Well, of course not. You have to make arrangements for a sitter and all. And you'd have to close the shop. But I promise it'll be worth the trouble, Mrs. Flint. And it's for a very worthy cause . . . Mrs. Flint?"

"What?" she looked down at last. "Oh, yeah. Okay," she said, taking the card. "I'll do my best."

R uth stepped onto her porch and locked the door. It occurred to her that she might not be allowed to come home again for . . . who knows how long? Maybe never. She had meant to pay her bills last night, so the power and water would stay on for another month, no matter what. Oh well. Too late now. But opening the door again, she reached inside and switched on both the hall light and the outside light that hung from a chain above the porch. There. If they locked her away, at least the stained-glass transom would glow in the night to make the place look occupied.

Ruth descended from the porch in the soft morning glow and limped along a short concrete sidewalk between two small patches of lawn. She lingered at the top of the three steps that led down to the street, wondering if the police would emerge from one of the cars parked along the curb. A mourning dove cooed from a power line overhead, competing with the distant murmur of traffic on Interstate 10. Across the street, the caretaker had already opened the bronze door to the mausoleum. A neighbor woman emerged from her house four doors down, wearing a robe and slippers. She bent beside an azalea beneath a window, then straightened with a garden hose in her hand and began watering her lawn. Ruth suddenly felt ashamed. She did not know the woman's name. She should know her neighbors' names.

Ruth felt as if she were not inside her body but standing a few feet away, watching her own actions with the casual interest of a stranger. When the police did not immediately appear to take her into custody, she descended to the sidewalk. The last step was taken on faith, since the ground lay obscured beneath a mantle of mist. To distract her attention from the real threat of the morning, she found herself creating fanciful ones. Perhaps the earth had opened up below and spewed forth a sulfurous vapor, leaving a yawning chasm concealed beneath the mist, ready to swallow both her and her sin. Or perhaps a poisonous snake, freed from the zoo, lay coiled and ready to strike just below the opaque blanket of fog. That would be appropriate. She thought of the Torah as she often did in moments of pain, but this time, the words did not comfort. Instead, God's words to the serpent in the Garden of Eden merely confirmed her fears: "'I will put enmity between thee and the woman, and between thy seed and her seed; it shall bruise thy head, and thou shalt bruise his heel.'" Her foot slipped into the fog and settled on solid ground.

Certain that this merely delayed the inevitable, Ruth set out for her car with the shroud of vapor swirling around her ankles.

S ol sank low in his seat, surprised to see Rabbi Gold emerge from her front door. Somehow, she had managed to come home last night without his noticing. His eyes darted to the surrounding cars and houses, searching for signs that someone other than he had observed her movements. His hand gripped the door handle and rested there, waiting.

She descended her porch steps and crossed her little front lawn. Sol noticed she had a slight limp. He wondered why. Had she been shot yesterday after all? The rabbi stopped at the top of the concrete steps and stood there like she was waiting for someone. Sol watched her looking left and right, up and down the street. He slid lower behind the steering wheel, even though he didn't think she could spot him from so far away. After a few minutes, she stepped to the sidewalk and set off in the opposite direction.

What was she doing? Where was her car?

Rising up in the seat, Sol removed his hand from the door handle and stroked his beard. When the rabbi was a block and a half away, he twisted the key in the ignition and the old truck rumbled to life. Shifting into gear, he rolled forward very slowly, keeping pace with Ruth Gold's leisurely stroll along the sidewalk. Two blocks from her house, she turned left. He sped up as she disappeared on the far side of a dense cluster of shrubbery in a neighbor's front yard. When he reached the corner, Sol slowed to a stop and peeked around the shrubs just in time to see the rabbi's strange little car pulling away from the curb.

How had she eluded him last night? Sol Cantor wrinkled his forehead in thought as he turned the corner to follow Ruth Gold. He would not let it happen again.

I t wasn't until Kate and the kids were safely home that she thought about the gray-haired man's final words. *He knows about the shop. He knows my name and the kids' names. He even knows John's name.* Filled with a deepening sense of dread, she wondered, *Who is he?*

Kate went to her backpack on the kitchen counter. Rummaging through it, she found the card Orvis Newton had given her and read the penciled words again. The address he had written for the "community outreach event" seemed familiar. She thought it might be Temple Brit Yisrael. The time he had written confirmed this guess. Instead of an hour, it simply read, *Before sunset.* Flipping the card over, she found Reverend Orvis Newton's name printed in simple black letters beneath the words, *Sister Nan Smith Crusade for Jews.* And below his name, she read, *Apostle to the Hebrews.* Remembering the familiar way this disturbing evangelist had referred to her pastor by his first name, Kate felt certain Reverend Cahill would be able to tell her more about Orvis Newton. She decided to schedule an appointment with her pastor as soon as possible.

Replacing his card in her backpack, Kate thought about Orvis New-ton's strange eyes. She had seen such eyes before, but where? Suddenly, an image flashed unbidden in her mind. At first, she had no idea where it came from or what it meant, but it was not a fantasy; she was certain of that. The image was elusive, refusing to reveal itself as a fully formed memory, but Kate felt she should work at remembering, so she chased it through the dark labyrinth of her past. . . .

Little Katy saw a crowd of people standing close together. She saw their faces very clearly, most of them purple with rage, but she did not think they were angry with her. She seemed to be floating through them, moving without effort. The people shouted things she did not under-stand. Ugly things. She remembered one man yelling the word *Jew* over and over again, his huge, horselike teeth exposed by thin curled lips, spittal flying with each expulsion of the word. In the ugly man's mouth *Jew* sounded like one of the bad words her parents didn't want her to say. Katy knew Ruth was a Jew, but it had never occurred to her that there might be something wrong with that. She turned her frightened eyes toward the sky. Daddy's face hovered above her, staring out and away at the crowd. He held her very tightly. A woman pushed up close and called her name. A strange lust shone in the woman's eyes. "Katy, honey, tell us what *really* happened!" Katy stared at the woman mutely, certain she was not really there beneath her makeup, thick as clay, certain she was a hollow illusion.

"Daddy?" she asked. "Is *Jew* a bad word?"

Without answering, he carried her on through the crowd. They climbed the steps of a large building. Looking up, Katy saw tall, fluted columns tilting together as they soared toward a stained white pediment. Her daddy passed between the columns and into the coolness of a cavern-ous room with lofty ceilings. She saw a sparrow swoop through the air just below the ceiling. The people outside tried to follow her and Daddy, but large men wearing uniforms blocked their way. Only she and Daddy and a very few others got through. The sparrow flew to a windowsill way up high and perched there, looking out. Katy knew the sparrow did not belong in that place. Looking back, she saw the others pressed against the glass outside. They wanted in. The sparrow wanted out. Was this a place where nobody got what they wanted?

Echoes of her daddy's footsteps lingered in the shadows high above. Katy enjoyed being carried. Daddy had not done so for a long time, claiming she had grown too heavy, but today Katy rode with her arms around his neck, feeling his strong hands linked beneath her bottom. Katy knew it was the safest place in the world. Then she glanced at her daddy's profile and saw an expression she knew only too well, his lips turned down at the corners, the lids of his eyes squeezed close and narrow.

Uh-oh. Somebody's in big trouble.

Daddy carried her up a sweeping staircase and into a long wide hallway lined with wooden benches and a pair of tall doors. A man rose from one of the benches and approached them. He spoke to her daddy. She heard some new words: *arraignment* and *testify.* Her daddy listened quietly. She felt the familiar scratch of his whiskery cheek when he nodded his head. She tightened her grip around his neck. Grunting, he stooped and set her on her feet. Ignoring his conversation with the man, she took his hand and stood leaning against his leg just a little, looking around.

All kinds of people sat on the benches against the walls: men, women, black people, white people—there were far more black people—entire families dressed in fancy clothes and single young men with long hair or afros, dressed in bell-bottom jeans and tie-dyed T-shirts. Everyone looked worried. She did not like this place! Men with long sideburns and wearing somber suits with wide lapels and fat, colorful ties sat among the people, quietly reading pieces of paper, searching through briefcases, or speaking earnestly to those beside them on the bench. Katy wanted to run away, although she did not know why. It was just a feeling she absorbed, a mood that began with the sparrow and rippled out from the people like the way things felt at home, now that Mommy was so sick. Katy stood a little bit closer to her daddy's leg, gripping the fabric of his trousers and wishing she could be somewhere else, playing with Ruth. A deep sadness washed over her at the thought of Ruth. Why wouldn't their parents let them play together anymore? It had been so long.

A man came through the tall doors. He wore a uniform like the other men who had stopped the people outside. The man called her name, but he was not looking at her. He was looking the other way.

How did he know her name?

Still holding her hand, Katy's daddy led her toward the tall doors. The man in the uniform opened one of them and stood with his back to it, waiting. A big black gun dangled from his belt. He looked down at her without interest. She did not want to go in. Something bad was on the other side of those doors. She stopped, planting her feet stubbornly against her daddy's momentum. He looked back.

"I don' wanna go in there," she said.

He knelt beside her. "Sugar, we have to do this. But don't worry. I'll be with you the whole time."

"But I don' wanna!" she said, her voice rising.

"Sugar girl," he said, stroking her hair, "I don't want to either. But this is something we have to do."

"Why?"

"We've been all through this."

She stared at the gun hanging from the man's hip. "It's not like you said."

"Sure it is. You remember how I told you the judge wants to hear what happened? About the bad man and the poor lady in the kitchen? I told you we were going to the courtroom to see the judge? Remember?"

"Sure I do."

"Well, this is it. The courtroom."

"But I don' *wanna!* Can't we come back later?"

"No, sugar. The judge is waiting for you now, inside these doors."

"Why can't Mommy come too?"

He sighed. "We've talked all about that. She wanted to come with you. She just couldn't."

"Please don't make me do it."

Daddy cupped her cheeks in his hands. "Sugar girl," he said, "I'll take care of you. Please don't be afraid."

So they went in.

As they entered, a man passed them, walking out. He frowned, looking down at her, and Katy saw one of his eyes change colors. What happened after that was all a blur.

TWENTY-SIX

Sergeant Andy Collins stared at a crossword puzzle in Sunday's *Times-Picayune*, trying to come up with five letters starting with *P* for "over a yard, under a foot."

A thin, metallic voice said, "Excuse me."

Sergeant Collins looked up. He had not heard the woman enter. This was not unusual, since an inch of bulletproof glass separated him from the sally port.

"Yes?" he said.

The woman lifted her chin, placing her mouth level with the small round speaker mounted in the glass between them.

"Is Lieutenant Washington here?"

"He don't work Sundays." Ah! He had it. Carefully writing within the boxes, Sergeant Collins penciled the word *patio* on the puzzle.

The woman said, "I really need to talk to him. Could you call him at home, please?"

The sergeant sighed and lowered his pencil. "What for?"

The woman ignored his question and wouldn't meet his eyes. Andy Collins took stock of her automatically: five-foot-two or -three; short black hair; Caucasian, olive complexion; average build; nicely dressed in black slacks, a cream-colored blouse, wide patent-leather belt, and matching purse—a good-looking woman but agitated, rubbing her hands together, having trouble standing still. She seemed to have a serious problem.

"Ma'am? I can't call the lieutenant unless it's an emergency. Maybe someone else can help you. Detective Baxter is on duty. He works pretty close with the lieutenant."

"No. No, I need the lieutenant. He knows me. He'll treat this . . . I mean, he'll know I'm not a . . ." She stopped speaking and took a deep breath. "Listen, just tell the lieutenant that Rabbi Gold stopped by, all right?" The woman was already walking away.

"Hey!" called the sergeant.

She stopped and looked back.

"Can you help me out with something?"

"What?" asked the woman doubtfully.

Andy Collins lifted the newspaper enough to show her the puzzle. "I need a nine-letter word that starts with a *T* for 'at the head at the end.'"

The woman wrinkled her brow for a moment. Then she said, "Try *tombstone*."

Sergeant Collins lowered his eyes to the puzzle. By golly, *tombstone* worked. "Thanks," he said.

"Thank *you*."

"What for?" asked the sergeant.

"You've reminded me of something."

She walked out the door. The sergeant stared after her for a moment, then shrugged and returned his attention to the puzzle. After penciling *tombstone* into the appropriate squares, he moved on to the next clue, but his mind wouldn't focus. Instead he found himself thinking about that woman. A rabbi with a purse . . . who would have thought it? A very worried rabbi, if his instincts were worth anything. Sergeant Collins considered his options. There were upsides and downsides either way, but he decided it'd probably be best to let the lieutenant know.

He reached for the telephone.

ol followed her from the police station to a Jewish cemetery back over
near her house, on Canal across from North Anthony.

Muttering, "Stupid woman," under his breath, he watched her park
and enter the cemetery alone. Everyone knew better than that. The cemeteries had become popular with muggers in the last few years. Only tourists entered them alone. Locals knew better—or ought to. He'd met an
old boy in Angola who told stories of what happened to women in the
cemeteries. Remembering the man's jailhouse tattoos and the soulless joy
he took in retelling his exploits, Sol marveled at Ruth Gold's foolishness.
He stepped from his truck and searched through the assorted pieces of
metal in the back. Selecting a short piece of black iron pipe, he tested its
balance in his hand. With any luck at all, the bad guys were working
another graveyard today.

ey. Am I early?" Jake Singer stood outside Kate's open front door,
smiling.

"No," she said, standing barefoot in the hall. "I'm late. Can you give
me just a minute?"

"Sure."

"Okay." Kate started to close the door. Then she realized what she
was doing. "Oh," she said, "I'm sorry. Would you like to wait inside?"

He smiled again. "That would be nice."

She blushed. "I don't know what I was thinking. Come in, please."

Jake stepped into her home. He wore a crisp pair of chinos, a short-
sleeved plaid shirt with a button-down collar, and a pair of brown loafers
with leather tassels. Withdrawing his right hand from behind his back,
he offered her a single yellow rose. As he held it toward Kate, she noticed
the thick, ropy muscles of his forearm and the way the blond hairs lay
tightly curled upon his tanned skin.

"Thank you," she said, taking the flower and lifting it to her nose.
"Ummm. Smells wonderful."

"I know. I sniffed it all the way over here."

"Would you like something to drink? I have sodas, mineral water,
Kool-Aid—"

He laughed.

She looked at him curiously, then realized what she'd said. Covering her mouth with her palm, Kate laughed too, the flower bobbing in her hand. "Sorry," she said. "I'm so used to offering drinks to the neighborhood kids. You're the first adult guest we've had around here for . . . well, for a while."

He stopped laughing. "That's a shame."

"I don't mind."

"No? Well, I'm glad you're making an exception in my case."

She stared at the Star of David around his neck. A silence rose between them, awkward and ill defined.

Finally, Kate said, "So . . . you want some iced tea or a Coke or something while I get ready?"

"That Kool-Aid sounds good, actually."

"Oh, come on."

"Really," he said, pale eyes sparkling. "I used to love the stuff. Might be fun to try it again."

"Really?"

"*Really*, Kate. Why not?"

Touching the tiny gold cross on her necklace, Kate felt herself relax a little bit. "Okay," she said. "Why not?"

Even behind her sunglasses, Ruth squinted against the sunlight's reflection on the bleached marble tombstones. The roar of a jet descending toward the airport and the hiss of traffic on Canal added to the harshness of the environment as Ruth made her way through the tombs toward her parents' humble grave. In spite of the soaring temperatures and noisy aircraft, and the fact that it had only been a week since her last visit, she felt a deep need to be here. Ever since they had laid her parents side by side, this had been the one place in all of New Orleans where she felt she truly belonged. The noise and heat didn't matter. Nothing could rob her of the cold comfort she felt near their graves.

Ruth followed a circuitous path through the cemetery, hardly noticing her surroundings. She knew this was a dangerous place for most people but somehow felt it was not so for her. She believed *Hashem* in his mercy protected her here. Some rabbis avoided cemeteries because they were *tref*—unclean—but like most Reform rabbis, Ruth ignored that particular bit of biblical law. In the best liberal tradition, she chose to observe the traditions that seemed to fit her life as *Hashem* had created her, and she respectfully declined to be bound by the others.

Reaching the concrete bench beside the Rosenbergs' tomb, Ruth sat and faced her parents' final resting place. She thought of Steve, so recently placed in the ground. Even now, she did not understand her feelings for him. Had it been love? Perhaps. All she knew for sure was that she missed him and wished she could believe that he was somewhere better now, waiting for her, instead of dead and in the ground and simply . . . gone.

The Torah did not speak of a life after death, at least not clearly. There was much rabbinic debate in the Talmud on the subject, and of course the references in the prophets and writings were well known, but one had to stretch the text very thinly to arrive at a teaching of afterlife in the five books of Moses. When pressed by an instructor at Hebrew Union College several years ago, she had taken the position that this life was all we could expect. If heaven wasn't in Torah, it probably didn't exist. Several times since her ordination, congregants and fellow rabbis had challenged her on that. She always returned to the Scriptures to defend her position, and yet, as Ruth stared at the carved names of her mother and father, her heart filled with an undeniable longing. Each time she visited this place, the feeling rose more strongly than before—a vague and inexpressible desire, like hunger for a particular kind of food that she had never eaten. Ruth noticed it most strongly at moments of transcendent beauty. Just the other day she had seen a crimson waterfall of sweet-gum leaves flowing to a verdant lawn and suddenly, inexplicably, she had longed to be somewhere else—somewhere beautiful. Yet in that moment, with the emerald lawn blanketed by the vivid red leaves, she *had* been in a beautiful place. Why the odd desire for something else . . . some other splendor?

When hunger or fatigue overtook her body, it was because she needed food or sleep. *Hashem* had created her with those needs and provided the means to satisfy them. The longing itself was proof that the thing she desired actually existed; wasn't that also true for thirst and boredom and loneliness? For those, *Hashem* had created drink and work and love. So if she felt this deep longing for . . . how could she express it? Some other life? Yes, that came as close as anything. Some other life. If she wanted that so intensely, did it not follow that her desire itself indicated the other life existed somewhere, somehow?

Ruth shut her eyes.

Hashem, I know Judaism is about making a difference here and now, but you have also filled me with a need to be rid of this world, to enter into something better. As Abraham and Moses rested with their fathers, I want to see my parents again. But I'm afraid. What if this is nothing but selfishness or egotism? What if I only feel this way because of my troubles?

She sighed.

Hashem, please show me the truth.

Opening her eyes, she blinked against the sunshine and sat with her hands clasped together in her lap, awaiting God's answer. If she had to live with the knowledge that her family and the only man she'd ever seriously considered taking as her husband were all cold and in the ground, if she had to live with the fact that Sol Cantor wanted to put her in the ground beside them—it would be nice to believe in a world to come. Maybe later she could find something in the Torah to offer reassurance. Ruth Gold believed all of the answers were there, if only she could understand.

It turned out that the aquarium stayed open later than Jake thought, so they decided to do both: go to the aquarium *and* see *Moby Dick*. Jake called it a "big fish date." The remake of Melville's classic had been wonderful, with modern special effects and breathtaking underwater photography, but throughout the picture Kate had been plagued by a recurring sense that she should be doing something important. For days now, the nagging feeling had been there. She had almost brought it to the surface once or twice, but the thing, whatever it was, always slipped away unseen. It had ruined the show for her.

Now, after the movie, Kate managed to ignore the feeling and enjoy the drive to the aquarium. They rode in Jake's locksmith van, with the kids in back among the shelves and equipment. Paul asked a dozen questions about Jake's work, and Jake answered them seriously, going into great detail. Paul and Jilly walked ahead through an underwater tunnel of glass with their heads thrown back and mouths wide open as a school of brilliant blue fish swam over them. Kate and Jake followed close behind. "It's beautiful," said Kate, looking around as they passed sea life to the left and right and overhead.

"Yes," agreed Jake, pointedly keeping his eyes on Kate's profile. "Beautiful."

"Oh, look! What *is* that?" asked Kate.

"I think it's a blowfish."

"Look how it moves. See those little fins?"

"Uh-huh," Jake said, still looking at her.

She noticed, and smiled. "You're missing it."

Ahead, Paul and Jilly emerged from the glass tunnel and stood waiting impatiently. "I wanna see the baby sharks," said Paul. "They let you pet them and everything."

"Okay, honey," Kate said. "We'll get there. Let's just walk around until we find them."

"But I wanna go there *now*."

"There's lots of other things to see. Giant turtles and electric eels and things. We don't want to miss them, do we?"

Paul frowned. "I don't care about them."

"I wanna see the giant turtles," said Jilly.

"There you are," said Kate to Paul. "Some of us like things other than sharks, honey."

"But I wanna *go* there!" His voice rose. "Right *now!*"

Kate stepped closer, lowering her voice. "Come on, honey. Please don't be this way."

Jake watched the two of them carefully.

Kate placed her hand on Paul's shoulder, but he jerked back, pointedly turning his back on her with his plump arms crossed and his jaw jutting out defiantly like a little Mussolini. He began walking away. Kate said, "Where are you going?"

The boy ignored her.

"Paul, please wait for us."

Paul disappeared around a corner.

Kate turned to Jake. "I guess we'd better—"

Jake nodded, heading toward the corner. "Sure. I've seen enough here anyway."

A few minutes later, as Jilly and Paul stood a few feet away watching sharks cruise silently beyond a giant glass wall, Kate said, "I'm sorry about that."

"No need to be," said Jake.

"He's been acting that way a lot lately. I don't understand it."

"Maybe he's feeling a little bit threatened."

She looked at him. "By you?"

He shrugged. "Maybe."

Kate returned her gaze to the school of fish on the other side of the glass. "I guess it's possible. This is the first time we've been anywhere with a . . . uh . . . with a man, since John died."

Jake did not reply. They stood silently, watching the fish. Then he said, "I'm honored."

"Huh?"

"That I'm the first. I'm honored."

She looked at him. "I guess it does make you sort of special, doesn't it?"

"Oh," he said, "there's nothing special about me."

After a while, Jake walked over to Jilly and Paul and pointed to something in the tank. Soon, the three of them were absorbed in conversation as Kate looked on. Paul became more and more animated, enthusiastically responding to Jake's observations.

Smiling, Jilly glanced back at Kate. Seeing Jilly standing there with Paul and Jake, Kate felt something stir inside, a slumbering giant of a feeling that she'd nearly forgotten. Almost immediately she put it back to sleep. But not before she'd allowed herself to enjoy the awakening, just for an instant.

Washington hung up the phone and walked across the room to increase the volume on his stereo. A set of shelves containing thousands of jazz and classical recordings on compact discs obscured the wall behind his sound system. As he twisted the volume control, Ruth Brown's husky voice streamed from eleven speakers strategically placed around the room. Next to Ella Fitzgerald and Billie Holiday, he figured Ruth

Brown was the best there ever was. In fact, there were moments when he would put her ahead of Ella and Billie, like right now, as he matted a photograph while "5–10–15 Hours" crooned from the stereo. He remembered taking this particular shot in St. Francisville last winter: a black and white of a picket fence alongside a sidewalk where two children squatted next to each other playing pitch the penny. Right now it was his all-time favorite, like Ruth Brown. You could scout locations for days, spend hours considering the light and selecting the right lens and filter and so forth, but sometimes it all boiled down to being in the right place at the right time. Dumb luck.

He had driven up to see his elderly Aunt Luella one Sunday last winter and gone for a short walk around her neighborhood in the old river town. Turning a corner, he'd spotted these kids, and the scene had been perfect. Without thinking about it much, he snapped a few shots with his Nikon and kept walking. By the next day he'd forgotten all about it, but a week later when he developed the contact prints, there was this one frame with the kids and the sidewalk and the fence . . . man, it was flawless. The sense of timelessness and peace just drifted off the paper and into your mind. So Lincoln Washington had played with it in his darkroom, pushing up the contrast. When it got even better, he decided to include it in a show coming up at a little gallery uptown.

Washington loved to do this on his days off. Whether shooting around the city, or in the swamps with his Walkman headphones on, or hanging around the house listening to his stereo and fiddling with his shots, these twin passions—jazz and photography—were all it took for him to enjoy a relaxing Sunday afternoon.

Then Collins had to call about that rabbi.

He tried to pick up where he'd left off. Positioning the white mat board on his cutter, he slid the knife across it twice to trim the outer edges to the correct size. Then he adjusted the knife to the forty-five-degree position and began his cuts in the center to frame the image. The first three went just fine, but he overcut on the fourth, ruining the mat. Sighing, he threw it in the trash.

Why did Collins have to call on a Sunday? Now he couldn't get Ruth Gold off his mind. Not that it was really Collins's fault. For some reason, the rabbi's far-fetched accusation that Solomon Cantor was a serial killer had lodged in his brain like a splinter, worrying its way into his subconscious to prick his thoughts at the most inopportune moments. But he had an unidentified woman in Audubon Park killed by big cats and racist punks firing automatic weapons at tourists in the Vieux Carre, both on the same day. Why should he think twice about some paranoid woman with persecution fantasies?

Washington had checked this Solomon Cantor's record. The Nan Smith murder had been Cantor's one and only problem with the law. He hadn't even been cited for a traffic violation until the other day, and Cantor never caused a ripple of trouble in all those years at Angola. He spent most of his time working in the prison library. Never had a beef with another con, or if he did, he settled it quietly. To Washington, he sounded like a very unlikely candidate for a serial killer.

Still, Rabbi Gold's worries kept coming back to haunt him.

Lincoln Washington crossed the room and stood before a sliding-glass door, staring out at his backyard. It wasn't much, a few square feet of sun-baked Bermuda grass and some honeysuckle on the chain-link fence along the alley. Between the job and his photography, Washington didn't have time for yard work. He paid a neighborhood kid ten bucks a week to mow the lawn and tried to remember to get out there every spring and fall to fertilize. Now and then he had to kill some poison ivy. That was about it. But he did find it helpful to stare outside while he tried to organize his thoughts.

Okay, so her boyfriend was murdered by cyanide poisoning. Ruth Gold had been the obvious prime suspect, but her story about the apples being delivered had checked out. They'd originally come from some outfit in Washington State. Sort of a fruit version of Omaha Steaks. The fruit company's records showed the order was placed by Rabbi Gold and charged to her Visa card, but the rabbi denied ordering the fruit; and the thing was, they'd been shipped via overnight express two days before the rabbi said she received them. They should've arrived the next day, and the delivery service's records claimed they had. So. Was the rabbi lying about ordering the apples and when she got them, or had someone used her credit card number, then intercepted the shipment, poisoned the fruit, and replaced the package at her door? The rabbi had no history of mental health problems, and as far as he could tell, she and the victim had no beef whatsoever. She didn't stand to profit from his death. Could have been some kind of romantic problem, of course, but nobody they'd interviewed had ever heard the rabbi and the victim fight. In fact, the guy's friends all said he'd been crazy about her—a real one-woman man. So insanity, jealousy, greed, and heat of anger were all unlikely motives. Why would she kill him?

Washington tended to think the rabbi was clean. Which meant someone stole the apples from her front porch, poisoned them, and replaced them the next day, thus causing the delay in delivery and making Ruth Gold a targeted victim instead of a suspect or a victim chosen at random.

Or . . .

Maybe the delivery company just took an extra day for some reason, and the apples got poisoned up in Washington State, in an act of indiscriminate insanity, the toughest kind of case to crack. The cops up there were looking into the possibility.

Deliberate or random? Washington decided it was too close to call.

Then there was the old guy who shot his brother. Rothstein, Rothburg, something like that. How did you make that one for a serial killer? Somebody vandalizes the old guy's apartment; he gets scared and caps the first thing that moves. Now he's lying there in the psychiatric ward at the hospital, talking nonsense to anyone who'll listen. Nasty business for sure, but nothing like the MO of the boyfriend's murder.

And finally, there was that night when the rabbi's friend—what was her name? Kathy something . . . no. Kate? Yes, Kate Flint. Anyway, she'd had that B&E and attempted arson at her home. Again, completely different MO from everything else. But serial killers almost always followed a set routine. They didn't poison one victim, then con another into a shooting, then burn down another victim's house. Still, it was interesting that everyone concerned went to the same temple.

Except for the Flint woman.

There, see? Even that wasn't a pattern. Besides, it was a big temple. With a group that size, people were bound to die fairly often, even of unnatural causes. Washington figured if he checked he'd probably find the death rate in the rabbi's congregation was no greater than usual. On the other hand, it did bother him that the rabbi, her friend, and both of the old brothers had all been witnesses at Sol Cantor's trial. What were the chances of that? Pretty slim. Especially if you considered the fact that Cantor had only been out of prison a couple of weeks when all these things started happening.

A squirrel made its way in fits and starts across Washington's lawn, pausing in the middle to rise on its hind legs with its front paws tucked under its chin. It looked directly at him. The lieutenant's mind barely registered the presence of the animal as he pondered the timing of Cantor's release and the deaths. Then a huge brown bird with bright yellow claws and a viciously hooked beak swooped down from out of nowhere, spreading its wings at the last possible moment, seizing the squirrel in its talons and lifting it away. Washington pressed his cheek against the glass, straining to watch the bird of prey until it flew over the top of a neighbor's house and out of his line of sight.

Was that an *eagle?*

Okay, that's it. He turned away from the glass, crossed the room and lifted his car keys from the shelf near the stereo. How could he enjoy himself with all this craziness going on? Might as well go to work.

T hey had a late dinner at McDonald's. Jake had ordered the fish fillet sandwich in the spirit of their big fish date. Kate had ordered one, too, just for fun, but the kids wanted Happy Meals with burgers. Kate was relieved that Jake hadn't taken them somewhere nice. The French Quarter had some of the world's finest restaurants, and a lot of guys might have tried to impress her, especially on a first date, but with the kids along that just wasn't a good idea. Fortunately, Jake seemed to know better. It was a good sign. Kate liked men with common sense.

Jake took everyone's order and stood in line while she and the kids washed up in the rest rooms. When they came out, he already had everything set up at a corner table near the front, where they could watch the passing crowd. Paul and Jilly dug into their Happy Meals immediately.

Kate said, "Hey. Aren't y'all forgetting something?"

"Oh, all right," said Paul, replacing his burger on his tray.

Jake smiled. "What's up?"

"We bless every meal, don't we, kids?"

Jilly nodded. She already had her hands clasped together in her lap and her head bowed.

Jake raised his eyebrows. "Okay," he said. "Why not?"

Bowing her head, Kate said, "Paul, will you ask the blessing?"

"Oh, Mom."

"Come on, Paul. It's your turn."

Sighing elaborately, Paul bowed his head. "God, thanks for this food, and for the neat fish and all at the aquarium—" Kate peeked at Jake, who sat with his head up and his eyes open, watching her son—" . . . and thank you for our family. Please watch out for us, and take good care of Dad. In Jesus' name I pray. Amen."

Kate raised her head, still watching Jake, wondering how he felt about that last part—the part about John and Jesus. Although she had done her best to ignore it, in the back of her mind a small voice still whispered that she shouldn't be here with him. But Jake didn't seem to mind. He had already started eating his fish sandwich.

"Mmmm," he said, rolling his eyes, with his cheeks stretched comically by an enormous bite. The children both laughed.

Good, she thought. *Maybe it will be okay.*

CHAPTER
TWENTY-EIGHT

As the shadow from the Rosenbergs' tomb crept closer to her parents' graves, Ruth tried to remain focused, sitting with her eyes closed, listening from the heart for an answer to her prayer about life after death, but her thoughts wandered along old familiar paths to other times when she had come to this place, and other prayers she had offered up from beside her parents' graves. Some had been answered in immediate, obvious ways. Sometimes she had come here in turmoil and left in the peace of *Hashem*'s undying love, but many other prayers had not been answered as she would have hoped. Ruth's forehead creased as her mind entered darker regions, populated by events she would rather forget . . . .

The cancer struck Isaac three days after Ruth's second *Yom Kippur* in the rabbinate, the *Yom Kippur* when she had denied tickets to her brother. It had already metastasized into his lymph system, liver, and kidneys. They gave him very little time. They did not even attempt chemo or radiation therapy. It seemed that death had come for her brother and would not be denied.

She learned the details of Isaac's condition mainly through a series of telephone conversations with her mother, who spent day and night at Isaac's side on the fifth floor of the Touro Infirmary, reading to him, supervising the nurses who came and went with annoying frequency, and dozing in the reclining chair they had placed in the corner for that purpose. Her father visited Isaac every day for an hour on his way to his office and another four or five hours each evening. Ruth also stopped by every day or so, but only for a few minutes each time. She told herself she didn't want to tire him. She told herself Isaac had enough visitors already, people from New Orleans, of course, and his girlfriend, Sheryl something, down from Princeton. Apparently the young woman's relationship with Isaac was quite serious. She had taken a hotel room near Touro and joined Ruth's mother in her virtually round-the-clock vigil at Isaac's side.

Ruth remembered long days at temple, filled with a bone-deep grief that she refused to acknowledge, hiding behind an avalanche of work: budgets, programs, lectures, preparation for *Shabbat* services, visits to the sick—Isaac wasn't the only Jew in town with cancer, after all—and mundane tasks like supervising building maintenance and doing her own laundry. Anything to avoid the boy in the bed at Touro Infirmary. Anything to ignore the wall between them.

When the doctors could do nothing more for him, her parents took Isaac home. He died on a Sunday morning, less than a week later. Ruth was in bed when her mother called. She had been annoyed when the telephone rang so early. After she heard the words, those final words that seemed so normal yet so bizarre, she sat on the side of her bed above the Silversteins' garage in the Garden District and tried to cry. She felt she should cry. She made the noises, moaning and so forth, but the tears would not come. After a few minutes of that, it occurred to Ruth that she was acting without an audience, so she stopped and took a shower.

Isaac's body lay in the ground by Tuesday afternoon. Jews bury their dead quickly because they do not embalm the bodies. It is a tradition

handed down through the centuries, grounded in the hope that the resurrection will find the Jewish dead ready and waiting with their bodies
whole, including the blood. In the Torah it is written: "For the life of the
flesh is in the blood, and I have given it to you upon the altar to make an
atonement for your souls, for it is the blood that makes an atonement for
the soul." Since Ruth did not believe in resurrection, she did not care one
way or the other, except, perhaps, for the fact that the money saved by
not embalming the body could be given to the poor. That was something,
at least.

On Tuesday evening after the funeral service, they had gathered at
her parents' home: Mom and Dad, of course, and a few of their closest
friends, mostly from the Jewish community, although a few non-Jews
came too. One of those was Sheryl, Isaac's girlfriend, a lovely girl, tall
and slender, with perfectly straight, long brown hair that she wore down
and constantly tucked and retucked behind one ear or the other. A gold
chain with a small cross hung outside her dress of simple black. No
college girl would have such a dress in her wardrobe, unless she played
an instrument in a symphony orchestra or chamber ensemble or went
to a lot of funerals. Ruth asked if she was a musician. The girl seemed
surprised at the question, saying no, she couldn't carry a tune. Ruth had
then complimented her on her dress. Sheryl said she had purchased it at
the Riverwalk mall a week before. The unspoken gloom of what she had
done lingered in the air between the two young women, souring the rest
of their conversation. Shopping for a dress to wear to your boyfriend's
funeral while he was still alive—if you could call what Isaac had endured
those last few days living—doing that all alone in a strange city . . . the
mental image of Sheryl's brave and lonely act saddened Ruth far more
than any other part of that cursed day.

Ruth watched the girl closely for the rest of the evening, catching
glimpses of her chatting on a sofa or trying to be helpful in the kitchen.
Then, during an unguarded moment when Sheryl obviously thought no
one was watching, Ruth saw her face dissolve into utter anguish—her
eyes squeezed shut, her mouth a twisted, downward-pulling thing, like
one of those masks the Greeks once wore in their amphitheater melodra-
mas. Yet Ruth knew that Sheryl's grief-stretched face was no mask. Standing just outside an open door, peering into the room beyond, Ruth had

seen a person unafraid to bring her emotions to the surface full and undi-
luted. Nothing stood between Sheryl's heart and skin; she was whole in
her sorrow, perfectly connected inside and out, soul and body united,
swaying with complete abandon to a dirge that only she could hear.

Seeing Sheryl that way—spying on her—Ruth forgot herself for just
a moment and moaned aloud. Sheryl heard and looked her way. Their
eyes connected, and Ruth saw something rise within Isaac's girlfriend
that shamed her still, a decade later. This stranger who had traveled
down from Princeton, abandoned her studies at midterm, slept upright
beside Isaac's bed as he wasted away, showered in her hotel, and gone
right back to sit beside him again, read to him, and watched him dying
until she knew the time had come to take the streetcar alone across a
strange city to buy a plain black dress—this unwed widow who did all
of that—*she* extended sympathy and love to *Ruth* with her gentle eyes,
rimmed in red.

Choking, Ruth turned and ran from the house.

She never saw Sheryl again, but four days after Isaac's funeral, Ruth
received a letter postmarked Princeton, New Jersey. She did not open
it at first, telling herself she would get around to that as soon as she
finished washing the dishes, or tomorrow morning with her coffee. In
that way, she postponed reading the letter for almost a full day. But
finally, on Sunday afternoon a week after Isaac died, Ruth forced herself
to break the seal. The note was written in a spidery and artless hand.

Dear Ruth,

    *I appreciated your hospitality last week after the funeral. We didn't seem to
be able to get together while I was there, but I heard so much about you from
Isaac that I feel as if we're sisters, in a way. I hope that's all right to say.*

    *Anyway, here I am back at school, and I have one last thing to do. Isaac's
roommate, Grant, and I are going through his things, boxing them up to send to
you and your parents. It's what Isaac wanted. He told me to send you his books,
so those will follow in a few days. I hope you don't mind, but I thought I'd keep
his Bible. It's all I want to remember him by. Of course, if you want it, I'll send it
along as well. Just let me know.*

    *There's one other thing. Isaac told your mother and me that he wanted you
to see to his tombstone.*

Sobs racked Ruth's body. She flung the letter to the side and screamed at the top of her lungs in her belated grief. Those first tears she shed for her brother, when they came, were all-consuming. For over an hour, she beat the cushions and buried her face within them, until finally she was spent. Then she finished reading Sheryl's letter.

> *He told us he wanted something very simple. Just regular block letters, not too big. He wanted you to have them put only his name without any dates. And he asked if you would have them put a verse from the Bible under his name. Here it is:*
>
> 'Blessed are the pure in heart, for they shall see God.'
>
> *Ruth, he was worried that you might not do this for him, because the verse is from the New Testament, and he knew how you felt about his faith. But he told us he picked that verse specially, because it shouldn't be offensive in the Jewish ceme-tery, and as you know, he wanted to be buried next to your mom and dad's plot.*
>
> *Anyway, I don't know why Isaac wanted you to be the one to do this, but he did. I asked him why. He said you would understand. I hope you do.*
>
> *Yours truly,*
>
> *Sheryl*

Unbelieving, Ruth read the last half of the letter again, slowly at first, then faster.

What?

What?

As her mind soaked in the words, Ruth's outrage rose once more to stand in the place it had almost abandoned, damming the cleansing river of her grief, re-creating the parched and mordant landscape her freely flowing tears had almost washed away.

A decade had passed since she received Sheryl's letter, and now Ruth stared at Isaac's tombstone. She had caused it to be placed two months after his funeral. That had been a *mitzvah*. But on it, only Isaac's name appeared. The space below was blank. Since her mother had died, no one else could read the phantom words across that smooth and empty surface, but every time Ruth Gold looked upon the naked stone, some-thing of its flinty coldness touched her heart. She welcomed the indigna-tion, preferred it to the sorrow and humiliation that were her only other choices. As always when she stared at Isaac's grave, the familiar epithet rolled through her mind:

How dare he?

Nothing about this woman was easy.

Sol knelt behind the smooth marble of a five-foot tombstone and peeked around the corner. The rabbi sat on a bench about thirty feet away. She had been there over two hours. What was wrong with her, hanging around like a sitting duck, begging for it? She was smart enough to know better. Sol disliked foolish people.

He hefted the pipe in his hand, testing the balance again. Heavy enough to do serious damage but short enough to swing in the tight spaces between the tombstones. The marble felt cool against his cheek. Near his feet, pieces of plaster like broken bits of eggshell had fallen away from a low crypt, revealing an under-stratum of orange bricks worn thin by the erosion of a hundred years of rain. From the crumbling mortar between the bricks drooped a withered brown fern, dry and lifeless.

Sol's right leg ached. He'd been squatting behind this tombstone for too long—a ridiculous position for a man his age. Carefully, he began to straighten out his leg, but some of the feeling had gone from the calf down, and he accidentally kicked up some gravel. He froze, afraid she might have heard. That could ruin everything. When she did not react, he went ahead and straightened the leg all the way. Then a charley horse kicked in, a cramp so sudden and so violent, he moaned aloud without thinking.

Ruth heard the sound of gravel crunching underfoot, very close by. She opened her eyes and glanced around, but saw no one. Perhaps she was imagining things. Then she heard it again.

"Hello?" she called. "Is anybody there?"

Immediately she felt foolish. What if it was a mourner, come to pray on the anniversary of a loved one's death? Or—*O Hashem, please protect me*—what if it was one of those animals loose from the zoo?

She heard a grunt, very deep. It was the sound of a big man exerting himself.

Springing to her feet, all of her self-recriminations for yesterday's violence in the French Quarter gone in an instant, she jammed her hand into her purse, feeling for her gun. Then she remembered that she had left it at home, afraid to venture out with it again. She heard gravel kicked against gravel, a metallic ringing, and the moan of a man in pain.

"I'm calling the police!" she screamed, backing away with her eyes on the looming crypts across the cemetery. The sounds seemed to come from just beyond them, but she couldn't be sure. The source of the echoes could have been in any direction. As Ruth stepped backwards, frantically glancing left and right, she stumbled over a low grave, landing squarely on her bottom. Pain shot up from the cut in her leg. She rolled on all fours and scrambled to her feet. Abandoning all attempts at decorum, she dashed between two tall white tombstones, emerging onto a path that ran parallel to the one leading to her parents' graves.

A few yards away, standing squarely in the center of the path, she saw a large man with his back toward her. In one hand he held a short black pipe.

Ruth sucked in her breath.

The man turned.

Their eyes locked.

She screamed.

Ruth backed away from Solomon Cantor, refusing to take her eyes off him. Her heel struck a marble slab. She stopped, still staring at the man.

"Wait, Rabbi," said Solomon Cantor. "You don't get it."

Ruth did not answer. Instead, she sprinted between the tombstones to her left, charging headlong across the next path and between two more graves on the far side.

Behind her, she heard Cantor's voice. "Stop, Rabbi! We need to talk!"

Breathing hard and ignoring the pain in her leg, she looked back. At that instant, he stepped into view between the parallel walls of marble across the path, still clutching the black pipe. Afraid to look away from him but also afraid to stop, Ruth ran on blindly several more steps. Her shoulder slammed into a concrete pillar. She bounced off the pillar and staggered, almost falling.

"You don't understand, Rabbi!" Cantor limped toward her. "Gimme a chance to explain."

"Stay away from me!" she screamed, reeling from the pain in her shoulder. He said something else but she didn't understand. She stumbled on, holding her shoulder and turning to her right, placing a tall tombstone between herself and Sol Cantor, then turning again as soon as he was out of sight. Weaving left and right to throw him off her trail, she made her way across the graveyard, moving more slowly now, doing her best to be silent. She heard him following and calling out her name. Finally, just ahead, she saw the gate. Beyond it lay the safety of the street. Surely he wouldn't follow her out onto Canal in broad daylight. Abandoning all attempts at silence, Ruth broke into a run again. Behind her, his footsteps came closer as he chased her, scattering gravel with each stride.

She was through the gate!

Turning left, she charged along the sidewalk, praying for a policeman to drive by. Her Citroën stood at the curb on a side street, just twenty yards ahead.

"Stop!" called Solomon Cantor. "Lemme explain!"

Ignoring him, she ran on. Arriving at the driver-side door, she dug through her purse for the keys as his heavy footsteps drew near. Her hands closed on the car key. She risked a glance back. He was very close, walking now, with both hands extended at his sides, palms toward her. What had he done with the pipe?

"Come on, Rabbi," he said. "Gimme a break here. It's really not what you think."

Sobbing with fear, she jammed the key into the lock, frantically jerked opened the door, dove inside and slammed the door shut, punching the lock twice to be sure. He arrived outside the car just as the latch clicked into place and shouted through the glass, "I've been watchin' out for you, Rabbi. Followin' you in case somethin' happened. My leg fell asleep and I fell when I stood up. . . ." Her hand shook so violently she missed the ignition again and again. Reaching over with her other hand, she managed to insert the key two-handed. She turned it. The engine roared to life.

Sol Cantor tapped on her window. "Why won't you believe me?"

Refusing to look at him, Ruth slammed the car into gear and jammed her foot on the accelerator, speeding away from the curb with her eyes straight ahead, afraid to look back, afraid she would see him in her rearview mirror, following.

Ruth drove wildly for blocks, weaving in and out of traffic, using her horn when she would normally use her brakes. After a few minutes, she slowed somewhat, becoming more and more confident that she had lost him. She pulled to a stop at a traffic light and fumbled in her purse for her cellular phone.

Punching in a number, she thought, *Maybe* now *he'll believe me!*

TWENTY-NINE

I want another pie," said Paul.

"You already had yours, honey," said Kate.

"You said this was a special occasion." Kate blushed and Jake looked away nonchalantly, as if unaware that her son had just revealed Kate's true feelings about the date. Meanwhile, Paul continued to whine. "We always get seconds on special occasions."

Jilly said, "Yeah! I wanna 'nother pie too!"

"Okay, okay!" Kate laughed nervously.

"I'll get them," said Jake. He was up and heading back toward the order counter before she could object.

"Jake?" called Kate.

He turned.

"Bring some extra napkins, too, okay?"

"You bet."

The line had grown since they first came in to McDonald's. Jake joined the shortest one. He couldn't believe how well things were going. She really seemed to trust him, like he was a regular guy. Still, he couldn't make himself stop looking for signs that she was nervous. Surely she could tell about him somehow.

Jake shifted his weight from foot to foot, rocking left and right as he waited, getting impatient. That girl behind the register sure was taking her time. He felt the pressure growing inside his head. He bounced up and down on the balls of his feet to fight it off. Energy could be good or bad, depending on how you used it. Moving his body took his mind off things sometimes. He glanced back at Kate and her kids. She saw him and smiled. He smiled back.

Surely she could tell.

Two boys came in and walked up to the line. Each step they took was marked by a loud click. Jake glanced at their feet. They wore Nike athletic shoes. Both boys had used tacks to attach beer-bottle caps to the soles of their shoes, an old trick to create tap shoes on the cheap. The boys probably danced some pathetic excuse for tap on a street corner in the Quarter with a cardboard box on the ground for the tourists' money. A couple of Gregory Hines wanna-bes.

Click, click, click. Why don't they stand still?

Click, click, click. Jake felt the pressure rising fast. He bounced on the balls of his feet again, trying to let the energy go, but the boys' shoes were also in constant motion, tapping on the hard ceramic-tile floor, echoing from the walls, echoing from the ceiling, echoing, echoing. Jake shoved a finger in each ear but could not stop the noise. He shut his eyes, squinting them tight. Immediately he saw the black place of his dreams with the light at the end—the horrible light—and the thing pulling him along, *click, click, click.* Terrified, he opened his eyes and the vision went away, but the *click, click, click* remained. He began to hum, his own voice all he could hear, his fingers still jammed tight in his ears, his calves work-ing hard to keep him bouncing up and down. He hummed and bounced and tried his best not to let the pressure build.

What's that?

Jake jumped forward, spinning to face the thing that had touched his back. One of the boys stood there, hand frozen in midair, an astonished expression on his face. Jake looked at him wildly. The boy's lips moved. *Is he laughing at me?* Jake wondered. *Cursing me?* Summoning his courage, Jake removed his fingers from his ears, but the boy's mouth had already stopped moving. Instead, he heard a voice coming from behind his back. He spun again, facing the order counter once more, where the girl in the uniform stood behind the cash register and said, " . . . you all right?"

Jake saw the fear in her eyes and hated it.

"Hey, man, the sister wanna know what the matter wit' you," said one of the boys behind his back. "You trippin' or what?"

The other boy laughed uneasily. Jake shook his head like a dog, fighting to clear it. Then, wiping sweat from his brow, he stepped up to the counter.

"Pies," he mumbled. "Gimme two pies."

The girl behind the counter would not look at him as she filled his order and took his money. Behind him, the horrible clicking went on. He refused to look back, afraid of what he might see. Finally, a pie in each hand, he took one very deep breath and spun suddenly on his heels.

"Whoa!" said the boy closest to him. "What you doin' now?"

Ignoring him, Jake walked quickly away from the counter, willing himself not to run. As he approached Kate Flint and her children, he watched carefully for signs that they had seen his behavior at the counter. When he stood beside the table, Kate looked up at him and smiled without a hint that anything was wrong.

But Paul watched him closely.

W ashington checked the temple first and found Ruth Gold's boss, the senior rabbi, standing in the parking lot watching some guys fix the roof. The acrid scent of burning tar assaulted the lieutenant's nostrils as the rabbi told him Ruth Gold hadn't shown up for a class she was supposed to teach that morning. Glancing up, Washington saw a crew of men mopping the stuff on the roof. Man, it stank. He thanked the rabbi and got out of there as quickly as possible.

Still thinking about the way the eagle had attacked the squirrel in his backyard, Washington turned his '67 Mustang onto St. Charles and rolled past the park. Eagles were one thing, but a couple dozen seriously dangerous animals were still in the street. In the squad room, he had heard that a bear got into someone's house over on Prytania. Crawled in through an open window early in the morning. Apparently, when the lady of the house got up to make coffee, she discovered it sitting on the floor of her kitchen with its snout in a sack of sugar. Washington shook his head. Man, oh man. How would that be? Wake up with a *bear* in the house?

What's next?

The lieutenant followed St. Charles to Canal and turned his Mustang away from the river. Fifteen minutes later he rolled to a stop in front of the rabbi's house, right across from a mausoleum. Weird how people in New Orleans lived cheek by jowl with the dead. Little cemeteries all over the place. Kids took shortcuts through them; didn't give it a second thought. Sighing, he opened the car door and stepped out, heading for the rabbi's front porch. All this trouble on his day off. He sure hoped it was gonna be worth it. Then, just as he was about to ring the doorbell, Washington's cell phone beeped.

"Lieutenant? It's Baxter."

"Yeah?"

"I took a call from dat rabbi woman of yours a minute ago. She reported a two-four-five."

Assault with a deadly weapon, thought Washington. His grip tightened on the phone. "Is she all right?"

"Sounded okay to me."

"What's her location?"

"Said she got away in her car. She's driving 'round. Called on her mobile."

Washington made the sergeant repeat the number twice as he committed it to memory. Then he disconnected and called Ruth Gold. She answered on the first ring, sounding scared.

"The sergeant told me everything," said Washington. "Are you all right?"

"I'm okay."

"Where are you?"

"I'm just passing a bunch of apartments. Wait. Here's a sign. It says *St. Bernard* something. I can't read the rest of it. There's a lot of graffiti."

The St. Bernard Housing Projects. Washington groaned inwardly.

That area had one of the highest crime rates in the city. Definitely not a good place for a white woman to be driving around alone. "You need to get out of that neighborhood, Rabbi Gold. Listen. I'll meet you at the station, okay?"

"The one where I went this morning?"

"Yes, ma'am."

"It may take me a while to get there, Lieutenant. I'm sort of lost."

"Okay. Lemme give you directions . . . " As he entered his car, Washington reeled off a short list of streets, telling her which way to turn at each one. By the time he was done, the Mustang was in motion. "Have you got that?"

"Yes. I think so."

"Good. From where you are, we should be seeing each other in about twenty minutes. Oh, and lock your doors."

"Okay. Lieutenant?"

"Yes, ma'am?"

"Are you going to arrest me? I only ask because I'll need to call my boss and a couple of other people first, if you are."

"Why would I arrest you, Rabbi Gold?"

She did not respond.

"Rabbi Gold?"

"Yes. I'm sorry. I, uh, I guess you don't know about yesterday."

"What are you talking about?"

"The shooting. On Decatur."

It was Washington's turn to pause as he drove one-handed, wrist draped over the wheel, phone to his right ear. "What about it, Rabbi?"

Jilly peered out through a big clear bubble.

Kate smiled and gave a little wave, watching through the window as Paul's face joined her daughter's in the McDonald's play tower outside. Jilly waved back, then moved out of sight within the colorful midair tunnel, but Paul remained, staring at Kate and Jake. Paul had not wanted to go outside to play, but Kate had insisted, telling him he needed to watch his sister. Now, looking at Jake, she said, "They're having a ball."

"I'm glad. Do you think they like me?"

"Oh yes!"

"Paul seems a little distant."

"I know. But it's not you, believe me. He's just having trouble adjusting to some things."

"I see."

They both took a sip of coffee. Kate had been trying for thirty minutes to figure out what had gone wrong. Earlier, Jake had been very upbeat and fun. Then, sometime in the middle of their meal, he had become nervous and fidgety. *Maybe I'm boring him. It's been so long, I don't know how to act around a man.*

"Mind if I ask a personal question?" said Jake.

"Depends on the question, I guess."

"Okay. Well, if it bothers you to talk about this, just say so."

She waited, but he did not go on. Finally, she said, "Ask me, Jake."

"Uh . . . I was wondering about their father."

So that's the problem. Kate nodded, looking down at her coffee, feeling relieved. *At least it's not my company. It's my past.* She spoke her husband's name out loud, "John."

"John. Did you keep his last name?"

"Sure. Why wouldn't I?"

"Well, you know. Some women go back to their maiden names after a divorce."

"John died."

"Oh. I'm sorry."

"I don't mind talking about it," she hurried to reassure him. "It's been a while."

"Good."

Kate glanced up at him, eyebrows arched. Jake flushed. "I mean, it's good that you've had some time to . . . well, you know what I mean, don't you?"

"I think so, yes."

He sighed. "Oh, boy. I'm not very good at this."

"You're doing fine."

"I am?"

Meeting his eyes, she said, "Yes, you are." They sat silently for a moment, then Kate said, "He was a Jew."

"John?"

"Uh-huh."

"That's . . . interesting."

"He converted when he was eighteen. About two years before I met him."

"Converted to Judaism?"

"No. To Christianity." She paused. "His parents didn't speak to him for years."

"Not at all?"

"No."

Jake shook his head. "Some of us are so suspicious of your faith that we do some pretty mean things."

"*Mean* doesn't begin to cover it, Jake. And it wasn't just his family. Even some of his friends quit talking to him. He tried everything he could think of to get them to . . . to take him back, I guess you'd say. But a lot of them—friends and family both—acted like he'd done something criminal. They broke John's heart."

Jake had begun to bounce his leg up and down very fast beneath the table. She could feel the entire table trembling slightly. When he spoke, Kate thought she heard a bitterness in his voice that had not been there before. "I'll bet they said it was *John* breaking *their* heart."

"Yes," she said, watching him closely. "We heard that a lot."

"So how about now? Are you in touch with his folks?"

"When we had Paul, they came to the hospital. His mother wanted to hold her grandson. It was the first time John had seen his parents in over five years."

"Things got better after that?" Jake wrapped his plastic straw around his finger and pulled it tight. The end of his finger turned red.

"Sort of. We started seeing each other from time to time. But they tried to pressure us into raising the children as Jews. Of course, that was out of the question. I got pretty angry with them once or twice. But they kept trying. It was very awkward."

Jake nodded. The end of his finger had turned from red to purple. Kate could barely restrain herself from telling him to release the pressure on the straw. He said, "I'm really sorry, Kate."

"Thank you."

"No. I mean it. I want to apologize."

"Why? You didn't do anything."

"I know, but it seems like *someone* should apologize," he said, releasing the straw. She watched as his purple fingertip slowly paled. He noticed her watching his hands and balled them into fists, hiding the end of his finger. Beneath the table, his leg continued to bounce.

You're saying you took a shot at those punks?"

"Two shots, actually," said Ruth Gold, looking around his office.

Behind his desk, Lieutenant Lincoln Washington lifted a hand to his mouth to conceal his smile. "And after you shot at them, you just walked away?"

"Well, they were moving out of my range and into that other man's. I saw him shooting too, and knew he had a better angle. Plus I couldn't be sure I wouldn't hit people beyond the car once they got farther away, so I decided to cease fire."

"Cease fire?" Washington swiveled away from the rabbi to stare out through the wired glass window, the grin spreading irresistibly across his face. He knew a citizen had fired at the perpetrators, of course, but eyewitness accounts had described the shooter as everything from an elderly man to a girl of twelve or thirteen. Now it turned out that the shooter was a female rabbi, which was definitely one for the books. With his back still to her, he said, "Where'd you learn to shoot a handgun, Rabbi?"

"Uh, I visit a firing range down near Gretna every now and then."

"And you said you've got a nine millimeter Beretta?"

"That's right."

"I'll bet you're pretty good with it?"

"I . . . uh . . . I've been getting a three- or four-inch pattern at ten yards."

Washington laughed in spite of himself.

Ruth said, "I don't see what's so funny."

A detective out in the squad room called through Washington's open door, "Hey, Lieu, they caught another lion over by Lee Circle."

"Good," said Washington, still chuckling. "Good."

Ruth sat back against her chair and crossed her arms defensively.

"I'm sorry, Rabbi," he said, managing to keep a straight face. "It must have been very traumatic for you, and I shouldn't make light of the situation." Washington knew for a fact that the bullets they had removed from the driver had matched Detective Whitman's side arm.

Ruth said, "Does this mean you're not going to arrest me?"

"*Arrest* you?" asked Washington. "Ma'am, I'm gonna try to get the mayor to give you a medal."

Ruth stared at him suspiciously for a moment, then said, "Okay, if you say so. But what about Solomon Cantor chasing me with that pipe?"

"Oh," said Washington, "him we're definitely going to arrest."

THIRTY

The great-looking man on Kate Flint's front porch said, "I had a great time."

"Me, too," said Kate, her heart beginning to skip beats.

A mosquito buzzed past her ear, lured by the light streaming from the open front door and cheerfully out for blood. Behind her, Kate heard the too-bright voices of the television. Jilly and Paul had already become engrossed in a video, so she and Jake would have a fleeting moment of privacy, a moment she'd been dreading.

"*Moby Dick* was really something, wasn't it?"

"Yeah. I liked the special effects."

The feeling that she should remember something important rushed to the surface again from out of nowhere. Why at this moment of all times? For the briefest instant, she thought she had it, then the memory slipped away once more.

Meanwhile, Jake continued to talk. " . . . like to get together again sometime?" he asked. "Maybe just the two of us?"

"Sure," said Kate, forcing herself to refocus on the conversation. "That would be nice."

"Okay. Well, thanks for the day, Kate. It was great."

"Thank *you*, Jake."

He smiled, turned, and descended the steps. Kate watched him go, surprised to feel a mild disappointment. Was that *it?* After so much stress— wondering if he would ask her for a kiss, wondering how it might be to kiss a man other than John for the first time in years—he walks away without even a handshake? She'd been worried about what he would expect, what she should do. Should she offer her cheek or her lips? What if he wanted more? It had been so long since she'd been in this situation, Kate wasn't sure how to handle it anymore. She had talked herself into an episode of arrhythmia, worrying about this moment. Now, part of her was relieved, but she also found herself wishing he had offered some indication of how he felt. Questions of a kind she had not asked for years commanded her mind: Would he really call again? Did he find her attractive? Did he really like her, or was he just saying and doing the right things?

Maybe Paul's prayer at dinner had offended him. Maybe they should have skipped the prayer, just once.

As Kate watched Jake walk away, as her heart flopped within her like a fish out of water, she saw a week of self-doubt opening ahead, a week of loneliness more intense than what she'd felt since John's death. Gone were her earlier concerns about their different faiths. She did not care. She only knew she had to find out what he really thought, because a week of wondering would be torture. He was such a gentle man. So good with the children. So patient. So strong. All through the evening she had found herself stealing glances at his profile, his smile, his well-muscled arms. Suddenly, she knew that if she had the courage, she would call him back up the steps. She longed to be held as she so often held her children, to banish her loneliness with simple human contact, to feel safe within the arms of this beautiful, gentle man. Only her timidity restrained her. Nothing else.

As if he could read her mind, Jake stopped at the bottom of the steps and turned to look back. He stood perfectly still with his hands shoved into the pockets of his chinos. *Oh, why does he have to be so handsome?*

"Uh, Kate? I've got a question. It's really dumb, but I'm gonna ask it anyway."

"Okay."

"Do you . . . I mean, as a person, just as a person . . . do you think I'm . . . you know . . . likable?"

Relief flooded over her. He cared about *her* opinion of *him!* That meant he liked her! Kate realized she was thinking like a schoolgirl, but she couldn't care less. Struggling to keep her voice neutral, she said, "I like you a lot."

"No. I mean, do I seem like I fit in?"

She cocked her head. "Fit into what?"

"You know, with other people. Society."

Self-doubt crept in again. Had she misjudged him? "What do you mean, exactly?"

He paused before answering, as if searching for words or the bravery to voice them. Finally he said, "What would you do if you found out I'm not normal?"

Kate shrugged elaborately. "Who knows what 'normal' is, anyway?"

"I'm serious. What would you do?" He began to bounce slightly on the balls of his feet, up and down, up and down.

She said, "What are you trying to tell me?"

He raised his voice—not much, but enough to change the mood of the conversation completely. "Don't do that. Don't answer a question with a question. What would you *do*, Kate?"

Watching him stand there, face upturned, looking for something, Kate suddenly knew her answer was important to him. "I guess it depends on what you mean. There are all kinds of ways to be 'not normal.' Some of them are bad, but some of them are very good."

Her words did not seem to please Jake. "Look," he snapped. "I just want you to—" he stopped abruptly and took a deep breath—"I'm sorry. I shouldn't have asked you this so soon."

"Tell me what's going on, Jake."

"I . . . I shouldn't. Not until you know me better." He looked at her, pleading with his eyes. "But I'm a good person, Kate. Underneath, I'm *good*."

She forced a smile. "I believe you."

"You do?"

"Sure."

He nodded nervously, or was it just an illusion created by the strange way he bobbed up and down? "Okay. Okay. Well, the thing is, you know, *Yom Kippur* is coming up in a couple of days, and I was gonna go to temple. It's been a long time since I . . . well, anyway, I feel like I really need to go. To atone, you know?"

"I think so."

"Well, anyway, the thing is, I was wondering if you'd come with me? I mean, I know it's sort of a weird thing to ask, especially since we just met and all, and you're not even Jewish, but I really don't wanna go alone, and I don't have anyone . . . that is, I—I just would really appreciate it if you'd come."

The plea in Jake Singer's blue eyes was irresistible. Thinking that perhaps his invitation had been inspired by an aching loneliness just like hers, Kate almost said, "All right." Then reason took hold, and she thought, *What are you doing? Say no. Tell him you've got other plans.* But Jake's eyes were so incredibly clear. Part of her mind wondered what it would be like to look into those eyes every day. No more loneliness. Someone to be there for her. Just for her. So when her answer came, it was, "Yes. I'll come."

She regretted it immediately.

These feelings were not right. Instinctively she understood they could lead her to a painful choice between this man and her faith, such as it was. She had to get some space from him, to regain her perspective, but it was so difficult to resist, languishing as she was in this cruel sea of solitude. Then, remembering something Ruth had said, Kate thought, *Maybe there's a way out of this.* Summoning her willpower she said, "Can we get seats? I heard it was sold out."

Jake frowned, his previous happiness eclipsed by a sudden look of gloom. "Oh, yeah."

Then she felt him slipping away and could not bear it. Like a rag fluttering in the wind, Kate changed her mind again. He was so very, very gorgeous. She said, "Maybe if I ask Ruth, she'll save some places for us."

"All right!" He grinned at her. Their eyes met, and she shivered. Suddenly serious, he said, "Thanks for trusting me, even though . . . you know . . ."

She lowered her eyes for a moment, appalled at what she had done.

Her racing heart was a writhing thing, duplicating the inconsistency of her mind. She had no business dating a Jewish man. She had no business going to a temple on a Jewish holy day. She was a *Christian* woman!

I've made a mess of things. People will know I'm not Jewish, and they'll resent my being there, and I'll say the wrong thing and . . . oh, God, can't you just make life simple for once?

But then, looking back down at the color of the summer sky in Jake Singer's eyes, her confusion dissolved beneath a surge of relief. She would see him again. She would!

He wiped his forehead in a sudden, strange gesture, as if erasing a memory.

"Jake, won't you tell me what's the matter?"

He turned to look across the street at the moonlight dancing on Bayou St. John. "Can I explain some other time?"

"If that's what you want."

"Yeah. That would probably be best."

Gabby Cantor opened the door with a frown, wondering who would come to call at that late hour. In her right hand was a bourbon and water. Her fourth of the evening. "Yes?"

A small black man wearing an expensive suit stood on her front porch with four uniformed patrolmen. He seemed to be admiring her beautiful home. If he had asked, she could have told him it was a hybrid Italianate and Greek Revival style, circa 1859, with original, lacy wrought-iron fencing around the property in a rattan pattern unique to the residence, two-story fluted columns with ionic capitals, a twelve-foot-deep original cypress gallery and sixteen-foot ceilings on the lower level, with double-hung exterior windows tall enough for a man to step inside from the gallery without stooping. But Gabby Cantor wasn't interested in playing the real estate broker this evening. Gabby Cantor was frightened.

"What's happened?" she asked.

"Evening, ma'am. I'm Lieutenant Lincoln Washington, with the New Orleans Police Department." He showed her his badge, then replaced it in his inside suit coat pocket. "Is Solomon Cantor at home?"

"Why?"

"I need to ask him a few questions, ma'am."

"What for?"

"Is he home?"

The older woman's lips formed a taut, bitter line. Lifting her impeccably manicured fingers to a heavy gold chain around her neck, she said, "What's he done?" She slurred the s.

"Ma'am, if you'll just tell me whether he's here, we can get this over with a lot quicker."

"Well, he's *not* here," she snapped.

"Isn't that his truck parked over yonder?" Washington pointed at an old pickup parked at the curb between a sparkling new BMW and a top-of-the-line Mercedes Benz. It looked like the mechanical version of a migrant farmworker crashing a debutante ball.

Gabby took a slow sip of her cocktail before saying, "I don't have to answer that."

"We checked the tags, ma'am. It's his truck. And we have a warrant to search these premises for him if he doesn't present himself here at the door."

"I told you, he is not here. Now will you please go away before my neighbors see you?"

"Have it your way." Washington stepped to one side. Nodding his head at the door, he said, "Y'all go ahead."

The four patrolmen removed their side arms from their holsters and walked straight toward Gabrielle Cantor.

"Ma'am, please step away from the door," said Washington.

Gabby held her drink close to her chest, as if hiding behind it. The policemen filed past her, the one in front holding his weapon pointed forward, the three behind pointing theirs at the ceiling. Washington followed them in. He paused for a moment to look up at the glowing chandelier in the stair hall, over six feet from top to bottom, with a hundred beaded strands of cut English crystal fanning out to a circular perimeter so wide it almost touched the walls on either side. Six different colors of paint trimmed the hall, all of them perfectly harmonized in muted colors. The air reeked of cigarettes. To the left, the living room—in the old days it would have been called the parlor—was handsomely appointed with an eclectic mixture of furniture styles ranging from

Bauhaus to Biedermeir. To the right stood a wide cased opening trimmed
in thickly fluted molding. Beyond the cased opening lay a dining room
with a table of richest red mahogany lined with at least a dozen Second
Empire chairs. A monumental staircase ascended from the hallway immediately ahead, with a plush woolen runner restrained by brass rods at each
riser, and a fluidly hand-carved banister streaming down from the second
floor as if frozen in midcascade.

Washington whistled. "Ma'am, you mind if I ask what you do for a
living?"

Gabby downed the rest of her drink in a single gulp and crossed the
living room to the dry bar. Uncapping the Jim Beam, she said, "I sell real
estate."

"You must be pretty good at it."

"I am," said Gabby Cantor, turning back with a lift of her chin.
"I'm the best in town. Do you have to have those police cars parked
in front of my home? This will positively *ruin* my reputation in the neighborhood."

"I'm sorry, ma'am. We'll be gone as soon as we can."

Gabby held her glass in both hands to keep it from trembling. The
two patrolmen who had checked the ground floor returned to the hall.
One of them caught Washington's eye and shook his head. The other
two descended the stairs. Washington looked at them. They shook their
heads as well.

"Ma'am," he said, "we could get going much more quickly if you'd just
tell us where your husband is. We'll find him anyway, but if you help,
there's less chance of a problem."

The ice in her drink rattled against the glass. "Problem? What do you
mean?"

"I think you understand."

"Won't you tell me what he's done?"

"I can't do that."

"Well, I don't know where he is, Detective."

"I'm a lieutenant, ma'am."

"Oh? I'm sure you're a good one, too."

Washington smiled. "Best in town."

She stared at him. "Are you mocking me?"

"No, ma'am. I just want you to know I'm going to find your husband, one way or another. Be better for everyone if I did it the easy way."

"Well, I still don't know where he is. He's not living here."

"Why didn't you say so earlier?"

"You didn't ask."

"Where does he live?"

"Ask his parole officer."

"We did. He gave us this address. I need you to tell me where he is."

"If I knew, don't you think I'd tell you rather than letting you cause all this scandal? Now will you *please* get your cars and your men away from my house?" Turning her back on him, she drank deeply from her fifth cocktail of the evening.

The windows all across the front of the Christian girl's house glowed brightly. Orvis Newton watched them carefully, hoping for inspiration. He was out of stories. Oh, there were plenty more, but they weren't *right*. You couldn't use just anything. They should be in order if at all possible, and of course they had to have the desired result. Behind him, the bells of St. Francis Cabrini chimed their familiar tones, comforting him as he stood alone on the sidewalk.

Just then someone's shadow passed across one of the window blinds.

He held his breath. Was it her? Sometimes, with no one there but her and the children, he thought about how simple it would be to walk up and knock on the door and . . .

No. He had a strong sense that would be wrong. It was the Holy Ghost warning him away. He had not yet received a clear calling about this woman. She was a sister in Christ, after all. If he was going to do it at all, it had to be done the right way, exactly as he had been told. He had to follow the Plan. Orvis sighed and shifted his weight from one foot to the other and waited.

Something would be revealed to him.

Those little painted toenails tapping on the sidewalk nearly drove Solomon Cantor crazy, but Gabby seemed to appreciate his help with the dog. Besides, if they were ever gonna get back together, he'd have to get used to this little mutt, so he guessed he didn't mind too much.

Sol still couldn't believe the way Gabby had hit the big time, and he had to hand it to her, she didn't rub it in. Right from the start, she knew better than to offer him money. She hadn't even asked him to move in. He'd like to live with her, sure, but not until he got his own little business off the ground. There was no way he was gonna sit around on his can mooching off Gabby. Someday, he'd let her put a roof over his head. Stupid not to, with such a big fine house. After all, he'd done the same for her back before all the trouble. But since then, he hadn't leaned on anyone—not one single person for twenty-five years—and he wasn't about to start now. So every time he came to her house, Sol brought a load of groceries and cooked something up, or he made it a point to take her out for a meal. In her car, of course. Sure, he might use her washing machine, but at least he did his own laundry instead of asking for help from her maid, and if something broke around her house, he fixed it. No more of those high-priced repairmen. Half of those guys used the fix-it thing as a scam to case the joint anyway. Sol had heard all about it on the inside.

Who knows? Maybe some day, if they could get through this rough spot, he and Gabby could have things like they used to, with him wearing the pants in the family. But first, she had to readjust. Gabby wasn't handling him being out very well. Couldn't get her mind off what happened and the way it was before. She'd never been able to forgive him for the Nan Smith thing. She kept saying, "What if they find out, Sol? What if everyone finds out?" Gabby was way, way too concerned with that. Sometimes she talked crazy, about how her life would be over if people knew.

Sometimes she worried him.

Solomon Cantor passed a big green house with a black door. The other night the woman who lived there had stopped him and asked what he'd charge to walk her dogs. Sol wasn't proud. He'd thought about it, then said, "Fifty a week, once a day. Weekends off." She said he was high, but she'd think about it, and asked for his number. He didn't have a phone, so he'd written Gabby's number on a scrap of paper from his wallet. When the lady saw the Garden District exchange, she got curious.

"You live in someone's garage apartment or something?" she'd asked.

"Nope. My wife owns a house a couple of blocks over. Maybe you've seen it. Two-story, with big white columns and a wrought-iron fence that looks like bamboo?"

The lady got huffy and went indoors. Probably figured he was pulling her leg, a rich neighbor, offering to walk her dog and all. He smiled. She'd be surprised if she knew he was serious. But it was better the lady turned him down. Walking dogs for money in the neighborhood would be bad for Gabby's image.

Sol let the mutt do his business on a trash can. Then he tugged at the leash, and the dog went on down the sidewalk, little feet flying somewhere under all that hair. They were coming up to Gabby's street. The neighbors on the corner had a tropical garden growing in their front yard. Even in the dark he liked to look at it. African elephant ears, banana trees, palmetto palms . . . if you ignored the two-story mansion with all that frilly woodwork, the yard looked like a scene from a Tarzan picture, one of those old ones with Johnny what's-his-name and the good-looking brunette playing Jane. He used to pay a quarter to watch those shows down at that theater on Canal, the one with the fancy columns and the big inside-out dome in front. Quarter a show. Boy howdy. Now people would pay fifty dollars a week just to get someone to walk their dog.

When Sol reached the corner he turned toward her house. Then, seeing two police cruisers and an unmarked car parked under the streetlight, he quickly turned back behind the neighbor's lush vegetation. While the little dog sniffed at the corner of the fence, Sol peeked between some banana leaves. In a few minutes, he saw five men come out of Gabby's house. Four wore uniforms . . . cops. Two of them got in one of the cars and drove away. The other two walked over to his truck. Some little guy was with them. Black guy in plain clothes. The three men walked around his truck, then the plainclothes guy stopped and looked in the driver's side window.

Gabby's mutt started to growl. Sol yanked on its leash, but it strained to get at something in the bushes on the other side of the fence. It growled again, a funny little sound, not something Sol wanted to hear right now. He yanked harder on the leash. The mutt yelped and backed away from the bushes.

Now the guy turned a flashlight into the cab of the truck from every angle. Then he went to shining it on the stuff in the back of the truck. Sol got nervous.

Sure enough, the plainclothes guy walked around the back; Sol heard the metallic creak of the truck's tailgate being lowered. The guy climbed into the truck bed and squatted down, looking at whatever it was real close. He picked something up and shone the light on it. What was that? A piece of pipe? Why would he . . .

Oh no.

Suddenly Sol understood the fix he was in.

The detective spoke to the uniformed cops. The katydids sang too loudly for Sol to understand a word. In a minute or two the plainclothes dick hopped back down to the street, said something else to the uniformed cops, then walked over to the unmarked car, got in, and drove away. As the taillights of his car disappeared around the corner, Gabby's little dog inched closer to the bushes. Sol gave the leash another yank.

Thirty minutes later the uniformed cops were still there when a tow truck arrived, jacked up his pickup, and took it away. Gabby's mutt had been sitting with its ears perked forward the whole time, watching something through the fence. Sol didn't care, so long as the little cotton ball stayed quiet. He waited until the cops in the patrol car drove off, then tugged on the dog's leash and turned to take the back way down the alley. The dog wouldn't budge. He dragged it along as its little toenails clawed at the pavement, trying to get back to those bushes. It began to bark. Disgusted, Sol stopped and bent to pick up the mutt.

That's when he saw the snake.

Sol froze, his eyes locked on the thing. It must have been as big around as his thigh and fifteen or sixteen feet long. An anaconda, maybe, or some kind of python, all slick and scaly and wrapped around the lower branches of the neighbor's magnolia . . . exactly the kind of monster snake that Tarzan used to wrestle in the rivers, back when movies cost a quarter. Its black marble eyes stared right through him. Maybe it had plans for the dog. Slowly, Sol wrapped his hand around the mutt and straightened up, holding it close to his chest as the giant snake's forked tongue flicked in and out of its mouth. Safe in his cradling arms, the dog bared its teeth and barked. The snake just hung there, intertwined among the branches a foot or two above the ground. Using his thumb and first finger, Sol delicately squeezed the dog's mouth shut. It wiggled, but he held it tight. *Stupid little mutt.* Placing one foot behind the other, he backed off, facing the snake, keeping his eyes on it every moment. When Sol was thirty feet away, he turned and headed for the alley, casting glances back from time to time. Meanwhile, even though its tiny jaws were still clamped together by Sol's two fingers, Gabby's dog growled fiercely.

CHAPTER
THIRTY-ONE

Monday morning at ten-fifteen, Baxter walked into Lieutenant Washington's office. "Link, we might have an ID on that stiff from the park."

"I'm listening," said Washington.

"Okay. We got a missin' persons filed on a Helen Blumenthal this morning. Neighbor heard her cat howlin' an' got worried. Ain't seen her since Friday night. So he called the building manager an' they went inside her apartment. Found a few signs that she left the place intendin' to come back on Friday. The cat was out of food and water, the Saturday and Sunday *Picayune* was both outside de door, an' her bed ain't been slept in."

"Did you ask the neighbor to come in and ID a head shot?"

"Aw, Link."

Washington smiled. "Sorry. Of course you did. When'll he be here?"

"On his lunch hour. Round about noon."

Washington thought for a moment. "I don't wanna wait that long. Let's run over to her apartment, see what we can see."

"Okay. I'll get the car an' meet you out front."

How do you think the Jews who worship at Temple Brit Yisrael will feel about your presence here on *Yom Kippur*, Reverend Newton?"

Orvis smiled at the reporter as she moved her microphone toward him. It had been his idea to conduct the interview on the sidewalk in front of the temple, and the reporter had quickly agreed. Orvis felt they had established a good relationship. She was certainly comfortable around him, unlike lots of people who became intimidated when he told them he was a man of the cloth.

"We hope our Jewish friends will be touched by our presence, Julie." He held his smile. "After all, we're here to demonstrate our deep and abiding concern for the welfare of their immortal souls."

"The senior rabbi of the temple, Rabbi Samuel Gottlieb, has expressed outrage at your tactics. He called them—" she checked her notebook— "'the offensive and condescending acts of dangerously unstable fanatics.' Would you care to respond?"

"I'm not sure what the rabbi means by 'dangerous' or 'unstable.'"

"Could he have been referring to the murder of Nan Smith twenty-five years ago under similar conditions?"

"Well, if that's the case, it would seem that *we* are the ones in danger. After all, Sister Smith was killed by a member of Rabbi Gottlieb's congregation." Orvis lowered his eyes dramatically. "Her memory is an inspiration to us all. . . . " He allowed his voice to trail off, took a deep breath, and shook his head sadly. Then, perking up, he continued brightly, "That's exactly why we want everyone to know that Sister Smith's ministry continues today."

"I see, and—"

"And if I may, Julie, I'd also like to respond to Rabbi Gottlieb's remark that we are 'offensive.'" Orvis smiled directly at the camera. "The Lord Jesus Christ said his gospel would offend the world. He said it would be an affront to those who are *of* this world. That is why I take *pride* in causing the kind of offense that Rabbi Gottlieb describes."

"The rabbi has also described your founder, Sister Smith, as, quote, 'a zealot who had no regard for the sanctity of the Jewish community's right to worship as they please.' What do you say to those who remember her in that way?"

Orvis felt his face turning red. He knew it was happening but couldn't stop the anger. "Those words are lies, Julie! Whether the rabbi made them up himself, or whether he's repeating someone else's lies, I couldn't say, but they *are* the most vicious kind of lies! There have been other attempts by Jews to silence this ministry by impugning Sister Nan Smith's reputation. Of course, such slander will not stand. She was a saintly woman."

"Thank you, Reverend. I—"

"And I would suggest that Sister Nan Smith—who died doing the very work we are engaged in here today—Sister Smith would agree that the strength of the rabbi's concern about our efforts and the attacks he has launched against us by making inappropriate statements such as that are indications that we are successfully reaching a large number of his congregation. She'd be *delighted* that the rabbi is so upset. I am certainly delighted that he's upset. I want him to be even more upset, because I want him to look out one day upon an empty sanctuary. That day is coming, Julie, and when it does, I pray that the rabbi will swallow his sinful pride and come out here where Jesus Christ is waiting to cleanse him white as snow." Orvis smiled suddenly. "That's what we're about here, and we're doing our best, but much more could be done if our resources weren't so limited. So, if any of your viewers would like to support our work here, they can send checks or—"

"Okay, Reverend! Thank you." The reporter lowered her microphone and turned to the cameraman. "That's it, Billy."

Orvis said, "But I wasn't done."

She said, "Reverend, I thought we agreed you wouldn't mention fund-raising in this interview."

"I still don't understand why you won't let me talk about that."

Offering her hand, she said, "It's against station policy, Reverend."

Orvis shook her hand. The reporter seemed to withdraw it as quickly as possible. Saying, "Okay, well, thanks for your time," she walked toward the van, coiling the microphone wire as she went.

"But I didn't get a chance to talk about the goats."

She turned, eyebrows raised, and said, "Goats? What goats?"

Ruth entered The Other Day with a shopping bag in each hand and stood nervously near the front door, wondering if this was a mistake. Katy Flint was on the telephone with her back to Ruth and had not seen her enter. In the small shop, Ruth could not avoid overhearing every word Katy said as she arranged an interview with her pastor for later that afternoon. There was still time to leave, but just as Ruth was about to act on that thought, Katy hung up the phone and turned around.

Katy said, "This is a surprise."

"Is it all right? My being here?"

"Sure. I just thought after the other night . . . you know."

"I feel bad about that. I mean, there you were taking care of me, and I dumped on you." Ruth offered a smile. "I'm sorry."

Katy waved the apology away with the back of her hand. "Forget it. We were both pretty freaked out."

"That's for sure."

"So, what've you been doing?"

"Shopping, of course," said Ruth. "What else would I do on my day off?" Relieved at Katy's magnanimous attitude, Ruth dropped her full weight onto a seventeenth-century Windsor side chair as if it were brand-new, plopping the bags down on each side, throwing her legs out in front and leaning her head back to stare up toward the ceiling. The oaken spindles in the bowed chair back creaked, but they held. "I'm pooped."

"Want a cup of tea?"

"You bet."

Katy rose and switched on the hot plate. "Something tells me you've worked things out with the police."

"Would you believe it? That lieutenant thinks I did a *good* thing, shooting at those guys. He said he was gonna ask the mayor to give me a medal."

"They really didn't mind that you shot at those people?"

"Well," Ruth frowned, "I did have to promise not to do it again, unless it was absolutely necessary." Katy's laughter took Ruth off guard. She had not meant to make a joke, but she smiled just the same. "That wasn't even the best part. Turns out I missed. That other guy shot the driver, not me."

"Oh, Ruth. That's *wonderful*. I mean, not that the man got shot, of course, but—"

"Believe me, I know exactly what you mean."

The water began to boil. Ruth watched Katy pour it into a teapot, which she brought on a tray to a small walnut side table. Sitting across from Ruth on a primitive ladder-back chair, Kate poured steaming water into two matching Dresden cups. "We've got Constant Comment and Red Zinger," she said. "And Earl Grey."

"Gimme the Earl Grey. I need the caffeine."

They dipped their tea bags into their cups in silence. Ruth enjoyed the moment of peace and civility.

Then Katy said something she didn't expect. "I've missed you."

Before she could stop herself, Ruth said, "Oh, Katy. You don't really know me."

Katy's eyes fell to her cup. They sat together awkwardly, silence spreading between them like a contagious disease as Ruth cursed herself for her ungracious response. *What's the matter with me? Why can't I be nice to this woman?* Finally, without looking at her companion, Ruth said, "I'm sorry, but it's true."

Katy did not respond at first. Then she said, "All those years apart from each other . . . don't you ever wish we had them back?"

Ruth felt something ugly stir inside again, but this time she managed to push it back.

"Come on, Ruth. You know what I mean. I know you do."

Ruth lifted her cup to her lips and sipped, looking out through the window at the pedestrians on Chartres, letting the dreadful memories rise in spite of herself, thinking back to the moment their friendship died. . . .

It had been a rare, cool morning. Ruth remembered mist flowing like cigarette smoke from her mouth and nose. She remembered thinking back to an even earlier time, when she and Katy had played at being grown-ups, balancing bits of twig between their first two fingers, pretending to be smoking and wishing they were old enough for the real thing. They had discussed their favorite brands. Katy said she would smoke Marlboros. Ruth opted for Kents.

On that cool New Orleans morning, Ruth had longed to play at smoking with her friend again. "Papa," she had said, "can Katy come over?"

Her father shrouded the potted plants on the back porch in plastic, one by one. Even at her age, Ruth knew he would never have thought to cover the plants alone. It had been her mother's request. He wore a red plaid shirt and brown cotton pants rather than his unusual coat and tie. That too had probably been her mother's idea. The time of year did not matter. Summer, winter, spring or fall, he always wore his black or gray suit. Except for the festivals that originated with the harvest, her father's world bore no connection to the passing of the seasons. His universe overflowed with books and meetings, with the sixteen Jewish months from *Tishri* to *Elul*, with holy days, births, *Bar* and *Bat Mitzvoth*, and burials. He marked the seasons not in terms of weather but of *parashat*, the fifty-four divisions of Torah that must be studied in the lifetime *Hashem* has given for that purpose.

"Pumpkin," he sighed, "I have something hard to tell you."

And so Ruth learned that Katy might never come again. It was because of things Ruth could not understand now. Things she would only understand when she was older. It was not his wish, and certainly not her mother's, that she lose Katy's friendship. But it was necessary. It was for the best.

"Why?" She begged, not asking a question so much as pouring out her heart.

He drew her close with gentle hands soiled by peat. He reminded her of strangers on their front lawn with flashing cameras and shouted questions, of telephone calls that never stopped, of men and women calling through the fence by the school playground. As the acrid odor of pesticide rose from the pots, he reminded her of the many times she had asked him why those people wouldn't go away. Did she remember asking him that question?

Ruth nodded mutely, a sense of apprehension rising within her, although she did not know the feeling's name. She only knew that she wished her father would stop. Yet somehow a thing had happened, a thing that even her father could not control.

"Katy's parents agree with us, Pumpkin," said her father. "We all think it's best for the two of you to stay apart for a while. Until this blows over."

Again she asked her father why. Why did the people hold the signs? Why did the man stab the lady? Why did so many people care about her and Katy being friends?

And slowly, with infinite sadness, her father taught her four new words: *Crusades. Inquisition. Pogrom. Holocaust.*

Words no child should ever hear, but words no Jewish child could ever be allowed to forget. He spared her the brutal details. Those would be revealed far too soon without his assistance, and, after all, there are limits to what a father can endure. But he could not protect her from the simple fact of two thousand years of betrayal and hatred endured by Jews. Endured by her grandparents. By her blood.

"But Katy is my friend!"

"Yes, Pumpkin," he said. "Yes, she is. But she is also the child of Christian parents. You must never forget that she is not like you. You must never forget that we are Jews and she is not."

"No!" Ruth pushed away from him and planted tiny fists on her hips, spreading her feet wide and setting her jaw stubbornly against her father. "You're wrong! My friend Katy is *good!*"

"I know, Pumpkin," he said, nodding. "Many of them are. But in the whole time that they have existed—which is a very, very long time— there have never been enough of the good ones to stop the others."

Ruth cried herself to sleep that night, filled with longing for her friend. She waited for Katy to somehow reach out to her, to magically appear and save her from the loneliness. Ruth knew that Katy would do that. She knew Katy would not stay away for long. Katy *loved* her. Katy was her very best friend.

But Katy did not come, and in the months that followed, Ruth's sorrow slowly changed. She began to understand that the pain she felt had proved her father right. As the memory of her friend's voice and face and mannerisms slowly faded, her feelings for Katy shifted imperceptibly from longing to an unfocused bitterness, until, finally, the thing was accomplished.

She began to think of Katy as one of *them.*

Draping the string of her tea bag over the edge of her cup, the rabbi began rifling through her purse. She withdrew a single photograph. "Here," she said, extending it toward Kate. "Look at this."

Still wounded by Ruth's cool response to her openness about their old friendship, Kate took the photograph languidly, forcing the rabbi to extend it toward her a bit longer than civility allowed. When she took it, Kate did not even glance at the image.

"Well, *look* at it, Katy," said Ruth.

With a sigh, Kate lowered her eyes to the picture. It was a candid shot of a man and woman, sitting at a table, surrounded by several other people.

She glanced at Ruth. "So?"

"It's him. Sol Cantor. I came over to show that to you so you'd know what he looks like now."

Kate looked at the image again. He was so much older than she remembered, and now he wore a beard. He seemed . . . not smaller exactly, but less intense. The man in her memory was young and strong and clean-shaven, with a square jaw. She recalled his photograph on the front page of the newspaper way back then; he was staring straight at the lens, a glare in his eye, defying everyone. But the man in this photograph leaned toward the woman beside him as if drawing protection from her presence. The eyes above his beard were wary and defensive.

"He's changed," she said.

"Of course."

Annoyed at Ruth's curt tone, Kate glanced at her, then at the photograph. She began to feel a sense of recognition, not from twenty-five years ago but from much more recently. She wondered if her memory could be playing tricks on her.

"Where was this taken?" she asked.

"At *Mekhkar Torah* a couple of weeks ago. We took pictures for a brochure."

Kate passed the photograph back to Ruth.

"Well?" asked the rabbi.

"Well what?"

"Have you seen him recently?"

Kate shook her head. "No." Rising, she walked to the tiny rest room under the stairs and placed her teacup on the counter. "I need to close up." She removed a cloth from an old wardrobe, walked to the front of the shop, flipped the sign on the door around from Open to Sorry, locked the door, and began dusting.

Ruth remained seated. "Aren't you closing early?" she asked.

"I've got a meeting at four with the pastor of my church."

Ruth watched her wipe the furniture with the dust rag for a while, then said, "Katy, please try to understand . . . I don't have many friends. I'm . . . I guess I've been too busy these last few years."

"All right."

"Really. It's not you. It's me."

"I said all right, Ruth. I understand." Kate continued to wipe down her inventory, studiously avoiding even a glance in Ruth's direction.

"I was rude just now. I'm sorry." Ruth sighed. "It seems like I'm always apologizing, doesn't it? I don't mean to be this way. Is there something I could do to make it up to you?"

Katy paused. "Well, now that you mention it . . ."

"What? Just name it."

Kate's attention remained on her work. It was a way to distance herself from her actions, from the small voice inside warning her that she should not do this thing. In a carefully neutral tone, she said, "Jake Singer asked if I'd try to get some seats for *Yom Kippur.* Could you do that?"

"Jake Singer? The locksmith?"

"Yes."

"So you and he . . . "

"We had a date; that's all. What about the tickets?"

"It's sold out."

"I'm aware of that, Ruth. That's why I asked you to help."

"It's very unusual for a non-Jew to come to *Yom Kippur.*"

"So? I'll bet you don't invite a lot of us to your Torah study either. What's the difference?"

"The difference is enormous, but maybe this isn't the time to worry about that," she said. "I do have a few seats reserved for friends. All the rabbis do. They're right up front. You can have a couple."

"Could I bring the kids?"

"There aren't very many seats reserved . . ."

"With everything that's going on, I won't leave them with a sitter."

"They could stay in our day care."

"No."

"We have full-time professional people running the day care. Paul and

Jilly will be as safe as they are at school. They *are* at school right now, aren't they?"

"Yes, but everyone at the school knows about our situation. They're keeping the kids indoors during recess, and the principal agreed to have security guards sit in the hall outside their classrooms."

"It's good to hear they're taking this so seriously."

"I asked the principal to call Lieutenant Washington. That did the trick. But I'm not comfortable leaving them with strangers, Ruth. Not even at your temple."

"It's a long service. They might get a little restless."

"Look. If you don't want me to come, just say so. The only reason I'm asking is to make Jake happy."

"No. We'll work something out." The rabbi cocked her head, considering Kate. "Do you use your children as an excuse this way often?"

"*What?*"

"I'm sorry. That came out wrong. I just meant, you know, you mentioned them when I asked you to come to our Torah study too. As a reason not to come."

"Well, they need me with them right now!"

"Really? Katy, please don't take this the wrong way, but who needs whom, exactly?"

Kate turned on her. "*Who do you think you are?*"

Holding both hands up, palms out, Ruth said, "I'm sorry. I did it again. Of course they need you."

"Why would you say a thing like that?"

"I don't know. I . . . I would like to get together with you, Katy. Share a little bit, you know? But it seems like your kids keep coming between us. I'm wrong to see it that way, I know, and I'm sorry. Really. Maybe it's just because I'm single."

Kate stared at her for a moment, then began dusting the furniture again, rubbing a table top too quickly, as if trying to dig down into it.

"Listen," said Ruth, "I've got four seats reserved. You can have them all."

"You're not bumping someone else off the list to do this, are you?"

"No. I hadn't invited anyone yet."

"Were you going to?"

"Do you want to go to *Yom Kippur*, Katy?"

"Were you holding the tickets for anyone else or not?"

Ruth's voice became small and dreary. "There's nobody else to invite, all right?"

In spite of her indignation, Kate heard the sadness behind Ruth's words. She stopped her furious dusting. "Well," she said. "Thank you, then."

"You're welcome."

They exchanged tentative smiles.

Ruth spoke. "I say things sometimes . . . I don't know where they come from."

"It's okay."

"I had no right—"

"Ruth, don't worry about it. We're both under a lot of stress." Kate looked away, too proud to admit her deepest fear: *Could there be some truth in what she said?*

"This isn't how I want to be, Katy."

Katy sighed. "I know. Me either."

Ruth nodded, lowering her eyes. Kate resumed her dusting.

"Listen," said Ruth. "I'm not trying to be difficult, but are you absolutely certain about not seeing Sol Cantor lately?"

"Yes. I'm sorry."

"The police told me he drives an old pickup truck. It's always filled with junk."

Kate began to shake her head but stopped, wrinkling her brow. "Let me see that picture again."

CHAPTER THIRTY-TWO

Washington gazed at a framed photograph on a buffet beside the dining table. In it, two women faced the camera at some mountainous location. Maybe the Rockies or the Swiss Alps. One of them was definitely the woman they had found facedown in the lagoon.

He walked to the center of the room, slipped on a pair of latex gloves, and stood still, silently absorbing the feel of the place. He could hear Baxter in the bedroom opening drawers already, but Washington had learned long ago that you could tell a lot about the people who lived in a place by simply standing in the center of a room and taking it in. He took a deep breath. Let it out. This was almost as depressing as finding the body.

Here in her home, the few remains of Helen Blumenthal's life spoke to him—family photos, souvenirs, her taste in art, books, furniture. Washington turned slowly, eyes noting everything. The victim had copies of

Entertainment Weekly and *People* magazines scattered over the coffee table—frivolous pulp filled with stories about strangers. Yet most of her family photographs were on the far side of the dining room. They weren't placed on the way to the kitchen or the bedrooms where she could pause occasionally and look at the images. She would have to make a special point of walking around the dining table to get close enough to really see the faces in the photos. Washington had seen the same thing in many other homes. People tended to put the unimportant items within easy reach and the important things in less accessible locations.

He had no idea what it meant.

Washington crossed to stand beside a small, darkly stained table. The red message light on the woman's answering machine blinked. Washington tapped a button and the first voice that rose hollow and metallic said, "Uh, Helen, I just heard about that person they found in the park, and I thought, you know . . . well, you might not know about the person in the park. Uh, anyway, they found someone over there who was . . . you know . . . dead. Look, I know this is silly, but would you call and let me know you're okay? No, wait. You can't call me. I'll probably be in jail. I mean, at the police department. Oh . . . I've made a mess of this. Listen. I'll see you later and explain everything, all right? Bye."

The recording quality was bad, but Washington was pretty sure he recognized the voice. Reaching into his jacket pocket, he removed his cell phone and flipped it open. His finger was poised above the key pad when the phone beeped. He pressed a different button, lifted it to his ear, and said, "Washington."

"LT, I got a Rabbi Gold wantin' me to patch her through. Says she's got something new for you on a case."

Speak of the devil, thought the lieutenant. "Okay. Lemme have her."

The telephone hummed for a moment, then he heard her voice, same as the answering machine. "Lieutenant?"

"Rabbi Gold. What can I do for you?"

"Listen. Katy and I were just talking, and she remembered something about that drive-by shooting."

He frowned, "Mrs. Flint was there?"

"Yes." A pause. "I thought you knew."

"No. She didn't come forward as far as I know."

"Oh . . . uh . . . will you hold for a minute?"

"All right, but please make it quick. I'm in the middle of something here."

"One second, I promise."

He heard a bump and distant voices, then a soft rustle, and the voices were suddenly muted. He sighed and walked around the little table. Behind it was a padded chair. He stood by the chair as the muffled noises continued in his ear. On the table beside the answering machine were a coffee mug filled with pens and pencils, a couple piles of papers, a desk lamp, and a portable telephone. He rifled through the papers. Bills mostly, miscellaneous mail, a few letters, and a couple of things on letterhead from a hospital, addressed to a Dr. Helen Blumenthal. So she was a doctor.

"Lieutenant?" A different voice.

"Yeah? Who's this?"

"Kate Flint, Lieutenant. I'm sorry I didn't let anyone know I was there that day."

"Mrs. Flint, when you witness a felony—"

"I know, I know. But I had my children with me, and my main concern was to get them away before anything else happened."

"That's understandable. But you should have called us later." The table had a single drawer. He slid it open and looked at its contents. A small electronic calculator. More pens and pencils. A couple of keys. A date book. He picked it up. Date books were usually interesting.

"I *know*. I can't believe I didn't call. I'm so sorry."

"Why didn't you?" he asked as he flipped to the most recent entry.

A slight pause. Not long, but just enough for him to know she was either going to tell him something important or lie. He froze in place, focusing on what she would say next.

"I was afraid you'd make me tell you about Ruth."

Good. She didn't lie. He started turning pages in the date book. "Okay. We'll talk more about this later." He didn't want to let her off the hook too easily.

"I *am* sorry."

"We'll talk about it later, Mrs. Flint. Tell me why you and Rabbi Gold called."

"I saw Sol Cantor at the shooting."

He looked up. "You sure?"

"Absolutely. He was there in his truck."

He set the date book on the table, ignoring it. "What was he doing?"

"Nothing. Just watching."

"From his truck?"

"Yes. He was parked at the curb, a few yards up the street from the music store."

"Did he see you?"

"I . . . uh . . . I think so."

"Okay. What did he do during the actual shooting?"

"I don't know. When the guns started firing, I ducked down to hide with the kids."

"Okay. Listen. We definitely need to get together, but I'm gonna be out of pocket for the rest of the day. I want to see you tomorrow in the late afternoon. About three."

He picked up the date book again and scanned the entries for last Friday. This Dr. Blumenthal had been a very busy lady.

"Okay," said Kate.

"Good," he said, still reading from the book. She'd had a hair appointment, then lunch with someone named Cara. In the late afternoon, she'd scheduled a telephone call from another person named Evan, or maybe she was supposed to call him. Then he noticed the last entry: *See R. before service re: J. Cantor?*

"Mrs. Flint," he said, "would you please put Rabbi Gold back on the phone?"

"Okay." He heard the sounds of the phone being passed from hand to hand.

Then the rabbi came on the line again. "Yes?"

"Rabbi Gold, do you know a woman named Helen Blumenthal?"

She did not answer. He thought perhaps she had not heard his question, but then, in a low and fearful voice, Ruth said, "Why do you want to know?"

It was only the second time Kate had been in Reverend James Cahill's office at the church. The first time, their new pastor had officially welcomed her and John and six other people who had also recently joined the congregation. The tall, charismatic man who now came around his desk to shake Kate's hand had intimidated her back then. The bookcases on all four walls, stuffed to overflowing with everything from theology to Greek philosophy to socioeconomics, still impressed her with the extent of this man's knowledge and wisdom. But over the years Kate had come to understand that Jim Cahill was a gentle soul, and this time she was more at ease as she settled into a thickly upholstered chair across from him.

Kate felt she should make the most of this opportunity, but so many issues pressed upon her conscience; it was difficult to know where to begin. Maybe she should start by asking for her pastor's thoughts on dating Jake . . .

No.

She knew what he would say, and she did not want to hear it.

She could mention Paul's problem with anger, but there again, Kate felt the reverend's response might be uncomfortable. Maybe she should share her concerns for Paul's and Jilly's safety. But what if that led to a conversation about sending them away? Kate knew she must keep them near for their own safety. She was positive about that. Still, Ruth's question earlier that afternoon echoed in her memory: *"Who needs whom, exactly?"*

While considering all these problems, it suddenly occurred to her that they might be intertwined. In that moment, something dark and misshapen rose on the horizon of her mind, something she instinctively feared to face. She fled the shadow looming in the distance by asking an easy question, the question that had first inspired her call for an interview. Smiling at Reverend Cahill, Kate said, "Do you know someone named Orvis Newton?".

"Sure. He runs a storefront mission over in the Irish Channel. Our church supported his ministry for years. Why?"

Jim Cahill listened closely as Kate briefly explained about her chance encounter with Reverend Newton at Jilly's Sunday school class and the old connection with the Nan Smith tragedy. Then Kate asked, "What can you tell me about his work?"

"Well, until recently Orvis focused on aid to inner-city youth, but now he's changed the name of his ministry and shifted his attention to evangelizing Jews."

"Do we still support him?"

Reverend Cahill frowned. "No. Orvis is highly dedicated, but the elder board and I have some real issues with his methods."

Kate said, "I saw him at that Jewish temple over by Audubon Park, waving signs and shouting Bible verses."

"Then you know why we can't be a part of their ministry anymore. Of course, we all want Jewish people to accept Jesus, but . . . ." The reverend shrugged.

"So we dropped them?"

"Maybe it would be better to say we're not supporting them financially. I mean, we're still praying for them, of course." Revend Cahill leaned toward her. "Why are you so interested in Orvis?"

"Frankly, I'm a little nervous about him teaching Jilly's Sunday school class."

"Oh, I understand, believe me. Orvis can be . . . how shall I put this?" Reverend Cahill looked at the ceiling. "Intense. Yes, that's as good a word as any. But I've known him for years, and I'm sure he's basically harmless. On the other hand, nobody told me he'd be teaching children's Sunday school, and I don't think he's an appropriate choice for that. We'll find something else for him to do."

"Good." Kate sat back, relieved. "I appreciate it."

Kate's pastor spoke as he made a note on a pad on his desk. "Why were you at Temple Brit Yisrael?"

"I was invited to go to a Torah study by a rabbi I know over there."

He looked up from the pad. "How wonderful!"

Kate fidgeted in her seat. "Yes. Well, when I got there, I ran into one of Reverend Newton's people, and—"

"It must have been awkward for you, being at the temple with those folks waving signs and all."

Thinking of Martha Douglas and the rejection from the Jews she endured every day, Kate said, "I felt a little bit sorry for them."

"Yes, I often feel that way about my Jewish friends. After all the suffering they have endured, you'd think we Christians would be more sensitive."

"No, I meant . . ." Kate stopped herself, suddenly realizing that the reverend's perspective and hers were completely different.

"Yes?" he asked, waiting for her to complete her thought.

She shook her head. "Never mind."

"Well, it's a shame you had to experience Orvis Newton's kind of so-called evangelism." Reverend Cahill looked into her eyes. "But I'm glad you showed them a better way."

"What do you mean?"

"You know . . . there they were, shouting across the parking lot about the love of Christ, and then along you come, crossing over to get to know the people they're shouting at."

Thinking of Martha's arguments against going in to study Torah and of her own eagerness to get away from the temple, Kate said, "I think Reverend Newton's people have good reasons for witnessing the way they do."

"Uh-oh. Sounds like one of them bent your ear a little, right?"

"A little."

"I'll bet they tried to tell you that studying the Torah at the temple might be misinterpreted as support for the Jewish point of view."

"That's exactly what they said."

Nodding, Kate's pastor leaned back in his chair. "For what it's worth, I think you did the right thing. It must have been hard to go into that temple, especially with Orvis and his people standing outside telling you not to do it. Hopefully, your example will help them get past their fear."

"*Fear*? They hardly seem afraid to me. I mean, don't you think it takes courage to stand up for Christ the way they do?"

"Not at all. They live in their own little universe, with a sort of Fort God mentality, constantly reinforcing each other's narrow views of those outside. I think it requires a lot more courage to go beyond your comfort zone and engage people on their own terms, like you did."

Remembering how easily she had been convinced to leave Temple Brit Yisrael, Kate desperately wanted to defend Orvis Newton's approach. "I think you're being too hard on them. It takes a lot of faith to dedicate your life to evangelism like they do."

"If they have so much faith, why aren't they willing to listen to opposing points of view, really listen, without worrying that they'll be

compromised somehow? Why aren't they confident enough in their faith
to wait for divinely inspired opportunities to discuss Jesus, rather than
trying to force the gospel down people's throats?"

Ruth Gold's angry words surged up in Kate's memory: *"I wouldn't try
to cram good news down people's throats!"* Now that her pastor had said almost
exactly the same thing, Kate found she could not look at him.

After a pause, Reverend Cahill said, "Well, enough of that. Let's focus
on the positive, shall we? I see now why you wanted to get together so
urgently. Not many people are given an opportunity like this."

"I guess."

"You guess?" He smiled again. "Oh, believe me, I know about a hundred seminary students and ministers who would give their right arms to
trade places with you. The opportunities in comparative religion alone
are phenomenal, and who knows how many people you can reach with
the gospel if you stick with it long enough?"

Kate's heart began to race. "I wasn't planning to go back."

His face fell. "Did they retract the invitation?"

"Not exactly. Mainly I'm afraid I'll say something wrong."

"Such as?"

"Well . . . I believe so many different things than they do."

"Hey, they're Reform Jews, Kate. They pride themselves on being
inclusive and pluralistic. Just don't be pushy about your beliefs, and like
Saint Peter said, if someone wants to talk to you about Jesus, be ready to
explain the reason for the faith that you have. That way, if Jesus never
comes up, at least you're there, showing them that some of us are loving
and respectful. I don't have to tell you that's more than a thousand people
with signs and slogans could ever accomplish."

The conversation shifted to Kate's children and how things were
going at the antique shop. Reverend Cahill asked a few questions that
Kate answered automatically. Then he showed her to the door, reiterating
his hope that she would visit the Torah study again and calling it a "wonderful opportunity."

It was all she could do to give him a weak smile and a nod.

Several times on the way home Kate had to lift her hands from the
steering wheel to wipe her moist palms on her skirt. She had hoped her
visit with the pastor would relieve this pressure she felt building up inside,

but to the contrary, the atmosphere in her Jeep now seemed heavy, pressing against her chest, making it hard to breathe. Opening her mouth widely, she sucked in air like a fish out of water. Kate hadn't been this afraid since the day she realized that her husband was really, truly, going to die. She didn't want to go back to that temple, especially not for some major event like *Yom Kippur*. She had hoped all along that Ruth would deny her request, but with the rabbi's offer of four seats in the front, she was out of excuses. Even worse, now her own pastor expected her to start visiting Ruth's temple on a regular basis!

Well, at least I'll get to spend time with Jake. But if this is God's will, it's . . . it's crazy, that's all. I'm just a widow and a mother and a shopkeeper. He should send a pastor or a theologian to that temple. Someone with credentials!

As she wove her way through the rush-hour traffic, Kate found she was speaking to God right out loud, repeating the same words, over and over:

"Why me? Why me? Why me?"

THIRTY-THREE

Two days later, on *Yom Kippur* morning, a man in a dark suit and a black silk *yarmulke* stood in the alley behind Temple Brit Yisrael watching for just the right moment. Many in the congregation knew him, and his disguise was subtle at best, so it would not do to be spotted going in.

The temple buzzed with activity. Next to *Shabbat* itself, the most important holy day of the year had come at last. Men, women, and children, all in formal dress, approached from every direction, having parked along the residential streets nearby. Small groups arrived in vans at four- or five-minute intervals from the Catholic church parking lot half a mile away. Orvis Newton figured there must be a thousand people here, most of whom probably hadn't been to temple since last year at this time. They stored up their sins all year, hoarding them for this day, when everybody came to get rid of their guilt.

*The Day of Atonement. What hypocrisy! As if a few chants, an apology, and a
toot on the horn of a dead animal could make up for a lifetime of miserable failure.* Orvis
smiled. *Today they'll learn better.*

Soon there would be a moment when the path to the rear entrance
was clear. Then he would step from the alley and go inside, and when
he did, he would not bring atonement and a glimpse of their precious
world-to-come. What Orvis had in mind was retribution and a lesson . . .
a small, smoldering sample of what the afterlife really had in store for
such as them.

Kate took the children's hands in hers as they walked toward the temple
doors. She hoped Jake would be waiting for them beside the entry as
planned. They had arrived a little late and been unable to find a parking
place anywhere near the temple. The New Orleans police were out en
masse, directing traffic and enforcing temporary No Parking signs posted
in the lawns along the curbs of many of the nearby streets, so Kate had
driven to the church parking lot several blocks away and taken the shuttle. As they had ridden toward the temple, Kate watched her children,
trying to ignore the butterflies in her stomach.

Now, crossing the parking lot, Paul looked old for his age in a navy
blazer and khaki slacks, his straight brown hair still a bit wet and parted
as straight as a ruler. Jilly had chosen to wear her little pink dress, the one
all covered in tiny violet flowers. Her white stockings had already begun
to bag a little at the knees, but to Kate that just made her even more ador-
able, especially since the Barbie doll clutched in Jilly's free hand was
dressed just like Jilly, white stockings and all.

Uncertain whether the appropriate dress for the occasion should be
somber or celebratory, Kate had vacillated between a dark brown wool-
blend suit with a high-collared cream blouse, or a subtle floral-patterned
blouse with a billowy ruffled skirt and a wide leather belt. In the end, she
had decided it was better to overdress than to risk seeming disrespectful,
and now she was glad she'd chosen the brown suit. Everyone Kate had
seen so far looked like a million dollars. She noticed a lot of people wearing white. It had surprised her, though, to see a few people wearing
sneakers; even a couple of the men in suits wore Nikes. Kate thought it

was strange until she remembered that John had once told her that some
Jews, even the more liberal Reform Jews, would walk long distances to
temple rather than drive on *Yom Kippur*.

Suddenly, Kate's thoughts were disrupted by a loud voice calling
from the far side of the parking lot. "Where are you going?" Kate looked
for the speaker but could not see him over the cars and other pedestrians
making their way to the temple. "There's no atonement in that building!"
shouted the voice. "Open your Torahs! Read Leviticus! 'For the life of the
flesh is in the blood, and I have given it to you upon the altar to make an
atonement for your souls. For it is the blood that maketh an atonement
for the soul.' Where is the blood in this Day of Atonement of yours?"

People around Kate paused to stare in amazement toward the sound
of the voice. She saw white cardboard signs above the crowd, their
slogans shocking to see in that place on that day: Trust Jesus, Jesus Saves,
and Your Messiah Has Come. The shorter people in the crowd craned for
a better view. Some moved in that direction, but most hurried toward the
temple, faces set in grim and angry expressions. For an instant the crowd
parted, and Kate caught a glimpse of a small cluster of people loitering
on the sidewalk between the parking lot and St. Charles Avenue. Five
policemen with ever-moving, wary eyes stood behind the little group,
and just beyond the policemen a television crew aimed their camera at
the young man with the loud voice. He had short hair the color of coal
and a flushed, freshly scrubbed look to his pale face. His dark conservative suit contrasted surreally with the fact that he was restraining a pair
of snow-white goats at the ends of two ropes.

"Look!" called the voice, "we've brought a pair of scapegoats without
blemish, like the Bible says. But your own Torah says you can make
atonement only at the temple in Jerusalem, and God destroyed that
temple, just as the prophet Daniel said he would! So where will you
sacrifice these goats today? You have no temple in Jerusalem for your
sacrifices because only one offering is pleasing to God now, only the
crucifixion of Jesus Christ! Trust in your Messiah! Believe in his sacrifice
for your sake and you will be saved!"

The crowd had come together again, obscuring Kate's view of the
evangelists and the goats, but Kate could still hear the voice booming
across the parking lot unchallenged. Then a middle-aged man wearing a

cream-colored suit and a knitted *yarmulke* charged directly in front of
Kate, plunging through the crowd toward the evangelists. His momentum
seemed to draw others along in his wake. Kate and the children were
caught up and pressed forward. At first, she thought the Jewish man
would stride right up to the man holding the goats, maybe even strike
him down, but he stopped several feet away. The young evangelist
continued to shout, but the Jew silenced him with an even louder voice.
"You there! You with the Scriptures so loose in your mouth! You say we
need these *goats* to atone for our sins?"

"I only say your Torah demands it," cried the man on the sidewalk.
"But if you would—"

The Jew cut him off, yelling loudly enough for the whole parking
lot to hear, quoting the Psalms and the prophets. The evangelist quoted
Scripture in response, and soon, the two men were flinging Bible verses at
each other like stones. The television crew circled them. Kate saw Martha
Douglas standing tall among the little group of evangelists, casting fearful
glances at the hundreds of Jews surrounding her. The young man holding
the goats said, "All I know is—"

"Know?" shouted the Jew. "You seem to *know* very little, sir! I suggest
you go back to wherever you came from and study the Bible, since you
have apparently learned so little about it! And while you're at it, perhaps
you could learn a few things about common courtesy and respect!"

At that, the crowd erupted with shouts and jeers. Everyone called
derisively to the evangelists—some quoting verses, others taunting
them with questions, still others chastising them for their rude behavior.
The four policemen who had been standing nearby began to move
in between the Christians and the Jews. The camera crew fought for
position.

"Mommy, why is everybody yelling?" Jilly cried. "I don't like it!"

"Come on, kids," said Kate, backing away. She hurried toward the
front doors of Temple Brit Yisrael, glancing around uneasily.

That morning, Kate had agonized over whether to place the small
golden cross around her neck on the outside or inside of her blouse. In
the end, she had let it show, thinking, *I was invited by a Jew and given seats
by a rabbi. I have a right to be here. Besides, what kind of Christian would I be if I hid
my faith?* But now the cross felt like a beacon, drawing the angry eyes of

everyone in sight. When they reached the portico in front of the temple entrance, Kate slipped the necklace under her collar, glancing around to be sure no one saw. As she looked to the right, a large old woman standing nearby caught her eye with a puzzled expression. Certain the old woman had seen her hide the cross, Kate turned away, but not before she felt a strange sense of déjà vu, as if she knew the woman from somewhere. She was deep in thought, trying to place the woman's face, when Jilly lifted her voice, "Mommy? Why were those people mad?"

"I don't think they were mad, exactly—"

"The one in the beanie cap sure was," said Paul.

"Yeah. I guess he was." She felt a twinge of nausea. *Why didn't I listen to my instincts and stay away from here?*

"I bet he was mad 'cause there's too many people. How come there's so many people?" asked her daughter.

How can I explain this without getting thrown out of here? Kate said, "You know how you're mean to Diana sometimes? And when you're mean to her, you feel bad later?"

Jilly held her Barbie doll out to the side, pretending that it was flying through the air. "No."

"Come on, Jilly. You wouldn't feel good if you hurt Diana's feelings, would you?"

"I guess not."

"Okay. So what could you do to feel better?"

"Give her a present?"

"That might work, and would you say anything to her when you gave her the present?"

"Maybe I'd say I was sorry."

"Right. 'Cause that's what we say when we hurt someone's feelings, and that's what all these people are here to do."

Jilly looked around. "They were *all* mean to someone?"

"Sure. You don't think anyone is perfect, do you?"

Jilly nodded solemnly. "Yes. Daddy was."

Kate swallowed and looked away from her daughter. After a moment, she said, "I don't think Mister Singer is going to come. Let's leave."

Jilly said, "But you said we were coming here for Jesus!"

"Keep your voice down!" hissed Kate, glancing at a smartly dressed couple nearby. Kneeling beside her daughter, she spoke quietly. "Mr. Singer isn't here, and—"

"You just came to see him," said Paul. "The Jesus stuff is just an excuse."

She spun to face him. "Paul!" Her son stared at her defiantly. In his eyes, she saw no respect, none. She looked away. "That was a terrible thing to say."

Paul set out for the temple door.

"Paul Flint! Come back here!"

He stopped. "I'm not scared to go in there."

"You think I'm scared?"

He said nothing.

"Come on, Mommy," whispered Jilly, squeezing Kate's hand. "It'll be okay."

Kate felt her face go hot. Rising to her feet, she said, "I just thought you guys would want Mr. Singer here with us."

Paul snorted.

Suddenly, Kate wanted to strike him, to slap that insolent expression from his face. She took a step toward the boy, actually drawing her free hand back, but Jilly squeezed her other hand again and skipped ahead, pulling her and calling, "Come on!"

Kate held back, but Paul stepped forward to join the surging crowd.

"Paul! Come back here!" called Kate. But there was no way her son could return against the flow of so many people. "Hold on to me, Jilly," said Kate, clinging to her daughter's hand. Then, fighting her way ahead, passing those in front, mumbling apologies, Kate Flint made her way to Paul's side and took his hand as well and hung on to the Christian children of her Jewish husband as she was pushed against her will into Temple Brit Yisrael on the single most holy day of the Jewish year.

Rebecca Betterton stood outside the entry doors with her back to a column, watching the people crowd up to the door. Women and girls in their finest dresses trailed lingering tendrils of perfume in their wakes, while the multicolored *yarmulkes* of men and teenage boys bobbed along like silken bubbles on a river of humanity. Rebecca felt completely alone.

Wasn't that funny? Here she was, surrounded by all these people, and she
felt as if she were the only one there. Everyone she saw was a stranger.
Even the murmured voices of the passing crowd fell upon her ears as if
spoken in a language she had once known but had since forgotten. Now
and then a person bumped into her. Some of them mumbled apologies,
but mostly they offered only an expression of annoyance, as if she had no
business standing still in a place where the thing to do was to move along.
Rebecca knew their thoughts; she saw them very clearly in their eyes: get
to the sanctuary, sit down, stand up, sit down again, wade through the
Hebrew—does anyone remember what this stuff means?—do the thing,
get it over with, and get home so we can finally eat. That's the way it's
supposed to go, and anyone who bucks the system makes it a little more
difficult for the rest of us, so what are *you* standing around for, old woman?

She used to think that way herself, until the problems with Roy and
the Peeping Tom and her body getting older and the memories of Sidney
and regrets about Aaron and this terrible feeling she couldn't seem to
escape—this feeling of being alone.

God, I hope you're here today, she prayed, although she did not notice
she was praying at all.

That was when she saw the young lady standing off to the side with
two children. Rebecca Betterton felt an immediate affinity for the woman,
since they were both so obviously waiting for someone who had not
come. She watched the young lady closely, hoping to make eye contact,
and out of all the hundreds of passing people, she alone happened to
notice when the young lady slipped a slender golden necklace inside her
collar. It would have been an unremarkable act, except for the symbol at
the end of that necklace, so foreign to that place.

This office is growing smaller all the time, Ruth thought.

She smiled at her oxymoron. Growing smaller. A perfect description
of how she felt. Dressed in the clean white robes of purity, Ruth hid
behind her desk, using it as a barricade against the faithful thousand
waiting down the hall, each of them longing for the new start that came
through repentance and atonement. But how could she lead the congregation to such things when she could not find them herself?

Ruth sighed and pushed away from the desk, allowing her eyes to close and her head to fall back against the vinyl upholstery of her chair. Somewhere out there was a man she felt such strong aversion to . . . no, she must not avoid it, the word was . . . it was. . . .

She could not bring herself to identify the feeling she held for Solomon Cantor, who had killed that woman so long ago, and in killing her, had also destroyed something in a little girl whose only crime had been curiosity. Ruth told herself that Solomon Cantor would not dare to come to temple today, with the police searching for him all across the city, but if she really believed that, why did she feel rooted to her chair, physically unable to rise and proceed to the sanctuary where, at this moment, she should be taking her place alongside Rabbi Gottlieb and the others? Solomon Cantor had demonstrated absolutely no remorse since his release from prison . . . no remorse, no repentance, and no restitution. To the contrary, he was almost certainly killing people again. He had killed the man she might have married and her best friend. He had sent people to kill her and Katy. She owed him nothing—no forgiveness, no pity, no benefit of the doubt.

Why, then, did she feel so ill-equipped to participate in the coming service?

Something held her back, some failing in herself. It was not the usual sense of inadequacy that plagued her every time she officiated at *Yom Kippur*. It was . . . it was . . . what exactly? The word for this emotion rapped at the edges of her consciousness, demanding to come in, but she told herself she could not give it a name.

Then, suddenly, the emotion itself seemed to rise up and whisper, *Liar. You know me. You know exactly what I am.*

Moaning, Rabbi Ruth Gold rubbed her tightly shut eyes. She had to force her thoughts onto peaceful paths. But where was the way that led to peace? Her life was in danger. People she knew, had worshiped with, were dying. People she loved were gone forever. She dreaded sitting upon the *bima*, looking out across a sea of faces, seeing the missing ones, the ones that mattered most, the only ones she had ever truly loved: Steve, her mother, her father, and Isaac—especially Isaac, during these high holy days of awe.

And now Helen too.

Her dear, sweet, harmless friend, mauled by a creature that belonged behind bars, regardless of whether it was animal or human. Ruth thought of the last time she had seen Helen Blumenthal, dressed in a simple black shift adorned with a single strand of perfect pearls, jauntily setting out across the park. Ruth could not rid herself of Helen's image, a Jewish Evangeline passing into the darkness beyond the oaks and the beckoning Spanish moss.

When Lieutenant Washington had told her about Helen, he had said the animals were deliberately released, and whoever was responsible was legally accountable for Helen's death. *Legally accountable.* It was a phrase she understood all too well. A phrase for this day of all days, when Jews approached *Hashem* for forgiveness and inclusion in the Book of Life.

A knock at the door.

A man's voice, one she did not recognize, spoke. "Rabbi? They're ready to start. Rabbi Gottlieb asked me to come let you know."

She did not answer.

"Rabbi Gold? Are you there? Are you okay?"

"Yes!" she called to the closed and locked office door. "I'm on my way."

"All right," said the man on the outside. "I'll tell them."

Ruth stared at the door, surprised to see how far away it was, looming in the distance with all of the foreboding welcome of a masked executioner. Foreboding welcome. Another oxymoron, and yet it felt exactly so. *That's funny . . . just a minute ago, this office seemed so small, and now it's a mile across. I wonder if I can even make it to the hallway?* Rising, she gathered her white robes about her and set out for the final service of *Yom Kippur*, the *Neila*. She walked and walked and finally, as she reached for the doorknob, she realized why it had seemed so far to go. It was she herself growing smaller, pressed into a bitter little mold, a mockery of the Ruth she had once set out to be, pressed moment by moment into ever-shrinking proportions by her cold, cold rage and resentment.

See? it whispered again. *You know exactly what I am.*

Ruth Gold opened the door and stepped into the hall, smiling rigidly at the other tardy people rushing toward the sanctuary where the *shofar* and the Torah and the penitent masses awaited.

Yes, I know what you are, and may Hashem forgive me, I welcome you.

THIRTY-FOUR

The crowd pressed against them on every side. Kate tightened her grip on Paul's and Jilly's hands. Now and then she heard strange words mumbled somberly as people greeted each other, some in Hebrew, some in English. *"Shana tova,"* said one man. Kate recognized the words, having read them that morning in one of John's books on Judaism. The traditional greeting of the days of awe—"may your name be inscribed"—alluded to the Book of Life. That was the reason everyone was there: to atone for the wrongs committed in the past year, and hopefully, to attain God's forgiveness as symbolized by having their names written in the Book.

Someone tapped her elbow.

Startled, Kate jerked away and looked behind. An elderly woman standing near the wall beamed down at Jilly, then looked up to catch Kate's eye. Kate felt a shock of recognition.

"*Shana tova,*" said the woman.

Confused and unsure of how to respond, all Kate could think to say
was "Thank you."

Still smiling, the older woman touched Jilly's hair, a simple, grand-
motherly caress. In the next moment the crowd moved forward, Kate and
the children were pushed away, and the old woman was gone, left alone
beside the wall. Kate remembered that the old woman had seen her hide
her cross beneath her blouse. The woman had surely passed by those
people with the signs and the goats, and she obviously knew Kate was
a Christian, and yet with a kind word and a touch, she had wiped away
the near panic Kate felt, the almost overwhelming fear that someone
would condemn her for her faith. Kate's eyes welled with tears. She felt
that she should seek God's forgiveness for her weakness of faith and the
paralyzing fear it had caused.

And so it came to pass on *Yom Kippur,* the Day of Atonement, that
single Christian heart joined the millions of Jews around the world in
praying, *Father, I have sinned. Please forgive me.* Kate sensed that for once her
prayerful request had been heard.

But somehow, she also knew it was not enough.

Rabbi Shumish had not appeared, and Rebecca Betterton had grown so
tired of waiting. As each new face moved past Rebecca felt her depression deepen. These people were strangers, every one. This was the temple
of her youth, the place she and Sidney had brought their son to learn
about his heritage and to celebrate his *Bar Mitzvah,* but she had not seen a
single person she recognized. To make matters worse, as Rebecca had
walked from the shuttle van to the temple doors, those horrible people
outside had waved their signs and shouted at her, shattering any hope
she'd had of arriving with a proper sense of reverence.

Instead, she felt old and silly and alone.

Wait. There was a familiar face: that woman over there, the lovely
blonde lady who hid her cross before. She looked so nervous; Rebecca's
heart went out to her. How horrible to be invited to a new and unfamiliar
place, only to find those awful people outside being rude to her hosts in
the name of her own religion. Why, she must be mortified!

Someone has to do something.

When the woman drew near, Rebecca leaned forward just a bit from her stationary position beside the wall. *"Shana tova,"* she said, speaking those words for the first time in almost twenty years. They felt foreign to her tongue, like a wonderful spice she had tasted long ago, in a forever lost land.

What was that expression in her eyes, this beautiful woman? Was it unease? offense? "Thank you," she said, and Rebecca, feeling the strain behind her response, wondered if her own misery was so transparent that even the beautiful stranger saw it at a glance. Reaching down, Rebecca touched the little girl's hair. *God makes us perfect, but we make such a mess of things.* Then they were gone, pushed ahead by the hundreds more behind. Awash in a sense of failure, Rebecca cast a desperate look back over the heads of the remaining crowd. If Rabbi Shumish did not come, she had decided she would leave. She would not face God alone today. She did not have the courage.

They were inside and Kate still had not found Jake, but she saw Ruth sitting up on the platform in front, resplendent in a perfectly white robe. Beside her sat four other people, three men and another woman, all dressed in the same pure white. Seven more sat across the platform from Ruth and her companions. Between the two groups, a towering pair of shimmering gold lamé curtains hung from a simple rod mounted against the wall at the rear of the platform. The curtains fell to the floor where they gathered in abundant folds. A simple bronze dish hovered fifteen feet above the platform, suspended by wires just to the left of the curtains. Kate did not recognize its function until she saw a small flame flicker above its edge. In addition to the oil lamp, a large *menorah* stood against the brick wall beside the curtains. At the leading edge of the platform was a large podium, wide enough for two people to stand behind it side by side. Down on the sanctuary floor, folding chairs had been arranged along the aisles, reducing the walkways to half of their usual width. The empty areas along the sides and behind the fixed pews had also been filled with temporary chairs, until it appeared to Kate that over a thousand people were in attendance.

She led the children down an aisle, checking the small numbered pieces of paper temporarily taped to the ends of the pews, comparing the numbers to those on the tickets she had received from Ruth. A soft hum of voices rose from the congregation, but much lower and much more quiet than one would expect for a crowd that size. Even Paul and Jilly seemed to be affected by the solemnity of the occasion. Kate found their places near the front, and Jilly settled wide-eyed onto the pew, craning her neck to make out the dim heights above. Paul pored over the prayer book he had found in his seat, intrigued by the unfamiliar shapes of the Hebrew letters.

Kate watched the people nearby, some of whom reminded her of the strangers who came to her church on Easter and Christmas, checking their watches, emoting tension and discomfort. Probably, like their Christian counterparts, many of these Jews had come simply because of tradition, or to see and be seen, or to satisfy the wishes of a spouse or parent. Then she noticed other faces with prayerful, meditative expressions. Their piety evoked an unexpected memory of a time when Kate had sometimes experienced that same sense of reverence at church. In fact, the longer she sat among these people, the more she felt that the predominant mood here was the same, and for an instant, Kate felt herself surrender to a sense of overwhelming humility. Then with a shock of recognition, she remembered where she was and the moment died, but not before a surprising thought arose.

Why, these people really do love the Lord!

Someone slid into the pew beside her. Kate cast a sideways glance at her new companion and found Jake Singer there, grinning at her. He looked very proper in a black suit and matching black silk *yarmulke.*

"Hey," he whispered.

"Hi." She smiled, feeling her heartbeat quicken.

"Quite a place, isn't it?"

Lifting her eyes to the huge space above them, she nodded wordlessly. They sat silently for a few minutes as the last of the latecomers filed in. The air between Kate and Jake seemed to crackle with energy. Casting her eyes to the side surreptitiously, Kate stole glimpses of Jake's strong hands clasped in his lap. She felt a sudden urge to reach over and touch them. Then she gave a little start, shaking her head and

looking away, embarrassed. The tall doors behind them closed, and
a man in a white robe and prayer shawl rose to his feet to approach the
podium.

I t was impossible. Never before had Ruth fought so hard to focus her
thoughts on a service, to forget the outside world and lose herself in the
moment at hand, but she could not escape this . . . this ugly thing inside,
and that, of course, was the problem. Her distractions had nothing to do
with the outside world. She had brought them to the sanctuary in her
heart, brought them with her, right up onto the *bima*.

Sam Gottlieb rose to welcome the congregation. Then readings from
the *Union Prayer Book* commenced, and when Andy Bloom rose and blew
the *shofar*, lifting the ram's horn high in the ancient tradition of rabbis and
priests going all the way back to the Temple of Solomon, Ruth's rabbinic
training took hold. She named each blast silently as the piercing, mourn-
ful notes rang from the rafters:

Tekia, shevarim-terua, tekia.

Tekia, shevarim, tekia.

Tekia, terua, tekia.

For a moment, in the midst of the impossibly beautiful sounds, Ruth
saw an unbroken string of notes—pearls hanging from a golden thread,
rubies woven through time itself to connect her and this day with *Moshe*
blowing the first *shofar* on Mt. Sinai. That first time, the purpose of the
blasts had been to warn Israel not to repeat their sin with the golden calf
while *Moshe* remained high above, receiving Torah. Now, the *shofar* called
them to account for the sins they had already committed. Ruth closed her
eyes as the last of the notes echoed in her heart. For a moment, she saw
the path to repentance just ahead. She longed to set foot upon it. She
longed for *teshuva*—to return.

But then she thought of Helen.

How could she repent of hatred for a man who had killed people
such as Helen and Morton and Steve? Although the aching in her heart
felt so much like guilt, as far as she was concerned, she owed God no
apologies. In fact, as far as Ruth Gold was concerned, she owed *Hashem*
nothing at all.

Kate tried to follow along in the prayer book, matching the spaces between the clusters of Hebrew letters to the pauses in the voices of the congregation around her. She joined in when the readings slipped into English. The rabbi behind the podium paused and another man rose, holding a small, hornlike object. Lifting the object to his mouth, he blew. A sound rose boldly through the air in clear, sharp bursts. More short, bold blasts followed, an intricate series of them, offset by longer notes from time to time. It was wonderfully, chillingly, breathtakingly beautiful. It was not music. It was far more than that. It seemed to call to Kate from a realm beyond earthly experience. A thought unbidden rose to the surface of her mind: *That's the sound the world will hear when Jesus comes again.* Immediately, she realized how foreign that notion was to this place, and yet, in that moment, she felt it to be true beyond all other truths in the universe, and she longed to experience a sense of forgiveness, to be ready when Jesus came.

Why had her prayer gone unanswered? Why was she unforgiven?

Then, as suddenly as it had begun it was over, and the fellow with the horn returned to his seat, as a short bald man approached the podium. Without so much as a nod to the audience, he began to sing. Again, Kate had never heard anything quite like this before. One part Gregorian chant and one part *Arabian Nights*, it transported her to another, vaguely familiar place. Perhaps that place was Jerusalem.

The man paused and all those around her lifted their voices as one, the audible perfume of ancient Hebrew ascending to the heavens. Kate felt her heart rise as well. Although she did not understand the words, she thought she knew their meaning, and a pounding began within her chest, growing stronger and stronger as each new wave of mysterious syllables washed over her and up and away. She knew her heart was going into fibrillation, but she did not care. The growing tightness in her chest seemed to fit this occasion somehow, a divine reminder of her flawed humanity.

Kate could not say when Jake had taken her hand. He might have been holding it all along. She only knew that this too felt right—as if it were a part of a sacrament of some kind—and when she finally became aware that their fingers were intertwined, she was already holding on to him with all of her strength.

At that precise instant, Jilly rose to her knees in the pew, placed her lips near Kate's ear, and said, "I gotta pee."

Kate almost laughed aloud. What could be more perfect? Here, in the midst of this magnificent ceremony, nature called as yet another warning from God not to forget that she was merely mortal, after all.

"Can't you hold it?" whispered Kate, knowing full well that this service would last over two hours.

"No, Mommy."

Kate nodded. "All right."

Jake had opened his eyes to watch their exchange. Guessing, he whispered, "Does she have to go to the rest room?"

"Yes. Do you know where the nearest one is?"

He nodded. "Can she go by herself?"

Kate looked at him like he had lost his mind.

"I mean, once you're at the rest room, can she go in and use it by herself?"

"Oh, yes. Of course."

"Okay. Why don't you let me take her?"

"But—"

He leaned closer. "It'll be easier than trying to give you directions."

Kate started to protest, but the woman sitting in front of them chose that moment to turn and give them a deliberate frown. Even then Kate might have resisted, but the quiet intimacy inherent in Jake's offer touched her in a place she could not bear to deny. Oh, how she longed for her children to have a man in their lives whom they could trust. Could Jake be that man?

Kate leaned close to Jilly. "Mr. Singer's going to take you, okay?"

Jilly nodded urgently.

So Kate looked on with passive acceptance as Jake rose, adjusted his dark suit while his black silk *yarmulke* clung precariously to the back of his head, and set off up the aisle with the center of her universe in his arms.

A t least *I've done something right,* thought Ruth as she looked down upon Katy and Jake, holding hands. *Not that it makes up for the rest.*

Katy had the children with her, just as she had said she would.

Something told Ruth that Katy was hiding behind those children, using their needs as an excuse to avoid dealing with the loneliness of her own life. *Ah, well. We both have our problems.* Ruth herself could not elude the memory of Helen crossing the street and entering the woods at the edge of the park. Why hadn't she insisted on giving her friend a ride? It would have taken only fifteen minutes to drop Helen off at her building . . . fifteen minutes compared to eternity. The shameful thing was, Ruth remembered considering that option and discarding it because it had seemed like too much trouble.

And then there was Steve, whom she had refused.

And Isaac.

Always Isaac . . .

She felt a tear flow down her cheek.

Get a grip, girl. You can't start bawling in front of all these people.

Ruth dabbed at her eyes with the back of her hand. Beside her, Sam Gottlieb spotted the movement. Many people cried on *Yom Kippur.* Always one to be prepared, Rabbi Gottlieb removed a wad of tissues from a pocket beneath his robe and offered one to Ruth. She took it with a dreary smile, dabbed her eyes, and lifted her face toward the congregation.

So many people filled with guilt and hope. So much devotion and love. *Hashem, look how we adore you. Why must we suffer so?*

Then, for just a few moments, she managed to think like a rabbi again, lifting her heart in prayer as she joined in the liturgy. But try as she might, Ruth could not restrain the image of Helen disappearing forever into the park. It emerged, juxtaposed with the thought of Lieutenant Washington sitting at Helen's desk, his hands sifting through her private things, the unimportant accoutrements of Helen's life, which she would surely have arranged differently had she known they would be seen by strangers.

The cantor at the podium lifted his fine, clear voice to heaven and Rabbi Ruth Gold mentally replayed her conversation with Lieutenant Washington for the hundredth time, like a phonograph needle stuck between the grooves. Again and again he had asked if she knew anyone in Helen's life named J. Cantor. Finally, in frustration, she had replied, "Isn't it obvious? If the name is Cantor, she was talking about *him*." No, Washington had said. Solomon Cantor's middle initial was *F*. There was no *J* in his name. He had continued to ask in a dozen different ways until finally Ruth had refused to answer any more questions unless he told her why that initial was so important. He had paused as if deciding whether she could be trusted, then said, "I'm looking at her date book, and it says here, *See R. before service re: J. Cantor.* That's written for the night she died."

Then Ruth had told him about Helen's warning—the conversation that evening in the temple library about the patient she was seeing and the fears Helen had for the congregation's safety. Ruth remembered Helen's voice, wavering with frustration at her own professional ethics: *"I believe the patient may be dangerous."* Ruth had asked Washington if psychiatric counseling was a condition of Solomon Cantor's parole. He had said he did not know. She had snapped, "Well, I suggest you find out."

A motion in the congregation stirred Ruth from her memories. She saw Jake Singer rise from the pew with little Jilly in his arms. The position of Jilly's hands made the reason for their untimely exit clear to everyone. Ruth smiled in spite of her morbid mood.

Some things will not wait, even for you, Hashem.

Shifting the little girl so she rode easily within the crook of his strong left arm, Jake set off up the aisle. Most of the men and women ignored them, but a few glanced their way, smiled at Jilly's obvious situation, then returned their attention to the momentous ceremony. Ruth was about to do the same when she noticed something odd.

As Jake Singer passed a pew near the back, a woman reached out to touch him. He seemed to anticipate her gesture, moving as far as possible toward the opposite side of the aisle. The woman's hand lingered in midair for just an instant before it was quickly withdrawn.

A large man seated in the pew in front blocked Ruth's view of the woman's face. She craned her neck, straining for a different line of sight. For some reason, Ruth felt it was important that she know the woman's identity. Just then, the cantor reached a stage in the liturgy that required the congregation to rise. Ruth kept her eyes locked upon the large man, willing him to react slowly. Her silent entreaty was granted, and the woman behind him stood first, allowing Ruth to clearly see her face.

She was Gabby Cantor.

Ten minutes later, Orvis found the woman near the children's day-care center, standing beside a bronze plaque that read *Jacob Israel Cantor Children's Wing*.

"Come on, this way," he said.

"Okay," she said with total trust.

He had her alone, in the right place and time as they walked along the hall, empty now except for the guilty residue of the millions of little sins that had oozed between these walls just a few minutes before. The others had collected together in the sanctuary, their unholy brew of souls swirling in a cesspool of futile expectations, while Orvis alone moved straight and true, upstream as it were, toward the only real hope of salvation, and now, as the two of them walked up the hall away from their dreary little ceremonies and pretentious charades, she clung to him for dear life.

Orvis smiled at the irony.

THIRTY-FIVE

Kate kept thinking they should have returned by now. Although she hadn't checked her watch when Jake and Jilly left, it seemed to be taking far too long.

She turned to look back toward the doors.

A man—Kate thought he must be the chief rabbi at the temple—had been speaking for several minutes. She tried to listen in spite of her growing concern about her daughter, but she found it impossible to follow his words. Kate had been seized by a nagging feeling of anxiety almost from the moment Jake had walked away with Jilly in his arms. *Why did I let him have her? I don't really know him. I should have taken her myself.*

Kate decided she was overreacting, probably because everything she'd ever been taught cried out against her growing feelings for Jake, and now that he was not physically present it was more difficult to ignore the small voice of her conscience. Jake was a Jew and she a Christian. It would never work. Unless . . . perhaps his religious commitment was not as strong as hers. Perhaps he would convert.

No. That was a foolish hope. She could not abandon her faith, and she could not expect him to abandon his. Yet whenever she was with Jake Singer that stagnant logic evaporated beneath the warmth of his presence and the parched and lonely winds that moaned within her heart.

She smiled, remembering how much fun their date had been . . . the aquarium and the walk on the levee and the movie *Moby Dick*.

Wait a minute.

Moby Dick.

The old lady!

Of course!

That nagging déjà vu sense that she had forgotten something, the same feeling she had at the movie the other day with Jake. . . . The old lady *was* Moby Dick, the woman she and Ruth had seen in the locker room all those years ago, just before they heard Nan Smith's scream. She had been much larger then—obese, really, and of course, a lot younger—but Kate was certain that old woman was the one witness they had not called to the stand at the trial. The prosecuting attorney had never asked the woman to testify because she had not actually seen Solomon Cantor that day and because she had been too emotional. Maybe that was why she and Ruth had both forgotten. But it was definitely the same woman, so she and Ruth were *not* the last surviving witnesses. There was one more.

And she had to be warned.

At last, Ruth had something to take her mind off her grief. Like a drowning woman clutching at any bit of flotsam to survive, she seized the question and refused to let it go.

Why had Gabby Cantor reached out for Jake Singer?

And, even more intriguing, why had Jake avoided her touch?

Ruth Gold's beleaguered mind welcomed the puzzle. She knew she would find an answer sooner or later. When it came to puzzles, she almost always found the answer.

What Orvis really enjoyed was the total trust. She went along with him without question, meekly, in spite of the unusual nature of their brand-new relationship. It amused him to have such authority over her. He believed it was his right, and in fact, she was correct to trust him so. Just like her, he had no choice. Justice demanded what he was about to do.

He led her through a maze of hallways, searching for his goal. It wasn't far from here, he was sure of that. Just around the next corner, and then he could finish this thing.

"Here we are," said Orvis, opening the door.

She gave him a questioning look as they stepped out into the courtyard.

"Let's just go over there, shall we?"

He led her to the bench beside the wall and gestured for her to sit.

"Now then, I want you to wait here for a minute. I'll be right back."

She looked up at him with trusting eyes. "But why?"

He patted her hand. "You just wait."

The rabbi had finished speaking, and the singer had begun again. Kate could not stop looking back over her shoulder. How could she have let Jilly out of her sight? It had been at least twenty minutes. *Twenty minutes!* Something wasn't right, and she wasn't the only one who noticed.

"Where are they?" whispered Paul.

"I don't know."

"Do you want me to go find them?"

"No!" she said, too loudly.

The woman in front of them turned to frown again. Ignoring her, Kate leaned close to Paul. "I'll go," she whispered. "You wait right here."

Paul pursed his lips and frowned. She touched his arm. "I need you to stay in case they come back while I'm gone, honey. To tell them where I went. Please?"

He nodded, his eyes straight ahead.

"Good," she said. Giving his stout little arm another squeeze, she rose and started up the aisle.

Ruth watched the cantor. His name was Ernie Collins, and he was wonderful, with never a glance at the prayer book or Torah, and never an instant of hesitation, just an unbroken flow of pure and holy words.

Ernie really was quite a singer.

Singer . . .

Cantor . . .

She lifted her hand to her mouth as an idea took shape. Washington had said Helen's date book mentioned a "J. Cantor." Now Ruth struggled to recall her conversation with Gabby Cantor on the day Gabby had paid her a surprise visit at her house. There was something she should remember . . . yes! The name of Gabby's son, the name of the new children's wing, was Jacob Israel Cantor. They'd been talking about the Nan Smith murder, and she had asked how old Ruth was when it happened. Ruth had answered, and then Gabby said, *"Our son wasn't much older than that when he . . . well, basically, Izzy lost his father."*

Gabby and Sol called their son Izzy, which was short for Israel, of course. But it was just as true that Jake was short for Jacob, and just now, Gabby *Cantor* had reached out to Jake *Singer*. Katy had met Jake because Ruth had given her his locksmith card, and Ruth had gotten his card from Helen Blumenthal. Singer . . . Cantor. Jake . . . Jacob.

What if Jake Singer was the "J. Cantor" in Helen's date book?

What if Katy was dating Jacob Israel Cantor?

Ruth remembered Helen's words that night in the temple library: *"I don't have a specific reason to think you're in danger. I'm talking about all of us. Everyone here at temple."*

Ruth was on her feet before she knew what she had done. Seated beside her, Sam Gottlieb reached for the sleeve of her robe. "Not yet, Ruth. It's your turn in a minute."

But Ruth shook off his hand and darted for the steps.

Kate had already reached the outer hall when Ruth burst through the doors. "Oh, Ruth," she said. "Thank goodness you're here."

"I've got to tell you something."

"It'll have to wait. I need to find Jake and Jilly. Something's wrong."

"I know. That's what I'm trying to tell you."

"What?"

"Jake is Sol's son. He's changed his name from Cantor to Singer."

Kate paled. "How do you know that?"

"Just trust me, okay? You're right. We've *got* to find them." Ruth pointed down the corridor. "See that hall to the right up there?"

Kate nodded, heart swelling against her lungs, constricting her breath as it pulsed irregularly.

"Okay," said Ruth. "That leads around the temple toward the south. This one here goes in the same direction, only on this side of the building. On the far end, there's another hall that runs east and west to connect that hall with this one. It's a big, connected rectangle. Got it?"

"Yes."

"I'll take this hall; you take the other. Check every room you pass along the way. We'll meet at the far end of the building. There's two of us and only one of him. Whoever finds him first will scream like crazy. Then the other one will come running."

"But shouldn't we get more help? What can we do against—"

"There's no time!" shouted Ruth as she set off down the hall.

God's demands had horrified him at first. He was not a bloodthirsty man. In fact, Orvis had resisted the calling for many days, telling himself it could not be God's will; it must be something else: Satan, the opposer, or even something gone wrong in his mind. But in the end, Orvis had known he was neither insane nor the victim of deception. In giving him the vision of his Bible pressing back against Gabrielle Cantor's door, God had called him to these violent acts. Who was he to resist? Still, by obeying the Voice, he disobeyed other commandments, sacred words spoken to all Israel from the top of Mt. Sinai.

It gave him pause from time to time.

To obey was to disobey, much as Abraham was given a choice between committing murder by sacrificing his son or refusing a direct command from God. What could you do in a case like that, except obey the command with faith that the sin you had been ordered to commit was somehow acceptable in God's Plan? Faith demanded action, so he would do as he was told and let God sort it out in the end.

Unafraid of being seen, Orvis stood full height upon the roof, slipping on a pair of black leather gloves. The thick aroma of liquid tar assailed his nostrils. Perfect. All according to the Plan. Perhaps even an improvement, since Orvis had assumed the roofers would leave the portable tar kettle on the ground when they came to repair the rips he had made in the roof. The reverend had been fully prepared to carry buckets full of hot pitch up the ladder to accomplish his task, but upon his arrival just after dawn this morning, he had been delighted to find the device had been lifted to the roof with a small crane. The kettle was the kind Orvis had seen roofers use a hundred times: two tires, a trailer-type yoke, gas canister underneath, and dried black tar smeared on every side. His one concern had been that the thing might require too much time to melt the tar, but raising the lid he saw a bubbling caldron of superheated pitch, ready and waiting. When he had ignited the gas burners this morning, he had also repositioned the kettle along the edge of the roof, carefully adjusting its position until he was certain all was just as it had to be. Several large cylinders of solid tar stood nearby, wrapped in kraft paper and ready to be added to the melter when the roofing crew returned tomorrow to finish their job. He had placed one of the cylinders on its side and rolled it to the proper position. Now all that remained was to slip the end of a timber under the kettle and, using the cylinder as a fulcrum, let a basic law of mechanics do the rest.

"Are you still there?" he called, not bothering to look over the edge. "Are you on the bench?"

She paused before answering, just as he'd known she would. To her, his voice would seem to come from nowhere and from everywhere, like an utterance of God Almighty. That, too, was according to the Plan.

"Yes . . . " came her reply, thin and weak and trusting. "I'm on the bench. Where are you?"

"I am very near," called Orvis Newton as he pushed down upon the lever.

Ruth's mind raced as fast as her feet, putting the pieces together. Why would Sol and Gabby Cantor's son change his name? Why would he refuse to acknowledge his connection to Gabby in the sanctuary?

"Jilly!" she screamed, pushing open another door. Again, like the fifteen rooms before it, she found the room empty. "Jilly! Where are you, baby?" she called again, not caring that her voice could probably be heard in the sanctuary on this most holy day.

Had she been wrong about Sol Cantor all this time? Was *Jake* the murderer?

For the sake of Katy Flint's child, she earnestly hoped not.

Kate abandoned every pretense of respect and silence. She had already checked the bathrooms and found them empty and looked behind a dozen other doors as she made her way up the hall. With each unoccupied room, her panic grew. Now as she ran from door to door, flinging them open and shouting Jilly's name at the top of her lungs, Kate's irregular heartbeat pounded well out of control. In spite of the weakness caused by her condition, knowing a stroke was possible but not caring, Kate willed herself to keep moving.

Bawling like a baby, she reached the end of the hall. Her pulse was now a raging wind in her ears, akin to the sound of a hurricane. There were no more rooms to search. But there *had* to be more! She hadn't found her precious Jilly yet!

Kate brought herself up short at the end of the corridor and wiped her tears away. No more! She would curse her Maker before she let him make her cry another tear. Lungs heaving, Kate stood up straight for dignity's sake and prepared to unleash the pent-up fury that had been building in her ever since the moment John's malignancy was confirmed in spite of a thousand earnest prayers, a fury that had mounted with each pitiless indignity and grinding agony her man had endured while she uselessly begged on her knees for mercy, a fury that had clawed its way deep into Kate's defective heart when her love of loves had exhaled his last breath. She longed to curse the heavens, to rage against God before all creation, but in the final erratic heartbeat before she released her rage, a lingering remnant of her faith aroused the sobering recollection that there is an unforgivable sin, a point of no return. Kate Flint's courage failed. When she gave voice to the wrath in her soul, it was not with an outraged roar but in the soft, pitiful tones of a beggar, and in that instant, she hated her cowardice almost as much as she hated God Almighty.

"Don't take Jilly, too," she whispered. "Don't do that to me."

There! Just down the hall, a row of windows along the far side glowing with the afternoon sunlight, and beyond them, an atrium. Hoping against hope, Kate flew to the glass and pressed her palms against it.

Outside on a bench, alone and forlorn, sat a living memory. With her palms and her sniffling nose pushed hard against the window, Kate saw the old woman who had greeted her in the hallway earlier, the woman she and Ruth once saw on the day of a murder, the woman they'd called Moby Dick. It was Mrs. Friedman, the witness they never called to the stand. Instead of wearing a white towel as she had in the locker room all those years ago, the old woman wore a touchingly simple pure white dress, but it was her all right, sitting on a bench just as she had on that terrible day.

This can't be a coincidence. This must have something to do with my baby!

Heartbeat still screaming out of control, Kate ran along the hall and shoved her way through the outside door. A pair of dark spots grew before her eyes like melting film in a motion picture projector. Kate had seen those spots before, when she had worked out too hard at the gym in the early days of her condition, before she knew her limitations. She knew her brain was crying out for oxygen, knew she would lose consciousness soon unless she stopped, but Kate kept on. Although she did not believe for a second that God would really answer, once again she prayed, "Don't do this to me . . . *please*." And as she stepped into the silence of the courtyard, a disembodied voice answered from the heavens above. Like Abraham, Isaac, Jacob, and Moses, she heard it with her own ears. God himself said, "I am very near."

Kate sobbed with relief. The Lord had answered her at last. He would save her baby girl!

Then the boiling tar fell from the sky, scalding everything it touched, and Kate knew that she had been horribly deceived. It was not God's voice she'd heard, but Satan's, spewing his black and sulfurous drool down upon the woman from her past.

THIRTY-SIX

After sprinting from room to room along the hall for almost a hundred yards, Ruth stood panting at the intersection of the corridor. She had heard Katy calling for her daughter earlier, but now the frantic mother's voice was silent. As Ruth's breathing slowly returned to normal, she considered the options. She should probably run down past the courtyard and hope to meet Katy at the other end. After all, that had been the plan. But what if Jake had taken Jilly outside? Even now, he could be driving away. Shouldn't someone check the parking lot and the street?

Ruth decided Katy could wait. She ran for a side exit, robes flying. Stiff-arming the panic bar on the door, she dashed into the afternoon sunshine. Ruth ran flat out, her low-heeled pumps pounding the pavement at a tempo twice as fast as the rhythm of the somber voices rising from within the sanctuary. There should be police out here to help with the traffic. They could look for Jilly, and the private security guards could help. She would get everyone looking!

Circling the exterior of the sanctuary, Ruth reached the first of the cars and cast about for a police officer, but there were none in sight. She crossed the lot, slipping sideways between the closely parked cars, glancing left and right at each cross drive. Finally she came to the street.

"Where are they?" she wondered aloud, staring south along the road, shielding her eyes from the sun. The familiar band of Christian fanatics marched along the sidewalk about fifty feet away. Up to then she had escaped their notice, but now they saw her and began shouting their evangelical slogans and moving in her direction. One of them appeared to be dragging a pair of goats. *Goats?* She loosed a short, mirthless bark of laughter. Why not? They'd had wild beasts from Africa and the Yukon crossing the parking lot in the last few days. What difference did a few farm animals make?

Obviously, these people were crazy.

An engine roared to life behind her. Ruth spun on her heel just as a dark sedan peeled out from its parked location about thirty yards away. The setting sun glared from the car's windshield as it sped in her direction, obstructing her view of the driver until the car came alongside. For a fraction of a second, Ruth glimpsed the profile of the man behind the wheel. The glass was heavily tinted, and the man's face turned away slightly, but she saw enough to know that the driver could be Izzy Cantor.

"Stop!" she screamed, running out into the road. "Stop!"

The car sped away without pausing.

As Ruth stood in the middle of Walnut Street staring after it, two of the Christians reached her, a young man dressed in a dark suit and an extremely tall blonde woman wearing a modest cotton dress. The young man held the goats at the ends of a pair of ropes.

"Ma'am?" he said. "Did you know your Messiah has already come, and he's coming again one day?"

Ruth did not seem to hear.

"Ma'am? Would you like to know your Messiah?"

"What?" asked Ruth, looking vaguely in his direction.

"Are you ready to meet your Messiah?"

By now, the entire group had reached them, nine or ten in all.

"Oh . . ." said Ruth, stiffly pounding her hips with her fists and looking beyond them at the distant, retreating automobile. "Oh . . ."

"Ma'am?" asked the earnest young man. "Are you all right?"

Ruth stared right through him, her mind running down possibilities like a mouse in a maze, stumbling into dead ends at every turn. Helen had said her patient might harm anyone in the congregation. Helen had given her Jake's card. Jake Singer was really Jacob Cantor. Obviously, Jake was the patient, and now he was loose with Katy's child. What could she do? What could she *do?* The evangelist's mouth continued to move, but Ruth did not hear his words. Maybe Jake and Jilly had been in that car. She hadn't seen them clearly, but it could have been them. Then again, maybe not. Oh, what could she do, alone, with so many places to search?

She had an idea.

Ruth focused her attention on the young man and said, "I need your help."

"Praise God!" said the tall young woman standing beside the man.

"Yes, ma'am," said the earnest young man. "That's what we're here for." He drew closer, tugging the goats behind. Their hoofs tapped on the concrete.

"No. You don't understand. I really do need your help."

"It's not our help you need," replied the tall woman. "You need Jesus Christ."

"Will you please listen!" screamed Ruth. *"I need your help!"*

Suddenly, the young man stepped in front of the tall woman and said, "Martha, I think this lady is in some other kind of trouble."

"Finally!" said Ruth, lifting her face toward the sky.

Ruth gave them all the details, and in less than a minute the evangelists had fanned out across the parking lot, crossing it in an organized line, pausing to check the interior of each vehicle, calling Jilly's name, even getting on hands and knees to look beneath the cars.

Ruth began to hope again. "Thank you," she whispered, watching them. "Thank you."

Rabbi Sam Gottlieb was more than a little angry.

For some time now, Ruth Gold had been acting strangely. Leaving Torah studies in the middle of class, screaming at congregants in hallways, insulting Gabby Cantor, one of the temple's most generous supporters . . . and now this. Leaving the *bima* in the middle of *Neila.*

Sarah Onheimer, the chair of their new membership committee and active supporter of perhaps a dozen other regular programs at the temple, approached the podium for the day's sixth and final Torah reading. Ruth should be here. It was she who had lobbied so persuasively that Sarah should have this high honor. But the time had come, and Rabbi Gold was missing the moment.

Yom Kippur was the second most sacred day in the Jewish calendar, next to *Shabbat* itself. The Torah required that desecration of the Sabbath be punished with death, and desecration of *Yom Kippur* with excommunication . . . a fate some would consider worse than death. He himself had once officiated at a *Neila* while running a fever of a hundred and two. Yet here was one of his rabbis, clearly healthy, dashing off in the middle of services with no explanation. Sam had no doubts about Ruth's piety, but this was a very serious business. The Talmud allowed only one excuse for such a blatant violation of the high holy day, and after Gabby Cantor's complaint, he knew the board of directors would probably accept nothing less.

For Ruth's sake, someone had better be dying out there.

As she reentered the temple, Ruth heard the sound of footsteps staggering down the hall, then Katy rounded a corner and collapsed to the floor. Ruth ran to kneel at her side. "Have you found Jilly?" she asked.

Katy shook her head and spoke between ragged breaths. "We . . . need . . . help."

"I know. I've got some people looking for her outside."

"No . . . medical . . . help," panted Katy.

Ruth took her shoulders in both hands. Katy looked terrible. Pale, sweaty . . . this was more than simply the result of running through the halls. "What's wrong with you?"

Shaking her head, Katy said, "Not me . . . a woman . . . in courtyard . . . roofing tar . . . boiling . . . all over her."

"*Hashem*, be merciful. What about Jilly?"

"Haven't found her. Got to keep looking."

"Okay. Try the second floor. There's a set of stairs around the corner up here. You'll find some empty rooms if you make a left at the top. I'll call for an ambulance."

Nodding, Katy tried to stand. She was halfway up when she fell back to the floor.

"Katy," cried Ruth. "What is this?"

"Heart," gasped Katy. "Old problem. I'll be okay. You go."

"But—"

"Go!" begged Katy. "*Run!*"

Ruth jogged toward her office. As she went, Katy's ragged voice echoed along the hall behind her. "O God, don't do this to me," she was saying. "Not again."

Even as she ran for help, Ruth could not help but wonder why this desperate mother was praying for herself and not her child.

Martha noticed a dense row of wax-leaf Ligustrums beneath a broad expanse of windows overlooking St. Charles and decided to check underneath them. A little girl could easily hide behind those leaves. The tall woman wound her way between the rows of cars and approached the shrubbery. "Jilly?" she called, hitching up her skirt and kneeling to look under the bushes. "Jilly, honey? Are you there?"

She was answered by an inhuman scream. At first, Martha feared the cry had come from behind the shrubbery, but then she realized her ears had mistaken an echo from the masonry wall beyond the shrubs for the source of the cry. Turning from her kneeling position to look back, Martha found her vision blocked by the first row of cars at the edge of the parking lot, so she stood to peer over the vehicles. She saw a security guard and a police-man and a couple of her friends from the Sister Nan Smith Crusade for Jews searching for the little girl farther along the wall of the temple. Shading her eyes to see all the way to the sidewalk, Martha noticed that one of the goats was missing.

Both of them had been left tied to a stop sign post, but now only one was there and the poor thing was frantic. Straining against the rope, it kicked and charged away from the sign again and again, violently brought up short each time by the rope around its neck. Where was its companion? Why was it so upset?

Moved by the goat's pitiful cries, Martha Douglas brushed leaves and grass from the knees of her ruined hosiery and hurried back across the parking lot. As she neared the sidewalk, she heard the scream again, much lower and more plaintive. Without the brick wall of the temple nearby to echo the cry, she realized it had come from the park across Walnut Street. Martha turned that way just in time to see a tiger drag the bloodied second goat into the underbrush.

Speechless, she lifted her hand and pointed, working her mouth, trying to scream. Only the smallest of whimpers would come out. Fortunately, a policeman holding a cup of coffee had also seen the tiger. He dropped the foam cup, splashing his trousers, and reached for the microphone clipped to his uniform's left shoulder. Soon, the area swarmed with other men in uniform. Guns drawn, they stood in a line facing the park. Meanwhile, Martha had calmed herself enough to care for the remaining goat. She spoke to it in measured tones until it stopped raging against its restraint; then she knelt beside it, running her palm along its neck, petting it like a dog. The goat responded well, lowering its head to the ground to nibble nervously at the grass.

Martha shielded her eyes from the sun and stared at the park again. As she watched for the tiger, it occurred to her that there had been a sacrifice at Temple Brit Yisrael today after all . . . a sacrifice to whatever evil had possessed a human soul to let such mayhem loose upon the city.

Ruth hung up the phone. The paramedics were on their way. Now what should she do? A seriously injured woman lay in the courtyard of the temple, and a little girl was in the hands of . . . who knew what? Both were desperate situations, but she could only be in one place at a time. She needed more help. Lots and lots of help. But to whom could she turn? Everyone at the temple who was not performing an essential service was in . . .

The sanctuary.

There would be doctors there, maybe even burn specialists, and police officers—professionals who would know exactly how to handle both of these emergencies. One thousand people who might be able to help . . . and one thousand people to offend.

Did she dare?

The Talmud was clear: *Shabbat* and the holy days could be violated in order to save a life. Ruth had no other choice, and no excuse to hesitate. Into the hall she went, heart filled with a deep, expanding dread. Over and over again, she thought, *I have no choice. I have no choice.* Her pace slowly increased until she was running. *They may fire me for this. I may never be welcome in this temple again. But I have no choice. I have no choice.*

The twin mahogany doors loomed tall ahead, their curved bronze handles mocking her, daring her to enter. A woman's voice filtered through the narrow slit between them, Sarah Onheimer speaking Hebrew words of Torah, warning her off. Ruth paused a few feet away. It occurred to her that she had not actually seen the injured woman. She had only Katy's word that the woman was in dire trouble. Did she dare trust Katy enough to interrupt the *Neila?* What if Katy was mistaken, or worse, what if she was deliberately trying to mislead? Ruth stood facing the sanctuary doors, aware that her next action might very well end her career. Did she really trust Katy that much?

Swallowing once, she seemed to be watching from someplace outside herself as her hand reached out and gripped the handle. She pulled. The door swung out silently.

Before Ruth were the backs of one thousand heads in gently curving rows, each of them intent upon the woman at the *bima*. In her terror, Ruth fixed her attention on an old man, just to her left, rocking forward and back in time to the *aliyah*. He looked almost Orthodox with his black suit, long, scraggly gray beard, and his *talit* and *yarmulke*. Faced with three thousand years of tradition, Ruth Gold lost her resolve. She stood frozen just inside the closing door, staring wildly toward the *bima*. How could she do this? *How could she?* It was a transgression against the most holy moment of the year for the one thousand Jews who sat before her.

Oddly, Sarah Onheimer's words of Torah did not penetrate her thoughts. Instead, she thought of the portion read ten days ago on *Rosh Hashanah*. It was the *Akeda*, the binding of Isaac, the famous tale of God's demand that Abraham sacrifice his only son. Ruth had always marveled at the ease with which most people skipped over the nagging question at the heart of the story: How could God ask a man to kill his son, to break one of the Ten Commandments? And yet, how could a man refuse anything God asked? The answer, of course, was faith. *Hashem* wished to teach

Abraham that faith was more important than all of the commandments combined. It was both the root and the goal of them all, and so, filled with faith that *Hashem* would find a way to make this terribly wrong thing right somehow, Ruth filled her lungs with air and shouted, *"Excuse me!"*

The heads of the crowd turned in every direction. Sarah Onheimer stopped reading. Ruth's voice had echoed from the walls, its source impossible to identify. *I could still get out of this. If I just keep my mouth shut, they'll never know it was me who yelled.* But the thought of little Jilly would not let Ruth take the coward's path. Again, she lifted her voice. "Please forgive me," she began. "But we have a terrible emergency. We need doctors and nurses and policemen. Are any of you policemen?"

A thousand pairs of eyes turned to her in amazement and outrage, their silence a gigantic serpent coiled around her chest, squeezing with unrelenting, physical force, squeezing until bile bubbled up in her throat. She choked. She fought to breathe. Then, miraculously, a woman stood and said, "I'm a police officer. What's wrong?" Then another rose and said, "I'm a doctor," and another, and soon three dozen men and women were on their feet, facing her, waiting to be told what to do.

Clearing her throat, Ruth said, "There's a woman in the south courtyard who's been badly burned. Do any of you know about burns?"

"That's my specialty," called a gray-haired man near the *bima*. Already, he was stepping sideways past his seated neighbors in the pew, heading toward the aisle.

A general hum of voices rose from the congregation as Sam Gottlieb approached the podium. Sarah Onheimer stepped aside, and the rabbi spoke loudly. "The situation seems to be under control now. We will continue with the *Neila*."

Ruth raised her hand. "Excuse me!" she called. Rabbi Gottlieb stared at her across the sea of people, his brow wrinkled, as Ruth continued. "We also have a little girl missing. She's about five years old, is wearing a white and pink dress, and has blonde hair. Her name is Jilly, and we think a man named Jake Singer has taken her, because—"

"*Taken* her?" shouted someone from near the front. "I dropped her off at the day-care center!" The bile returned with the force of a tidal wave as Ruth saw Jake Singer—or should she call him Izzy Cantor?— rising to stand by his pew. Staring at her, he said, "You must be crazy!"

THIRTY-SEVEN

Kate's heartbeat was worse, the pulse much more rapid, the sense of outward pressure against her rib cage even more intense. Oh, how she hated this feeling! Sometimes, when she felt a rapid flurry of beats followed by a pause even longer than usual, Kate held her breath in anticipation, wondering, *Will it start again, or was that my last heartbeat?* But she had taken her medication, and the dizziness had begun to pass. She had almost caught her breath now that she sat on a leather chair in Rabbi Sam Gottlieb's darkly paneled office, watching Jilly play with her Barbie doll on the carpet.

They had found her daughter in a day-care class, just as Jake had said, and now Kate was concentrating on remaining still while Ruth sat with her eyes closed in another chair nearby and Paul stood at Kate's side, staring at Lieutenant Lincoln Washington with something approaching awe. The Lieutenant sat halfway on the desk, one leg swinging to and fro, the other planted firmly on the floor. He wore immaculately polished Italian loafers, a perfectly tailored, dark blue, worsted wool suit that would have been the envy of a Swiss banker, and his usual tiny gold earring, which twinkled in the light when he tilted his head a certain way. He held his hands clasped around the notebook in his lap, as if it contained a secret.

"So this Friedman woman . . . uh—" he looked at the notebook— "Rebecca Friedman-Betterton . . . she was a witness at Cantor's trial?"

Kate said, "She was supposed to be, but they never called her to testify." She had to pause to breathe. "Like I told you, that's why Ruth and I didn't remember her before."

"Okay," said Washington. "Tell me again about the voice you heard. You said it was a man's voice. No doubt about that?"

Kate shook her head. "No doubt. A man's voice."

"Did it sound familiar?"

"I already said it didn't."

"And what did it say again?"

Kate sighed and rubbed her temples, willing the throbbing in her ears to subside. "I think it was something like 'I'm close by' or 'I'm right here.' Something like that."

"You didn't recognize this voice?"

Kate stood suddenly. "Lieutenant, I've told you everything I can remember. Now, my children are here listening to these horrible things, and they're tired, and I'm tired, and we need to go home."

"Mrs. Flint," said Washington, "do you recall what we discussed when your house was vandalized? Sometimes people remember more than they think they do. Little things that don't seem important to them could help us catch the perpetrator or prove the case in court, but people forget details with the passing of time. That's why it's so important that we go over this again right now."

"But my kids need to get away from here."

"I can have an officer take them to—"

"No!"

"—a playroom in the day-care area if you like."

"No! They stay with me!"

He nodded. "All right, but we do have to go over this again."

Still on her feet, Kate said, "I've got a headache."

Someone opened the door. Several voices tumbled into the office, and Jake Singer took one step into the office, even as a woman outside called, "Hey! You can't go in there!"

Jake surveyed the room; then, turning toward Kate, he said, "Are you okay?"

Kate refused to look at him. Someone beyond the open door said, "It's like it was raining tar. . . ."

Staring hard at Jake, Ruth said, "How could you just take her daughter?"

"I didn't take her! Why do you keep saying that? I just left her in the day care. It seemed like a good idea to—"

"*Good idea?* To take a woman's child somewhere without her knowledge?"

"Jilly didn't want to go back to the service." His eyes were on Kate. "I was going to tell you as soon as I got back to my seat. But you weren't there."

"That's right," said Ruth. "She was outside, searching for her daughter along with me and everyone else!"

"I would have been back sooner, but—"

"But what?" interrupted Ruth.

"It took a while, because Jilly had a little accident on the way to the bathroom, didn't you, honey?" He smiled down at the child.

Jilly returned his smile and nodded, but Kate stepped to her side, kneeling to block Jake's view.

"Kate?" he implored.

Without looking at him, Kate gathered Jilly into her arms and said, "I don't even know who you are."

His shoulders slumped. "Come on, Kate, just because I took Jilly to the day care?"

Ruth said, "Why didn't you tell us about your father?"

Jake opened his mouth, but nothing came out.

Ruth turned on him. "What are you going to say, *Izzy?*"

Ignoring her, he continued to look at Kate. "I . . . I'm sorry, Kate. But I had good reasons. You've got to believe me."

"Good reasons to lie to us?" said Ruth. "To pretend to be her friend while the people who helped put your father behind bars are dying? What reason could you have that would possibly be good enough?"

"Kate," implored Jake. "Please . . ."

Kate felt him watching her, but she would not meet his eyes. She had not looked at him since he entered the room. Finally, Jake lowered his gaze to the floor, turned, and left.

When the door closed behind him, Washington asked, "What was that all about?"

Ruth said, "That man is Solomon Cantor's son. But he's been lying about his name, pretending to be someone called Jake Singer, and he's been sucking up to Katy."

Without reacting, Washington turned his penetrating brown eyes back to Kate. "Sucking up?"

"We had a date," she said. "Just one."

"Tell him about the locks," said Ruth.

"Locks?" Washington raised an eyebrow.

Eyes on the floor, Kate mumbled, "When they broke into our house, he changed the locks. He's a locksmith. That's how I met him."

"How did you come to call him for that?"

"I suggested him to Katy," said Ruth.

Washington turned toward the rabbi. "Okay. How'd you meet him?"

"Helen Blumenthal gave me his card."

"You don't say." Washington stared at the rabbi for a moment. "How come you didn't know he was Cantor's son? Haven't they been members of your congregation for a long time?"

"There are almost two thousand families in our temple, Lieutenant. I can't keep track of them all."

"Yeah, but this is Solomon Cantor's family. Seems like you'd have a particular interest."

"Actually, it's the other way around. I avoid his wife as much as possible, and I think she avoids me too, for obvious reasons."

"You never saw Mrs. Cantor with this Izzy Cantor around the temple when you were growing up?"

"Lieutenant, like I said, it's a big congregation. It's not hard to dodge someone here if that's what you both want to do. Besides, I don't think Jake has gone to temple for some time. I would have at least noticed him sitting in the sanctuary. He's too good-looking to miss."

"Okay," said Lincoln Washington, lifting his weight from the desk and straightening the sharp crease in his slacks. "Y'all hold on a minute while I step outside and handle a little business."

I n the waiting area outside the senior rabbi's office, men and women stood talking in several groups. A few of them took notes. Two or three used the temple's telephones. Some wore NOPD uniforms, but the rest were plainclothes cops. As Washington walked past a large man with a flattop haircut and a brown-and-orange-plaid sports coat, he tapped the man on the shoulder and inclined his head in his direction of travel. Sergeant Baxter detached himself from the conversation he'd been having and followed Washington a little way down the hall.

"Whereyat, Link?" asked Baxter.

"All right," said Washington. "See that guy up there?"

"Yeah," said Sergeant Baxter, glancing at the departing form of Jake Singer.

"Tail him, would you?"

S olomon Cantor could barely restrain his joy. At long last, there before his eyes was Izzy. He recognized his son from photographs he had seen in Gabby's house. Oh, look at him! So handsome in his dark suit and *yarmulke*, with Gabby's sandy hair and the wide shoulders of his father. Solomon's chest felt light all of a sudden, as if filled with helium.

My son, he thought. *My son!*

Most of the congregation had left the temple long ago, but Solomon remained, hiding across the street in the park, watching Ruth Gold's Citroën. It had been touch and go for a while, avoiding the men who had searched the park and avoiding the tiger. Earlier, Solomon had glimpsed the animal through an opening in the undergrowth as it crept up to the tree line, eyes intent upon the goats tethered to the stop sign. Fortunately, Sol had been downwind. He had almost convinced himself it was a trick of the light when the huge cat suddenly dashed into the open and seized one of the goats. The capture was over before anyone on the temple grounds had noticed.

Sol had immediately climbed a tree. What a ridiculous situation. A man his age, sitting up in a tree.

Then, after maybe two hours, Izzy had emerged from the temple. Sol had barely dared to hope the task of protecting Ruth Gold might lead to this. He had followed her day and night since the first murder, scarcely sleeping, praying constantly that he would be able to intercede when the time came. He had longed to protect the other little girl too—funny how he still thought of them as little girls—but it was impossible to be there for them both, and so he had chosen to focus on Ruth.

Now at last Izzy had appeared, as Solomon had hoped.

As Solomon had feared.

He had sworn to protect Ruth and Kate even if it cost the life of his only son, but perhaps it need not come to that. All Solomon had to do was follow him, find out where he lived, and look for a way to connect with him. If they could somehow be reconciled after all these years, maybe Solomon could begin to undo the damage Gabby had done. It was worth a try, and it made more sense to follow Izzy than to follow just one of his potential victims, never knowing when or where he might strike. Sol descended from the tree, moving as quietly as he could because of the police across the street. Not to mention the tiger.

H ello? Hello there!"

Oh no. Not now. Muttering under her breath, Ruth quickened her pace, crossing the parking lot toward her Citroën. She had spent all afternoon fielding Lieutenant Washington's questions, unlocking doors for police, working with them to allow the congregation to leave, explaining herself to Rabbi Gottlieb, and answering the same questions to different policemen all over again. After everything she'd endured, the last thing she needed was one of the evangelists' mini-sermons as she left. All she wanted now was a quick meal alone, a few minutes of escape curled up with a good book, and twelve solid hours of dreamless sleep in her own comfortable bed.

But it was not to be. The woman continued to call to her insistently as she crossed the parking lot. Ruth actually had the key in her car door when the tall blonde arrived at her elbow.

"Ma'am?" said the woman with a smile. "May I ask you a question?"

Opening the door, Ruth said, "Look. I appreciate your help earlier, but

I'm a rabbi. Understand? A *rabbi*. You're not gonna talk me into becoming a Christian, so please, could we just go our separate ways in peace? This has been a very tough day for everyone."

The woman's smile evaporated. "I wasn't going to say anything about that."

Ruth took a deep breath, paused, then closed the car door and turned to look up at the woman. "All right. What can I do for you?"

"Well, everyone else has gone home. I mean, all of my friends. But I didn't see you leave and I was hoping to ask, you know, how your little girl is doing?"

"*My* little girl? Oh. You mean Jilly. She's not mine. She's a friend's daughter."

"Is she okay?"

"Yes," said Ruth, considering the woman before her. After a pause, she continued, "Are you saying you waited here all this time just to ask about Jilly?"

"Uh-huh," said the woman, nodding her head.

Ruth sighed. "It's been so hectic, what with the service interrupted, and we had a . . . a terrible accident. An elderly woman died today, and—"

"So that was why the ambulance came?"

"Yes."

The woman squeezed her eyes shut. "Thank God!" Then, opening her eyes wide, she exclaimed, "Oh, I'm sorry! I mean, I'm not thankful that the lady passed away, of course, but I am grateful the ambulance didn't come for the little girl. That was what I thought, you know."

Ruth considered her for a moment. "May I ask you something?"

"Sure."

"Don't take this the wrong way, but why are you so worried about Jilly?"

"Why, I . . . I had to know for sure if she's all right. I mean, the police said so, but I wanted to make extra sure, you know?"

"But you thought she was Jewish, right?"

The woman looked confused. "What difference does that make?"

Ruth examined her face, searching for signs of insincerity. All she saw was genuine concern. Finally she said, "It was wrong of me not to come

back out to let you know. I'm sorry. It's just that so much happened after
I went back inside, I completely forgot."

"Oh, that's okay. I understand. On a day like today, your people
needed you with them, not out here."

"Yes. Well, thank you for your help."

"You're welcome, Reverend." She gasped and covered her mouth.
"I mean *Rabbi!* I'm sorry. I meant to say Rabbi!"

Ruth smiled and patted her arm. "Relax. It's okay."

The tall blonde Christian flushed bright red. Lowering her hand,
she said, "Please, tell the little girl . . . Jilly?"

Ruth nodded.

"Okay, well, please tell Jilly we're all so glad she's okay, and we'll be
praying for her. We'll be praying for the loved ones of the elderly lady
who passed away as well."

Opening her car door again, Ruth said, "I will. Thank you. That's
very nice, and thanks again for your help today."

"I'm just glad the Lord led us here so we *could* help."

Ruth froze, facing the interior of her car. When she spoke again, it
was through gritted teeth. "Just when we're starting to reach some kind
of . . . of . . . an understanding, why did you have to say that?"

"What? What did I say?"

"What did you say? You . . . you . . . oh, *forget* it!"

Moments later, as Ruth wheeled furiously onto the street, she glanced
in her rearview mirror and saw the woman standing all alone among the
police cars in the parking lot, watching her drive away.

The Lord had been satisfied once more. Orvis neared his room, avoiding the potholes in the alley, feeling free for the moment and emptied
of the need to act. Tonight he would sleep without dreams, alone in the
peaceful vacuum of his inner world. He approached his battered door,
looking neither left nor right nor upward at the tangled web of electric
lines crisscrossed overhead like slender cracks in a collapsing sky. As he
passed a pile of plastic garbage sacks, a drunk lying on the asphalt stirred
and looked his way. "Mistah," he said, "you gotta quattah?" Orvis paused,
slipped a tract into the man's shirt pocket, patted him on the shoulder,

then walked on, leaning forward slightly at the waist to push his way through the stench from the overflowing Dumpster just beyond the rear entrance to his building. The drunk climbed to his feet and staggered after Orvis, saying, "Will ya gimme a dime at least?"

"Get away," said the reverend.

A few seconds later Orvis stood in his room removing his clothes. It was good that his suit was pitch-black, since some of the tar had splattered on his trousers as it poured over the side of the roof. When he had stripped everything away, he crossed to the tiny bathroom and stepped into the shower. Steeling himself, he twisted the cold-water knob.

As the frigid liquid spewed from the rusty showerhead, Orvis sucked in his breath, feeling the pain. His teeth began to clatter. He hugged his arms to his pale white torso. After a few minutes, he reached for a bar of soap, trembling violently. He rubbed himself with the soap, slowly at first, then faster and faster, until his hand passed furiously over his body, batting at his skin like a man in a swarm of bees. A small smile played across Orvis's face as the bar of soap made a little whishing sound.

Whish. Whish. Whish.

He thought about the cyanide in the apples and the applesauce. Cyanide comes from fruit. Apples and peaches. The seeds. He thought about how perfect that would have been, because of the Plan, of course, but also because the Jews eat fruit on the Day of Atonement.

Whish. Whish. Whish.

He thought about the bear and the zebras. He thought about the big cats. He thought about those other animals, the human ones with their tattoos and their pierced tongues and their shaved heads.

Whish. Whish. Whish.

He thought of flinging the bust, the radio, and the revolver from the top of the Rothstein's apartment, each object carefully calculated to terrorize, to drive a man over the edge. They were the firstfruits, the choice kids from his flock. His offerings had made such satisfying crashes through the windows down below.

Whish. Whish. Whish.

The *Times-Picayune* had reported that one of the tigers remained at large. Dogs and cats had been disappearing by the dozen. The authorities were amazed that an animal of that size could elude them for so long, but

they did not understand the role God played in these events. It was the
Lord who kept the tiger free, and since the beast had tasted human blood,
it was a miracle there had been no other victims. Only the Lord's inter-
vention could account for that.

Whish. Whish. Whish.

What were Eliot's words? Oh yes, 'Swaddled with darkness. In the
juvescence of the year came Christ the tiger.' Orvis smiled. He had always
liked that line. *Whish. Whish. Whish.* Well, the year was no longer young, but
the tiger still came. He would teach that to the Jews. Come, Lord Jesus.

Whish. Whish. Whish.

Orvis watched as soapy water spiraled down the drain. At the center
of the spiral was a black hole. At the center of the hole was a tiny spot of
light. As Orvis stared, he felt the light coming closer, growing in his
mind, until he saw forms and shapes within the light. It was his dear,
sweet Nan, smiling, reaching up for him. Orvis stopped rubbing his body
with the soap and stood unmoving, looking down at the rising light, at
Nan's face growing as it came, and now he heard her patient voice within
the gurgling water, her voice softly saying, "Brother Orvis, nothing you
can say will change my mind. You can't call this love, all this shouting
from a distance. You're wrong to be here, wrong to do this, and I'm going
in there to apologize and to beg forgiveness." Staring at the light, Orvis
whispered, "Please don't." But the apparition joined the swirling water and
receded into darkness.

Whish. Whish. Whish.

He rubbed himself more furiously, cleansing the false memories from
his consciousness, driving the angelic demon back down in her hole. This
vision at his feet was a liar. Nan had been beside him, all along. They had
never disagreed about his methods. She had *not* gone inside to apologize
to the Jews. He had *not* driven her to do that. He had *not* driven her inside
that day. He had *not*. He had *not!*

Whish. Whish. Whish.

The Reverend Orvis Newton rubbed himself until the entire bar of
soap had shrunken completely away in his hands; then he stepped dripping from the shower, opened the medicine cabinet above the sink, and
removed a fresh bar.

Unwrapping it, he stepped back inside the shower.

This time, she had to listen to him.

Breathing rapidly, Jake Singer approached Kate Flint's front door. Behind him the lights on Moss Street shimmered on the liquid black Bayou St. John. A cricket pulsed brightly from somewhere in the dark below the raised porch. Jake wiped his palms on his shirt and lifted his hand. He froze with his finger half an inch away from the doorbell button. His hand shook. He lowered his arm and clasped his hands together, steadying them. *What if she won't talk to me? What if she sends me away? I don't think I can face that.*

Turning, he crossed the porch and began to descend the steps. *Wait.*

I have no one else. I have no other choice.

Lifting his chin, he turned again and strode back across the porch and punched the doorbell before he could change his mind again. The chimes rang somewhere deep inside the house. He waited. He thought he heard someone approach the other side of the door. He watched as the tiny glowing peephole dimmed to black. Someone was blocking the inside light, looking out at him. He shifted his position so she could see him clearly. As a pair of june bugs circled the light above his head, he waited. He tried to smile.

She did not open the door.

"Kate?" he called. "It's me, Jake."

Suddenly, the tiny light shone through the peephole again, but still, the door did not open.

"Come on, Kate. At least give me a chance to explain. . . . Kate? Kate? I . . . I need a friend right now. Please."

He waited five full minutes, but she did not answer, so Izzy Cantor slowly descended the steps to the ground.

ink, I think we gotta little something here," said Sergeant Baxter as he stood across the street from the hotel, speaking into his cell phone.

"Go ahead."

"Okay," said Baxter. "Me an' Doris O'Denny been tailing that Cantor guy all evenin'. He been busy. Drives round for a while, then he sits on a bench at City Park for an hour or so, then he goes to the Flint woman's house, but she don't come to the door. So he leaves and we been tailin' him in an' out of a bunch of bars ever since."

"Uh-huh."

"Now we over here at the Poisson Hotel. You know it?"

"What a dump."

"You got that right. Anyway, he gone inside there. So Doris goes in, 'cause he mighta made me at the temple earlier, when he went into that rabbi's office, ya know?"

"Uh-huh."

"And the desk guy, he tells Doris this guy been livin' there a week or two."

Washington said, "That's interesting. His mother stays in a small mansion over in the Garden District. Why would he pick a dive like the Poisson?"

"I was wonderin' that too."

"Okay. Thanks, Baxter."

"Wait a minute. I got more."

"What?"

"Well, me an' Doris is standin' round here, talkin' it over, when along come this other guy. Looks kinda familiar, an' walks right into the Poisson like he own the joint."

"Who is it?"

"I don't know his name. But I seen him round somewhere. I'm thinkin' it was at that Jewish church."

"Temple."

"Whatevah. So anyway, Doris goes back inside again . . . hang on, she comin' out now. . . ." Washington heard a muffled conversation, then Baxter was back on the line, chuckling. "Link?"

"Yeah."

"She heard him give his name to the desk guy. It's Jones. John Jones."

"Rings a bell."

"He related to the Smith family, I think."

"Oh yeah. *That* John Jones."

"Well, anyway, I'm pretty sure I saw him hangin' round that Jewish church."

"It's a temple, Baxter. They call it a temple."

"Whatevah."

The light on Jilly's bedside table cast a soft cone of yellow on the pages of the picture book in Kate Flint's hands.

"'. . . the rainbow stretched across the sky, just like he promised Noah and his family,'" she read. "'So every time you see a rainbow, just remember God put it there so you will know he's watching over you. The End.'"

Closing the picture book, Kate looked at Jilly, sound asleep, with her stuffed rabbit snuggled tight against her chin and the sheets pulled all the way up. Paul had probably dropped off to sleep as well, among the rock-and-roll posters and plastic airplane models and photographs of tanks and missiles in his room across the hall. Kate touched Jilly with the back of her fingers, drawing them gently across her daughter's warm, rosy skin. *What would I do without them? How could I go on?*

Even though there was absolutely no evidence that Jilly had ever been in any danger today, Kate could not bring herself to leave Jilly's side, and now that those panicked moments in the hallway of the temple had proven to be unwarranted, she did not feel so guilty for refusing to consider sending the children away.

I'll just stay for a while and watch her sleep.

Kate rose from the edge of Jilly's bed, crossed the room, and lowered herself onto an old wooden rocking chair. Her own mother had nursed her in that chair more than thirty years ago. Her grandmother had nursed her mother in the chair as well, and Kate had used the rocking chair for that purpose when Paul was born. Seven years later, when Jilly came into the world, John had moved the chair into this room, across the hall from Paul's, and again, the sturdy old rocker had become a part of the earliest memories of another member of her family. Kate pushed her feet gently against the floor, setting the rocker into motion. One of the runners creaked with each gentle to and fro. The regular rhythm of the chair seemed to mock the erratic beating of her heart. Would her pulse never return to normal? How she hated this feeling of weakness, of always being slightly out of breath. Most of all, she hated the constant reminder of her own mortality.

She kept her eyes on Jilly and directed her thoughts away from her wounded heart, determined instead to travel well-worn paths toward the special moments in their lives, but she stopped short of thinking about John. That way lay madness.

For three long years Kate had made it a rule to forget all that had gone before, and all that might still come. Often in moments like this, when her children lay snug in their beds and she was alone, she had pretended it was enough to live in the present. But now she could not seem to escape her memories of that charmed existence before John's death, when she had been blithely indifferent to the tenuous thread binding her happiness together. Jake Singer had roused a longing she could not deny. She would give anything for just one more instant of that former life, a moment as it was before the snapping of the thread, a single perfect point in time to express the depth of her loneliness. Jake Singer had given her heart a delicate caress like her daughter's eyelash fluttering against her cheek, and Kate had broken her own rule, glancing forward, soul sick of the present and daring to hope the future held something better. Compared to all the other experiences of her life, Kate's few hours with Jake should have been as insignificant as a raindrop in the Mississippi, but those moments had awakened her sleeping heart to the potential of union with another man. Now, like it or not, Kate realized as she rocked in her grandmother's chair, life was back—sloppy and noisy like a newborn baby, making no promises, bringing birthing pains, but filled with possibilities nonetheless.

How typical that it all came from a lie.

Jake Singer might be a liar, might even be much worse than a liar, but she had him to thank for returning her to the land of the living, or, more precisely, she had him to blame. Earlier tonight when Kate had watched him through the peephole with her hand on the doorknob, she had struggled with her warring desires. He had been so beautiful, standing in the soft light, his cheeks beginning to show a day's worth of whiskers, his thick hair tousled, his soft, kind eyes staring at the door, almost as if he knew she was there. He had called to her: *"I need a friend right now."* In that moment she had nearly forgotten his lies and her panic at the temple. She had nearly opened the door. Then the memory of his words the last time he stood there on her porch arose in warning:

"What would you do if you found out I'm not normal?"

He was *not* Jake Singer, the man she had met and been attracted to beyond all proportion or common sense; he was Jacob Israel Cantor, son of Solomon, the murderer. He had tempted her to step beyond the boundaries of her faith and lied about his ancestry. What other secrets did he hide? What other dangers?

So, in spite of her aching loneliness, Kate had removed her hand from the doorknob and softly walked away.

Now she lifted both of her palms to her face and held them there for a moment, pressed against her eyes. She dropped them to her lap and laid her head back against the chair. She was tired. So tired. This unpredictable galloping heart sapped her energy just as these circumstances burdened her spirit. She longed to drift away for a while, even if it was just to sleep. . . .

Behind closed eyes, Kate saw the tattooed and pierced countenance of the maniac with the machine gun on Decatur Street. Laughing and dangling his tongue obscenely, he removed his features like a mask to reveal the shiny tar-covered face of Rebecca Betterton, writhing in pain.

Kate awoke with a shudder and looked around, surprised that she had fallen so easily to sleep, surprised that her nightmares lay so close to the surface. On the little round table beside her lay one of Jilly's picture books, the one about Noah and the Flood. Desperate for something benign to occupy her thoughts, she picked it up and scanned the book's back cover. On it was a list of the other titles in the series, based on famous stories from the book of Genesis: Adam and Eve, Cain and Abel, the Tower of Babel, Sodom and Gomorrah. . . .

Then, for some reason, she remembered the words of the policeman at the temple that afternoon: *"It's like it was raining tar."*

And from out of nowhere, another image came to her, a mystery wavering in the distance of her imagination. Kate didn't settle on the thing directly, but saw it on the periphery as an incidental detail, something that should not be ignored. Maybe it came from that weary halfway place between this world and her dreams, maybe it was something she had felt for days but not yet brought to consciousness, or maybe it was a gift from above. Whatever its source, the image in her mind—still too hazy to identify—was enough to make Kate rise and cross the hall to her own bedroom, where she lifted her Bible from the bedside table. Breathless from her heart's arrhythmia, she sucked in air through her open mouth and turned the pages quickly until she found chapter nineteen, verse twenty-four of the book of Genesis: "Then the Lord rained down burning sulfur on Sodom and Gomorrah—from the Lord out of the heavens."

Taking quick, shallow breaths, Kate read those ancient words again and again until finally they blurred and ran together and she knew with a terrible certainty that she was looking into the mind of a murderer.

THIRTY-NINE

Ruth Gold lay awake with her head propped upon interlaced fingers, searching the ceiling of her bedroom for peace. Outside, the wind blew strongly enough to remind her that it was still hurricane season, but hurricanes were nothing to Ruth compared to the turmoil in her mind. She could not seem to forget the way those people—those pompous, fanatical, insensitive, sign-waving Christians— had joined her search for Jilly. Ruth did not know what to make of their eagerness to help. At first, she had assumed they knew Jilly was the child of a fellow Christian. It was a straw to be clutched. But then the tall woman in the parking lot had told her she believed Jilly was Ruth's daughter. She had waited alone outside the temple for hours, worrying the whole time about a rabbi's child. Probably, they all believed the lost girl was a Jew. Of course, the tall woman's parting remark had been insufferable— as if God would "lead" someone to stand outside a temple and disrupt

Yom Kippur! But no matter how she tried, Ruth could not summon enough anger to overcome the fact that she *had* waited all that time, alone, simply because she was worried about a stranger. A Jewish stranger.

It was very confusing.

Those people had always seemed so hostile. Indeed, Ruth had taken perverse comfort up to now in the thought that they were enemies. Given their outrageous behavior, it was easier to think of them that way. But the police said that several of them had risked their lives searching the woods for Jilly in spite of the escaped tiger, and as Ruth had described Jilly's dress and hair that afternoon she thought she saw tears form in the eyes of the tall blonde woman.

Why does that threaten me so?

Ruth rolled onto her side, punching her pillow. The digital clock on her bedside table read 3:00 A.M.—the most solitary hour of all. Ruth knew she should get some rest for what could only be another tiring day tomorrow, but she simply could not stop thinking about the way those people had surprised her. Finally, lying awake at that loneliest of late night moments, the mask of her bravado slipped just enough to allow a rare glimpse into the mirror of her soul. There, Rabbi Ruth Gold saw a bitter truth: In defending herself from the blatant prejudice and insensitivity of her Christian neighbors, she had allowed herself to make the same mistakes.

Suddenly she sat up. Sleep was impossible and lying there just made things worse. What she needed was a diversion, or at least a drink.

Rising, she wrapped herself in her robe and shuffled toward the door with scotch on the rocks in mind, but just as she reached for the doorknob, the bedside telephone rang. Ruth turned to stare at it. A call at this hour could only be bad news. Should she answer it? Without moving, Ruth let it ring again and again. It had just begun to ring for the fourth time when she picked it up. "Hello. Who is this, please?"

The caller spoke in a rush. "It's Kate. I think I've got it figured out! Or some of it. I mean, not all of it, but maybe enough so they can catch him. It's a start, anyway. More than we had before. I—"

"Katy!"

"Yes?"

"Will you please slow down? I mean, it's three in the morning, and I—"

"Oh. I'm *sorry*. I did it again, didn't I? I'll call back tomorrow."

"No! Katy? Are you there?"

"Yes?"

"You can't just call and tell me you've got it all figured out and then hang up."

"Well, I don't have it *all* figured out. I said that, didn't I?"

"Yes, you did. I'm sorry. You were very clear about that."

"Good. Because I wouldn't want to take credit for something I didn't do."

"Katy?"

"Yes."

"Will you please shut up and tell me what you called to say?"

"How can I tell you and shut up, too?"

"Katy . . ."

The voice on the other end laughed. "I'm sorry. It's just . . . well, I'm so proud of myself."

"This must be good."

"Oh, it is, I think." She paused. "Let me ask you a question. Did it ever occur to you that there might be a pattern to all these murders?"

"But they're all different. That's why the police had so much trouble believing they were connected."

"What if I told you there *is* a pattern, and you of all people should have seen it a long time ago?"

"Go on."

"Okay. Think about the first murder. How was it done?"

"Poisoning."

"Right. But how was the poison delivered?"

"Come on, Katy."

"Humor me. How did your friend get the poison into his system?"

Ruth sighed. "Steve ate an apple, as you very well know."

"Okay, and we both think there's a good chance I was almost poisoned with *apple*sauce, right?"

"So what?"

"Well, think about the next one. What happened?"

"The murderer tricked Benny into shooting Morton."

"Yes! Get it?"

"No."

"Come *on*. Think about it, Ruth: Benny and Morton were *brothers*."

"Okay . . ."

"And your friend Steve ate poisoned fruit."

"Okay . . ."

"Think like a rabbi! It's so obvious when you see it."

"It's the middle of the night, and I don't feel like playing guessing games. Why don't you just spell it out for me?"

"One more clue—"

"Katy!"

"Come on, Ruth. This is fun."

"Maybe for you."

"Look, the third murder—or almost murder—when they tried to shoot you. Where did it happen?"

"You know where it happened, Katy. It happened in the Quarter."

"Yes, but where, exactly? Where were you?"

"At that music store."

"*Tower* Records, right? With that music blaring so loudly you couldn't hear yourself think."

"Yeah. So?"

"Oh, Ruth. Do I have to hand it to you on a silver platter? Think Torah, Ruth!"

Suddenly, it came to her. Ruth gripped the telephone tighter. "It's Genesis! He's following the stories of Genesis!"

"Exactly! Adam and Eve, and Cain and Abel, and—"

"And after the Tower of Babel, there's the Flood, with all those animals and Helen drowning in the lagoon!"

"And next comes Sodom and Gomorrah, and poor old Mrs. Betterton dying in fire and brimstone from the sky!"

Ruth lifted her hand to her mouth as her mind spun through the implications. Finally she whispered, "Katy, you're a genius."

Do Jews have any kind of tradition that might explain this pattern?" asked Lieutenant Lincoln Washington.

Ruth Gold's eyes flashed. "If you're asking whether serial murder is a Jewish tradition, the answer is no."

"Rabbi, I'm just exploring all the options here, all right?"

"That is not an option."

"Why not? Are you saying Jews don't murder people?"

"Of course not. Every now and then we get a David Berkowitz among us. We also steal and lie and covet our neighbor's ox occasionally. I'm just saying our religion doesn't have a tradition of mass murder. We leave that to you Christians."

Washington's face turned to stone as Kate sipped her coffee uncomfortably. In order to avoid waking the children, Kate had suggested that the three of them sit outside on the elevated front porch of her home. A cool front had blown in overnight, and a soft shroud of fog lay upon the Crescent City, deadening sounds and dimming the gathering glow of the rising sun. Here and there across the bayou lights came on in the bedrooms of the early risers, their fuzzy yellow windows floating unsupported in the mist, the tranquil surroundings a surreal contrast to the mood of the three people on the porch.

Ruth said, "I'm not sure why I said that. I apologize."

"We're all under a lot of pressure," said Kate.

"No. It's not that. Something's happening to me," whispered Ruth. "Things are . . . changing."

"What kind of things?"

Ruth glanced at Kate. "It's not important. We can talk about it later."

"Okay," said Washington. "Let me ask this a different way. Is there a . . . ah . . . a precedent in your history for a reenactment of portions of the Bible?"

"Well, we have *Sukkot*. In English it's called the Festival of Booths. It's an annual holy day when we live in temporary shelters or 'booths' to remind ourselves of the life our ancestors led in the wilderness. And there's *Purim*, when we dress in costumes and make fun of Haman, from the story of Esther. Haman was the first person to try to wipe out our people."

"How about a more personal tradition? Something you do alone?"

Ruth sipped her coffee, savoring the chicory flavor and gazing out into the fog. "No . . . there's nothing like what you mean."

Kate said, "What are you thinking, Lieutenant?"

"I'm not thinking anything specific, but you're right; there's a religious pattern here. These deaths and the Bible stories are too similar to deny the connection, and when you add the fact that almost everyone concerned with this case is Jewish, it seems to me that we need to look harder at the congregation of the temple."

Ruth said, "It's Solomon Cantor. Or his son."

"Yeah," said Washington. "Probably."

Nobody spoke. They listened to the sounds of the wakening city: a train whistle in the distance, the dull impact of a pedestrian's hard-soled boots on the footbridge across the bayou, the tolling of St. Francis Cabrini's bell. A car passed by, motoring slowly through the fog. Then, in the distance, the unmistakable sound of a big cat's roar. The three people on the porch said nothing, as if none of them wanted to admit what they had heard. But a moment later another ominous roar rumbled through the mist, undeniable.

"Could that be what it sounds like?" asked Kate. Washington was already reaching inside his jacket for his cell phone.

Ruth said, "The zoo's all the way across town. How could it come this far without being seen?"

"I have no idea," said Washington, punching buttons on his phone.

"Maybe it's the one that attacked Helen."

"It's possible," said the lieutenant. "They haven't caught all of the big cats yet. Wait a minute . . . hello? Yeah, it's Washington; who's this? Hey, Julie, whereyat? Good. Listen, I'm over here on Moss Street near City Park, and I just heard a lion. You heard me, a *lion*. . . . Roaring, what do you think? Okay . . . so if they caught the lions already I guess it's a tiger or something. . . . How would I know? No. No. Listen to me. Somehow, the thing has made it all the way over here. . . . That's right. . . . Okay, you do that right away. See ya."

As Washington slipped his cell phone back into his pocket, Ruth asked, "How could it live this long in the city without being caught?"

Washington said, "I asked a guy at the zoo that question. He reminded me that this is what they do in the wild. Blend in. They stay alive because their prey doesn't see them till it's too late. They're very good at hiding. Tigers especially, and their eyes are six times as good as ours, which means they usually spot you a long time before you spot them. Also, although they don't like to do it, when they're very frightened like this one probably is, they've been known to climb trees in the daytime to hide." He paused. "Ever notice how many huge old live oaks we got in this city? I've been making it a practice to stay out from under them lately."

Staring into the impenetrable fog, Ruth shivered. "It's got to be killed."

Washington nodded. "The guy at the zoo told me they'll have to do that to the one that attacked Dr. Blumenthal. Once they view humans as food, those animals can't be handled safely."

Ruth blanched.

Washington touched her arm. "I'm sorry. That was a lousy thing to say."

Ruth nodded. After a pause, she said, "How will they know which one's responsible?"

"I have no idea."

"But they'll kill it?"

"Yes."

"Good," said Ruth, nodding. "Good."

Washington said, "Rabbi?"

"What?"

"I get all the connections between the murders and the Bible stories, but how does the break-in here at Mrs. Flint's house fit the pattern?"

"I've been thinking about that. One possibility is, when he failed to kill her with the poisoned applesauce, he tried to burn her house down because of the angels God placed outside the Garden of Eden after Adam and Eve were ejected. The Torah says the angels had something that's often translated as 'flaming swords.'"

"All right," said Washington. "And that story, Sodom and Gomorrah? I'm trying to remember what comes next in the Bible?"

"Well, let's see. . . . Lot's wife looks back at Sodom as it's burning and turns into a pillar of salt."

"Yeah, I remember that. But it's part of the Sodom and Gomorrah thing, right? We need a new one."

"Hmm. . . . Lot's daughters get him drunk and sleep with him to become pregnant."

Washington stared at her. "I don't remember that."

"It's not one of the better-known stories."

He shook his head. "Not what I'm after. What's next?"

"Abraham tells a king that his wife is really his sister in order to avoid being murdered."

"Why would that keep him from being murdered?"

"He was afraid the king would kill him in order to marry Sarah."

"Are you saying Abraham put his wife on the street to save his own skin?"

"That's one way of looking at it, I guess."

The lieutenant shook his head. "I'm amazed that's in the Bible, but it's still not what I need. What comes next?"

"Sarah gives birth to Isaac. Then she becomes jealous of Hagar's son and convinces Abraham to send them away into the desert to die. But they survive, so that can't be it. After that comes the *Akeda*."

"The what?"

"Oh, sorry. The binding of Isaac. You probably know the story. It's when God tells Abraham to sacrifice his son."

He nodded. "So maybe with this *Akeda* thing we're looking at something to do with children."

Ruth said, "You think Cantor will model a murder on the idea of a father killing his own child?"

"Maybe," said Washington. "Except it doesn't have to be a father. The killer hasn't followed these stories precisely. He's just using them as a general guideline."

Hugging her elbows, Kate turned to look at Paul's dark bedroom window. "It could be a mother killing her son?"

Washington shrugged. "Or a mother killing her daughter. Who knows?"

"Well, he'll never make *me* do that."

The lieutenant looked at Kate. "You should keep in mind that this person found a way to make Benny Rothstein kill his brother." He paused. "Mrs. Flint, may I ask you a personal question?"

"Of course," said Kate.

"I don't understand why you didn't send your kids somewhere safe a long time ago, back when this guy tried to burn down your house. Don't you have any family or friends out of town?"

"No. Nobody."

Ruth looked at her oddly. "I thought you said there were grand-parents in Atlanta or somewhere."

Looking out into the fog, Kate said, "They haven't exactly been help-ful in the past."

"But they *are* the children's grandparents, right? I mean, if you told them the kids are in danger—"

Kate spun on her. "We don't know that!" she snapped.

Ruth stared in shock. Wildly, Kate turned to the lieutenant. "Tell her we don't know that for sure!"

"Mrs. Flint," said Washington quietly, "I think Rabbi Gold has an excellent point."

An electric convulsion yanked Kate to her feet too quickly, tipping her chair backward to the floor.

"I can't send them away! *They need me!*"

Neither Ruth nor the lieutenant would meet her eyes, so she looked down at the chair, then back at Washington and Ruth, and then back at the chair. She bent to set it upright, but what was the point of that? She straightened herself without touching it. Finally, leaving the fallen chair behind, she ran inside her home, slamming the screen door shut.

As Kate fled, the distant tiger roared once more.

FORTY

T humbtacked to the wall by Orvis Newton's narrow bed was a black-and-white photograph, Nan Smith's final portrait, taken at Sears Roebuck and used in the ministry's fund-raising brochure. Her eyes were large and soft behind her glasses as she stared forthrightly at the lens. She wore a hat with a half veil covering her forehead and a simple dress with a high collar. She was not smiling.

Beneath the photograph on the bedside table lay an open Bible, filled with notes in the margins written in a small but flowing cursive script. Orvis Newton had drawn thousands of solid red lines across each page, boldly obscuring the words. Nan Smith's Bible was now Orvis Newton's second most treasured possession. Next to it was the one thing he valued more: a small bundle of letters, all addressed to Orvis, written in the same hand as the margin notes in the Bible and tied together with a thin blue ribbon. They spoke of a future, with children and a home together. They

spoke of things taken away from Orvis on the day his dear, sweet Nan
was murdered by a Jew.

The Reverend Orvis Newton sat in his underwear on the sleep-tossed
sheets of his narrow bed. Beneath Nan Smith's impassive countenance, he
lit a match and reached for the single candle on a small plastic plate beside
the Bible and the letters. It was a short votive candle, the kind usually seen
at altars in Catholic churches. Being a Protestant, Orvis did not understand
why he kept the candle there, but it felt right somehow. He lit it each
night before he went to sleep and replaced it with another every morning.
He had done this every day without fail for twenty-five years.

Orvis gripped the wooden match so tightly his knuckles turned as
white as bones. The match shook as he held it to the wick. "I won't let them
get away with it, Nanny," whispered Orvis Newton, alone in his room. "I'll
stop them all. I promise." The scent of sulphur lingered in the air.

The ends *did* justify the means. Those who denied that fact were poor
Bible scholars indeed. How often had Orvis taught his little flock from the
story of Exodus, where God struck an entire nation—guilty and innocent
alike—with horrible plagues in order to free the Israelites? Orvis smiled. If
it was good enough for almighty God, it was certainly good enough for
Orvis Newton.

Now, as the shaking match fired the candle Orvis remembered that
other morning, not long ago, when the Lord had spoken so clearly, as if
they were side by side right here in this room. It was the day after that
Jewess told him her sordid lies about Nanny and Solomon Cantor. He'd
been wrestling with the Holy Ghost, groaning in agony at the damage her
lies could cause, but what could he do? He was a humble missionary to the
destitute in the poorest section of one of the poorest cities in the nation.
He had no funds and very few helpers. He had cried out to the Lord in
desperation, pounding his head with both fists. That was when he'd heard
the Voice:

*I am your help, Orvis, as you are my servant. Deal with them from my Word . . .
from my Word shall you measure out my judgment.*

And a verse had flashed into his mind: Daniel, chapter nine, verse
eleven: *"Yea, all Israel have transgressed thy law, even by departing, that they might
not obey thy voice."*

Transgressing. Departing. Yes. *It is so true.*

"Therefore the curse is poured upon us, and the oath that is written in the law of Moses the servant of God, because we have sinned against him."

The curse, written in the Law of Moses . . . he had understood immediately. The Jews must endure the same things their ancestors had endured. They had failed to understand the truth the first time, and dared to slur his dear, sweet Nanny's reputation into the bargain. Only one thing could break through their stubborn refusal: they would live the curse of their law once more.

So he had embarked upon this course the Lord had set. Beginning "in the beginning," of course, with the poisoned fruit for the two girls, his "Eves." He had failed twice so far, with the fruit and the Tower of Babel, but last night Orvis had made up for one of those errors, and tonight he would finish with Cantor's boy and one of the women, the Jew. She would be his witness at the sacrifice of Isaac, and then she would join the boy on the altar. The old man would also be dealt with, of course. Everything would be brought together in a perfect circle, exactly as it had been all those years ago, when his darling Nanny had been martyred for the Way.

'm not going!" Paul stomped his foot. "Not unless you tell me why!"

Kate knelt and pulled her son close, embracing him in the midst of a swirling mass of travelers at the New Orleans International Airport. Jilly stood at her elbow, clutching her fire truck to her chest as if to protect it. She pressed herself against her mother. Kate reached for her too, hugging both of her children at once, the three of them forming a motionless island in a rushing stream of passengers pouring toward the entrance to the jet way.

"You have to go," she said. "It's not safe here."

"Then you come, too!"

"I wish I could, honey."

"Why can't you?"

Kate filled with the urge to unburden herself, to tell somebody—anybody—about the unfair burdens life had thrust upon her. She knew he was far too young, yet who else was there? And so she spoke to her twelve-year-old son of the debt his father had assumed to start the shop, the monthly checks that must be written to the bank, the shop landlord, the home mortgage, the auction houses, the utilities. Looking him right in the eyes, she shared the harsh facts that his father had left them with no savings, and worse, had borrowed against the little equity they possessed in their home. October through December were the best sales months in the French Quarter—sometimes better than the entire rest of the year—and if she left now, it could cut their annual income in half. They might as well leave forever, because there would be less than nothing left when they returned.

But as she spoke, Paul seemed to drift away to that inside place all children have, where life is a fantasy and grown-ups cannot follow. Bitterly, Kate thought, *He can't even listen to me for two minutes!*

So she stopped before explaining the worst of it, sparing Paul from the knowledge that his mother wasn't welcome at his grandparents' home. John's parents loved their grandchildren to a fault, showering Paul and Jilly with toys and attention whenever they could, and of course the kids loved their only surviving grandparents. But when it came to Kate, John's folks were formally polite at best. She wished to speak of these things as well, but even if Paul had been listening, how did one explain such anger over religion to a child?

Kate touched her son's hair, gently pushing it up and away from his forehead. He jerked his head away, embarrassed. She said, "Listen. I'll call you every night, and you can call me anytime you want. This isn't for a long time. It's just until some things get straightened out around here."

"Mommy?" said Jilly.

"Yes, baby."

"Why are you crying?"

Kate wiped her eyes with the back of her hand and forced herself to smile. "I'm not crying, baby. I guess I got something in my eye."

"Oh," said Jilly. She returned her attention to her fire truck as the flight attendant came close to lead the children aboard.

"You have to go with this nice lady now, kids," said Kate, rising to her feet. "Remember to call me."

"We will," said Jilly.

"Okay. Y'all hold hands now."

Jilly took Paul's hand, but Kate's son remained standing with his back to the flight attendant, facing her defiantly.

"Go on, Paul."

"No."

"Please, honey. Do this for me."

"No! I have to stay here to help you! I'm the man of the house!"

Kate's emotions threatened to overcome her newfound resolve. She longed to wrap him in her arms again, to hold him, to lean on him, to keep him there in spite of the danger. Then she remembered the raw contempt she had seen in Ruth Gold's eyes this morning. She looked straight at the flight attendant and said, "Take good care of them," and turned and walked away.

R olling onto her side, Gabby Cantor squinted at the clock on her bedside table. It remained a blur. She reached for the cursed thing and held it close to her face. Almost noon.

Moaning, she dropped the clock to the floor. How long had it been since she'd lain in bed until noon? Thirty years? Forty? Bright New Orleans sunlight tilted through a narrow gap between the heavy plantation shutters across her windows. Specks of dust danced in the beam, like fairies come to pay their respects. She frowned. She did not believe in fairies, although there were more than a few people in this necromantic city who did, and Gabby Cantor would have appreciated even the company of mythical beings that morning . . . afternoon, rather.

Her head pounded from too much Jim Beam last night. Way too much. But who could blame her? Her son wouldn't acknowledge her existence, and her husband, lost to her for over two decades, was now lost to her again, out there somewhere, hiding from the authorities like a common criminal.

Criminal.

That's what Sol had become, whether he had chosen to or not, and his other choice . . . well, in many ways, *that* was even worse.

Gabby wasn't sure how she felt about him now. For years, she had assumed that the love they once shared was long dead. During those first few months after Sol went away, imprisoned as she was in her own solitary confinement of aching loneliness, it became clear that love was the source of her suffering, so, always the practical person, Gabby had shut off that emotion—choking it to death like the murderer they said he was. It was her way of becoming free again.

During the rest of Sol's time in prison, the real estate business had become her reason for living. She had poured herself into it, surprised at first to discover her natural ability, gaining confidence, and finally surpassing everyone until she virtually owned the New Orleans high-end residential market.

None of which had left much time for Izzy.

Of course, now she knew that was only an excuse. She had begun to understand—too late—that it wasn't a case of failing her son because of her business. It was really the other way around. She had chosen to focus on the business specifically because she had wanted to avoid her son. With his betrayal, Sol had taught her that love was an enemy, and retreat her only defense, so she had run from her love for Izzy as well, using the business as a shield against him, something to guard her back while she stumbled from the battlefield to tend to her wounds. Yes, perhaps she had gone too far in concealing the truth from her son. She had done more than conceal it. She had planted a new truth, a more acceptable truth, and plowed it into Izzy's fertile mind. But although she had only meant to protect him, it seemed that Sol was right: she had forced too much upon her boy. Real damage had been done. No wonder Izzy had changed his name and moved away and refused to see her at all . . . especially now that Sol was out.

For all these years, she had convinced herself it was Sol's fault, the direct result of his horrible choice twenty-five years ago. Gabby had convinced herself she hated him. But then, after dinner just the other night, she had seen him standing at the back door, silhouetted by the moonlight as he stared outside. He had not known she was watching. He had lifted his head toward the stars. She had seen something then, the Solomon of her youth, in the tilt of his chin and the slope of his shoulders and the easy way he stood with one hip cocked and his arms loose at his sides, and she had known he really *was* the boy she had married, and she, for her part, became a girl again . . . until she caught herself and retreated once more to regroup and reconnoiter this disturbing turn of events.

He left that night with the usual perfunctory kiss on her cheek. She had come just that close to reaching for him as he turned, to latching onto him and leading him back inside. But the fear would not die so easily. It had been bred into her from birth, a legacy of two thousand years. How did one escape such a history?

She had thought, *Tomorrow will be soon enough. Tomorrow we'll start again.*

Of course, tomorrow had brought policemen to her door, and Solomon gone once more, but that brief moment of surrender had opened Gabby's heart to possibilities she'd thought were long dead. Yesterday at temple, when she saw Izzy walking up the aisle holding someone's little girl, it had occurred to her that she could simply reach out and touch him as he passed. She had found her arm extended, her fingers straining toward her dear lost son before she realized what she was doing, but Izzy had stepped sideways at the last minute and continued past without so much as a downward glance.

So. She had been drawn out of her carefully constructed defenses by a clever feint of the enemy. Beaten while her guard was down. Her fingers clutched the sheets, drawing them into tight folds radiating out from each hand, like puppet strings leading nowhere. The spoils of her so-called success littered the room around her—the Second Empire bedroom furnishings supported a hundred thousand dollars worth of antique bric-a-brac. Her other rooms also overflowed with articles of great value. Yet she had been defeated. She and Sol had struck a bargain a generation ago. He had honored his part, but she . . . she had failed them all.

Gabby threw back the sheets and sat up. Her stomach roiled immediately. She flung herself to the side of the bed, hanging her head over the edge. It was touch and go for a moment, but the nausea passed. Moaning, she sat up again, this time more conscious of the throbbing in her head than the turmoil in her belly. Through watery eyes, she noticed a bottle of aspirin on the bedside table. Next to it was a glass of water. Had she really had the presence of mind to place them there last night? She used to do that, years ago. Amazing how old habits returned so easily. Groaning, she reached for the aspirin. Her hands trembled as she struggled against the childproof lid on the aspirin container. Finally, she got it open and shook four tablets into her palm.

She lifted her hand toward her mouth, drawing the tablets near. At the last moment, she stopped. She sat with her hand frozen in midair for several minutes, thinking. The aspirin would make her feel better in a little while, but then she would remember what she had done to Solomon and Izzy, and she would think about that horrible man who had come to her door, and the lies that she had told him, and poor Morton and poor Benny and the rabbi's boyfriend and Helen Blumenthal, and she would drink again. And tomorrow she would wake up just like this again, terrified at the evil she had set in motion, but too ashamed of herself and too ashamed of Solomon's decision to confess her sins and see it stopped. Gabby thought and thought and then she rose, the aspirin tablets falling to the silken sheets unnoticed. She crossed to her bathroom. A moment later, she returned with a different bottle full of tablets. She climbed into the bed, moaning at the pounding in her head, and shook some pills into her palm, a dozen pills or more. She put them in her mouth and reached for the glass of water on her bedside table. She swallowed them all, wincing as they scraped their way down her throat. She sat still for a moment, fearing the nausea would make a mockery of her efforts. Then, composed, she shook another dozen sleeping pills into her palm.

The level rays of the setting sun shot just above the green copper dome of St. Francis Cabrini across the bayou, glittering golden bright in the windows and casting long live oak shadows onto the slate roof of Katy Flint's house. Ruth arrived at the curb in front just as Katy closed the door of her Jeep and headed toward the wrought-iron sidewalk gate.

From her Citroën, the rabbi heard the gate's hinges creak. "Hey!" she called.

Startled, Katy spun toward her.

"Sorry," said Ruth from the open window of her car.

Katy passed a hand over her forehead pushing back her thick blonde hair. "That's okay," she said, smiling weakly. "What's up?"

"Did you get the kids off all right?"

"Uh-huh."

Ruth frowned, looking closely at Katy. "You don't look so good."

"It's hard."

Ruth said, "Listen, how's about staying at my house tonight?"

"Oh, Ruth. I don't know . . ."

"Come on. I'm turning over a new leaf here, trying to be nice." She smiled sheepishly. "Besides, it's for your own good." As Katy looked at the ground, Ruth rushed her words, eager to convince. "Actually, it's for my good too, Katy. I'm scared to be at home alone. Okay? Please?"

Katy glanced up. "Really? You're scared?"

"Petrified."

A squirrel chattered overhead. Ruth looked toward the sound. The squirrel peered down at her through a curtain of gray-green moss, its jet-black eyes sparkling in the afternoon sun. *She's going to say no. Oh, please, Hashem, I need this chance to make amends. Please, don't let her say no.*

Katy leaned against the brick post beside the gate. "I don't know if we should be more afraid of Solomon Cantor or of Jake."

"Or both of them."

Katy nodded. "He fooled me so . . . completely."

"I'm sorry, Katy." Ruth paused. "But we should stick together."

"Yes. You're right."

Watching her closely, Ruth said, "You gonna be okay?"

Katy shrugged. "Sending the children away and Jake lying that way . . . you know."

"Yeah. Listen, you probably don't wanna leave your home on top of everything else, so why don't we both stay here? We can watch each other's back."

"No. Let's go to your place. It makes more sense. I mean, I'm on the corner here, so they could come at us from two directions. Plus, this house is too large. He could be inside for an hour and we wouldn't even know it."

Baxter walked in without knocking. "Hey, Link. Got those shots you asked for."

"Lemme see them," said Washington, holding out his hand.

Baxter passed a manila envelope to him, then took a seat in the hard wooden chair beside Washington's desk. He said, "I still ain't been able to figure out who that fella is, but I know I seen him around."

The lieutenant grunted as he opened the clasp on the envelope and shook out six color enlargements showing a man in several positions: approaching the Poisson Hotel, reaching for the door handle, and entering. The best shot showed his face full front as he glanced back toward the street before going into the building.

"So, you make that dude or what?" asked Baxter.

Washington stared at the photograph of Orvis Newton for a moment before answering. "Oh yeah."

"Well? Whaddaya think?"

Washington was already rising from his chair. "I think we've got some work to do."

Is the room okay?" asked Ruth, standing in the door.

Kate placed her two bags on the floor beside the bed and looked around, a little out of breath. Suspended from the twelve-foot ceiling, a fan turned at a lazy pace. An olive green-and-black-plaid quilt on the bed matched half a dozen pillows of various patterns and sizes, as did the complementary colors of the upholstery on a white wicker chair and bedside table set. Wooden plantation shutters at the windows, a potted palm, and a gauzy mosquito net hanging over the bed completed the room's tropical feel. Kate's heart continued to pound erratically. She tried to ignore it, but this was the first time it had gone on so long, and Kate had begun to worry that it would never stop.

Or rather, that it would.

"It's lovely," she said. "Your whole house is lovely."

"Thanks."

They stood facing each other, Kate beside the bed and Ruth in the doorway with her back to the hall. Their eyes met and held, just for a moment, then both of them looked away and spoke at the same time.

"I was gonna—"

"Do you think—"

"You go first."

"No, you."

"Okay," said Ruth. "I, uh, I'm sorry for that thing I said this morning."

"What thing?"

"You remember. About Christians and mass murder."

"Oh."

"That was so *mean*. I don't even know why I said it. It's just, lately, I keep feeling . . . angry, you know?"

Kate nodded, "Well, since you bring it up, I have noticed a little bit of that."

They stood in silence for a moment, then Ruth said, "Let's get something to drink. I've got some sweet tea made."

"That sounds good, but I can't take the caffeine right now. Do you have some juice or something?"

"Sure."

Moments later, Kate sat on a barstool at a short counter in the kitchen. The sound of clinking glasses and a whirring refrigerator felt comforting. Ruth began to speak as she busied herself with the drinks. "Listen, since we're getting to know each other again, there are some things I need to get off my chest."

"All right."

"There's no easy way to put this, so here it is." She drew a deep breath. "I was raised not to trust you."

"Whoa!" said Kate. "What did *I* do?"

"Not you, specifically, but Christians in general."

"But why?"

"Lots of reasons, going back for centuries. The Crusades, for example. Did you know the Crusaders slaughtered every Jew they could find on their way to the Holy Land?"

"No."

"It's true, and the church blessed them for it." She set a tall glass of orange juice in front of Kate. "Then there's the Inquisition. The church in Spain forced thousands of us to convert to your faith. Our other choice was torture. Most Americans think of 1492 as the year Columbus discovered America. We think of it as the year the Catholics drove us out of Spain and stole our homes."

"Well, I'm a Protestant. We're very different from Catholics."

"Different in theology maybe but not in how your people have treated mine. Let me see if I can remember something I memorized back in rabbinic school." Ruth closed her eyes and stood still. When she spoke again, it was in a monotone that underscored the horror of her words. "'The Jews, being foreigners, should possess nothing, and what they do possess should be ours. . . . Their synagogues should be set on fire. . . . Their homes should likewise be broken down and destroyed. . . . They should be deprived of their prayer books and Talmuds. . . . Their rabbis must be forbidden under threat of death to teach any more. . . . Passport and traveling privileges should be absolutely forbidden to the Jews. . . . Let the young Jew and Jewess be given the ax, the hoe, the spade, the distaff and spindle, and let them earn their bread by the sweat of their noses.'"

Ruth opened her eyes and turned toward Kate. "That's from something called *Against the Jews and Their Lies*, written in 1542 by Martin Luther."

"Martin *Luther*? Are you sure?"

"Absolutely." Ruth sipped her tea. "Of course, that was a long time ago. But many pastors of the German Lutheran church supported the Nazis during their rise to power. Did you know that?"

Unable to speak, Kate shook her head.

"Yep," said Ruth. "And here's another quote for you. The pope at that time—I think his name was Pius the Twelfth—received a letter from a Vatican representative in Germany about the rumors of the death camps. The pope wrote back, saying that he would not call for an investigation of the rumors. One of the things he wrote was 'Do not forget that millions of Catholics serve in the German armies. Shall I bring them into conflicts of conscience?'"

Kate sat completely still, eyes focused on a bead of condensation trickling down the side of her glass as her ears roared with the sporadic coursing of her blood. She remembered Jake's words: *"Some of us are so suspicious of your faith, we do some pretty mean things."* Could this be why John's parents disowned him? She said, "I don't know if I told you this or not, but when my husband converted, his family pretty much kicked him out." Ruth did not respond, so Kate continued. "Things just got worse when he married me. They wouldn't talk to him at all. He used to call them from time to time, whenever anything important happened, but they were so distant—"

"I'm sure they had their reasons," snapped Ruth.

Surprised, Kate looked at her. "Have I said something wrong?"

Ruth opened her mouth to speak, then closed it and turned away for a moment. "No. It just hits a little close to home. In my family, we . . ." Her voice drifted off. She shook her head. "Never mind."

Watching Ruth, Kate thought of Jake's earnest brown eyes, filled with sympathy the last time she'd spoken of John's parents. What were his words? *"It seems like someone should apologize."* She could always say she was not responsible for what prior generations of Christians did, any more than she was responsible for American slavery, but that argument rang hollow. Kate believed that Christians were connected in one large body of believers spanning continents and centuries. She was a part of every other Christian going all the way back to the apostles. That idea had often been a comfort to her. It would be hypocrisy to deny it now that it was a burden, so, with some measure of sincerity she said, "I'm sorry. For the pope, and Luther and all the rest of it. I'm so sorry."

"I didn't tell you those things to make you feel guilty, Katy. I mean, it's not like I think any of it's *your* fault. But if we're gonna be getting to know each other again after all these years, it's important for you to understand some things about me."

"I think I do. You grew up in a culture that sees my faith as the enemy."

"No, that's overstating it. Most of us don't think of Christians as enemies, and that's not what I meant, anyway. I'm talking about you and me." Opening the freezer, she reached inside, withdrew a single ice cube and dropped it into her glass. "I mean, imagine how we hate to tell our children these things. It's much more delicate than the birds and the bees . . . having to deliberately begin the end of your child's innocence in order to protect her."

"It's like when John and I had to tell the children he was dying."

"Oh, Katy," said Ruth. "That must have been awful."

Kate looked down. Her heart paused, then started beating again.

"Well," said Ruth, "my parents chose to tell me all these terrible things when you and I got involved in Nan Smith's murder. They told me and then they split us up. They used the murder and the press frenzy and everything that happened afterward as a way to teach me about anti-Semitism, so when you and I quit seeing each other, I blamed you."

"But I was your best friend!"

"You think that made me feel *better*? All of a sudden everyone was talking about me being a Jew and you being a Christian and you wouldn't see me, and—"

"My parents wouldn't *let* me see you!"

"I know that now, Katy. I'm just trying to get you to see how things seemed back then. How I grew up thinking about you. How it all got mixed up in my mind." She paused. "I mean, Daddy would show me people at temple and tell me how they were in the camps, how they lost their husband and their children, and I would think about losing you. Then I would blame you. I was confused . . . you were my first loss to anti-Semitism, and my first betrayer, both. Do you understand?"

"I think so."

"Good. It's important, I think. We need to be honest with each other." The rabbi stared at her glass of tea. "Seeing you again after all these years has brought back so many old feelings. I mean, suddenly I feel so angry about . . . some other things. Family things that have nothing to do with you, but seem to be all caught up in this mess we're in." Ruth looked at Kate directly. "And I keep taking it out on you, and I don't want to do that, Katy. I really don't want to hurt you."

Kate said, "I believe you."

Ruth held her eyes for a moment, then looked away.

Kate said, "There's something you have to understand too. Those horrible things that were done in the name of Christ . . . none of that had anything to do with him."

Ruth said, "I know that."

"Maybe you do, but it's important to me that I say this, okay?"

Ruth nodded.

Kate felt the familiar sudden tightness in her chest, then just as quickly, the feeling went away. "Okay. It's just . . . Jesus taught us to love everyone. Even enemies. That's the point of the story of the Good Samaritan. Do you know it?"

"Of course I've heard the expression."

"The expression is based on a parable that shows what real love is. Jews and Samaritans were enemies back then, and in this parable a Jew gets mugged and left for dead beside the road. Some other Jews pass him by because he's a mess and they're too busy being all high-and-mighty to get involved. Then this Samaritan comes along. He knows the guy's a Jew, he knows most Jews hate his people, but he stops and helps him anyway."

Ruth took a couple of steps, placing some distance between them. "That's a nice *midrash*, but I'm not sure I see what it has to do with us."

"Those so-called Christians, the people who did such terrible things to Jews . . . they're like the ones who passed the man on the road. They claimed to be religious, but when something came along that forced them to practice what they preached, the truth rose to the surface. They're exactly the kind of hypocrites Jesus taught against, the ones who killed him."

"Are you saying Martin Luther and Pope Pius weren't Christians?"

Kate frowned as the rapid pulsing in her ears surged again. Would her heart never return to normal?

"No," she said. "I can't tell you they weren't Christians. But you shouldn't be judging Christianity on the basis of popes and theologians anyway. Jesus said the meek will inherit the earth . . . not the people at the top of the religious ladder, but those at the bottom. The difference he makes is mostly in people we never hear about, nobodies who are easy to miss because they live quiet lives for the sake of God and their neighbors. I mean, even Jesus was a nobody if you look at him in human terms. A manual laborer from a hick town in a third-world country. But I believe he was also God, who became one of us, one of the *least* of us, so that nobodies like me could know he really understands our pain, and believe in him, and be saved from just the kind of thing you're—"

"You're preaching to a rabbi," snapped Ruth. "Don't try to convert me. It's insulting."

"I'm not trying to convert you! I'm just trying to get you to understand that you can't judge Christianity by what Christians say and do;
you have to judge it by what Jesus said and did. Nobody's perfect—
religion or no religion. Even Jews do evil things sometimes. Does that
mean your religion makes them evil? I mean, I know I'm not exactly
perfect. So what? Does that mean I'm not really a Christian? Does it
mean Jesus lied? If I'm a bad friend or . . . or a bad mother, does that
mean God doesn't care about me? If I'm a little selfish now and then,
does that . . . I mean, if I . . . if . . . " Kate's voice faded as she inhaled
rapidly through her open mouth, trying to catch her breath, trying not
to cry.

Ruth spoke very softly. "Forgive me if this hits a little close to home,
but I have to ask: What good are the things that Jesus said and did if
they make no difference in how people live?"

FORTY-TWO

S ince the nightmares had stopped, Jake felt the need to sleep often, sometimes taking two naps in a day, and he slept very deeply. That is why he did not awake until the cloth was already covering his face. It felt wet and smelled sharply of some sort of chemical. Opening his eyes, he saw the sunshine from his hotel-room window shining through the fabric. His eyes burned. He shut them. He tried to push the assailant away, but his hands were heavy weights. Shaking his head from side to side, he fought to breathe, as gradually, consciousness began to fade away.

Then there was nothing at all.

T he sunset cast a rosy glow through the fly-specked window of Jake's room, dancing in the lenses of Orvis Newton's glasses as he stared

down to the street below. Spreading the venetian blinds a bit farther apart
to improve the view, he watched Solomon Cantor approach the building.

Orvis had been watching the hotel all day, hoping Cantor would
try to contact his son. Moments ago, when he'd seen the fugitive on the
street in front, Orvis knew the time was finally right. He had hurried up
here, worried about beating Cantor to the room and prepared for a struggle from the young man, but Cantor's son had been deeply asleep in spite
of the early hour, and the door wasn't even locked, and Cantor took his
time, circling the hotel to come in the back way.

Everything had worked out perfectly, as it always did for those who
served the Lord.

Still watching the street below, Orvis said, "'Slothfulness casteth
into a deep sleep; and an idle soul shall suffer hunger. He that keepeth
the commandment keepeth his own soul; but he that despiseth his ways
shall die.'"

Behind him, the young man snored. The ether wouldn't keep him
unconscious for long, but that was all right. Orvis needed the boy to look
drunk, not comatose.

I n spite of the unmarked police car parked in front, Sol had smelled the
cops a mile away. Feigning interest in a used television for sale behind
the cracked glass storefront of a pawn shop, he stopped walking, turned
his back to them, and watched their reflection in the filthy window for
a moment before heading back the way he'd come. Half a block up, he
ducked between two decrepit brick buildings and followed a trash-strewn
alley to the other end, where he emerged onto another squalid street.
Near the back entrance of the hotel he passed a '73 Cutlass, the only car
in sight, sprawled belly-down on the asphalt, all four wheels stolen, hood
and trunk open, rear window smashed, and a couple of drunks lolling
together in the backseat, arguing over a bottle wrapped in a brown paper
bag. He knew the police might also be watching the rear entrance. His
pulse increased in direct proportion to his proximity to the door. By the
time he wrapped his fingers around the handle, the blood roared in his
ears with each beat of his heart, reminding him of surf pounding the sand-
bars at the desolate tip of the Mississippi Delta.

Sol paused, just for an instant, and thought how nice it would be to fish those delta waters with Izzy once again, poling through the bottoms along narrow inlets and sloughs, filling a live well with redfish and bonefish. He and the boy had spent many peaceful days down in Plaquemines Parish before the murder, but it had been—what?—twenty-six years since he'd dropped a line in the water. If they caught him now, it could be another twenty before he had the chance again. He'd be eighty-something before they let him out this time.

For Izzy's sake, he couldn't let that happen.

Inside the hotel's rear entrance it took a moment for his eyes to adjust to the darkness. Sol stood at the end of a narrow hall leading to the lobby beyond the stairs. Beside him were a pair of rest room doors, both of which bore crudely printed Out of Order signs. The dismal yellow stain of nicotine coated the walls and ceiling, and the stench of vomit and disinfectant assailed his nostrils. A television game show blared from the lobby around the corner. Someone belched loudly.

Oh, Gabby, he thought. *Look what you've done.*

Solomon Cantor walked very slowly along the dark hallway until he reached the corner, out of sight of the lobby and the manager's counter. There he stood perfectly still, waiting for a chance to get Izzy's room number. Waiting was something he had learned to do very well at Angola.

F or a few minutes, Orvis Newton thought he had used too much ether, or maybe held the cloth over his face too long, but then Cantor's son moaned. That was good. He hadn't planned to knock the young man out completely, just daze him into docility. Fortunately, Cantor's son had been napping in his clothes. All Orvis had to do was put on his shoes. As he tied the laces, Orvis praised God for the time he had saved, not having to dress a semiconscious man. It was one more proof of the holiness of his task.

Placing his hands behind Jake's back, Orvis pulled him to a sitting position, then swung him around until his legs fell over the side of the bed. He sat beside him, raised one limp arm to drape it over his shoulder, wrapped his own arm around Jake's waist, and lifted him to his feet with a grunt. Jake instinctively tried to stand. That was good, but they had to hurry. Orvis couldn't afford to let Cantor reach the room. Everything depended on him spotting them leaving and deciding to follow.

Staggering under the man's weight, Orvis moved toward the door, opened it with his free hand, and shuffled out into the hall. The two of them meandered toward the stairs, weaving and almost falling several times, like a pair of drunks. That was good, too. Exactly what he'd hoped. Two bums helping each other to remain upright was a common sight in this neighborhood. No one would give them a second look.

Except for Solomon Cantor.

Baxter said, "Link . . ."

"I see them."

Washington observed the hotel entry where two men pushed awkwardly through the single door. Both of them tried to exit simultaneously, wedging themselves tightly in the opening. They backed up, and one of them almost fell, sagging in the other's arms. They tried again, exiting sideways this time, with one of the pair literally shoving his companion outside. The first man out could not stop his momentum, staggering across the sidewalk, dragging his companion behind. He teetered on the curb, one foot waving in the air as the second man pulled back on his arm. Finally, the pair managed to change their direction, setting off along the sidewalk arm in arm.

"They plastered," said Baxter.

"No fooling."

"Don'tcha think that's strange?"

"Why?"

"One a them's a man a God."

Washington looked at Baxter. "You saw what he had in his room."

"Yeah, but . . . well, yeah." Baxter shifted uncomfortably in his seat.

Both policemen redirected their attention to Orvis Newton and Jake Cantor. The two zigzagged up the street, now threatening to fall from the curb, now ramming into the wall. Near the corner, they stopped. The evangelist assisted the younger man as he slid down the face of the brick to assume a sitting position, arms and legs akimbo. Then Reverend

Newton approached a public telephone a few feet away, shoved a hand in his pocket, withdrew a coin, and after repeated attempts, managed to drop it into the coin slot. Slumped against the telephone enclosure, he punched the buttons and began to speak into the handset. Once he had to stop speaking as he dissolved into a long paroxysm of coughing.

"Hard to believe a guy that drunk could remember a phone number," said Baxter.

"Good point," said Washington. "Check out the call."

"You got it."

Baxter spoke softly into his cell phone as Washington continued to watch the drunks.

V an Morrison's "Moondance" jazzed from the speakers mounted high on the walls of Ruth's living room as she lounged against the multi-colored pillows of her sofa, reading Avivah Gottlieb Zornberg's excellent commentary on Genesis. The telephone rang. She continued to read. It rang twice more. Kate stepped into the room, heading for the phone.

"Ignore it," said Ruth.

"What if it's Paul or Jilly?"

"We can listen to the machine."

"All right."

They waited through two more rings, until Ruth's answering machine announced, "Hello. This is Ruth. When it beeps, you'll know what to do." The machine whirred for a few seconds, then clicked twice and beeped. A metallic voice filled the room.

"Hello, Ruth? This is William Onsler? From the JCC?"

The man on the telephone coughed loudly for a long time, then, "I'm sorry. I've got a terrible cold, or the flu or something. Anyway, I was calling to ask for a favor, but I guess you're not in, are you? Ruth? Ruth?"

Ruth rose with a sigh and crossed to the telephone. Picking up the handset, she said, "Hello, William."

"Oh, Ruth! I'm so glad you're there!"

"You sound awful. You don't even sound like yourself."

"Really?" He coughed again, not so long this time. "I don't feel like myself, I'll tell you that for sure."

"What can I do for you?"

"I hate to ask, but the police just called me. They're down at the JCC. Apparently someone broke into the Center and vandalized the place."

"Oh no."

In the background, Van Morrison sang about magic and moonlight. Ruth had a little trouble hearing the man on the telephone with the music turned up so high.

"Are you having a party?" asked William Onsler.

Ruth said, "Oh, can you hear the music?"

"Yes."

"I'll turn it down."

"No, that's okay."

"I'm sorry to hear about the vandalism. Did the police say it was bad?"

"I'm not worried about that, Ruth. It's probably nothing a little elbow grease can't handle. But they want someone to come check it out, you know, officially, and I'm just not up to it, and I was wondering . . . " He dissolved into coughs.

Ruth looked at Kate and rolled her eyes. "Okay, William. I'll go."

S omething white descended toward Jake's nose and mouth. He smelled that chemical again.

"It's a wonderful Plan, you see," said the man. "You and the Jewish girl will die, Solomon will go back to prison for killing you, and your lying mother will have to live with the knowledge that she caused it all."

The wet cloth covered his nose and mouth. Jake heard the man's words but could say nothing in reply.

"I know all about you, Jake. I read your file, you know. I followed you to your psychiatrist's office because you seemed on such friendly terms with Rabbi Gold. Imagine my surprise when I found out who you really are! An unbeliever might call that a coincidence, but we know better, don't we? It was certain affirmation that the Lord's hand is at work in my ministry. He led me straight to you." Orvis clucked his tongue. "But you told the doctor entirely too much, young man. She might have pieced things together."

Jake coughed feebly.

"Jake? That psychiatrist seemed to believe you have a strong dislike for your mother. Is that true? Do you hate your mother? I hope not. 'Honor thy father and thy mother,' you know. That's one of the Big Ten."

Jake felt darkness descending on him with each breath, but it did not seem to matter anymore.

T he drunks had been inside the station wagon for a couple of minutes now. Washington decided they were not going to move. He had his hand on the door handle of his unmarked car, ready to approach the suspects, when he sensed motion in the periphery of his vision and shifted his eyes to the front entrance of the Poisson Hotel. To Washington's surprise Solomon Cantor had just emerged and stood at the curb, frantically waving at an approaching taxi. The cab pulled over and Cantor jumped in. At that moment, the station wagon farther up the street pulled slowly away from the curb.

Baxter replaced his cell phone in his coat pocket and said, "They gonna get back to us on tracin' that call. Wanna roll?"

"Yeah."

"Which car you wanna tail?"

Watching the cab set out right behind the station wagon, Washington said, "Both of them."

G azing at Garden District mansions through the side window of Ruth's Citroën, Kate stole glimpses of well-lit interiors as Ruth carefully negotiated the traffic on St. Charles. Tulane or Loyola must have been sponsoring some event, because the cars had almost stopped along the avenue, and parking was nonexistent as they neared the JCC.

"Guess we'll have to park on one of these side streets and walk over," Ruth said.

"Now you know how your neighbors feel on *Yom Kippur*," said Kate.

Ruth smiled.

They found a spot on a narrow road lined with oaks, locked the car, and set out at a brisk pace. After a minute, Kate said, "Can we slow down a little?"

Ruth glanced at her. "Are you all right?"

"Yeah," lied Kate as the blood roared in her ears. "Just a little out of shape."

Reaching St. Charles, they turned under the yellow glow of a street-light. Kate said, "Hope the damage isn't too bad."

"Well, if it is we can always have it cleaned up."

O rvis did his best not to lose Cantor's cab in the deepening twilight. As he drove down St. Charles Avenue, the station wagon rocked pleas-antly from side to side beneath mossy old trees holding hands above the road like raggedy men playing London Bridge. Traffic was very thick. He had to pause by the curb once when the taxi got caught at a light behind him. The sunlight faded, and it became more and more difficult to pick out the cab's headlights from those around it, but he managed. Arriving at the JCC, Orvis turned into the street just to the west, managing through pure luck to find a parking place across from the rear entrance. Switching off the ignition, he turned and said, "Hey, we're here."

"Mundy widdle hinterlu," mumbled Cantor's son.

"I know," said the evangelist, stepping from the station wagon.

Cantor's cab pulled to a stop half a block away. Pretending not to notice, Orvis Newton opened the rear door and stuck his head into the compartment behind the seat. He gripped Cantor's son, dragged him roughly out of the old Vista Cruiser, and propped him up on the ground beside the rear tire. Orvis was in a hurry now. The trick was to get the boy inside the building before Cantor could stop him. That way, Cantor would have to follow.

Reaching inside the station wagon again, Orvis removed a crowbar. The solid metal heft of the bar felt comfortable in his hand as he turned back toward Jake. Orvis wrapped the younger man's arm around his shoulder, helped him to stand, and set out along the sidewalk next to the tall blank wall of the JCC. As they stumbled along he saw two women turn the corner and approach the parking lot across the street.

"Oh, look," he said to the semiconscious man at his side. "She's brought the Christian girl, too!" Orvis felt his heart soar with gratitude at this unexpected gift. God was good.

Hurrying now, he crossed the street and rounded the fence at the pool in back, pausing just long enough to force open a chain-link gate with the crowbar. He entered the swimming pool enclosure and crossed to the rear door, where he dropped the younger man to the pavement none too gently. At that moment, Orvis heard a nearby car door slam shut.

The Reverend Orvis Newton smiled, certain it was Solomon Cantor, taking the bait.

Baxter cursed the traffic. "We lost 'em! How'm I supposed to keep up in this mess?" he shouted, beating the steering wheel.

"Settle down," said Washington. "I think I know where they're going."

"Where?"

"That temple is near here. So's the Jewish Community Center. It's got to be one or the other."

"Yeah," said Baxter, nodding his head. "Maybe."

"Take the next left. We'll cut over to Prytania."

"Okeydoke."

Baxter spun the wheel hard to the left, narrowly cutting off an oncoming Dodge Caravan. The driver of the van shouted an obscenity.

"Baxter."

"Yeah?"

"Don't do that."

"What'd I do?"

Washington sighed. "Never mind."

U sing the crowbar, Orvis pried the steel door open with a loud screech. Immediately he dropped the crowbar and stooped to lift Jake to his feet. Together, they staggered into the darkened hallway. Orvis hoped the sound of the steel door giving way would draw Solomon Cantor in.

Suddenly the building's burglar alarm began to wail. Ignoring it, Orvis shouted into his companion's ear. "Just like old times, huh?"

The man said, "Kiney hudden tack."

"My sentiments exactly," said Orvis as they headed for the kitchen with its wide assortment of knives and cleavers.

T hey heard the burglar alarm a block away from the JCC but did not realize its source until they drew closer. Pausing to look up at the building, Ruth said, "I guess that's been going on since the kid broke in. Bet the neighbors and the cops are sick of it by now." She glanced around. "Speaking of that, where are the police? I thought they'd be out front to meet us."

"Maybe they're in back, by the pool, or over at the side entrance."

Ruth looked at Kate. "You remember this place pretty well."

"How could I forget?"

Ruth had her key ready when they reached the doors. She twisted it in the lock and entered quickly with Kate pulling the door closed behind them. The instant the latch clicked into place, Ruth turned to the security system keypad beside the door and punched in a four-digit code to neutralize the alarm.

Kate felt a palpable silence settle on the building. She marveled that Ruth could not hear her heart. To her, it had the sound of random blows on a bass drum.

"Come on," said Ruth. "Let's go find them."

Their footsteps echoed on the polished terrazzo floor with the hollow resonance of an undertaker's condolences. After a few yards, a strange sound, like a human moan, rose from deep in the bowels of the building. Kate stopped dead in her tracks. "What was that?"

"I don't know," said Ruth.

"I have a bad feeling. Let's get out of here."

"Wait a minute."

They stood together listening, but the sound did not repeat itself.

"Ruth . . ."

"It was nothing. The ice maker in the kitchen or an air conditioner kicking in."

"*Ruth* . . ."

"Okay, okay. Just gimme one minute, will you? I have to see about this damage."

Kate nodded reluctantly and together the women moved on, passing doors on either side of the hall. Some were closed, concealing who knows what. It seemed to Kate that the open ones whispered warnings. She felt the pressure in her chest increase still more, although that hardly seemed possible. Would she have to admit what was happening? Would she have to ask for help? Oh, how she loathed the very idea. Somehow, Kate felt as if her condition would remain a phantom unless she acknowledged its existence. So long as she denied it, so long as no one knew, she could pretend it was nothing serious.

Ruth walked slightly ahead, flipping lights on as they entered new corridors and flipping them off again at the opposite end. As they continued to move deeper into the network of hallways, Kate's premonitions began to fade, and with them, the tightness behind her ribs subsided just a bit. Nothing had happened. She told herself that nothing *would* happen. She would be fine.

Her secret was safe.

T he black windows of the temple stared blindly out into the unseasonably warm New Orleans evening. Washington and Baxter returned the stare, watching closely for any sign of activity.

"Maybe we beat them here," said Baxter.

"Maybe."

"Whaddaya think they're up to?"

Washington did not respond. His mind was elsewhere, walking the hall of Benny and Morton Rothstein's shattered apartment, kneeling beside Helen Blumenthal's savaged body, scenting the odor of burning tar long after Rebecca Betterton had been carried away, trying to make sense of the strange altar to Sister Nan Smith that he had found in Orvis Newton's pathetic little room.

He could not shake the feeling that they should have arrested Newton the moment they laid eyes on him at Izzy Cantor's hotel. But Washington had waited in the hope they'd get more evidence by watching him. Now the freak was out there somewhere with Cantor's son, and Cantor was right behind. Where were they? What were they doing?

No good will come of this, that's for sure.

Baxter's cell phone beeped. Washington continued to survey the temple, deep in thought, while his colleague spoke to the caller. Nothing moved beyond the dark windows of the temple. On the night after *Yom Kippur,* all was quiet.

"Link?"

"Uh-huh."

Baxter slipped the cell phone back into his pocket. "They traced that call the guy made."

With a deliberate effort, Washington roused himself from his reverie, turning to face his companion. "Who was it?"

"He called that rabbi woman."

For once, Washington's face betrayed his emotions. The fear arose too quickly to conceal.

T he Reverend Orvis Newton held a long knife in his right hand, pointing toward the floor. He stood perfectly still, listening to the girls. He could see them clearly, but they would have to look hard to notice him, standing as he was in the dark behind the louvered closet door.

"I just had the strangest thought," said the Christian one.

"What's that?" said the Jew.

The other one glanced around. They stood in the women's locker room near the rear of the building. "Isn't this exactly where we were when we heard that scream?"

"Oh, stop it," said the Jew. "You'll scare us both silly."

"But it's just like that time. I mean, here we are in the exact same place, and we heard that noise a minute ago, just like we heard the scream back then, and now we're walking around all alone trying to find out what made the sound, just like we did, and . . . doesn't this spook you out just a little bit?"

"All right. I admit it. I'm scared. Are you happy now?"

"Absolutely not."

"Look. Just let me check out the conference wing and we're outta here."

The Christian one sighed and followed the Jew out to the hall.

Immediately, Orvis stepped from the closet and crossed to press his ear against the door. He heard their footsteps fade as they walked away. After a moment, he opened the door and peeked out, just in time to see the girls turn right at an intersecting corridor that led to the kitchen and the meeting rooms. Orvis left the locker room and quickly slipped along the hall after them, moving with an odd, mincing grace that belied his age and conservative appearance, dressed as he was in an immaculate dark suit. At the intersecting hallway he paused, then bent to look around the corner, watching Kate and Ruth walk away as his fingers caressed the plastic handle of the knife.

Leaning close to Ruth's ear, Kate whispered, "Listen."

They stood stock-still. At first, all Kate heard was the low rumble of the air-conditioning equipment. Then her ears caught a soft, gurgling noise, and the unmistakable hiss of a human whisper. Careful to avoid making a sound, Ruth slowly lifted the flap of her purse, reached inside, and extracted her handgun. At the sight of the weapon, Kate sucked in her breath. Speaking very quietly, she said, "Let's get out of here!"

Ruth shook her head.

"Ruth . . . ," entreated Kate, but the rabbi had already set out along the hallway on tiptoe, with her small automatic gripped firmly in her right hand, pointed straight ahead. Kate stood where she was for a moment. Then, with a series of quick, shallow breaths, she followed.

Jake Cantor's eyes turned toward the man at his side with a flicker of recognition. "Like . . . last . . . time," he said.

"Shhh," whispered Sol. "Don't try to talk."

"This . . . where . . . happened." Each tortured syllable brought fresh blood bubbling to the surface around the knife in his chest.

"Hush now, Izzy," said Sol.

The young man's eyes remained solidly fixed upon his father. The words that came next seemed to cost him dearly. "I . . . remembered."

"Shhh. Be quiet now."

As Sol began to rise, Jake's right hand gripped him with surprising strength. Drawing another agonizing breath, he asked, "Why?"

Sol looked directly into Jake's eyes. With his free hand, he touched his son's hair, gently pushing it up and away from his forehead. "Oh, Izzy. Don't you know?"

The son would not release his grip on the father's arm, and he would not look away. He did not speak again, but after a moment, a tear escaped from his eye and traced a path sideways, along his temple.

Solomon Cantor wiped it away.

They reached the corner, with Ruth closest to the kitchen door, and Kate pressed against the wall behind her. Ruth looked back at Kate and nodded. She took a deep breath and stepped suddenly into the kitchen, bent at the knees with her automatic aimed ahead.

"Don't move," said Ruth, her eyes locked on someone out of Kate's line of sight.

Kate inched closer and peeked around the edge of the wall. What she saw drove her mind spinning back twenty-five years. A bleeding body sprawled upon the kitchen floor, just there, the man—the *same* man—also there, beside the body, staring up at them with fear and surprise. It was as if all the years had simply vanished and she had slipped back in time, doomed to repeat the worst moment of her life.

"Move away from him, Sol," said Ruth.

Kate sucked in air like a panting dog, desperate to catch her breath. She could not see the wounded person's face, hidden as it was behind Solomon Cantor's large frame.

"He's been stabbed," said Sol. "Call an ambulance."

"We're going to do that. But you get away from him first."

"I can't."

"You have to!"

"No. I can't."

"What's the matter with you? Don't you see my gun? Now, get away from him!"

Instead of answering, Sol turned to look back down at the man on the floor.

Ruth screamed, "Sol! Move away!"

Sol ignored the rabbi, not even glancing in her direction.

"Katy," said Ruth, "go dial 911!"

"Okay."

"Tell them to send an ambulance," said Sol.

"Tell them to send the *police*," said Ruth.

The pulsing in Kate's ears was almost intolerable. She said, "Where's the telephone?"

"Over there," said Ruth, using her weapon to briefly point beyond Sol and the man on the floor. "In the kitchen manager's office on the right."

"I'm not walking past him!"

"You hear that, Sol? She won't go near you. If you really want her to call an ambulance, you have to move."

At first, Kate thought he had not heard. Then he stood slowly and faced them. Kate could not pull her eyes away from his face.

"Get over by that wall and sit down with your back to it, facing me," said Ruth.

Sol followed her instructions, assuming a seated position several yards away from the wounded man. Kate's eyes followed his every move. When he had lowered himself to the floor, Ruth said, "Okay, Katy. Better hurry."

Kate kept her eyes on Sol as she inched along, sticking as close as possible to the stainless steel worktable opposite him. Her chest was bound in steel rings, ever tighter, as her heart raged like a trapped animal. It was not until she came directly alongside the wounded man on the floor that Kate risked a glance at his face. She froze. An army of emotions seized her: surprise, fear, pity, and even, perhaps, love.

Kate whispered, "Oh, Jake."

"Katy!" said Ruth. "There's no time. Call 911 *now!*"

But Kate had already dropped to her knees, drawn to him by something as irresistible as gravity. She laid her palm on Jake's forehead and whispered his name again. *He's dying*, she thought. The revelation pierced her with an unbearable finality and in an instant she truly saw him as if for the very first time, not as a means to an end but as a flawed human being, just like her.

"Katy!" shouted Ruth, "You have got to *go!*"

Jake did not respond to her touch, but Sol watched Kate carefully. "All right," she said, rising to her feet, fighting a tingling dizziness. "All right."

On the other side of the hallway, Sol slowly rose as well, mirroring Kate's actions. Kate did not notice, so total was her concentration on his son.

"You get back down!" shouted Ruth.

Startled, Kate lifted her eyes from Jake's face to where Sol now stood fully upright, looming over her just three strides away. With a little cry, she pressed herself back against the worktable.

"Sol," said Ruth, "if you move one inch toward her, I'll fire. Believe me, I *will* shoot you."

Sol stared at Kate. She found she could not look away. She felt hypnotized by his eyes, deep brown and moist, overflowing with a sentiment she could not fathom. Was it tenderness?

An inner voice whispered, *Don't be fooled.*

Then Sol lowered his gaze to the man on the floor, and what Kate saw was undeniable. No actor on earth could project the passions playing across his features, and in that glimpse of raw emotion, the widowed mother sensed a wounded soul who also saw the wholly human person lying there and loved him for all the right reasons.

Sol raised both of his hands slightly from his sides. The rabbi adjusted her aim. "You keep your hands off her, Sol!"

Ruth's voice rumbled obscurely in some distant portion of Kate's mind. Sol had her full attention as he continued to reach, not for her but for his son, with grief and love vying for dominance in his features. He took one step closer. She heard Ruth's voice rise again, but paid no attention to the words.

When it came, the shot slammed into Kate's thoughts, even as Sol spun violently and fell against the wall, the explosion impossibly loud in the confines of the kitchen. She watched in horror as the big man slid down, fingers clawing at the joints between the tiles until he came to rest beside his son.

"No!" screamed Kate, reaching for him.

"Stay back!" shouted Ruth. "Katy! What are you doing?"

Someone's insane laughter echoed down the hall. Kate heard the sound of running feet slapping the floor, fading with a manic giggle. She glanced at Ruth but the rabbi had turned away, pointing her weapon in the other direction, toward the hall.

"Who's there?" shouted Ruth. "Show yourself!"

A door slammed somewhere deep in the heart of the building, and the laughter stopped completely. "Katy," said Ruth. "will you *please* go dial 911?"

Kate looked at her blankly.

"What's the matter with you?" asked Ruth.

Kate felt a sense of lightness as the dizziness grew and stars twinkled before her eyes. The beginning of the end. Her brain, with insufficient oxygen, shutting down. She tried to speak, but all she could manage was "I . . . I . . . "

"Oh, never mind. I'll do it!" Ruth charged around the corner, out of sight.

Kate fell to her knees beside Sol, bending over him, whimpering, touching his back with her palm. Above the incessant roaring in her ears, she heard a pounding in the distance; the sound of metal slamming into metal; the beat of leather soles upon the floor, drawing closer; voices, frantic and calm, shouts, movement . . . but all these things happened in some other world. Kate had become a frightened little girl again, standing at her dying mother's bedside, searching for sanity after witnessing another violent death in that very same place. It was as if God's hand had drawn back the curtain of time so Kate could relive the sorrow of that long-ago moment and remember the question that had sabotaged her life. . . .

"Was she bad?"

"I don't know. Probably not. She was a minister, after all. A missionary."

"But she's dead."

Kate watched Solomon Cantor's eyes never straying from his son just three feet away. She watched Sol move his lips, his cheek pressed firmly against the floor. She leaned closer. His lips moved again. In spite of the blood rushing in her skull, Kate heard the words he whispered: "Save him. Dear God. Please. Save him."

Oh, she thought, *is this what love looks like?*

And suddenly Kate understood how wrong she had been all those years ago when it occurred to her that God's love was a dangerous thing, that it was better not to let him notice you especially, better not to stand out one way or the other. Because if Solomon Cantor could look like this and say these words even as he lay bleeding to death, if love of *any* kind could give him that much courage, then it was truly best to be the one to help the sick, to feed the poor, to be the missionary, and brave the Lord's attention.

A moan escaped her lips.

She jammed a knuckle into her mouth, filled with the certain knowledge that this wild, erratic lurching in her chest was merely the final throes of a heart that was already three years dead, a disembodied organ preserved by the frozen solace of her children's company. Faced with the selfless love of Solomon Cantor for his son, Kate saw at last that she had fashioned her children into a rock, an anchor, an excuse for her own life where once they had been a happy little boy and girl. Love—all love—had died for her with John Flint. She thought of Ruth Gold and her temple and the Jews there seeking God with love written large upon their faces. She remembered feeling surprise that Jews could love the Lord as much as she.

She . . . love?

Oh, the irony of it! She had *not* loved, and she had loved God least of all. What pompous selflessness, what hypocritical sincerity, what defiant contrition she had so piously born away from that temple! No wonder her prayers for forgiveness had gone unanswered. It was a marvel she was not struck dead where she stood.

Kate drew up her knees in a slow series of shaky movements until they were tucked beneath her chin. Wrapping her arms around them, she huddled against the cold tile wall, making herself as small as possible, watching as the stars before her eyes collided and merged to form twin black holes of nothingness.

Oh, how I hate this fickle heart!

Since John had been torn away, she had encompassed herself with herself, placing Kate Flint all around and at the center of a world with room for no one else. How cleverly she had disguised that little idol of herself, playing the part of devoted widow, faithful mother, devout Christian. But each of those persons was a lie, told to herself in self-defense. Self. Self. Self.

And she had stooped still lower, cloaking her raging ego with the image of Jilly and Paul—even hiding in a room filled with Jewish strangers—anything to avoid looking at who she really was. She had not kept her children at her side for their protection; she had kept them close in spite of the danger, leaving them in harm's way just to soothe her loneliness. She had camouflaged her neediness in everything from bigotry to benevolence . . . everything but the truth.

As the twin black spots before her eyes merged to obscure Kate's vision, Ruth Gold's words returned once more with merciless candor: *"Who needs whom, exactly?"* She remembered her easy little prayer of repentance at *Yom Kippur* and the hollowness she felt then, the certainty that God had not answered. She remembered her outraged prayer as she desperately searched the corridors for Jilly: *"Don't do this to me!"* Not "save my daughter," but "don't do this to *me.*" Kate saw herself placing Jilly in Jake's arms, doing that willingly even though she knew there was a killer loose, risking her daughter's life rather than taking the chance of offending a handsome stranger.

Something whispered that she had offered Jilly to a god without a name, but Kate laughed through bitter tears and beat her head against the wall once, very hard. Oh, what hypocrisy still lingered, to think such a thing!

A god without a name?

She knew its name; she knew it well, for it was Kathryn Flint.

"Oh no," she said, "what have I done?" whispering so the starving idol she had become would not overhear. Then she realized even that concern was merely more of herself at the center, so, finally, Kate Flint called out loudly to her Creator, loudly enough for all the world to hear, even above the pounding of her feeble heart.

"Dear Jesus," she cried, "please forgive me."

And this time, she knew it was enough.

FORTY-FIVE

Kate knew her heart would not allow her to go for help, so she did what she could. Bending close, the young widow began to pray for both men, begging for their lives. The older man's eyes lingered on her face for a moment, filled with hope, then his lids slowly closed. She turned to Jake, but he too was unconscious. The blood of father and son intermingled beneath Kate Flint's knees as she knelt, one palm on each man, pressed against their wounds, praying with all of her might. She did not know how long she lingered there.

Then Ruth's voice broke through. "Katy? I'm so sorry."

Before Kate opened her eyes, it was in her mind to say, "There's no need for sorrow. They'll both be fine. You'll see." But as she looked toward the sound of Ruth's voice, Kate's response died in her throat. Ruth stood pale and trembling with Orvis Newton close behind her, his left arm around her chest and her shiny steel automatic in his right hand, pressing hard against her temple.

"Hello again, Mrs. Flint," he said. "I can't say I'm surprised to see you here. It was in the Plan."

Kate did not understand what inspired her words. Something in his voice perhaps. A sense of reverence or fanatical insanity. She said, "The plan? You mean the Genesis stories?"

The fluorescent lights flashed in Orvis Newton's glasses, obscuring his multicolored eye. "How do you know about that?"

"It just came to me, like a revelation."

"Really?" He seemed excited. "He spoke to you, too?"

"Yes," said Kate, somehow rising to her feet. "He explained everything, beginning with the forbidden fruit."

"I failed at that," said the Reverend Orvis Newton.

"No," said Kate, "you didn't."

"Really? Even though she did not die?" He pressed the gun harder against Ruth's temple.

"We can't know the Lord's full will," said Kate. "It must have happened as he planned."

"Oh, if only I could believe it was so!"

"It is." Kate took one step closer. Where did these words come from? This courage? Kate said, "She is not supposed to die."

"No!" shouted Orvis Newton. "No! The Lord told me they all must burn in fires of eternal damnation for what they tried to do to Nanny!" Nodding at Solomon Cantor's fallen form, he said, "That one killed her flesh, and the others tried to kill her ministry. Her good name. They all have to die. The Lord has spoken."

Kate took a second step, as Ruth watched from within the evangelist's embrace, eyes wide with terror. "Those who must die have died already."

"But this one?" He glanced at Ruth's cheek close by his own, then flicked his eyes back to Kate, the gun never wavering from the rabbi's temple.

"She must live. I was told she must live. It's why the fruit failed."

He looked at her. "And you?"

Kate felt absolutely calm. "You mustn't harm one of your own."

"I knew it!" he shouted. "Hallelujah! I knew that all along! I stood

outside your house watching so many times, trying to summon the courage, but it was the Holy Ghost who stopped me, wasn't it?"

"Yes."

Orvis Newton's voice changed, becoming authoritative and strong,
as if he stood before a congregation. "I did not seek this burden," he said.
"I am Abraham, climbing Moriah with sin to the left of me and sin to
the right, and no possibility of a righteous resolution, for God himself
commands me to commit an evil beyond imagination. Yet he is the Lord,
so I must climb." He looked at Ruth Gold, continuing to speak in an
oratory style. " 'Thou shalt not kill.' Don't you think I struggle with that?
I am a man of God. But I have been *commanded* to kill, like Abraham.
To obey is to disobey. So I must climb, and only when I have proven
that I will sacrifice even righteousness itself on the altar of God's desire,
only then will the Lord say, 'It is enough.' "

Kate said, "But I've received a revelation too. The Lord sent me to
tell you he does not want her harmed." She took a third step, shifting
her eyes to Ruth.

It was her first mistake.

"No!" screamed Orvis Newton. He removed the weapon from Ruth's
temple, pointing it directly at Kate's face. "You're a deceiver! The Lord
commanded me to sacrifice this woman! I know he did!"

Released from his grip, Ruth slipped to the ground as if her legs had
turned to water. She covered her head with her hands and rocked back
and forth, whispering, *"Shema Yisrael Adonai Elohim Adonai echad. Shema Yisrael
Adonai. . . ."* The words poured from her lips, on and on, as Kate stared
into the black circle of death at the end of the gun in his hand.

"You cannot sacrifice her," said Kate. "Who will be your witness
then?"

"Witness?"

"Yes. You know the Lord expects a witness. It's part of the plan.
Someone must tell the world the good news about what you've done."

"Good news. Yes . . . " Orvis nodded. "But I can do that."

"Not alone. The Scriptures say there must be two or more." Where
was this coming from? How did she know what to say?

He continued to nod. "That's true, that's true. 'At the mouth of two
witnesses, or three witnesses, shall he that is worthy of death be put to

death; *but* at the mouth of one witness he shall not be put to death.'
Deuteronomy seventeen six."

"Yes. You see? You mustn't harm us. Who will be your witnesses?"

He stared at her, one eye shifting colors like a kaleidoscope beneath
the stark fluorescent light. For a moment, she thought she had won, but
then he said, "I'm one. You can be the other." He swiftly turned the gun
away from her, placing it an inch away from Ruth Gold's head, his finger
tightening on the trigger.

"No!" screamed Kate. "Not her! Take me! *Take me!*" She ran the final
steps toward him, ran full speed into him, knocking him away before he
could raise the gun to stop her, falling to her knees and covering Ruth as
best she could with her own body—to protect her, to keep her safe, to
wait for death as Ruth prayed, *"Shema Yisrael Adonai Elohim Adonai echad.
Shema Yisrael Adonai . . . ."*

Kate Flint fiercely hugged her childhood friend, enveloping her,
rocking forward and backward with her, eyes shut tight, braving the
Lord's attention, whispering a little prayer of her own: "Take me, take
me, take me." But just as she could almost feel the fleeting, flashing
bullet hitting home, someone screamed and shots were fired. Kate
heard footsteps pounding past and felt a touch; she flinched and heard
a new and close and gentle voice say, "It's okay now." She opened her
eyes and saw Lieutenant Washington kneeling at her side, and she
noticed that her heart was finally beating strong and steady, the way
it used to do.

atching the paramedics slam the doors on the second ambulance and pull away from the Northside Jewish Community Center with siren roaring and lights flashing red and blue against the ghostly canopy of Spanish moss draped from hundred-year-old oaks, Washington inhaled the humid New Orleans air deeply through flared nostrils and asked, "What happened?"

Baxter seemed embarrassed. "Link, I swear, I was right behind him. He was there one second, then he was gone. Somewhere over in the middle of the park. I'm sorry, man."

"Don't worry about it. We'll get him."

Lieutenant Washington had other concerns. He couldn't shake the notion that one of those ambulances wouldn't be speeding toward Touro Infirmary right now if he hadn't been so easy on the rabbi after the last time she fired her automatic. *Now look what she's gone and done.*

The Flint woman huddled in a patrol car around the corner, her story being taken by a detective who usually worked the Broadmoor and Mid City beats but had come over to help out with the mess. Rabbi Gold slouched alone on a bench by the entrance. Near her stood a uniformed cop with orders to keep the rabbi at the scene.

Washington crossed the dimly lit pavement, told the patrolman to give them some space, and sank to the bench beside the rabbi. "You okay?" he asked, adjusting his tie.

She laughed once, curtly. "Oh, yeah. I'm wonderful."

Washington nodded in the dark. "Hard to shoot a person."

The rabbi did not speak.

"All these years, I've only had to do it once. Couldn't sleep for weeks."

Ruth glanced at him, then away. "Did the person die?"

"No. Came close, but he pulled through."

She said nothing.

After a moment, Washington said, "Why'd you come here tonight?"

"I got a call from William Onsler, the director of the center. He said a policeman called him about a vandal breaking into the center, but he was sick, so he asked me to come."

"Are you sure it was this Onsler fella?"

"Of course. I—" She fell silent . . . then, "I'm an idiot."

"No. He's very good at what he does."

"But why does he do this? I mean, I know he's crazy, but . . . *why?*"

"We entered his home this morning—he lives in back of a little storefront mission over in the Irish Channel—and we found a real strange setup. He has an old photograph of Nan Smith pinned to the wall beside his bed, with candles and personal letters from her, and her Bible open in front of it. Like an altar or something."

"But we all—I mean everyone he's killed or tried to kill, except for Sol Cantor—none of us hurt that woman. Most of us helped put Cantor away for her murder." She shook her head. "It just doesn't make sense."

"That's what I'm trying to say. You should've seen his place. Very weird. In that Bible, on the page it was open to, he circled a verse with a red pencil about twenty times, real boldly."

"What verse?" asked the rabbi.

The Lieutenant checked his notes. "Daniel nine eleven. Do you know it?"

"Believe it or not, I don't have the whole Bible memorized, Lieutenant."

"Yeah. It's pretty obscure, I guess." Still looking at his notes, he read, "'Yea, all Israel have transgressed thy law, even by departing, that they might not obey thy voice; therefore the curse is poured upon us, and the oath that is written in the law of Moses the servant of God, because we have sinned against him.'"

Ruth shivered.

"It gets weirder," said the Lieutenant. "He circled other verses that describe the forbidden fruit and the ones about Cain murdering Abel, and all the rest of the stories that fit the pattern, but every other line in the whole Bible was crossed out."

"Every line?" She paused. "That would take days."

"It's consistent with an obsessive personality, that's for sure."

Leaning forward, Ruth looked at him, struggling to read his eyes in the dim light. "Am I under arrest?"

"Should you be?"

She watched his silhouette against the amber glow of a streetlight in the St. Charles neutral ground beyond. After a moment, she said, "You would've done the same thing."

Washington shrugged. "Maybe."

"He's twice her size. I warned him. I warned him several times. But he wouldn't stay on the floor. He stood up and reached for her and I had to fire."

Still Washington remained silent.

A deep green streetcar with maroon trim rumbled along the neutral ground, its single headlight jerking with each *clump-clump* of the steel wheels rolling over buried ties. Watching the streetcar, Ruth said, "He was kneeling there with the knife when we came around the corner. He was right beside Jake, and he had blood on his clothes, and it seemed obvious what he'd done."

The streetcar slowed to a stop with squealing brakes, and two young women, wearing small backpacks and carrying armloads of books, stepped down. Both cast curious glances toward the small crowd of police milling around in front of the JCC, then hurried away toward Tulane or Loyola.

Washington asked, "What was so obvious about it, Rabbi?"

"Think about it. The *Akeda*. The binding of Isaac. It looked like Sol was reenacting the next big story in the Torah, just like you said. Except he went all the way and stabbed his son." Her voice got softer, pleading with him. She was shaking. "You would've done the same thing. You would've."

Washington remained silent for a while; then he covered her hand with his and said, "Yeah, I probably would have."

Ma'am?"

At the sound of the voice, Kate awoke with a start. "What?"

"Wake up, ma'am," said the nurse. "You can see him now."

Rubbing her eyes, it took Kate a moment to realize she was lying on a vinyl sofa in the hospital lounge with a thin blanket drawn across her shoulders like a shawl. "He's awake?" she asked, looking up at the ebony face floating against a sterile background of stark white ceiling tiles and rectangular fluorescent lights.

"I don't imagine he will be for long. You might wanna get moving."

Kate threw the blanket aside, found her espadrilles, slipped them on, and followed the nurse out to the hall, patting at her sleep tousled hair and trying to smooth the wrinkles in her blouse. "Have the police seen him yet?"

"Yes. They walked out of his room a minute ago."

"Has anyone found his mother yet? Is she here?"

"I don't know about that, ma'am," said the nurse.

Jake's room was the third on the right. Lieutenant Washington's partner, Detective Baxter, the big one with the porkpie hat and orange-plaid sport coat, stood outside the door. "Missus Flint," he said. "Y'all let us know if he says anything more 'bout what happened, all right?"

"Yes. Is he okay?"

"He's real lucky, all things considered. I can't believe he's up an' talkin' after bein' stabbed like that."

Kate nodded, squared her shoulders, and went into the room.

Jake lay covered by a sheet from the waist down, his hospital gown bunched under his armpits and his thick sandy hair pushed up on one side. A soft spray of whiskers powdered his chin. His eyes were shut; disappointment washed over her. Had he gone back to sleep? Had she missed her chance?

"Jake?" she whispered. "Jake, are you awake?"

He did not answer.

She sighed. After staring at him for a moment, Kate crossed to the window and looked down upon the city. Below her lay a verdant tapestry of treetops, the interwoven limbs of centurion oaks spreading as far as the eye could see, a living fabric penetrated here and there by delicate church steeples and the soft gray slates of Garden District mansion roofs. Halfway to the horizon and slightly to her right sprawled the central business district, a jagged row of glittering glass and concrete jutting up through the urban forest. It occurred to Kate that any significant change for the better in such a view would require a person's entire lifetime to accomplish, but a madman's single act could wreak destruction upon it in an instant. Why was evil so easy and good so hard? She contemplated the impersonal character of this Crescent City, rising from the untamed swamp, unbeholden to any person, made by man yet under no man's control. It would remain just so, or change completely, no matter what happened to Jake or to her. She wondered what *would* happen.

Behind her Jake lay fighting for his life, his wounded chest rising and falling with labored breaths, and she stood watch, her own chest wounded in another way, the victim of emotions she had savored, yet knew she must not feel. Reaching up, she pressed her palm against the glass. The wind blowing past so high above the ground had chilled the surface. A frosted aura formed around her fingers, condensation encircling the warmth of her flesh. The first signs of autumn had settled onto New Orleans. She removed her hand and saw its silhouette drawn in condensation on the glass, hovering ghostlike above the city. People in caves ten thousand years ago had painted just that pattern on the rocks. Nothing significant had changed in mankind since.

No.

That's not true.

She had been dead inside for three years, but over the last few weeks, she had reached for a new life, had been prepared to sacrifice a vital tenet of her faith to find it, had placed her children at risk for it. She had rationalized each visit to Temple Brit Yisrael as a service to the Lord, when the truth was she had hoped somehow to find happiness there with Ruth and Jake. She really did not understand what she had found instead. It was not a new life. Looking back, she realized it had been within her all along, buried deep beneath the selfishness and sorrow but always there in the faith of her youth, never gone. She had simply remembered where she left it, in that moment when she begged for forgiveness and knelt to sacrifice her pride at the altar of Solomon Cantor's love for his son. Since that moment, she had felt something different at her center, at the very heart of what she was. She had changed. She had thought she needed relief from loneliness, a man for her children, a way to serve her God, but what had she received instead? What was it really? She had not felt this way for so long, she couldn't say for sure, but her new sense of peace and empathy was undeniable. Standing there with the city down below, consciously defining what she had received for the first time, she thought perhaps the best single word for this peculiar peace was . . .

Love.

Kate Flint knew that she could be alone in the world and the love of God would still be there. She knew whatever life her children must endure, the love of God would still be there. She knew at last that she could be the kind of mother her children deserved, the kind of woman a good man might desire, the kind of friend that people need in darkest moments, and all because she had given that place at the center of her life back to the source of all love. Without God, she was nothing, but with him there at her center she felt that she could be . . . magnificent.

Jake cleared his throat.

Kate turned toward him. He lay with his head tilted toward her, his eyes slightly open, squinting against the sunlight. "Do you want me to close the drapes?" she asked.

"Uh-huh."

She pulled on a plastic rod, and the curtains slid across the window with a whisper, obscuring the disinterested outside world and the frosty handprint on the glass. Crossing to his bedside, she said, "How do you feel?"

"I'm sorry."

She smiled. "What for?"

"For lying to you. I'm so sorry, Kate."

"Let's not talk about that now."

"No. I need to. I don't want to . . . I don't want anything to happen to me before I tell you why I did it."

She brushed his hair away from his forehead. "You can tell me later if you like. I mean, it doesn't really matter."

"It had nothing to do with you. It was my father."

"Okay."

"He's . . . he was . . . I thought he was a monster. I didn't want people connecting me with him. So I changed my name."

"I know."

"But it had nothing to do with you. I've been Jake Singer for a long time."

Stroking his forehead, she said, "It's okay."

"You seem so calm," he said, looking up at her. "I wish I had that."

"I wish you did, too, Jake." She paused. "I could explain it if you like."

He let a silence build between them, then: "You're talking about Jesus."

"Uh-huh."

Looking away, he said. "That's hard for me, Kate. I'm not much of a Jew, but still . . ."

"Sure. I understand."

Again, they lapsed into silence. After a while, Jake said, "We're not going to be together, are we?"

She did not say the words. It was not necessary.

He sighed. "I'm not crazy, you know."

"It's not that," she said.

"Different worlds?"

"In a way."

Kate felt something akin to heartbreak, but she knew the gift of love she had been given would prevail. In facing the fact that she and Jake could never be, she had also somehow said a final good-bye to the need she'd had for John, and although it felt like freedom, still it brought the small sorrow of all good-byes. It was grief's last, desperate attempt to keep a comfortable place at the center, the birthing pains of the rest of her life, the price of peace.

"I'm sorry we can't have more, Jake."

"I'll be fine."

And so will I, thought Kate. *At last, so will I.*

A nurse entered. Smiling at Kate, she crossed directly to Jake and stood beside him, taking his pulse. Then she checked the fluid levels on his IV, injected something into a plastic tube hanging there for that purpose, and made a note on the chart at the foot of his bed. Turning to Kate, she said, "I just gave Jake something for the pain. He'll be drifting off to sleep soon. You'll need to let him rest."

Kate nodded. "Just another minute or two?"

"Okay," she smiled. "But he'll be talking foolishness in a minute."

When they were alone again, Jake said, "I had good reason to hate my father, Kate. I thought he killed someone a long time ago. I really did. I've thought so all of my life."

"Nan Smith," she whispered.

His eyes widened. "How do you know that name?"

"I was there."

"What?"

"Ruth Gold and I were swimming. We went inside to use the rest room. There was a scream, so we walked down the hall and . . . we saw your father."

"You're Katy O'Connor?" he said incredulously. "The girl from the trial?"

"That's who I used to be."

"Well, you're wrong! It wasn't him!"

Kate frowned slightly. "I know what I saw, Jake."

"You were wrong. Everyone was wrong! Even me. Especially me."

"You don't have to be ashamed of your father anymore." Kate leaned close to him. "He's changed. I saw it in his eyes."

"No!" moaned Jake. He grimaced and reached for his chest, taking a series of rapid, short breaths. Kate stood beside the bed silently, wondering if she should call the nurse back in, but after a minute his breathing slowed. He whispered, "You don't understand. He didn't have to change. He didn't do it! He was always a good man! A *good* man!"

Tears slowly traced the outline of his cheeks, mingling with the stubble of whiskers on his jaw. Kate wiped them away. "Oh, Jake . . . he can't

help what he was, but last night I saw who he is *now*, and believe me, your
father has become a gentle man who loves you very much."

Jake closed his eyes and lay silently. She stood by him until the drug
had taken full effect, then walked softly toward the door. Before she
reached it, he moaned. She looked back. His eyelids fluttered and half
opened, covering the upper half of his irises. He spoke in a strange monotone. "All those years . . . the same nightmare every night. Over and over
and over . . ." Jake twisted the sheets at his chest.

"Seriously, Jake, I don't think you should—"

"I remember you were cutting up potatoes, and the knife made that
awful sound every time it hit that metal table. *Click-click-click-click-click!*"

"Jake," said Kate, becoming frightened. "Please stop."

A new voice said, "Let him talk." Kate turned back toward the door.
Ruth stood there, holding it open, staring at the man on the bed.

Jake continued. "You were cutting up potatoes when the lady came,
remember? And then you started screaming." Kate lifted a hand to her
mouth, listening. "You cursed her and you hit her hard, right across the
mouth. She just stood there while you hit her. It was hard to think. You
were screaming so loud." He seemed to stare straight through Kate.
"You can't make me forget it anymore, Mother."

Kate gasped.

"I saw the lady lift her arms. She was gonna hurt you. You were
screaming so loud, saying those awful things. She was gonna hurt you.
So I ran up and I did it. I picked up your knife, remember? You were
slicing potatoes before. In the kitchen. *Click-click-click.* She fell down, and
I did it again. Right in the belly." He closed his eyes again and continued
in a strange, faraway voice. "Why were we angry with her, Mother? Why
did we do that?"

Jake fell silent. For a moment he lay with his eyes closed, perfectly
still. Kate thought he had finally fallen fully asleep, but then he rocked
his head slowly from side to side. "You made me think Daddy did it.
You told me everything was a dream—everything I remembered. You
told me over and over and over and over and over. . . . And then it *was*
a dream, and I couldn't tell the truth anymore, and you let me live with
those nightmares . . . all those nightmares. I need to know why, Mother.
I . . . I need . . . I . . ."

Horrified, Kate looked down on him, her shoulders arched, one hand covering her mouth and the other clasped tightly to her chest. She stood huddled as if for protection against the cold. She grieved for Jake, tortured all these years by the smoldering coals of a personal holocaust he was not permitted to acknowledge. She grieved for Nan Smith, dead at the hands of a child, and she grieved for her own son, Paul, standing in a room filled with policemen, clutching a knife as Jake once had, ready to defend their home as little Jacob Israel Cantor had once defended his mother. But more than any of these poor broken people, she mourned for Solomon Cantor, who had spent a quarter of a century imprisoned for a crime he did not commit. She thought of that big man with his uncontrollable hair and perpetual five o'clock shadow, so obviously uncomfortable in the coat and tie they had made him wear to court that day, sitting behind the defendant's table, watching her. She saw herself as the jury had: a sweet little girl, a little blonde Irish girl with a ribbon in her hair, so tiny in the witness box, so frightened of the big dark man over there, the Jewish man, speaking softly, barely able to say the words for fear of him. What chance did Solomon Cantor have against a girl like that? No chance. None at all. She made herself remember how he had looked at her. Not frightened. Not angry. Not even sad. As Katy had spoken the words that sent him to a hell on earth, Solomon Cantor had smiled a gentle smile, a father's smile, a smile that said, "Don't worry; I understand. You can't help it. It's not your fault."

"My God!" moaned Kate Flint. "What have I done?"

Suddenly, Ruth was there beside her; Ruth's arms were around her, holding her, pulling her close, and Ruth's voice was in her ear; Ruth was crying too, but soothing her. "Oh, Katy. Don't cry, Katy. We didn't know. We just told them what we saw. We didn't know."

And Kate leaned heavily on Ruth.

And Ruth leaned upon Kate.

And there they stood, together again at last.

FORTY-SEVEN

The Reverend Orvis Newton whistled "Onward Christian Soldiers" very softly as he lay covered with magnolia leaves deep within a cluster of trees and bushes near the center of Audubon Park. He had been there all night, listening to the sounds of the police on foot crossing back and forth across the grounds, listening to the heavy *whomp, whomp, whomp* of the helicopter passing high above, and listening to the unrelenting voice of God, chastising him for failing yet again. He did not fear the police. His fear went much, much deeper. He had wept in the darkness, ashamed of his ineptitude. He had begged God for forgiveness, promising a myriad of penitent acts if only he could be given one more chance to complete the Plan. He did not understand these repeated failures. What if he was wrong about the Plan? If so, Orvis feared his very faith could disappear, and with it, his immortal soul.

It was morning now. The police were still out there, but in fewer numbers, and the helicopter was long gone. Orvis Newton felt frustrated, lying still when there was so much work to do. The work was the only way to build his faith, to push his fear aside. The children who relied upon his ministry for food and clothing would receive twice as much as ever before. He had promised it. Their parents would be taught to use computers. He had promised he would find the machines somehow, and Bibles would be given out to all—he had promised to find good Bibles, with study notes and commentary and leather covers and gilded edges. He would sleep no more than three hours at night and would reduce his food allowance to one small meal each day. He would give away his extra suit. He would kill the girls.

He had promised so many holy things last night to keep away the fear.

Now, as sunlight fell through the thick canopy above, sliced by branches into sharply angled rays alive with pollen, Orvis peered up from beneath the magnolia tree, whistling softly on and on, because one of the other things he had promised was to praise God every second of every day, no matter what may come. *"Onward Christian soldiers, marching as to war."* Orvis whistled his praise because he feared to sing, in case the police were still nearby. He whistled very softly, certain no one could hear him outside his little refuge. He tried to feel the joy of God. It was appropriate to feel joy when one praised him in song, but Orvis Newton felt only fear of not remembering. He had promised so much. Keeping the list straight in his mind was difficult. What if he forgot something? What if he failed to honor his promises? What if he did not do his work?

He had to get to work. Serve the Lord. Fear him.

Orvis Newton sat up, brushing magnolia leaves from his black suit. He listened and heard nothing except for the distant traffic on St. Charles Avenue. Slowly, grunting with the effort, he stood, both knees popping when he straightened. A sunbeam shone upon his face. He lifted his eyes toward it, looking up toward heaven through the deep green cover of the branches. He could see heaven through a parting in the leaves. It was beautiful. As he looked at heaven, his eye changed colors from green to blue and back again. He whistled softly. *"Marching as to war."*

Then he heard the low, rumbling noise, like a prolonged grunt, or maybe the purring of a cat. Yes, more like a cat's purring. But much deeper than a cat would make. Unless of course . . .

Orvis Newton looked higher, up beyond the parting of the leaves that had shown him heaven, and swaddled with darkness there among the branches he saw the black-and-orange stripes of death descending.

FORTY-EIGHT

Kate had left Paul and Jilly at home alone, with Paul in charge. He was thirteen now, and she thought he could handle things alone for a couple of hours, but he had wanted to come along, to feed his morbid curiosity by watching them put Gabrielle Cantor in the ground. After repeatedly telling Paul he could not come, the boy had set his jaw and followed her out onto the front porch, dragging Jilly by the hand, defying her openly. "I'm not staying here and watching her," he said, inclining his stubborn chin back toward the house. "You can't make me."

From longstanding force of habit, Kate had almost surrendered. What harm would it do, really, to have the children at the funeral? But in a sudden moment of clarity, she saw the plea behind Paul's bluster, saw it clearly for the very first time, and she knew what she must do, what she should have been doing all along. Although her heart ached at how hard it was, Kate put some steel into her voice.

"Paul, it's time you started doing what I say without talking back. I'm the grown-up here, and I know what's best. Now you turn around and take your sister into the house right this instant, just like I said."

Paul had continued to stare at her, and for a moment Kate thought he would resist, but then she saw something change in his eyes—was it relief?—and he nodded, turned, and walked inside. It had been a minor victory for them both. He had received permission to be a boy again. She had found her self-respect. Of course there was much more work to be done, but Kate knew at last what was required to save her son.

So now, here at the cemetery Kate smiled in spite of the circumstances. She stood apart from the mourners, taking shelter from a brisk breeze in the lee of a groundskeeper's shed. Winter had come early, edging out the summer with no autumn in between. This was no surprise in New Orleans, a two-season town. There were days when everything baked beneath the unrelenting Louisiana sun, and humidity basted the citizens like a million dripping hams, and there were days like today, when a brisk wind nipped at Kate Flint's body. She pulled the collar of her coat closer to her chin.

After the discoveries of Gabby Cantor's and Orvis Newton's bodies, someone had leaked most of the story to the press. Given the murderous pattern from the Bible that the killer had followed, it was the kind of news guaranteed to boost subscriptions. The *Times-Picayune* had run headlines for three days straight, heralding new developments in the "Genesis Murders." Gabby Cantor's death had officially been declared a suicide, and today, more than three weeks later, they were finally laying her body to rest. It had taken three weeks because the police forensics team had kept the body for some time, and then there had been several days of debate on where to inter her. Solomon Cantor had insisted on Gabby's right to lie beside her family in the Jewish cemetery at the end of Canal, but a small group of Orthodox Jews with relatives interred there had objected. Jews, they insisted, do not bury suicides among the faithful. The issue had been resolved at last—Kate did not know how— and here they were, laying the woman's body down.

Kate thought the delay might have been for the best. Three weeks ago neither Gabby's husband nor her son could have attended the funeral, but today Jake was here in a wheelchair, with Solomon standing beside him, pale and gaunt, but on his feet. About fifty people had assembled with them. No doubt some were Temple Brit Yisraél congregants who had known Gabby Cantor, and others were employees in her firm, but Kate thought some might be strangers; there in genuine sympathy for the pain of a family they did not know. It was a *mitzvah* to mourn the dead. Ruth had told her so.

Many of the older women wore black lace veils. Most of the men wore *yarmulkes*. Solomon Cantor, oddly, did not. A group of ten men stood in a circle around the grave, chanting in unison, rocking back and forth slightly. Kate did not understand the Hebrew words, but the grief that rose with each syllable cast its bitter shadow upon her. Rabbi Samuel Gottlieb stood at the foot of the plot, leading the ceremony. Unlike his dress at most religious services, the rabbi did not wear his simple black robe with the gleaming white strip of fabric draped across his shoulders, something Kate had learned to call a *talit*. In the weeks since Gabby Cantor and Orvis Newton died, she had come to understand that many of the trappings of Christian worship had their roots in the Jewish culture. A bishop's skull cap and robe, a minister's prayer shawl, the Christmas candles, the Lord's Supper, and a new believer's baptism—all of these icons of her faith had been borrowed from the Jews. Kate felt proud of her new knowledge and had vowed to learn more, to build as many bridges as she could between her faith and theirs for Jake's sake, as well as for Ruth, and Paul and Jilly, and herself.

The service ended. The first of the mourners filed past her, walking toward Canal Street and the huge, spreading oaks above the wrought-iron cemetery gate. Jake reached up as he rolled past, brushing her fingertips with his, but Kate was saddened when Solomon Cantor, pushing Jake's wheelchair, took care not to acknowledge her. Since the night that Ruth had shot him, Solomon Cantor had not been seen at Temple Brit Yisrael, nor had he allowed visits at the hospital. She and Ruth had tried to speak to him many times, to express their regret for the wrongs he had suffered in part because of them, but he would not return their telephone calls or answer the door of the Garden District mansion he had inherited from his wife. Kate watched his broad shoulders bent slightly over the wheelchair as he pushed his son away. Just outside the cemetery, Solomon helped Jake rise and enter a black limousine. The big man's hands were tender on his boy.

Some of the other mourners met her eyes as they walked by. A few nodded, their greetings mutely communicated by the gesture. She saw anger in the faces of others. A pity, but it was understandable. Too many Jews from their congregation had been buried these last few weeks, too many dead at Christian hands, and by now, many of the people of Brit Yisrael knew about her religion, since Ruth had introduced her to the entire *Mekhkar Torah* class last Saturday. In spite of Ruth's assurances that she had more right to attend the funeral than most, Kate felt uncomfortable. She was, in the final analysis, still a stranger among them.

Maybe that will change some day. God willing.

When everyone else had departed through the low iron gate, only Ruth Gold remained beside Gabby Cantor's grave. Kate approached her. Ruth reached for Kate, and the two of them stood arm in arm, the fabric of their skirts fluttering in the breeze as they looked at the just-carved tombstone. A mourning dove called gently from the branches of an ancient live oak. On the far side of the cemetery, an old black man in a green uniform clipped a nandina hedge.

Kate felt a deepening sense of peace, standing with her new old friend in that quiet place, but Ruth's voice interrupted her mood.

"That night, when he was going to kill us, all those crazy things you said to him . . . how did you know what to say?"

Kate shrugged. "I think that was a God thing."

Ruth nodded. They listened to the dove and the old black man's clippers. Then, "Lieutenant Washington said Newton was on the verge of shooting you. Half a second later, and we'd be burying you today."

"I know."

Ruth turned to stand directly in front of Kate, facing her just half a step apart, their eyes level. Kate met her gaze evenly. Ruth said, "You put yourself between him and me. You said, 'Take me.'"

Kate said nothing.

"How could you do that?"

"Oh," Kate smiled, "that was definitely a God thing."

After a moment, Ruth pulled Kate to her in a hug. They stood that way for a while, then Ruth pushed away. She laughed, a brief expression of embarrassment. She wiped her eyes and took Kate's hand. "I've noticed everyone else calls you Kate."

"Yes."

"But I've been calling you Katy all along."

"Uh-huh."

"Why didn't you tell me?"

"I want to be Katy to you."

They stood hand in hand a while longer, smiling, and then Ruth's eyes shifted slightly. "Will you look at that?" she said in wonderment, staring across the cemetery.

S olomon Cantor had crossed the line between the Jewish and the Christian sections of the cemetery. The Jewish plots were low and humble. Basic headstones and footstones marked each resting place, along with low borders of cut marble that restrained the soil a foot or two above grade. There were one or two larger, more ornate tombs, but they were the rare exception. On the Christian side however, monumental crypts predominated, each competing with the next for attention, some constructed of multicolored marbles from around the globe, others ten to twenty feet high. Carved columns, life-size angels and lambs, intricate wrought-iron doors, and overstated neoclassical motifs were the rule.

Arriving at his destination, Solomon entered the tiny prayer chapel hesitantly, pausing a moment to allow his eyes to adjust to the darkness before he crossed the ten-by-twelve-foot dark and simple room. The light gray limestone walls, blue slate floor, and dark brown wooden ceiling imposed a somber atmosphere. Ahead lay a small plat-form bounded by a low cushioned step. A delicate amber shaft of light sloped in through a stained-glass window facing east, the only source of illumination. The musty scent of damp stone possessed the air. Along the edge of the platform, beside the padded step, a wooden railing rose just high enough to support Sol's elbows as he knelt before the simple wooden cross upon the wall. He clasped his hands together and bowed his head.

The rabbi walked to the door of the chapel and pulled. Groaning hinges futilely resisted the iron panel's outward swing. She took a single step into the tiny space and stopped. Solomon Cantor turned to peer back at her, then returned to his former position of prayer. A moment later, the door protested again, and Katy stepped inside. Without moving or speaking, both women watched Solomon Cantor's back.

Finally, the old man muttered, "Amen," and rose to his feet with some effort. He turned toward them. Ruth noticed with a start that he seemed to have aged ten years in the past three weeks.

"What do you want?" he asked.

It was the moment Ruth had waited for—the chance to repent and ask forgiveness for the guilt that weighed so heavily upon her soul. But what she had just seen drove all thoughts of reconciliation from her mind. "Mr. Cantor," she said, "what are you doing here?"

"That's none of your business."

Unaffected by his defensiveness, she asked, "Have you converted?"

He stared at her defiantly. Then something in his face relaxed. "I guess with Gabby dead, it doesn't matter anymore."

Solomon turned to look at the window on the side wall. Ruth followed his gaze. The stained glass illustrated a beautifully rendered scene. Ruth wasn't certain, but she thought it might have been the Christian story of Jesus calling Lazarus from the grave. Solomon looked at it silently for a long time. He was still staring at it when he began to speak.

"I'll bet you've been feeling bad about me, and your part in the trial and all. But you shouldn't. There were things going on you girls didn't know. I didn't want you to know. Now . . . I guess you got a right to hear it all." He turned to them, his eyes fierce. "But nobody else. I want your word on that. Nobody else can know."

Ruth lifted her chin. "I won't keep a secret that causes harm to anyone."

Solomon returned his attention to the stained-glass window. "The time for that is past."

"Then you have my promise," said Ruth.

"Me too," said Katy.

Ruth watched as Solomon seemed to draw strength from the image on the glass. The amber glow bathed his face with youth, filling wrinkles, concealing the plodding footprints of time. For a moment she saw the man that he had been more than two decades before. The illusion drew her back in time as well, and Rabbi Gold felt as if she were that little girl in a sticky wet swimsuit again, fearfully tiptoeing toward her destiny.

Solomon Cantor began with a most extraordinary statement.

"Nan Smith saved me," he said. "Maybe that's not the right way to say it, but that's what she did. She led me to Jesus. I came here today to remember that, and to ask God to be good to her in a special way for what she did for me, and to pray for Gabrielle's soul."

He turned back toward Katy and Ruth. The illusion of youth fell away as his face moved out of the light, but Ruth the shivering child remained, suddenly very afraid.

"Gabby saw us hugging and crying on the day I was saved," said Solomon. "She never understood. At first, she thought Nan and I were having an affair, but I convinced her of the truth soon enough. Only thing was, for Gabby, the truth was worse." He sighed. "She made me move to the spare bedroom. She did her best to keep me from being alone with Izzy, 'cause she thought I'd try to convert him. She wouldn't talk to me unless our friends were around, and then she was scared to death I'd tell them. She threatened me. She said if I didn't keep it quiet, she'd take Izzy and disappear. That she couldn't bear the shame . . ." His voice faded as memories overtook him.

Ruth felt rooted in place, terrified, yet too fascinated to move.

"I tried to explain to her," said Solomon Cantor. "I said I felt like Abraham. I mean, in a way it made sense, what Orvis Newton said in the kitchen. God tells a man 'you shall not murder,' but he also says 'sacrifice your only son.' How do you make a choice like that? What do you do? I told Gabby I still believe *Adonai* is one. I'm still a Jew. I *am*. But I believe in Jesus, too. I believe God is one, and I believe he's three. It makes no sense, but who am I to understand? I mean, he's God Almighty. You don't understand God. You just believe. That's what I told Gabby, and then that day— you know, the day it all fell apart—I found Gabby and Izzy there beside Nan in the kitchen, and Gabby looked me right in the eyes and said, 'Izzy's killed her, and it's your fault, Solomon. You're to blame for this.' I didn't understand till later why it happened, how Gabby beat on Nan and screamed at her for helping me find Jesus, how she scared poor Izzy into doing what he did. All I knew was we couldn't let them see my boy that way, covered with Nan's blood."

Solomon rubbed his face with a callused hand, sighing. "You have to understand, there was this other kid back then, up in Utah. He had killed his mother when she tried to paddle him. Stabbed her, just like Izzy did to Nan. It was all over the papers. They took that kid away from his family and put him in a mental hospital. He was only eight." Solomon passed his hand across his face again, stretching it out of shape like a rubber mask. "So I told her to take Izzy home, and I stayed to help Nan, but it was obvious she didn't have much time." He paused. He took several quick, shallow breaths in through his nose. He wiped his eyes. Finally, he continued. "Nan kept tellin' me she didn't hold it against Izzy. She kept sayin', 'Sol, don't worry. He didn't mean it. I forgive him.' She said that over and over. 'Don't worry. I forgive him.' While she was dying, Nan was worried about me and Izzy. I . . . I . . . when I saw how she was at the end, it made me even more certain—" Sol waved his hand back toward the cross on the wall—"about that."

Katy said, "You took the blame to protect your son?"

Solomon Cantor simply shrugged.

Twenty-five years in prison for love of someone else, thought Ruth. *What kind of a man is this?*

Solomon continued. "I thought they'd put Izzy in a foster home or juvenile detention or take him away to some mental hospital like they did that kid in Utah. I thought that would be the worst thing that could happen to him." He hung his head. "After what Gabby did to my boy while I was inside, I know better now."

"What did she do?" whispered Ruth.

Solomon's words took on a new edge, each one clipped and sharp. "She brainwashed him, right from the first. Told him it was all a dream. That it never happened, not the way he remembered it. Said I killed Nan, and he wasn't even there. Made him live his entire life with the same nightmare every night. Drove him into therapy to make the nightmares go away. Never let him know how much I loved him, or what I gave up for him. Left my boy so eaten up with feelings that he couldn't explain, he threw away his name!"

Katy asked, "Why did you keep your faith a secret?"

He stared at her with his arms stiff at his sides and his hands clenched into fists. "I've wanted to tell everyone about Jesus all these years, but I was afraid they'd figure out the truth about Izzy if I did. I mean, the case against me made no sense if word got out that Nan led me to Christ. So I kept quiet, thinking I could pretend to convert after I got out. But when they let me go, Gabby kept beggin' me not to say anything about being a Christian. Kept sayin' it would hurt Izzy, maybe drive him further over the edge, and hurt her, too. Then people started dying and Gabby said it could be Izzy doing the murders. I didn't know but what she might be right. So I tried to protect everyone. I slept in the truck every night, trying to keep up, but I just couldn't. There were too many people to watch."

He looked directly at Ruth. "I finally settled on just taking care of you."

As Solomon Cantor spoke, a dreadful suspicion stalked Ruth's heart . . . a foreboding sense that this man's story would be her undoing. Thinking of his sacrifice—of what he did for love—she suddenly remembered her own words, flung at Katy once in anger: *"What good are the things that Jesus said and did if they make no difference in how people live?"*

Katy asked, "Do you know why Orvis Newton killed those people?"

Solomon Cantor sighed. "All these years Newton has been telling everyone that Nan was all for waving Jesus signs in front of temple. It wasn't true. If she had been that kinda person, I never would've listened to her. In fact, the only reason Nan was at the JCC that day was to apologize about him and his ways."

He stopped speaking and turned away from them, lifting his head to look at the wooden cross. Ruth knew somehow that his next words would indict her very soul.

"Anyway, I think maybe Nan told him about me before she was killed. He found out somehow, because when he heard I was getting outta the joint, he went to Gabby's place to try to recruit me. Said he was gonna tell everyone Nan led me to Jesus. 'Course, that idea terrified Gabby, so she told him that story about me and Nan having an affair in order to keep him quiet. Told him everyone connected with my case knew all about it. She probably would've done anything to keep him quiet about me and Jesus."

Ruth's past had tracked her down at last, standing squarely in her

path, undeniable, unavoidable. Gabrielle Cantor had sacrificed son
and husband to an ancient fear, and now Ruth could no longer flee the
haunting memory of a very young woman, a foolish, untested rabbi who
once did much the same. She whispered, "Are you saying all these evil
things have happened because Gabby was angry when you converted?"

With his back to her, still looking at the cross, Solomon Cantor
simply nodded.

The nameless evil Ruth had battled at *Yom Kippur* overwhelmed
her then. *Liar!* it shouted. *I am not nameless. You know exactly who I am.* And
in her mind, Ruth Gold saw the pitiful form of her brother Isaac on his
deathbed.

She began to choke.

Desperately she stumbled to the door and tried to open it, yanking
hard again and again, but there was no escape.

"Ruth!" cried Katy.

She moaned and wildly shook her head, pulling frantically on the
unyielding door. She heard Katy coming to help. She heard Solomon
call, "Wait!" She heard Katy's footsteps stop.

Solomon Cantor asked Katy, "You're a Christian, aren't you?"

Katy whispered, "Yes."

"I need to know something. . . ." said Solomon.

Ruth glanced back. What could it be? What new horror must she
face? Behind her, Solomon Cantor stood once more with the golden
glow of a risen Lazarus shining full upon his face. Imploring Katy with
liquid eyes, he said, "Do you think I made the wrong choice? Hiding my
faith all this time?"

The wrong choice?

Katy said, "Who am I to judge?"

Ruth Gold moaned aloud. *"God tells a man 'you shall not murder,' but he
also says 'sacrifice your only son.' How do you make a choice like that?"* Had Isaac's
choice been between 'Do not kill,' and 'Offer up a sacrifice'? Between
belief that God is purely one and belief that he is also three? *Did I make
Isaac face that kind of choice alone? Oh, what have I done?* Ruth moaned again,
yanking hopelessly on the chapel door. *Adonai,* she prayed. *Forgive me!*
And finally, she thought to push instead of pull, and the door flew open,
and a brilliant white light came flooding in.

FORTY-NINE

John Donaldson enjoyed clipping the
hedges. He did it three times each year, once when spring arrived, once
in midsummer, and once near the end of fall. He was the only full-time
groundskeeper at the cemetery, and he took his responsibilities very seriously. People came to his place of employment to remember their loved
ones, and it was John Donaldson's job to see that things looked as nice as
possible for them.

Snip. Snip. Snip.

The muscles of his forearms flexed beneath tightly curled gray hairs
as he worked along the hedge with his long trimming shears. People
wondered why he didn't use an electric trimmer, but John Donaldson felt
the noise would be disruptive. He even used an old-fashioned, manual
lawn mower to cut the small patches of grass between the concrete path-
ways and the elevated graves.

His concern was lost on some, of course. They were the ones angered by their grief, whose visits to the cemetery stirred old feelings of guilt or betrayal, or who simply raged against the finality of death. Even the smallest blade of grass out of place might infuriate such a person, and John Donaldson would bear the brunt of their dissatisfaction. It had happened many times over the years. That's why he tried to avoid the mourners, working by the far side of the grounds whenever they came to visit the deceased. But today, unfortunately, he didn't notice the small woman kneeling by a nearby tombstone until it was too late.

"Sir?" she called. "May I speak with you?"

At the sound of her voice, he stopped clipping the hedge and turned, taking in her short dark hair, the conservative cut to her clothing, and the perfection of her olive skin. All in all, a very attractive young white woman.

John Donaldson smiled. "Of course, ma'am. What can I do for you?"

"I was just wondering," asked the young lady, "are you a Christian?"

John Donaldson lifted his eyebrows. What kind of question was that for a stranger to ask, especially in a place like this? Still, there could be only one answer. "Why, yes, ma'am. Have been for over fifty years."

She nodded and looked away from him and placed her palm against the tombstone at her side, pressing it flat against the broad blank place below the name of the deceased. "I was trying to remember a quote from your Scriptures," she said. "I think it begins, 'Blessed are the pure in heart.' Do you know it?" She kept her eyes upon the stone.

"Yes, ma'am," said John Donaldson. "I surely do."

"How does it go? The rest of it?"

"I believe it's, 'Blessed are the pure in heart, for they shall see God.'"

The woman nodded. "Yes. That's the one."

He stood still, watching her. She closed her eyes and drew a deep, shuddering breath. "Did Jesus say those words?"

"Yes, ma'am, he surely did."

The attractive woman lifted her palm from the stone and began to trace a pattern upon it with her index finger. As she drew her finger across the surface, she slowly said, "'Blessed are the pure in heart, for they shall see God.'" Suddenly, she looked directly at John Donaldson. "There's nothing wrong with that, is there?"

"Why, no, ma'am. I don't believe there is."

"Where can I find a stonecutter?"

"You mean a monument company, ma'am?"

"Yes. Where's the closest one?"

He pointed. "Just next door, on the other side of this hedge, ma'am."

She glanced in the direction he had indicated, rose to her feet, and hurried away.

John Donaldson lifted a hand to his forehead, shielding the sun from his eyes to watch as the woman joined a blonde lady who had been waiting near the cemetery entrance. She took the blonde lady's hand just as natural as you please, and the two of them stepped out through the gate. He shrugged and returned to his work.

Snip. Snip. Snip.

After a minute or two, he heard a voice from the far side of the hedge.

"Sir?"

It startled him. He stared at the bush for a moment before answering. "Yes, ma'am?"

"Thank you."

He smiled. "You're welcome, ma'am."

"It's a lovely thought, isn't it?"

"The verse you mentioned?"

"Yes."

John Donaldson nodded, although she could not see him through the hedge. "Yes, ma'am," he said. "I believe it's a *very* lovely thought."

"Okay. Well, good-bye."

"Good-bye, ma'am."

He waited for a moment to be sure she had really gone this time, then returned to his work. But now he was thinking about that verse.

To see God.

Snip. Snip. Snip.

It was a lovely thought indeed.

EPILOGUE

What follows is not fiction.

In New Orleans, Louisiana, near a freeway and a little flower shop lie a pair of cemeteries divided by a busy avenue and shaded by ancient live oak trees. At the foot of the rusty iron gate guarding one of them, ceramic tiles have been imbedded in the sidewalk to form the words, *Cemetery Dispersed of Judah*. Compared to the towering crypts for which the so-called "cities of the dead" in New Orleans are famous, the graves in these two cemeteries are modest in size and ornamentation. What may be the oldest tombstone in them is inscribed with the words *Jacob Hart, March 28, 1781–December 20, 1812*. Many of the other inscriptions are in Hebrew. Some bear dates in accordance with the Gregorian calendar; others are inscribed with dates such as *Tebeth 5606* or *Adar 30, 5630*—the months and years remembered in accordance with the creation of the world, based on the Orthodox Jewish interpretation of the Torah. The older graves are the final resting places of

immigrants. This is apparent in the towns and nations of birth listed
on their tombstones: Amsterdam, Holland; Kingston, Jamaica; Crakau,
Galiezion; Moravia, Austria; Bavaria and Prussia. The names of those
residing in the coffins below also reveal their widespread origins: Moses
Aletrino; Henrietta Joseph; Virginia Lazarus; Shmuel Peixotto; Phineas
Solomon; Isaac Herdman; Abraham Marx; Samul J. Buxbaum; and Menszer
Pincus. Most of the tombstones are marked only with the name of the
deceased, the dates of birth and death, and the place of birth, but a few
bear added inscriptions. One such epitaph reads *Meek as Moses, Loving Peace
Like Aaron, He Spent His Days Teaching the Law of Which He was a Modest Student
and a Devoted Servant.*

None of this is unusual in a place like New Orleans. After all, the
cemeteries near the little flower shop lie in a city that has served as a port
of entry for peoples of every race and religion for almost three hundred
years. But one of the old graves in this Jewish resting place bears a most
unusual inscription, even for the Crescent City. The words are not from
the Torah, but were first spoken two thousand years ago on a small hill-
side in Israel:

Blessed are the pure in heart, for they shall see God.

No one remembers why or how a weathered old tombstone in a
Jewish cemetery came to bear the words of Jesus, but if it's true that God
wants us to love our neighbors as ourselves, one thing seems certain:

They're bound to be telling the story up in heaven.

GLOSSARY OF HEBREW, YIDDISH, AND JEWISH TERMS

NOTE: Non-English terms are Hebrew, unless specifically noted otherwise.

AKEDA Binding. The first word and name of the portion (or *parasha*—see below) in the Torah which describes the near-sacrifice of Isaac by his father, Abraham, at God's command.

ARBA KANFOT A type of small *talit* worn under the shirt at all times by some ultra Orthodox Jews, including *Chasidim*. (See *talit* and *Chasid*.)

BAT MITZVAH The ceremony introduced in recent years to commemorate twelve-year-old Jewish girls' transition into womanhood. Similar to a *Bar Mitzvah*.

BETH House.

BIMA The stage or platform at the center or head of a synagogue or temple. Tradition attributes its presence in synagogues to the platform from which the High Priest offered his daily Priestly Benediction at the Temple of Jerusalem. Also called a *duchan*.

BRIT Covenant.

CHASID (Plural: *Chasiddim*) Literally means, "pious ones." Sometimes written as "*Hasid*," and "*Hassidim*." A sect of ultra-Orthodox Jews which formed in the 18th century in Eastern Europe and took the name of an earlier group of Jews who resisted Hellenism before the time of Jesus Christ.

CONSERVATIVE JUDAISM A denomination of rabbinic Judaism that falls between Orthodox and Reform Judaism on the theological spectrum from conservative to liberal, respectively. See *Orthodox Judaism* and *Reform Judaism*.

EREV Evening, or, the evening of.

GOYIM Plural form of *goy*, a non-Jew.

HASHEM Literally, "the name," this word is used by many Jews as a way to refer to God without using his name, thereby avoiding the risk of taking it in vain.

IBN EZRA ABRAHAM BEN-MEIR Spanish port and biblical scholar, 1089–1164. Also an astrologer and mathematician. His biblical commentaries were intended to reveal the plain meaning of the Hebrew scriptures. They are considered the first exegesis to use the scientific method. His work strongly influenced the famous Jewish philosopher Spinoza.

KADDISH Jewish prayer of mourning for the deceased.

KASHRUT The body of laws found in the Talmud which stem from the Torah's instructions on "clean" and "unclean" foods. Laws concerning "keeping kosher."

MECHITZA A curtain which is hung around the women's section of Orthodox Jewish synagogues. The intent is to avoid eye contact between the sexes, thereby ensuring that worshipers' minds remain in a state of purity.

MEKHKAR Study or research.

MENORAH A lampstand (often a candelabra), modeled after the one described in the biblical book of Exodus. All synagogues and most Jewish homes contain a menorah for use during certain holy days.

MEZUZAH A piece of parchment inscribed with certain Hebrew scriptures and placed in a small container usually made of wood, ceramic, or metal, which is affixed to the door frame of a Jewish home or business. The tradition stems from Deuteronomy 6:9.

MINYAN A group of ten Jewish adults who have gathered together for religious purposes. Some prayers require that this minimum number of Jews be present.

MITZVAH (Plural: *mitzvoth*) Law, or commandment. Also popularly understood as a good deed. Rabbinic Judaism lists a total of 613 mitzvoth drawn from the Torah, of which 365 are negative and 248 are positive. Many have been rendered impossible to observe since the destruction of Herod's Temple.

MOSHE Moses.

ORTHODOX JUDAISM A denomination of rabbinic Judaism which tends to take a very conservative or "literal" position on biblical interpretation. In practice, this means understanding the scriptures as inerrant and divinely inspired, and attempting to observe the 613 traditional *mitzvoth* (see above) as strictly as possible given the destruction of Herod's Temple. Many Orthodox Jews believe that Jews of the more "liberal" denominations are sinners, that their rabbis are not truly ordained, and that converts to the other denominations are not Jewish.

PARASHA (Plural: *parashat*) Portion. A word used to describe rabbinic Judaism's traditional 54 divisions or "portions" of the Torah which are read over the course of each year in the same order, and on the same days, by all religious Jews. Each *parasha* is given a Hebrew name, usually taken from the first significant word in the portion.

PASKUDNYAK　Yiddish for a young hooligan, or "punk".

PESACH　Passover. The Jewish holy day commemorating the release from slavery in Egypt of the Hebrew people under the leadership of Moses, as accomplished when an angel of death (or "destroyer") "passed over" Egypt, killing the firstborn children of all humans and animals, except for the Hebrews and their livestock.

RABBI　Literally, "my master." A title generally analogous to the English term *minister*.

RABBINIC JUDAISM　A religion based upon the Torah, or first five books of the Hebrew Bible, as well as the balance of what is commonly called the "Old Testament" by Christians (collectively called *Tanakh* by Jews). It differs from Mosaic, or biblical, Judaism in that it reflects a body of traditions, collected in a document called the Talmud, which stem from, but are not specifically found in, the Hebrew Bible, and which were codified long after the writing of the Torah. (See *Talmud.*) Observance of Mosaic Judaism became impossible with the destruction of the Temple in Jerusalem by the Romans in the first century. While the roots of rabbinic Judaism predate that event (synagogues were already in use, for example), it is nonetheless partially a response to the theological issues raised by the destruction of the Temple.

RASHI　Popular name based on the initials of Rabbi Shlomo ben-Isaac, 1040?–1105, French founder of a Jewish academy and author of the first Jewish commentary on the Torah written in the west. Rashi's commentary is arguably the most widely respected in rabbinic Judaism.

REFORM JUDAISM　One of the more liberal denominations of Rabbinic Judaism which was founded in the nineteenth century on the premise that Rabbinic Judaism is a progressive religion in a continuing state of development. In practice, this means Reform Jews feel they are free to interpret the Torah and Talmud in light of their own individual revelation, and respond with personal choices regarding which of the *mitzvoth* they observe. (See *mitzvah.*)

ROSH HASHANAH　The Jewish new year's day, and first of the "High Holy Days" or "Days of Awe." Initiates a ten day period of penitence which culminates in the Day of Atonement, or *Yom Kippur.*

SHABBAT / SHABBOS　Hebrew and Yiddish, respectively, for "Sabbath," which is the heart of all Jewish worship. Required in the Ten Commandments and other biblical scriptures, the day begins at sunset each Friday, ends at sunset on Saturday, and is wholly devoted to rest, Torah study, and worship of God. Exodus gives the reason for *Shabbat* as commemoration of God's creation of the universe, while Deuteronomy gives the reason as commemoration of Israel's delivery from slavery in Egypt.

SHAIGETZ Yiddish for a non-Jewish boy.

SHALOM Commonly translated as "peace," but has a meaning much more complex, which includes the concept of "wholeness."

SHEHECHEYANU A blessing or prayer in which God is thanked for allowing or enabling an individual or family to reach a certain special point in life. It is recited on several holidays, and at other occasions which are usually "firsts" in life or in a season.

SHEMA A Bible verse, Deuteronomy 6:4, which has become perhaps the most important Jewish prayer. The *shema* declares the oneness of God and is named after the first Hebrew word in the verse, which means "hear."

SHIKSEH Yiddish for a non-Jewish girl.

SHOFAR A ram's horn blown like a musical instrument. It is sounded every day for several weeks up to and including *Rosh Hashanah*, and then again on *Yom Kippur*, to remind Jews to repent and return to God.

SHUL Yiddish for synagogue.

TALIT Prayer shawl. Its use in Judaism is suggested in Numbers 15:37-41.

TALMUD The codification of a body of "oral law" (which Judaism traditionally teaches was given to Moses on Mt. Sinai at the same time as the Torah), combined with a commentary on that oral law. It is written in Aramaic, contains some two and a half million words, and is composed of two parts: the *Mishnah*, (meaning, to "repeat" or "teach"), which is essentially a commentary on the written Torah, and was codified in the second century; and the *Gemara*, (meaning, "completion"), which is a commentary on the *Mishnah*. The Talmud was codified over several hundred years, ending in the sixth century. In reality, there are two Talmuds, one composed in Babylon and the other in Palestine over roughly the same period of time. The Babylonian Talmud is considered more authoritative.

TANAKH An acronym formed from the first letters of the Hebrew words for "law" (*torah*), "writings" (*nevi'im*), and "prophets" (*kethuvim*). Known by Christians as the "Old Testament." Although arranged in a different order, the texts canonized in the Jewish *Tanakh* and the Christian Old Testament are identical.

TESHUVA Return. The concept of *teshuva* lies at the heart of rabbinic Judaism's teaching on achieving atonement for sin, and unity with God. It is similar to the idea of repentance, except it involves more than simply "changing the mind" (which is the literal meaning of repentance). It also includes the idea of redirecting one's attention to God.

TORAH Literally, "law" or "teaching." The Torah is the first five books of the *Tanakh*, or Old Testament, which are Genesis, Exodus, Leviticus, Numbers, and Deuteronomy. Traditionally, these books were revealed to the prophet Moses directly by God. They include a narrative spanning from the creation of the universe to the Hebrew people's entry into what is now Israel, along with a significant body of laws governing secular and religious life. See *Tanakh*.

TZITZIT Fringes. The tassels on the four corners of a *talit*, worn in obedience to the commandment given in Numbers 15:37-41 and Deuteronomy 22:12.

YAHRZEIT The anniversary of a death. It is often observed by fasting, visiting the grave of the deceased, and burning a *yahrzeit* candle, which symbolizes the human spirit and is based on Proverbs 20:27: "The spirit of man is the candle of the Lord, searching all the inward parts of the belly."

YARMULKE Yiddish for "skullcap" (*kipa* in Hebrew). Traditionally believed to be based on the Hebrew words *yaray may'Elokim*, meaning "in awe of God," and usually worn during Torah study and the saying of prayers, (although worn by some Jews at all times) as a reminder that God looks down from above.

YISRAEL Israel.

YOM KIPPUR The Day of Atonement, the second most holy day of the Jewish year after the Sabbath, is the culmination of ten days of penitence, and second of the "High Holy Days" or "Days of Awe." (See *Rosh Hashanah*.) Commanded in Leviticus 23:27, Jews fast and confess their sins to God on this day in order that their names may be written in his "Book of Life" for another year (i.e. in order that they might be forgiven).